Pike Logan is

ONE ROUGH MAN

"An intense and intriguing character,
Logan is definitely an action hero to watch."
—*BOOKLIST*

"Taylor's protagonist, Pike Logan,
is one rough man who is one bad dude—
as a superhero, Pike ranks right up there with
Jason Bourne, Jack Reacher, and Jack Bauer."
—*NEW YORK TIMES* BESTSELLING AUTHOR JOHN LESCROART

"Brad Taylor has created a feisty,
devil-may-care hero in Pike Logan."
—*NEW YORK TIMES* BESTSELLING AUTHOR STEVE BERRY

Praise for
One Rough Man

"Taylor's debut flows like the best of Vince Flynn and Brad Thor. An intense and intriguing character, Logan is definitely an action hero to watch." —*Booklist*

"An auspicious, adrenaline-soaked rocket ship of a debut novel. Taylor's protagonist, Pike Logan, is one rough man who is one bad dude—as a superhero, Pike ranks right up there with Jason Bourne, Jack Reacher, and Jack Bauer."

—*New York Times* bestselling author John Lescroart

"Anyone who admires America's fighting forces and appreciates a page-turning read as much as I do is sure to find Lieutenant Colonel (ret.) Brad Taylor's debut thriller exciting. *One Rough Man* is authentic and gripping."

—Newt Gingrich, *New York Times* bestselling author and former Speaker of the U.S. House of Representatives

"Brad Taylor has created a feisty, devil-may-care hero in Pike Logan. . . . A coiling plot, crisp writing, and constant braids of suspense make *One Rough Man* one exciting read."

—*New York Times* bestselling author Steve Berry

"A fast and furious tale with a boots-on-the-ground realism that could only have been evoked by someone who intimately knows combat. Brad Taylor spent decades fighting America's enemies in the dark corners where they live, and his experience shows. Pike Logan is a tough, appealing hero you're sure to root for."

—*New York Times* bestselling author Joseph Finder

continued . . .

ONE ROUGH MAN

BRAD TAYLOR

A SIGNET SELECT BOOK

SIGNET SELECT
Published by New American Library, a division of
Penguin Group (USA) Inc., 375 Hudson Street,
New York, New York 10014, USA
Penguin Group (Canada), 90 Eglinton Avenue East, Suite 700, Toronto,
Ontario M4P 2Y3, Canada (a division of Pearson Penguin Canada Inc.)
Penguin Books Ltd., 80 Strand, London WC2R 0RL, England
Penguin Ireland, 25 St. Stephen's Green, Dublin 2,
Ireland (a division of Penguin Books Ltd.)
Penguin Group (Australia), 250 Camberwell Road, Camberwell, Victoria 3124,
Australia (a division of Pearson Australia Group Pty. Ltd.)
Penguin Books India Pvt. Ltd., 11 Community Centre, Panchsheel Park,
New Delhi - 110 017, India
Penguin Group (NZ), 67 Apollo Drive, Rosedale, Auckland 0632,
New Zealand (a division of Pearson New Zealand Ltd.)
Penguin Books (South Africa) (Pty.) Ltd., 24 Sturdee Avenue,
Rosebank, Johannesburg 2196, South Africa

Penguin Books Ltd., Registered Offices:
80 Strand, London WC2R 0RL, England

Published by Signet Select, an imprint of New American Library, a division of
Penguin Group (USA) Inc. Previously published in a Dutton edition.

First Signet Select Printing, January 2012
10 9 8 7 6 5 4 3 2 1

Copyright © Brad Taylor, 2011
Excerpt from *All Necessary Force* copyright © Brad Taylor, 2012
All rights reserved

 REGISTERED TRADEMARK—MARCA REGISTRADA

Printed in the United States of America

To my daughters, Darby and Savannah, for all the times your mother had to say, "Daddy won't be here. . . ."

People sleep peacefully in their beds at night only because rough men stand ready to visit violence on those who would do them harm.

George Orwell

PART
ONE

1

The target took a shortcut, unwittingly shaving another four minutes off of life as he knew it. His appearance surprised me, because I had parked in an alley specifically to get out of his line of march, figuring he'd go the long way around the block. He was about fifty feet back and walking at an unhurried pace. A minute later he passed me, unaware of my existence. He was so close that I could have flung open the door and knocked him to the ground. From there, it would have been easy to thump him on the head, throw him in the back, and haul ass. That would have been a bit extreme even for me, so I let him go. Better to stick with the plan.

I keyed the handset of my radio. "All elements, this is Pike. Target just passed by my location and intersected Twenty-second Street. He's crossing it now."

Pike's not my real name. It's my call sign. We use them because nobody in my unit wants to use military ones like "Victor-Bravo Three-Seven." I'd like to say that I got mine for doing something badass, but you don't pick your call sign. It picks you, and usually for something that's not flattering. In my case it came from a stupid comment I'd made during training. I grew up in Oregon, spending my time hunting and fishing. I was trying to describe how we should do an ambush, but wasn't communicating things right. I finally said, "You know, like a pike attacks when it catches another fish." Everyone looked at me for a second in silence, then broke out laughing. For the next two days every time I tried to suggest something, someone would say, "You mean like a pike would do it?" The name stuck. It's not too bad as call signs go. I suppose I could have been "Flounder." All in all, it's much better than my given name, which I despise.

The Foggy Bottom street in front of me was starting to clog up with the noontime lunch crowd, all out enjoying the summer sunshine. This would make it easier for my team to track the target without compromise, but the heat was turning my car into a sauna. Why the hell this guy liked wandering aimlessly around outside was beyond me, but the pattern he had created would be his downfall. Humans are creatures of habit. What looks absolutely random once will look like the same ol', same ol' over time. We had reached the same ol' stage with this target and were within minutes of taking him down.

After crossing the street, the target entered a coffee shop and took a seat at an outside patio. *Right on schedule*. I saw the team settle around him like an invisible blanket. The crowd flowed around them all without a clue what was going on. That always gave me a perverse sense of pleasure. While rushing to catch the Metro or get lunch, they were brushing past some of the finest predators on earth and didn't even know it. Sometimes I'm tempted to grab one of them and yell, "Don't you know what's going on here? Can't you see what's happening? You ought to get on your knees and thank the

Lord that people like me are out here protecting your sorry ass." Yeah, that's arrogant and unfair. I suppose executing the operation without anyone knowing is pleasure enough. After all, if they did know, that would mean we had failed. In the end, they could go about buying their Starbucks or bitching about the price of gas because my team and I would have prevented something much, much worse, like a suicide bomber at their kid's school.

In my mind, the world is split neatly into two groups: meat-eaters and plant-eaters. Nothing is wrong with either one. Both are necessary. One contributes much, much more to society than the other. The other is necessary to protect the contribution. I'm a meat-eater. My existence allows the plant-eater to contribute. Some plant-eaters, living in a so-called civilized world, call me evil, but at the end of the day, when the bad man comes and the plant-eater's praying for a miracle, I'm what shows up.

I scanned behind me after the target passed and was surprised to see another man at the entrance to the alley, large, bald-headed, and looking out of place. He loitered for a couple of seconds, then began moving my way. *He's following our guy.*

"All elements, this is Pike. We've got a trailer with the target. Stand by."

Bull, the trigger for the takedown, said, "You sure it's not a ghost?"

Bull was asking if I was seeing things that weren't really there. "No, I'm not sure, but he refused to enter the alley until the target was clear, then walked at a pretty fast pace to catch up."

If he was tracking our man, I had no idea why. We had no intel indicating the target had any security, or that anyone else wanted him. The guy could be police, a rival group, or even a countersurveillance effort protecting the target. Or he could be a lost tourist and I was jumping to conclusions. Either way, Baldy—and anyone else with him—would have to be separated from the target. If he was a tourist, it would take care of itself. If not, that left my team. And once we executed, we would need to be pretty damn swift, because after we got rid of this guy, his people would know someone else was on the ground and interested in the same target.

I gave a description of the trailer and watched him take a seat in the coffee shop, confirming my fears.

"Okay, listen up. We're going to keep the plan. If Baldy's not a ghost, he'll follow our target into the planned kill zone. We'll let the target go through, then take him out. Acknowledge."

"Pike, this is Knuckles. . . . We can't duplicate this hit twice in one day. We're going to lose the target. We need to develop the situation, not start thumping people willy-nilly."

"We won't lose the target, because you're going to tag him at his table. Using that beacon, we'll take him down at the parking garage to his apartment. That was our contingency plan anyway. It'll just be two hits instead of one."

"Pike, that damn beacon hasn't worked yet. We keep getting false positives. We're liable to take out some old lady."

Knuckles was my second-in-command, or 2IC. He's a Squid, but I don't hold that against him, since he's a SEAL. He's just like me, only he picked the wrong branch of service. His call sign was Knuckles, but it should have been Mother Hen, at least while we were preparing for operations. Once we were engaged it would be something like DeathDealingSlaughterMonster. Right now, Knuckles was in mother hen mode. He was a finicky perfectionist. Someone who wanted to ensure that every piece of kit, tactic, or technique was absolutely perfect before being used on an operation. It wasn't that he was rigid, since he was one of the best on fluid operations, and he did have a point. If everything's perfect when you start, then working through contingencies, or what we call "flexing," is that much easier. If you start with something that's faulty, then you'll be flexing from the get-go. The thing is, every operation goes to shit at one point or another—like right now. Doesn't matter how much you plan. You can either handle the curveball or not.

"Look, I get the risk, but we're running out of time. We don't have enough people to track both guys. Just tag the target and use your judgment. If you can't get him, you can't get him."

"What if the trailer's not alone?"

Knuckles was thinking right along with me. "I hear you. We'll develop the situation enough to confirm or deny he's alone. If he's got someone else working with him, we'll pass. If not, we'll take him down in the primary kill zone, leaving you and Bull with the contingency for the target."

There was a pregnant pause, then, "Roger. Out."

"Bull, keep your eyes on Baldy and see if he makes commo with anyone."

I watched a homeless man approach our target. *Jesus, now what?* This was turning into a circus. I was about to call Knuckles and warn him when I realized that was who I was looking at. Pretty damn good job of camouflage.

He shoved a cup at the target, begging for some change. The man ignored him. Knuckles grew belligerent, bringing out the manager. *I'm never going to hear the end of this.* Knuckles was breaking the cardinal rule of surveillance by interacting with the target. On top of that, he was creating a scene that would be remembered after the hit. He was going to be pissed that I forced this on him.

The manager came out shouting. Knuckles waved his arms, slinging coins from the cup all over the place. Bending down around the target's ankles, he scrambled to get his precious money. In the blink of an eye, I saw him slip something into the cuff of the target's pants.

The size of a micro-SD card, it was a passive beacon that worked like an E-Z Pass on a toll road. It would register every time it passed a special receiver. The good part was that the card didn't need GPS or transmitting capability, along with the requisite battery source, so it could be made very, very small. The bad part was the beacon wouldn't give a specific location. It would only confirm our suspicions as the beacon passed our receivers, which we had placed throughout the target's habitual route. The final receiver was in the stairwell of the target's parking garage. A team, hidden in the shadows, would deploy when the beacon signaled. Unfortunately, with the receivers' track record, it could trigger if the wind blew the wrong way.

After watching Knuckles get chased away, I gave Bull a call. "Anything going on?"

"No. He's looking at the target, but so is everyone else thanks to Knuckles's little play. Hasn't communicated with anyone."

"Roger. Retro, you guys ready?"

"Yeah. We just don't know what the trailer looks like."

"Don't worry about that. I'll trigger. If it's no good—"

"Break—break. This is Bull. Target's on the move."

Shit. That was quick. Ready or not, the target was going to force our hand.

2

Colonel Kurt Hale was almost run over by the scrum of advisors leaving the Oval Office. A few years ago, when the West Wing was still a novel experience, he would have felt a little awe. Today, he just felt annoyed that they didn't bother to say excuse me, too intent in their own little world to notice him.

The president's personal secretary saw his annoyance and grinned. "You leave the military and you could be just like them."

Kurt smiled. "No, thanks, Sally. Can I go in?"

"Sure. You and his wife are the only ones he never makes wait."

Kurt entered and saw President Payton Warren with his back turned, looking out the window, apparently deep in thought.

"Sir, you want me to come back later?"

He saw the president start a little, then turn with a smile. "No, no. Come in. I could use a discussion about something that's truly important."

The president shook Kurt's hand warmly. "Let's go to the study so we won't be disturbed."

Following the president, Kurt once again felt a little amazed at the position he was in. Originally he'd been just one of many men trying to help the president defend the nation, but their relationship had grown into a true friendship—albeit one still grounded in their respective positions. While the president had never served in the military, he had shown Kurt a keen grasp of the application of military power, using it as a scalpel when he could and a sledgehammer when he had to, but always only after he had analyzed all other options. As was not the case with other politicians Kurt had dealt with, he trusted the president's judgment and commitment.

After Kurt was seated, Payton handed him what looked like a Hallmark card.

"What's this?"

"Something I want you to take back to the boys as a token of my thanks. Happy anniversary."

Kurt noted the date on his watch. "Yeah, I guess it was today, wasn't it?"

"Three years ago today. I'll tell you, I figured I'd be impeached or in jail by now, but Project Prometheus has been pretty much flawless. And largely because of the efforts of you and your men, the country has remained safe."

"I appreciate that, sir, but they're your nuts on the chopping block. Not mine. And you were the one with the vision to see that the Cold War system in place wasn't working for a war in the shadows."

President Warren shrugged. "Come on. You never take any credit for the success. It's the three-year anniversary. Take a damn moment to enjoy what you've done. I know what happened before I took office. That's how I found you in the first place."

Before 9/11 there was little need for an element like

Project Prometheus. Everything was clear-cut. Everything was clean. The Department of Defense focused strictly on military endeavors and the CIA focused on what's called "national intelligence." For Kurt and men like him it was the good ol' days. *You tell me if the Soviets are going to attack, and I'll tell you how to defeat them in battle.*

After 9/11, the lines became blurred. Instead of focusing on state systems, everyone focused on the terrorist threat, with both the CIA and DOD thinking it was *their* mission. Kurt could see both sides, but the architecture in place had no room for the debate. Built for the Cold War, the system wasn't designed for hunting individual men or small teams. Kurt watched the two organizations push and shove, unilaterally building up their own capabilities. At the time, he didn't worry. The U.S. had figured out how to win before and would figure this out as well. Right after 9/11, he took the fight to the enemy in Afghanistan, figuring it was only a matter of time before the U.S. got serious on a global scale. Two years into the war, he had still been waiting.

To his disgust, he saw the sense of purpose begin to drift, watching the CIA and DOD do more fighting against each other than against the terrorist threat. He was convinced that they had spent so much time apart during the Cold War that they didn't even understand each other, let alone trust each other.

Kurt voiced his opinions and waited on someone above him to fix the problems, but nobody seemed willing or able. When terrorists affiliated with Al Qaeda conducted the Bali bombings in Indonesia barely a year after 9/11, killing more than two hundred people, he realized that the status quo wasn't going to work. He banded together with like-minded men in the intelligence community and set out to change things on his own.

Their initial proposal was simple: a true joint organization—a blending of both CIA and DOD clandestine assets on a habitual basis. Eliminate the duplication of effort and mistrust at the grassroots level. The end result would be a fusion of intelligence and direct action, a capability that could follow a trail until it died, literally. They eventually got the ear of the National Command Authority and the green light to give it a try.

Kurt smiled at the memory. "Yeah, that first effort was a lesson in futility. I can't believe how naïve I was. We didn't get a damn thing accomplished, unless you count making enemies. If you hadn't come along, I'd have retired and would probably be working at Walmart."

Instead of hitting the ground running, the unit immediately ran into problems. A new unit, no matter how good, still had to deal with the bureaucracy built for the Cold War.

Kurt had spent an entire year pulling his hair out trying to get men out the door, running into one problem after another. If the military members weren't denied a deployment order by some pinhead in the Pentagon, his CIA members were denied participation because of a lack of a presidential finding for a covert act. He had felt like he was trying to run a marathon in waist-deep water. No sooner did he break through the red tape on the DOD side than he'd run into issues on the CIA side. Once he got past the Washington bureaucracy, he'd be kicked in the gut by the ambassador of the country in which he wanted to take action. Time after time, the ambassador, either a political appointee or a career diplomat, decided that the current elections in that country, or the coffee harvest, or the latest *New York Times* article, made it a bad time to go after a terrorist. Kurt knew it was nothing but a bunch of bullshit political quibbling, but there wasn't a damn thing he could do about it, since the ambassador had the final word on anything involving the U.S. government in his domain.

Kurt finally got fed up. The Taskforce existed for twelve months before he threw in the towel. Not a single operation had succeeded. The unit was disbanded, with great fanfare and hooting inside the clandestine world, as the Cold War assholes reveled in its demise, their little bit of turf now free from threat.

"Yeah, sure," said President Warren. "You're not the retiring type. That first effort wasn't futile. You made a lot of waves. Enough to be remembered, to get your name passed along to me as someone with an idea. The rest is history."

After the failure of his first attempt, Kurt had taken an assignment to the Joint Staff at the Pentagon and had brooded for a while, trying to enjoy the status quo. He probably would simply have retired if it weren't for the Madrid train bombings in 2004, which caused a presidential candidate named Payton Warren to begin a serious study of radical strategies to defend the nation.

Kurt remembered their first meeting well. When asked for his opinion, he hadn't held back. Kurt *knew* things had to change. Al Qaeda wasn't going to wait for the system to fix itself. What was needed was a shortcut, a revolutionary change. A task force capable of conducting operations on its own, outside the purview of the Department of Defense, the director of national intelligence, or any ambassador. The thought was compelling but dangerous. He knew he was talking about subverting the very thing that made the country what it was—the United States Constitution.

Surprisingly, Warren had listened, and eventually gave Kurt the backing to get it done. Project Prometheus would operate without official government sanction, but with a safety net. Should something go terribly wrong, the president would step forward and take responsibility. The flap would make Watergate look like a glass of spilled milk, but the threat was deemed worth the risk. The price of failure would be the presidency itself, with the repercussions shaking the Republic to its core.

The task force was implemented quietly. Nothing they did had the stamp of the U.S. government. Every action was under deep cover in the guise of an independent business, either American or something else. All the members were assigned to other units around the United States, with the permanent core cadre of logistics, communications, and command either "working" at CIA headquarters or "assigned" to J3 Special Operations Division in the Pentagon. Should the wrong people discover the unit's existence, they would attack it without remorse. But so far it had operated for three years without a hiccup.

Kurt said, "Yeah, we've been pretty lucky. Let's just make sure that history stays in the shadows. Hopefully I can keep you out of jail for a little while longer."

President Warren chuckled. "Sounds good to me. Speaking of jail, you got anything going on right now I need to be aware of?"

Kurt was glad to leave the reminiscing behind and get down to business. "Yes, we do. You remember we've been tracking a facilitator in Jordan for close to a year, and we're close to executing a takedown?"

"Yeah. Azzam something-or-other?"

"That's him. Well, you know we got execute authority for Jordan, but the target's gone to Tbilisi, Georgia. Ordinarily, I'd just recommend sitting in Jordan with the team in place and waiting on him to return, but I think we need to go after him in Georgia."

"Why? What's the rush?"

"We think he's trying to get nuclear material."

3

hy would the target leave so soon? I called Bull. "What happened?"

"Don't know. Maybe Knuckles spooked him, but he's leaving."

"Keep on the trailer and let me know if he moves. Retro, be prepared to go either way. If the trailer's a ghost, take the target on my command."

"Roger."

Bull came back on. "Trailer's paying his bill."

I felt the sweat start to build. This was going to be close. I had about a ten-second window to trigger the assault on the target—or pull off the assault team and wait for the trailer.

"Roger all. Showtime."

I exited my car and headed in the direction the target had habitually gone. If he went the other way, the whole thing was off anyway. Knuckles came on. "Target just passed, no deviation."

Bull said, "Trailer's going the same way."

"How far back?" I had to make sure the target was out of eyesight of the takedown. If he saw us thump the trailer, he'd haul ass.

"You're good. About a hundred meters. If the target

follows his pattern, he'll be out of sight by the time the trailer's in the kill zone."

I posted on the corner of the narrow road the target had always turned down, on the other side of the street that he habitually used. From here, I could keep an eye on him without having him pass right by me. We had picked this location because there wasn't any parking at all on the side road, with the exception of one handicapped spot midway down the street, currently occupied by a van. No parking meant little to no foot traffic, and no witnesses. Once he was on that road, we could take him out. I couldn't see the trailer, which was good. The target turned the corner, heading down the street away from me, right into the kill zone. I had about five more seconds to confirm Baldy wasn't a ghost.

"Bull, where the hell's the trailer? I don't see him."

"He's on your side of the street, about forty meters away."

Shit. Of course he wouldn't walk right behind the guy. He was about to bump into me. I started walking away, calling Retro as I went.

"Retro, Retro, let the target go. I say again, let the target go. Knuckles, stay on him."

Both acknowledged.

"Bull, I can't turn around. Tell me when the trailer turns the corner."

I kept walking at a slow pace, starting to wonder if time had stopped. Finally, Bull confirmed Baldy had his back to me. His call was immediately followed by Knuckles.

"Target's stopped. He can still see the kill zone."

I turned around and saw the trailer stop as well, proving what he was after. "No issue. Let me know when he moves. Retro, get ready."

"Okay. He's moving. Kill zone's clear."

"Roger that. Retro, you have execute authority. Bull, Knuckles, the garage is yours. Haul ass."

I watched the trailer walk down the sidewalk, approaching the van. A man exited the driver side and moved to the sliding door adjacent to the sidewalk. He opened it to reveal another man in a wheelchair. Both began struggling to get the wheelchair onto the sidewalk, with the chairbound man doing what he could to help. When Baldy came abreast of the sliding door the driver asked him for help. He agreed and leaned into the van to get the right side of the wheelchair. When his neck was level with the top of the wheelchair, the man in the chair miraculously wrapped his legs around the target's waist and crossed his hands, grabbing the man's right and left collar and violently pulling out. I watched the target try to react as the operator scissored the fabric of the man's shirt into his neck, cutting off his blood flow and choking him out. While they were locked in the embrace, the driver simply pushed the wheelchair into the van and closed the door. *Man, that was probably a surprise.*

Retro came on shortly after. "We got him. He's down."

"Roger. Knuckles, you copy?"

"Yeah, we're on the way. Should beat the target to the garage by a few minutes."

"Good to go."

"You'd better hope that fucking beacon works."

4

President Warren took a moment to process what Kurt had said, then asked the obvious question: "What do you mean by 'nuclear'? He has a bomb?"

"No, nothing like that. We think he's attempting to get some radiological waste from a contact in Chechnya. But, as you know, that would be bad enough. Setting off a dirty bomb would cause incredible panic."

"Panic would be the least of our concerns. It could render whole blocks of city into a dead zone. Even if we could clean it up, we would never be able to convince anyone the area was safe. The economic impact would be huge."

Kurt smiled. "I'm glad you see it that way, sir. Since the target's changed location, I no longer have execute authority. I need to brief the Oversight Council tomorrow and was hoping for some help."

Even though Kurt had been given carte blanche to create Project Prometheus, he was cautious in its construction. He knew it went against everything that the United States stood for, and such activities in every country in history had ended up repressing the very people they were ostensibly designed to protect, something he'd promised Warren, and himself, would not happen. To that end, he worked with the National Command Authority to develop the Oversight Council, made up of thirteen people, including the president. They were the only ones who knew of the Taskforce's existence, and they approved every mission as a single body. All the council members were either in the executive branch of government or private citizens. None came from the legislative branch. Kurt had worked very hard to ensure the right people were chosen. He didn't mind members who were leery of the unit and its mission—in fact he welcomed them—but wanted to take politics out of the equation. He only needed a body that fully understood the threat and the implications of action. He almost achieved his goal.

President Warren said, "Well, you're on your own there. You were the one who specifically asked that my vote not have any more weight than any others. I can't throw my weight around for a specific target. It would set a dangerous precedent and defeat the whole purpose of the council."

"I wasn't referring to the council as a whole. I'm talking about Standish."

Out of the thirteen council members, Harold Standish was the only one who had absolutely no experience in anything related to what he was overseeing. No foreign-policy, intelligence, military, or any other experience that would give him the ability to make qualified judgments on Taskforce activities. That didn't stop him from thinking he knew better than anyone else, including the president. Given a do-nothing political appointment to the National Security Council by the president, Standish had taken the job and turned it into something dangerous.

He had created what he called the "Deputy Committee for Special Activities." Kurt thought it should be called the "Deputy Committee for fucking with anything I want," because Standish provided no useful service but had his fingers into every covert operation the U.S. undertook. DEA, DIA, CIA, you name it. And now, using his position in the NSC, he was involved with Prometheus.

Kurt saw the president bristle but plowed ahead. "Come on, sir, you can't think he's an asset for this kind of work. I don't understand why the hell you appointed him to anything in the first place."

"Slow down. Not everyone gets to live in the black-and-white world of the military. The political world has its own unique laws. I agree that Standish is a weasel, but that weasel played a significant part in getting me elected. He can just as easily play a significant part in hurting my administration. Prometheus isn't the only thing on my plate."

"Jesus, sir, listen to yourself. You'd let a weasel in on the most secret things in the U.S. arsenal? I'm telling you Standish is a threat. He needs to be reined in."

Kurt saw the president's face cloud over and knew he had overstepped his bounds. "Kurt, I didn't get to this position by being blind. I've seen Standish's type over and over again. He's power hungry, but he does have his uses. Just deal with him, and remember—if it wasn't for his work, there would be no Project Prometheus, because I wouldn't be president."

Kurt started to say something else, but the president held up his hand. "That's it. End of discussion.

I'll have Palmer keep him in check, but I'm not going to fire him."

Kurt backed off. "Okay, sir. But the immediate problem is the guy in Tbilisi. No telling what Standish is going to say about that. He'll probably only agree if we say we're going to smoke every Arab within twenty miles."

Warren laughed. "Come on. He isn't that bad, and he's only one vote. Who's in the hopper for the mission?"

"Pike's team. He doesn't know it yet, but I'm recalling him now."

Kurt had handpicked every member of Prometheus, and the president had made it a personal duty to meet every one of them. He knew Pike, which meant he knew his reputation.

"And you're worried about Standish. I've never seen Pike's team do anything without drama."

"Yeah, but he's the only one with a perfect record." Kurt smiled. "Terrorists can run from him, but they just die tired."

"Well, there you go. Let me handle Standish. You handle the terrorists. It's worked pretty well so far. We haven't had another major attack in close to ten years."

Kurt grew somber. "Don't kid yourself, sir. We've been lucky. Ever since 9/11 we've been hunting terrorists more concerned with their place in history than conducting a well-thought-out attack. They've been happy just to shove some explosives in their underwear. This guy getting so close to radiological material scares the shit out of me. Some lone wolf gets his hands on WMD and his place in history won't have to be well thought out."

"I know. It keeps me up at night, too, trust me."

"What keeps me up at night is another Khalid Sheikh Mohammed. Someone who understands the second- and third-order effects of an attack and has the patience and skill to make it happen. Someone who isn't satisfied with just bringing down a single airplane."

Kurt went to the windows overlooking the Oval Office patio. "That man is out there. Planning right now. Studying our weaknesses. If he gets his hands on a weapon of mass destruction, we'll learn the real meaning of terror."

5

Knuckles was coordinating the garage hit when I felt my pager vibrate in my pocket. I pulled it out and saw a word I never would have expected: ENDEX. *Huh. That's never happened before.*

We were on our culmination exercise, something that was considered sacred. This was the final exercise after three months of working out tactics, techniques, and procedures before deploying overseas on a specific mission. Now we were being ordered back in the middle of our last training run. It's like someone telling the Super Bowl team that they had to vacate the field on their final practice before the game.

"Break—break—break. All elements, all elements, this is Pike. ENDEX, ENDEX, ENDEX. We got an alert. Return to home. Head straight to the conference room. Acknowledge."

Four of them replied with their call sign and a simple "Roger." Knuckles was last, and I knew I wasn't getting a one-word response.

"ENDEX? What the hell? We won't get an ENDEX in a real-world situation."

I smiled, knowing he had spent the better part of the day dressed like a homeless man, stinking of whatever disgusting filth he could find to smear on his body. "I hear you. I just got paged. I don't know what it's about. I'll swing by and pick you up. I don't think anyone else wants to ride with you."

Before Knuckles could answer there was a chorus of calls claiming their cars were full or they were already moving. He finally broke in. "Okay. Fine. What about the Rabbit? What do you want to do with him, turn him loose?"

"No. Bring him along. I don't know what the page is about, but we might be able to pick up where we left off. No sense burning the team by letting him go."

Knuckles acknowledged the call, then gave directions where to find him. He was only a couple of blocks away. I cranked up the car and pulled into traffic. I rounded the corner and spotted him a block away. He was standing two streets up holding a cardboard sign that said: "Homeless Veteran. Will work for someone who understands what's important." I pulled over, allowing him to climb in.

"Funny sign. Unfunny stench. Maybe you should take the Metro."

"Ha-ha." Knuckles was silent for a minute, which told me he was pissed. I was unsure whether it was the exercise or the page, but he didn't waste any time leaving me wondering.

"What the fuck was that call back there about tagging the target? Dumbest damn thing I've ever heard. There was no reason to do that. It's not like we were in a Jack Bauer scenario."

"I know, but these exercises never have a guy carrying a nuke. We never get pressure to get it done at all costs.

I decided to make it a Jack Bauer scenario—see how the team reacts. We don't want that to happen on a real-world without doing it once in practice."

"Yeah, sure. There's a reason Jack Bauer's on TV. It doesn't happen real-world. You pull that shit on a live mission and we're spending the rest of our lives in a shit-hole foreign jail."

"Ease up. It's better to be prepared."

Knuckles switched the subject, telling me he was good. "What's the story? We've never had a culmination exercise called off. We're due to deploy in five days and we haven't even worked the kinks out of the new kit."

"I don't have a clue. We'll find out soon enough."

Knuckles began rubbing off his filth with a packet of wet wipes from his pocket. "This had better be good, because we aren't ready to deploy."

It was good.

WE CROSSED THE KEY BRIDGE, leaving Washington, D.C., and entering Virginia. Minutes later, we pulled into a parking garage under a nondescript office building near Clarendon. The small plaque on the single door leading into the building read "Blaisdell Consulting," making it sound like we were some sort of think tank or government contractors. It was a great cover, because consulting firms are all over D.C., and no one can figure out what the hell they do.

The entire thing was a façade. Outside of the initial foyer, manned by little old ladies who would take your number and ask you to return at a later date, the building was dedicated to one thing—finding and killing terrorists. It was a block long and four stories tall, incorporating everything from an indoor twenty-five-meter firing range to an isolation facility that could house twenty-four men. The unit inside had no official designation and no official affiliation with the U.S. government—only a top secret crypt that would never see the light of day. Because we had to call it something, it was known simply as the Taskforce.

We badged in from the underground garage and moved straight to the primary conference facility on the second floor. Paneled in dark wood, it was dominated by a large oval table with small speakers in front of every chair and a large plasma screen on the far wall. The lighting was muted. It would have looked like the conference room in any law firm except for one difference: Instead of being surrounded by bookcases full of law texts, the walls held souvenirs from past operations. Kaffiyehs, flags, framed letters in Arabic, and various weapons hung around the conference table. I had had the pleasure of hanging about a third of them.

I never really understood why so much money had been spent on the room, since we were so classified we wouldn't be giving briefings to congressmen or anyone else. If it had been done for our sakes, they could have left it bare concrete. We wouldn't have cared. In fact, speaking for myself, I would have liked it better. I was told it was to encourage us to start thinking like corporate types. Get us into the cover and away from the knuckle-dragging killer-commando past we all had.

The rest of the team had beaten us back. When we entered, they all looked at Knuckles and me as if we had gleaned some secret knowledge on the drive over. Before anyone could ask, I threw it right back at them. "Well, someone know what's going on? Anyone say anything about Johnny's team? Something happen in Jordan?"

Bull spoke up. "Nobody's talking. Duty officer said to wait here. The boss will be down in about five minutes."

Our lead intel analyst entered the room, moving straight to the computer system in the rear without saying a word. Ethan and I were pretty good friends, so I figured I wouldn't have to wait for the commander.

"Ethan, what's up?"

"Change of mission. You're headed to Tbilisi." He turned his back and began loading stuff onto the computer, which annoyed me.

"Tbilisi? What the fuck for?"

Speaking over his shoulder, Ethan said, "Pike, I don't have time right now. The boss is on the way down. All I can say is that you won't be coming to my house for dinner tonight."

6

Before I could ask anything else, the element leader for Omega Operations, Lieutenant Colonel Blaine Alexander, entered the room. His appearance really caused the team to perk up.

He walked over to Knuckles and me. "Glad you guys could get back in so quick."

"Well, we're here. What's the story? Something happen to the team in Jordan?"

"Nothing bad's happened to the team," Blaine said, "but something bad is about to happen with the mission. Your target is headed to Tbilisi, Georgia."

Knuckles frowned. "Why's that a big deal? This will be, what, his third trip? Didn't we already analyze that and decide to focus on Jordan, where he lives?"

Mustafa Abu Azzam was a confirmed leader of a terrorist cell affiliated with Al Qaeda. Living in Jordan, but born and raised in Oman, he was hell-bent on doing irreparable harm to the United States. Had he been focused on other targets, such as the country of Jordan itself, the Taskforce would have quietly passed its intelligence into the system, letting the Jordanians handle it. As it was, he lived and worked in Jordan as a reputable citizen, leading a double life that allowed him to plan attacks in relative safety. We had worked for close to a year to put a face to the name the Taskforce had been tracking. A year of hard, slow, boring—but necessary—work. Nobody wanted to kill an innocent man. My team had flip-flopped with Johnny's over and over again, trying to get a handle on this guy, and we were very close. Our next deployment had a good shot at finishing him. Starting with just a name, then with cell phone numbers, building into e-mail addresses and Internet traffic, finally into addresses outside the virtual world, we had pinpointed the man called Azzam. Johnny's team had taken the first confirmed photographs, and was simultaneously building a pattern of life for an operation while we prepared to deploy for the final takedown.

Before I could ask anything else, Colonel Kurt Hale entered the room, followed by a scrum of analysts. A large man with jet-black hair, my wife says he would be handsome if his nose weren't bent at an angle, like it had been flattened and sprung back out of whack. I always laugh at that, because I'm the one who flattened it. Don't get the wrong idea. It was during routine combatives training. I could show you a scar on my elbow where I had to have surgery because of something he did. I would never say a cross word to the man otherwise, because he's the finest commander this country currently has. Of course, I'm biased.

Kurt shook my hand and apologized for interrupting the team's training. I shrugged it off. "Thanks for throwing in the trailer. It caused a little high adventure."

Kurt grinned and said, "You guys need a wrinkle every once in a while. A few more days and you'd have figured out what he was doing."

"We didn't wait. We took him down. Would have had both targets if you hadn't paged."

"You took him down? He just entered the exercise today. Where is he?"

"In the parking garage."

Kurt was flabbergasted. "Jesus, Pike! You brought him here?"

I held up my hands. "Sir, don't worry. He's blind-folded in the back of a van inside a dog kennel. He has no idea where he is."

Kurt turned to one of the men with him and barked out instructions. I watched him get the van keys from Bull, then scurry out of the room. The way I was looking at it, *Return ASAP* meant get my ass here as soon as possible, so I wasn't too upset at the breach in security. Kurt knew me pretty well, so he shouldn't have been too surprised. More like business as usual.

Years ago, Kurt had been my first troop commander at a Special Mission Unit on Fort Bragg, and pretty much kept me from letting my arrogant attitude get me fired. He looked past the arrogance to the raw talent, and while everyone else wanted to get rid of me as trouble, he managed to channel my energy until I had sloughed off the bad and kept the good. Well, mostly.

Kurt shook his head and said, "We'll talk about this later. Have a seat."

After getting the team's attention, Kurt said, "Sorry for cutting your culmination exercise short, but there's been a significant change to the mission profile. Your target, Mustafa Abu Azzam, is currently traveling to Tbilisi, Georgia. This is his third trip, and, yes, he has always returned to Jordan, but we think we've finally figured out what he's been doing in Tbilisi. Intelligence indicates that he's been attempting to purchase a quantity of radioactive waste from some contacts in Chechnya. Apparently, he's been successful, and is planning on conducting the transaction within the next few weeks."

He paused to let that sink in, then continued. "Now, obviously, Azzam getting material for a dirty bomb isn't something we can allow, so things have sped up a bit. We can't be sure he'll return to Jordan with the material, so we have to stop him before he gets it, which is where you come in."

I didn't have to be told why we were the ones who were going to Tbilisi instead of the team in Jordan. The cover plan used by Johnny's team, the same cover plan that we were going to fall in on, was specifically built for that region of the world, down to a particular commercial sector in a specific city. The cover wouldn't transfer to Tbilisi without a significant chance of compromise.

"What's our status in Tbilisi? We've all been prepped for Jordan."

Blaine answered, "Alias shop is working that now. Luckily, we had built a plan for Tbilisi, so we just need to dust it off. Your new documents will be ready by the time you fly."

Knuckles spoke up. "What sort of support package can we expect? We haven't done any infrastructure development in Tbilisi. Seems we're going to be running the ragged edge on this."

"Believe it or not, we're sitting pretty good. We began

some preliminary infrastructure development on Azzam's first trip to Tbilisi as a precaution, so we aren't
starting from ground zero. The support team that was
flying to Jordan tonight will divert to Tbilisi. You'll have
a complete package."

I cut to the chase, asking the question on everyone's
mind. "Are we at Omega now?"

Kurt said, "No, not officially. Since the target's
changed location, I have to brief the Oversight Council
tomorrow, but I can't wait on their approval to get your
team moving. Worst case, I should have an answer before
you land. Given the ramifications of what he's trying to
do, I see no issue."

The Taskforce called each stage of an operation a different Greek letter, starting with Alpha for the initial introduction of forces. Being at Omega—the last letter in
the Greek alphabet, symbolizing the end—meant we
were ready to execute the mission. The missions themselves could take anywhere from three months to a year.
Getting to Omega was hard work, with an enormous infrastructure behind it. There were generally three or four
different missions canceled for every one that made it to
Omega. It was the crown jewel of our profession, the
gold at the end of the rainbow.

"Good enough," I said. "When do we leave?"

Kurt said, "Well, your team'll be flying with the support package tonight, along with Blaine. The flight plan's
already been filed, so a few extra people won't cause a
spike. *You*, however, will deploy on Monday, as scheduled." He grinned. "Don't worry—you'll get the leave I
promised."

I heard what he said, my face betraying the struggle going on inside. Kurt noticed my discomfort but didn't ask for my opinion. "Okay, before I turn it over to Blaine, remember, we don't have execute authority on this. I expect it but don't have it yet. Don't go Rambo on me."

7

It would have made things a hell of a lot easier if Kurt had simply ordered me to go. Now I would have to make a choice about whether to leave the team on the night they deployed, or abandon my family after I had promised I would be home for my daughter's birthday. Nothing was more important to me than Heather and Angie, but as the team leader the mission took priority. It was an impossible choice.

My deployment was nothing new for my family. I had married Heather after I was accepted into the Special Mission Unit on Fort Bragg, so she was used to frequent absences. Even so, leaving is like twisting a knife each time I do it, especially now that Angie is old enough to know I'm gone. Our last night together before the culmination exercise hadn't been a very good one.

I had been out grilling steaks when I heard a thump inside the house, like something had crashed. I went inside to find Heather staring at the thermostat on the wall, clearly upset. I asked her what had fallen.

"That was me kicking the damn wall. The air conditioner's broken again. That's just great. Right before you leave. Perfect. Something else I'll have to deal with."

This wasn't a good way to start our last night together

for at least six months. I tried to mollify her. "I'll have Paul handle it. I'll call him right now."

Paul was our next-door neighbor. He was a good guy, but I really didn't care for him. He was always upbeat, always helpful, to the point where it was sickening. I'm probably jealous because he spends more time with my family than I do. He's the one that Heather turns to for any immediate help, and that hurts. But that's not his fault; it's mine.

Heather waved her hand. "Paul couldn't fix a leaky faucet. Don't bother. I'll get Tim to help. He's a lot better with his hands, and he's home now."

She started to say something else but held her tongue.

I could tell she wanted to get something out but wasn't sure I wanted to hear it tonight. I needed to avoid a fight at all costs. While I, personally, didn't really fear what the future held, I couldn't predict what would happen on a deployment, and couldn't allow Heather's last memory of me to be a fight. We both knew the job was dangerous. We never talked about it out loud, but the potential consequences were there all the time. Tonight it was worse, because I was leaving. It was like a heavy presence that surrounded everything in the room. I took a gamble, hoping whatever she wanted to tell me would be a simple thing that I could smooth over before I left.

"What? What were you going to say?"

"I've said it before." She sighed, brushed a strand of hair out of her face, then let it out. "Why do you have to go? Why is it always you? You've been gone since 9/11. Isn't it someone else's turn?"

Shit. That gamble hadn't paid off. "We've been over this. I can't just up and leave. I'm the team leader. It takes time to train a replacement. This is my last tour. I promise."

Taskforce tours were a little different from anything I had done before. They were six months long, followed by three months of downtime, followed by a three-month ramp-up prior to deploying again. During the last month of the ramp-up, we deployed permanently to D.C. and dropped all contact with our past, so for the family it was more like a seven-month rotation. The final month was lockdown. It was when we were completely cleaned from our past and prepped to become whatever was called upon by the mission. Tonight was the last night before the lockdown in D.C., the last night before my final seven-month absence. I was stepping down after this tour, something I had promised Heather I would do.

She gave me a bitter look. "Yeah, just like your last rotation at the Unit. And then you go and volunteer for this new thing. What'll it be next, Pike? At least when you were with the Unit I had other wives to talk to, people I could call who knew what I was going through. Now I don't even have that. I have to run around telling everyone you're some sort of communication technician in the Eighteenth Airborne Corps. Do you know how stupid that makes me sound? You're never here, and when you are, you never put on a uniform. It's ridiculous."

"Honey—"

She continued, speaking so fast her sentences began to run together. "Angie's learned how to swim and you've never been in a pool with her. The damn next-door neighbor's teaching her to ride a bike. She's going to be six in a month and you haven't been to a single birthday she can remember."

She stopped, clearly wishing she hadn't said these things on the night before I deployed. She began to cry. "It's not fair. Why is it always you? Tim left the Unit. Why can't you do the same?"

Tim was a friend who had just retired from the military and started his own security consulting business. It would do me no good to tell her that Tim was still conducting dangerous work—maybe more so because he no longer had the backing of the U.S. government. I embraced her, whispering in her ear, "It's not always me. There're plenty of guys like me. I've told you I'm done. This is my last tour."

She began to sob. "You've said that before. . . . I worry all the time. . . . I'm afraid when the phone rings. It's always the same man telling me you're okay. I think to myself, *Why would I think he's not okay?*, then realize the call is because someone else is dead. One of these days he's going to tell me you're dead. I can't do this anymore. . . ."

I knew then that something had broken; something inside Heather had collapsed under the strain. She had always known the importance of my work, and had given me unwavering support through absences at Christmas, birthdays, and anniversaries. She had been my biggest cheerleader, but something had changed. It sank in for the first time that this really was my last tour. I love the mission with a passion. More than just a job, it defines who I am. But make no mistake, I love my family more.

I held her close, stroking her hair. "Shhh. That's not going to happen. Look, I'll talk to Kurt, see if I can get a weekend at home after the lockdown, so I can be at Angie's birthday. That'll be a start, won't it?"

Heather looked at me, her face softening. I had hoped that night that committing to come home for Angie's birthday would be the first step toward Heather's believing in our new future.

Before I could say anything else, Angie came scampering in from outside. "Dad! The food's on fire!"

Heather broke the embrace and looked into my eyes. "I'm sorry. I shouldn't have said any of that." She sniffled and wiped the tears from her face. She gave me a halfhearted smile. "Go save the steaks. You can save the world tomorrow. We'll see you in a month."

I smiled back, kissed her on the lips, and jogged out to the grill.

After dinner, Heather went to clean the kitchen and I took Angie to her room on my back. I turned out the lights and lay next to her.

"Dad, did you know Mr. Paul's going to teach me to ride a bike?"

"Mom told me that. I can't wait to see you do it."

I answered nicely but wanted to leap out of bed, run next door, and punch good ol' Mr. Paul in the mouth. Maybe I wanted to punch myself; I don't know.

"Will you watch me when you get back?"

"Of course I will, doodlebug. Go to sleep."

She closed her eyes but kept talking. "How long are you going to be gone this time?"

I felt an acid bile in my stomach. "Same amount of time, but this will be the last time for a while."

"How come you always have to go? Mr. Paul never goes away. How come he gets to play with Megan all the time?"

Angie was old enough to make connections between

my life and the lives of others. Looking at her by the glow of the night-light, I felt more torn than I ever had in my life, pulled in opposite directions by forces outside of my control. It was almost a physical pain.

I stroked her hair. "You know why I have to go."

"To keep the bad men away?"

I leaned over and gave her a kiss. "That's right, to keep the bad men away."

8

Memories of that night, and the commitment I had made to Heather, were interrupted by Blaine Alexander moving to the front of the table. He addressed the group. "Well, I'm lucky to be working with my favorite team on this one."

The comment caused the team to laugh. Whenever he became involved, the endgame had begun, so whatever team he was working with became his favorite team. Blaine and I had worked together on multiple operations in the Taskforce. He was a pretty switched-on guy, politically savvy and tactically sound. He had to be to keep the job. Before he could continue, I raised my hand. "Sir, I need to talk to Colonel Hale. Can you start without me? It won't take a minute."

He nodded, knowing what it was about. "Yeah, go ahead."

I left the room at a jog, seeing Kurt talking to his deputy commander, George Wolffe, outside of the Ops Center. George had come over from the CIA's National Clandestine Service. I don't know him near as well, but from what I've seen, he's calm and levelheaded. Unlike a lot of the folks at the CIA, Kurt said he was a meat-eater, so that was good enough for me. I didn't mind talking in front of him.

"Colonel Hale. Hey. Hold up. I need to talk to you."

"What's up?"

"I need to go with the team. I need to fly tonight."

Kurt looked at me like I was nuts. "What are you talking about? You're the one who begged me to break protocol and let you go home for your daughter's birthday. I broke every rule in the book to make that happen. People jumped through hoops to get you clean for the trip. Now you want to go to Tbilisi?"

"Sir, things have changed. The trip was planned because of our deployment schedule. The team's now deploying early. I need to go."

"You need to go home to your family. Come on, Pike, nothing's going to happen between now and when you get there. They'll just be building a pattern of life. This thing won't kick off for at least a week."

"You don't know that. We could be in a world of shit in twenty-four hours. I *need* to go. It's *my* team."

"Pike, think about this. You're the one who told me you haven't been to a single birthday of your daughter's since the first one. Go home. Azzam will wait. Even if this pops, there'll be other targets. Take the leave."

"No. This is it. I told you before. This is my last rotation. There won't be any other targets for me. My team's leaving. I need to go. We're at Omega, for Christ's sake. Don't do this to me."

Kurt said nothing for a beat, staring at me, mulling over the request. "Okay. You can go. But if you're flying tonight, you don't have time to get to a non-attrib phone for a call. Heather's going to get the usual notice from the Alias Shop after you're gone."

Heather had gotten this kind of impersonal phone call from operations plenty of times, updating her on my status. This time would be particularly difficult, but I knew she would understand.

"Good enough. She'll get over it. She knows this is my last tour. After this, it'll be Pike twenty-four/seven."

When I reentered the conference room, Knuckles gave me a look. I nodded, bringing a smile to his face. After that, we both focused on the man talking, spending the next four hours getting an in-depth briefing on the target, his templated actions, the Tbilisi environment, and the cover we would use to get the mission done.

Later, as we were packing our kit for the flight in the fourth-floor locker room, Knuckles broached the subject. "Heather's going to murder you for this. You promised her. It's the only reason she let you do this tour."

"She'll understand. The guy's trying to get a fucking dirty bomb. It's what I'm here for. It's not like I did this for a boondoggle to Hawaii or something." I started packing, saying again, "She'll understand."

Knuckles finished what he was doing and walked out of the room, saying, "That's what I said before my divorce."

I shouted at his back, "You married a stripper when you were nineteen! She left you three months after you tied the knot! Heather will understand."

Knuckles had already left the room, leaving me to say the last part as more of an affirmation than a fact. I stared at my kit, wondering if I was making a huge mistake. Knuckles was good. He was ready. I had been training him to take over after this tour anyway. I truly believed he could do it, but I also knew that the transition was six months early, and while he had the raw talent, he hadn't been a team leader inside the Taskforce. An Omega operation wasn't the time for him to figure out what that meant. The risks were too great. On top of that, the team—any team—develops its own personality, driven by the team leader. The members weren't plug and play. We were clicking because of my leadership style. I'm not saying it was perfect, or even the best, but that was irrelevant. They were used to me, and now wasn't the time to switch horses. It was one more birthday, but after this, I would be at them all.

9

I heard my earpiece crackle, then the words I was wait-ing for: "Pike, Hedgehog is on the move. Should be passing you in about one minute."

I was sitting on a patio just off Rustaveli Street in downtown Tbilisi, sipping my coffee like the seven other patrons around me. I had to physically fight to suppress a smile. I absolutely loved this work and would have done it for free. I looked at my watch, realizing with a pang of guilt that today was Angie's birthday. I consoled myself that I had made the right call. Kurt had been wrong. Azzam was going down tonight or not at all. If I had stayed behind, the team would have been forced to either conduct the operation without its full complement of people, including their team leader, or miss the op-portunity altogether. Given the stakes, they might have attempted it, but odds were they would have decided to pass, wasting a year's worth of work.

"Roger. Break—break. Knuckles, this is Pike. Hedge-hog's headed home. You have execute authority."

"Roger all. About time."

Muslim names are always long, drawn-out, impossible-to-say things. Being the Ugly Americans, we usually gave a nickname to whoever we were tracking just to clean things up. Sometimes it's simply his initials, as in UBL for Usama bin Laden, or AMZ for Abu Musab al-Zarqawi. Other times, it's because the guy reminds us of someone. We had taken to calling Azzam the "Hedge-hog" due to his remarkable resemblance to the porn star Ron Jeremy.

Azzam was currently conducting a complicated Inter-net dance of challenge and counterchallenge with the Chechen who was providing the radiological material to ensure that each was who he said he was, and that neither was the enemy. The Chechen himself had entered Geor-gia through the contested Pankisi Gorge, with onward travel into Tbilisi. Intelligence indicators showed they were planning on conducting the transaction no earlier than a week from now, which ordinarily would have given me plenty of time to plan a detailed operation.

Unfortunately, the Georgian interior police, with the help of a few choice pieces of intelligence from the United States, were set to arrest the Chechen tonight. This forced us to take down Azzam as well, as he would flee once he got word that the Chechen had been cap-tured. You'd think we could just tell the Georgians to hold off, but the truth was that, while Georgia was a staunch ally of the United States, my team was inside the country without their knowledge. The Georgians had no idea about Azzam, and I'd just as soon keep it that way. Let them have the Chechen. Azzam would lead to much bigger fish.

The patio I was on sat at an intersection, giving me a

commanding view down three of the four streets in front of it. Azzam should be walking toward my café, moving straight at me. It was still fairly early in the night, but the streets were already starting to pick up with partygoers hitting the bars and nightlife.

A rowdy group exited the Irish pub down the block, obviously already drunk. As soon as they cleared the sidewalk and crossed the street, I saw Azzam. I looked away. Call me superstitious, but from past experience, I'm positive that staring at someone somehow causes them to know you're there.

"Knuckles. I've got him. He's on schedule. No deviation."

"Roger."

Over the past four days we had developed a pattern of life on Azzam, and determined that the best time to snatch him was after his dinner meal, before he got back to his hotel. Each night, Azzam had eaten in the same restaurant, then walked the half mile back to the small, local inn he had found. He stayed on main thoroughfares through most of his route but took one shortcut down a narrow, one-lane road in order to avoid walking the extra four hundred meters the main road would have forced on him. This was where we intended to take him down.

I continued to sip my coffee like all the folks around me, without staring at the pedestrians to my front. I caught a flash of light out of the corner of my eye. Looking back to Rustaveli Street, the main four-lane thoroughfare that ran through Tbilisi, I saw a police car pull up on the opposite side, lights flashing.

Shit. That's going to cause a deviation.

10

It had been two days since the phone call with the robotic-sounding man telling Heather that Pike would be unavailable to come home this weekend. He had been unfailingly polite, but it had done nothing to blunt the hurt she felt. She hadn't had the courage to tell Angie her father wouldn't be here for her birthday. But then, Angie had yet to ask. In truth, she would probably take it better than Heather herself.

It was already past one, and she still hadn't picked up Angie's birthday cake at the supermarket. Before she did, though, she needed to go to Tim's to pick up the piñata. She had asked him to help with the birthday party when she found out Pike wouldn't be home, and he'd readily agreed. She had an ulterior motive for the favor: She intended to convince Tim to put some pressure on Pike to retire. Or at least find a less dangerous job. She wasn't even sure what it was that Pike did, but it had to be worse than the SMU, and that was bad enough. While not best friends, Pike and Tim got along well, and Tim was the only one with any experiences like Pike's. The only one Pike would listen to. In her heart, she secretly hoped Tim would offer him a job at his consulting company.

She hadn't told Angie about the piñata, but like children everywhere, Angie had picked up that there were secrets afoot and was sitting expectantly in the backseat. She rounded the corner to Tim's house and parked on the street. She recognized Tim's Blazer in the driveway, but not the two unfamiliar sedans behind it.

Angie asked, "Whose cars are those?"

Heather had no idea, and hoped she wasn't interrupting a meeting Tim had scheduled.

"I don't know. Probably salespeople."

Before Heather could stop her, Angie jumped out, racing to the back door, shouting, "Maybe it's Daddy!"

"Angie! Wait!"

Heather felt a pang of guilt. In keeping the piñata secret she had hoped to lessen the blow of her father's absence. Now it appeared she had only exacerbated it, as Angie had surmised her father was the surprise. Rehearsing what she would say as she walked up the driveway, she saw that the back door was open, with shards of glass on the ground. She heard Angie shriek and felt adrenaline fire into her body.

Heather's eyes dilated and her muscles became engorged with blood in a fight-or-flight response. She chose to fight, running into the kitchen through the back door. She saw a large man holding Angie by the hair twenty feet away.

Without conscious thought, Heather snatched a paring knife from a block on the counter and charged the man with a primal scream. She registered him flinging Angie away like a rag doll as he prepared to defend himself. Before she reached him she was knocked to the ground from behind, disarmed, and jerked to her feet. She noticed blood all over the room. Great washes of it, as if someone had slopped a bucket haphazardly about. Looking for the source, she saw Tim lying on the floor, wicked gashes all over his body, his intestines slopping out from a hole in his stomach. She felt faint, unable to assimilate the slaughter.

The man holding her said, "What the fuck are we going to do now?"

"Well, we can't take them with us."

She faced the voice and saw a handsome blond-haired man, his hands covered in blood up to his elbows. His eyes were purple and flat. Dead. Unbidden, a memory of her childhood dog came to mind—a large husky that had been hit and killed by a car. When Heather had found him, his lifeless eyes looked like those of the man in front of her.

The man restraining her said, "Whoa, Lucas, I didn't sign on for killing a woman and a kid. They're not on the target list."

Lucas said, "No shit. I fucking get that, but we need to get out clean. I didn't ask them to come here. Look at the bright side: It'll help confuse the authorities. It'll play right into our cover of random violence. They'll have so many threads to run down, it'll cover our tracks."

Another man Heather hadn't noticed, now holding Angie, said, "I ain't doing that. No way. No amount of money's worth this."

Lucas snarled, "The mission takes priority. Don't go soft on me. I'll do the work. Just hold them still."

Heather spoke for the first time. "Please. We won't say anything. Please don't hurt my baby girl."

Lucas looked at her with something bordering compassion and said, "I'm truly sorry about this. Just the wrong place at the wrong time. Unfortunately, I can't make it painless. It's got to look like something crazy happened here."

Before she could say anything else, Lucas shattered her jaw with a vicious right cross. She hit the ground on her hands and knees, feeling the blood spill out of her mouth. She heard Angie scream, "Mommy!" then felt something smash into her spine. She rolled over and surprised the men by rapidly crawling to her purse. Lucas grabbed her legs and jerked her back, but not before she had her cell phone. She hit 911 before he could stop her. He smacked the cell phone out of her hand, towering over her.

"You bitch. You just lost any sympathy from me."

He hammered her broken jaw again. Everything went black.

Three hundred miles away, inside the Taskforce Headquarters, a computer started bleating.

11

The Tbilisi police car remained where it had stopped.

"Knuckles, this is Pike. Stand by for a FRAGO. Azzam's about to deviate his line of march."

"Roger. You want me to stand down?"

I thought for a second. Ordinarily, unlike our training exercise, this would be an automatic rollover, as the chance of compromising the team far outweighed any hasty plan that we came up with. But with the Georgians taking out the Chechen tonight, a rollover wasn't possible. We would take him tonight, or start all over, waiting another six months to a year to get him—if we could even track him again.

"No, don't stand down. I'm going to pick up a follow. We know he's headed to his hotel. We just don't know the route. Keep the same plan. Pick your guys up and get ready to drop them off somewhere else. I'll see what road he commits to. Once I give you that call, do a map analysis and see what the most logical route would be to the hotel. Position on that route. If he takes it, take him down. If he doesn't, we'll wait for another day. You copy?"

"Yeah. I got it. I'm moving the assault team now."

I should have called Blaine before changing the plan, but things were moving quickly, and we didn't have time for a bunch of questions going back and forth. I knew the intent: Get the terrorist without compromising the team. I didn't need a call to HQ to confirm that.

I watched Azzam out of the corner of my eye. He rounded the turn in front of the café, paused for a second or two when he saw the police car, then began walking again. I threw some money on the table and left the café, holding thirty feet behind him. Before I reached Rustaveli, Azzam turned left.

"Knuckles, he's headed south down Rustaveli. I'm betting he'll cross at the next light—the street we couldn't figure out the name. You remember?"

"Yeah, I remember. It had that kindergarten school on it?"

"That's it. I'm thinking he'll walk up the street past the school, then head east toward the hotel."

"Got it. Doing the map reconnaissance now. Looks like he'll come straight up that street and get on his original route at the top, hanging another left. The only place to get him is at that turn. The road does a little zigzag up front, allowing us to snag him without anyone seeing the action from down the street."

"Sounds good to me. If there is any chance of compromise, let him go. Understand?"

"Yeah, I got it."

I looked at the kindergarten street, the one Azzam would use after crossing Rustaveli, hating what I was about to say. I said it anyway. "I'll trigger him crossing Rustaveli, but I'm going to have to stay on the west side or I'll get burned. From there, he's your target."

This was a major flex. I was supposed to follow Azzam up to the planned kill zone. That road was a well-traveled thoroughfare, the sidewalks on both sides used extensively by the local population. In the original plan, once he had committed to the shortcut, away from the pedestrians, I would prevent him from escaping the way he had come and provide command and control for the team during the assault.

The new road he was on was a thin, narrow hardtop without sidewalks and devoid of anyone at this time of night. I stood a good chance of compromising the operation by attempting to follow him, especially since his antennae were probably up looking for a threat. I would miss the assault, which sucked beyond words. It also put the entire assault in Knuckles's hands.

There was a pregnant pause before Knuckles responded, "Good to go. Standing by."

I knew Knuckles was now feeling the pressure, but decided that saying nothing conveyed more trust in him than any hokey attaboy I could give.

I watched Azzam stop at the next intersection, waiting for the light to change. I kept going, passing within five feet of him and continuing south down Rustaveli as if I had a different destination. I found a sidewalk food vendor about seventy meters away and got in line, awaiting my turn and watching Azzam.

I waited until Azzam was across Rustaveli and committed to the school street before calling Knuckles. I stepped out of line and brought my cell phone to my face so I wouldn't look like a nutcase talking to the air.

"Knuckles, Hedgehog's across. He's about five minutes out. I'm headed to my car."

"Roger all. We're set. If he takes this route, we have him."

"Roger. Once you have him, revert back to the original plan. Link up with me at my car and I'll run interference back to base."

"Got it. Next call will be jackpot or dry hole."

12

Knuckles sat in his van, his mind working at warp speed. He was parked on the zigzag road just to the east of the kindergarten street, facing the kill zone, the three-man assault team in position, but the plan was now going to shit. He had picked the zigzag road as the perfect kill zone based on Pike's following Azzam and triggering the assault as the team leader, something that was crucial to prevent the team from taking out the wrong person. They wouldn't have the time to identify Azzam before assaulting. They needed to positively know that the next man in the kill zone was the target, and Knuckles was now the man who would have to make that call.

Unfortunately, the zigzag road worked for the actual hit but caused problems with the trigger. From where he was parked, Knuckles couldn't see through the kill zone to the school street to alert the team, hidden in the shadows. The first he would see of anyone was when they were through it and in front of the van. He cursed silently. *Fucking Pike. Always winging shit.* He could abort, but the thought never crossed his mind. He turned to the teammate driving the van.

"Where's the Remington ball? We're going to have to trigger with remote video."

"In the small Pelican case right behind my seat."

Knuckles reached behind the driver's seat and found the box. Opening it, he pulled out what looked like a black, rubberized baseball. They called it a "Remington ball" because it was sold by the Remington Arms Company, the same people who make firearms. Invented and built in Israel, it was basically a hardened camera that could be rolled, dropped, or thrown. Knuckles had absolute faith in it, mainly because he had tried very hard to break it in the past. No matter how roughly he had treated it, the ball faithfully transmitted video to a handheld screen up to one hundred and twenty-five meters away—farther than he could throw it. What he found really unique—in fact a little creepy—was that the ball would right itself after it stopped rolling, putting the camera into operation as if it had a mind of its own. Once it did that, Knuckles could make the camera rotate a full three hundred and sixty degrees, seeing anything in the vicinity by remote control. In this case, they would only need to see down the street Azzam was walking up, allowing him to trigger the assault team when Azzam turned the corner.

But they'd need to get the ball into position. They drove as fast as they dared, hitting the street and doing a U-turn. Knuckles dropped the ball against the curb as the driver headed back to their original spot. Before Knuckles could orient the camera, Pike called and said Azzam was across the road and five minutes out. Knuckles cursed Pike again, taking a deep breath. Success or failure now depended on his actions alone. He didn't dwell on it. He confirmed the linkup plan with Pike and banished any fears, mentally preparing for the assault. He got the camera under control and began peering at the video screen, patiently waiting. Eventually he saw a fuzzy figure advancing on the camera ball.

"Two minutes out."

"Roger."

He watched the man get closer and closer, until he took up the entire display. The picture was clear enough for him to recognize Azzam. Knuckles rotated the ball as he passed, now watching the target's back moving into the first hitch.

"Thirty seconds."

"Roger."

Knuckles nodded to the driver, who started the van, pulling into the street at a slow pace. He rounded the first hitch in the road and saw Azzam bathed in the glow of the headlights. They were late. The driver inched the gas pedal forward just as the assault team deployed.

Knuckles saw one man move to Azzam's front, while the other two advanced from the rear. One held a Taser X26 stun device. He pulled the trigger from a distance of five feet. Firing two projectiles attached to wires, the Taser caused Azzam to instantly lose neuromuscular control. He fell to the ground with only a sharp exhale of breath, quivering, unable to move. The other men from the assault element fell on him, flex-tying both his hands and legs with zip ties much like those used on garbage bags, only much, much thicker.

The driver pulled the van up parallel to the downed terrorist, while Knuckles threw open the sliding side door. Two men outside heaved the terrorist into the van while the third kept the voltage going, preventing Azzam from doing anything but twitch. They climbed in behind him, sliding the door shut. Knuckles breathed a sigh of relief, feeling the clammy sweat on his body for the first time. They'd been working toward this moment for what seemed like years, but the entire operation had taken less than the planned five seconds. The van sped out of the area, stopping only momentarily to allow Knuckles to recover the Remington ball.

IT HAD BEEN ALMOST SEVEN MINUTES, and I was growing a little antsy. Maybe I should have had Knuckles confirm his plan. I was itching to break radio silence but wouldn't, mainly because I'd never hear the end of it from Knuckles. I knew better than to bug the team. He would do the right thing. I hoped. Finally, I got the call.

"Pike, Pike . . . this is Knuckles . . . Jackpot. I say again, Jackpot." Knuckles spoke in a calm monotone, as if he had just awakened from a nap.

I knew this was an act. He was probably hyperventilating when he put the handset down. I matched his cadence, because that's what cool commandos do, and replied, "I copy Jackpot. What's your ETA to my location?"

"Two minutes."

"Roger. Standing by."

I cranked the car and waited. Two minutes and fourteen seconds later they pulled up, not that I was looking at my watch. Knuckles was grinning like a teenager who had just egged the principal's house. He gave me a thumbs-up, and we pulled out of the parking lot with me in the lead. My car would now be a buffer vehicle for any contingencies that might happen en route.

Within minutes we were out of Tbilisi proper and headed toward a warehouse the support team had rented, not a single bit of evidence left that anything at all had occurred.

I called in the mission, alerting the reception team we were en route. Twenty minutes later, the car and van pulled into a vacant warehouse, the rolling door closing behind us.

I left the packaging of the terrorist to the support team, knowing he wasn't being flown out until tomorrow. In the meantime, he would be given a complete physical to make sure he wasn't on the verge of a heart attack, then sedated for the trip. My part of the mission, the fun part, was over. I grinned when I saw Blaine Alexander come out of the small office we were using for a tactical operations center.

"Another good one. No issues whatsoever."

I noticed that Blaine's face was grim.

"What's up? Did something go bad on the Chechen hit?"

"No. It's personal. Can I see you alone?"

My first thought was that he was pissed that I had altered the plan and taken Azzam without talking to him. I followed him into the office. "Yeah. Sure. What's up?"

Blaine closed the door. "Pike, I don't know how to tell you this. It's about your family."

After the first sentence I could no longer hear him. All I could hear was my daughter saying I kept the bad men away.

PART
TWO

13

Guatemala
Nine Months Later

Professor John Cahill gave an exasperated sigh and sat down, sinking into the fetid jungle soil. Sometimes he felt like he was trying to run a race in knee-deep mud. He was deep within Guatemala's Reserva de la Biosfera Maya—the Maya Biosphere Reserve—in the northeastern department of El Petén, and for some reason his workforce had decided to quit. He had been doing this sort of excursion into the heart of the Yucatán going on thirteen years now, all in a quest for his mythical Temple of Priests. He had been robbed by bandits, contracted malaria, and almost killed by an asp, but never had his workforce refused to continue.

Once a rising star in the Latin America department of the University of North Carolina, he was now teaching undergrads basic anthropology theory at the College of Charleston, his fall from grace complete. The school itself was a pretty good liberal arts college, but it didn't have a major in archaeology and didn't give a rat's ass about his theories of the Mayan demise, forcing him to fund these expeditions out of his own pocket.

As always, he had hired local Mayan laborers without going through the required steps with the Guatemalan government. Nobody had cared before, and surely nobody would now, but an unhappy labor force could bring unwanted scrutiny. The Biosphere, one of the last remaining uncharted rain forests on earth, was dotted with Mayan archaeological treasures. Because of this, his activities would not be looked upon as a prank. Disgusted, he called over the native leadership, determined to find out what on earth could cause his hires to give up a new set of thirty-cent rubber sandals.

The natives themselves couldn't articulate to the professor exactly what it was they feared, only that they wouldn't go any farther on this specific route. In the end, they were torn between their instinct and the bounty the professor represented. They weren't stupid. They still wanted a new set of rubber sandals. They just didn't want to pay for it with their lives.

WHILE THE PROFESSOR ARGUED WITH THE LEADERSHIP, Eduardo and Olmec, two of the younger members of the expedition, were having their own parley. Eduardo, a spindly nineteen-year-old, was sure this halt was an opportunity not to be missed. All he had to do was convince his partner.

"Olmec, now's our chance! The Elders still believe in the old ways too much. We can find this temple, take something of value, then get back here before dark. Tomorrow, at least we'll have something to show for it besides the professor's quetzals."

Olmec, one year younger than Eduardo, but rooted in

a much earlier time, responded, "We don't even know where it is. Only the professor knows. He never tells anyone more than the next hundred meters. There's no way we're going to find that temple by ourselves. If we could, why has our village signed on for these trips every year? We'd have done it by ourselves a long time ago. I'll tell you why—because there is no temple. There's only the curse."

Unlike Olmec, Eduardo had lost all semblance of Mayan instinctual heritage and saw such hesitation as complete idiocy. He was one of the few from his village who had made the trek as a migrant worker to the fabled United States. Some said that he did more than simply make the trek, but was in reality tied in to the illegal transport of workers into the United States.

"There is no curse. It's just an old wives' tale used to keep kids from wandering away in the jungle. Have you ever heard of anyone dying from some strange ailment out here or disappearing completely? Anyone at all?"

Olmec didn't say anything, prompting Eduardo to continue. "I saw the map on the professor's computer with the markings showing where the temple is. You could read the map and lead us to it."

Two years ago, while Eduardo was away, working in the U.S., a Presbyterian church from Santa Fe, New Mexico, had sent a "mission" to their village, spending a month building houses, wells, and sewage. One of the gringos was a scoutmaster. He loved his scouting job, and spent his evenings teaching the village boys scouting skills such as using a map, compass, and GPS. Olmec had paid attention.

Eduardo knew he was close to hooking his superstitious friend. All he needed to do now was convince him of the simplicity of the idea.

"I've been watching where the professor puts his GPS. I'll go take it. He won't miss it now, since we aren't going anywhere anytime soon. The maps too. He doesn't keep a good watch on either, because he thinks nobody knows how to use them."

Olmec sighed, then said, "If you get the equipment, I'll lead the way."

Eduardo slipped off, returning in minutes with a map, compass, and GPS.

Olmec reluctantly turned on the GPS and took a little time orienting the map.

"According to this, we're only five hundred meters from the temple, basically due north."

Eduardo said, "Let's get going. We've got about an hour of daylight left."

With Olmec leading, the young men slipped into the jungle. After thirty minutes of fighting through the foliage, Olmec called a halt. He had been diligently keeping his pace count, a method to measure distance by counting the number of times his left or right foot hit the ground, and had hit four hundred meters.

"We're pretty close to the professor's spot on the map," Olmec said. "Keep your eyes open from here on in. If the temple's here, we could walk right over it and never know."

They continued for no more than five minutes when Olmec hissed at his friend. He saw something in the jungle. A hump that didn't fit. A tangle of vines and shrubs that didn't seem natural. The gathering gloom was making him jumpy, like a child in bed at night who imagines the towel on the rack is a burglar. He was ready to return to the camp.

"We've gone far enough," he said. "Let's go back."

Eduardo nodded in agreement. "Okay. Let's just fan out a little and see if we can find anything."

Olmec had walked less than ten feet when he heard Eduardo trip and fall. He saw him sitting down next to a rectangular stone.

"Look!" Eduardo said. "This is man-made. The temple is here!"

Olmec, once reluctant to continue, became infected with the thought of discovery. He quickened his pace toward the hump he had seen. It was about eight feet tall and appeared to be a solid mass of earth. As he got closer, he saw that draping vines gave an illusion of mass, but that it was actually some sort of cave. Setting down the GPS and map, he moved the vines aside. A few meters inside the opening, just at the edge of light, was a gallon-sized sack made of woven grass encased in stucco.

"Eduardo! Get over here! I think we've found what we were looking for!"

"What is it? Is it gold? Jade? What?"

Olmec moved toward the sack, sure that it contained something of wealth.

14

The professor grew tired of the back-and-forth discussion among the men in the local Mayan dialect.

He addressed the shaman, who acted as the villager's spiritual leader. "Speak in Spanish. What's the problem?"

"There is no problem. We simply will not go any farther. The area you're leading us into is full of blackness and death."

This was the third time the shaman had made such a statement, without any elucidation of what he meant. The professor was about to explode into a tirade when it struck him that this could be proof of the temple's existence. He wished he had asked thirteen years ago where they didn't want to go.

He had always been fascinated by the Mayan civilization, and was convinced that all theories of their demise were incorrect. The Maya had reached their height at about 900 A.D., and had a civilization that rivaled any in Europe or the Middle or Far East. For reasons known only to Maya ghosts, they had simply ceased to exist. It was one of the enduring mysteries of human existence, and many theories attempted to explain their downfall, ranging from outlandish alien invasions to the more mundane. The professor thought that everyone was looking at the problem backward. In his mind, it wasn't outside influences that had caused the people to disappear, but something in the cities themselves that caused them to leave.

The professor's theory revolved around his interpretation of a fairly new Maya codex called the Grolier Codex. The last of four known Maya codices, it was found under suspicious circumstances in 1965 and was considered by many to be a fake. Others had determined it to be authentic and maintained that it detailed the Maya calendar as it related to the planet Venus.

The professor had reached an altogether different conclusion. At the time of the Mayan decline there were two ruling elites in competition with each other: the political royalty and the religious shamans. Both continually fought for control of the population of the Mayan city-states, and both were equally bloodthirsty. He believed the shamans had developed a weapon, mystical in the eyes of the average Mayan, which was used to seize power. He extrapolated that this weapon had somehow gotten out of control and had caused one or two dramatic wipeouts of various cities, which in turn led to an evacuation of other cities in a superstitious panic, and a wholesale destruction of the civilization.

He was convinced that the Grolier Codex detailed the location of a temple, restricted to shamans alone, that housed this weapon. He had no idea what the weapon could have been, and cared only about finding the temple. He dealt in a world of history, of dangers long since dead. It never entered Professor Cahill's mind that, if his theory were true, he was trying to find a weapon that the world was ill prepared to deal with.

*   *   *

EDUARDO REACHED THE ENTRANCE OF THE CAVE in time to see Olmec pick up the sack. A fine cloud, not unlike flour, puffed out, encircling Olmec.

"This isn't worth anything," Olmec said. "It's a bag of dirt."

Eduardo began to dig through some scattered pottery, looking for something else of value, when he heard Olmec trip and fall. He was about to ask if Olmec was all right when what he saw caused him to stumble back and fall himself. Olmec had dropped the sack and was thrashing around as if hooked to an electrical generator. His head was growing lumpy and distorted and his breathing sounded as if he were drawing air through a swizzle stick. As his metamorphosis continued, he began to froth at the mouth, gasping for air. All of his exposed skin appeared to be rippling, as if a band of cockroaches were running through his veins. Before Eduardo could recover from his initial shock, Olmec's eyes bulged obscenely, his mouth cranked open farther than any human's should, and he ceased to move. Eduardo screamed, finding that deep in his soul he was still a Mayan, and ran out of the temple.

He sprinted about fifty feet and stopped, torn between helping his friend and getting the hell out of there. He decided that his friend was beyond help.

THE PROFESSOR ASKED THE SHAMAN if he could speak to the men as a group, intent on overcoming their superstition with gold, like an age-old explorer from Spain. As the men gathered around they heard an awful shriek to the north of their position, then a desperate thrashing sound. They began to rumble, looking at one another as if their neighbor could explain the noise.

The racket grew in strength until it appeared to be just outside the camp itself. The men began backing up, moving away from the sound, like a herd of antelope one step removed from full-scale panic, tenuously waiting to see who would be the first to start the stampede.

Exasperated, the professor advanced to the edge of the camp, convinced the noise was man-made.

He saw the boy and shouted, "It's Eduardo! Someone get the first aid kit!"

Eduardo broke into the clearing of the camp, torn and bleeding from his pell-mell run through the jungle gloom. He fell to his knees, gasping for air. The men gathered around him, all shouting questions at once. The professor noticed that Eduardo was clutching his GPS in a bloody hand.

He snatched it away, shouting above the cacophony, "Where'd you get this, you little thief! Where'd you go?"

Eduardo looked up at the panic-stricken faces around him, eyes wild, showing more white than iris, and blurted out in Mayan, "The curse is real! It has consumed Olmec! He's been taken!"

That was enough to penetrate the thin veneer of modern logical thought, the words lancing the ancient suspicions hidden deep within each man. The trip wire broke. The men began to flee in all directions like a pile of leaves caught in a hurricane gale.

Within seconds the professor was alone. He slowly

moved in a circle, dumbfounded by the turn of events. Listening to the stampede grow fainter and fainter, he mumbled, "What did Eduardo say?"

The question was swallowed by the vast expanse of jungle.

15

Eighteen hundred miles away, inside Taskforce Headquarters, Knuckles zipped up his kit bag in preparation for his upcoming deployment. Unlike his last deployment, this trip was going according to plan, with no mad rush or changes in the mission. Now a team leader, his team had finished their culmination exercise this morning and was due to leave the next day.

He looked at the empty locker to his right, the dusty space bringing back memories of the last time he had done this, with Pike packing next to him. Knuckles couldn't help but smile. That mission had been pure Pike. *Talk about pulling success out of your ass.* Knuckles shook his head, thinking of the actual assault, remembering the final few seconds of absolute chaos. *"I'm not going to be able to cross. The target's all yours. . . ."* Looking back, Knuckles knew that Pike had just been coaching and mentoring, making sure he was ready to take over the team. Only Pike would do that on a live mission. The trust Pike had placed in him made him feel proud, but the circumstances made him chuckle. *What an asshole. Blaine would have ripped his head off at that decision if it had gone bad.* Knuckles wished he could talk to Pike before he deployed, let him know whom they were chasing and get a little verbal encouragement. That last mission had been almost a year ago. Since then, Pike had dropped off the face of the earth. Knuckles loved being a team leader but would have gladly given that up—and more—to have his friend back.

Pike had taken the loss of his family harder than anyone Knuckles had ever seen. He seemed to blame himself from the moment he found out. Knuckles had hoped that he would go through the grieving process and rebound, and had even told Kurt Hale that he would remain a 2IC in order to let Pike keep the team, hoping that would help him recover. Kurt had agreed, but it hadn't worked. Pike had just grown increasingly bitter, with anger being his primary emotion. His judgment as team leader had begun to falter, with him lashing out at any small mistake and constantly fighting with his superiors. It had come to a head when Pike irrationally took the initiative on a simple exercise and subdued a Rabbit through force, shattering his face in full view of a group of tourists at the Country Club Plaza in Kansas City, Missouri.

Knuckles felt like kicking himself every time he thought about it. He had known Pike was acting strangely. The final radio calls had been a clear warning that Pike was on the edge. He should have seen it. Should have stopped it.

The consequences of Pike's actions could have been severe. Besides the simple fact that he had harmed someone who had been recruited to help them train, the incident put the cover of the Taskforce in jeopardy. The Taskforce managed to prevent that, but Kurt pulled Pike from the team. Knuckles fought the decision, purely on loyalty grounds. The transfer only caused Pike to sink lower. Three months later he had demanded to be cut free from the military, and Kurt had granted his request.

After Pike left, Knuckles had called him twice a month just to check up, but two months ago the cell phone number had come back disconnected. Knuckles now had no idea where Pike had gone or how to contact him.

He finished packing and left the locker room, going down to the Ops Center on the second floor. He saw Kurt Hale and George Wolffe across the room gathering up data and talking with analysts. He knew they were leaving shortly to give the quarterly update to the Oversight Council. He was glad someone did it, or he wouldn't have a job, but he didn't think he could put up with the bullshit. Kurt waved him over.

"You guys ready? Any issues?" Kurt said.

"Nope. We're good to go. Hopefully we can get to Omega on this go-around. Don't worry about us. You should be worrying about the Oversight Council."

"No problems there," Kurt said. "They know we're doing the right thing. All I need to do is keep them up to speed. You do the work and I'll get the Omega authority. Lord knows we've chased this guy enough."

"I know. I can't wait to take this fucker out. This should be Pike's target. He's the one that found him years ago. I'm thinking of tattooing Pike's name on his ass before I turn him over to the support team."

Kurt laughed. "I was thinking that exact thing this morning. Not the tattooing, the fact that Pike's the one that got us here. You still talk to him? How's he doing?"

"I have no idea. His cell phone's disconnected and I don't know what he's doing now. I keep hoping he'll give me a call. I'm afraid that one day I'm going to see him on the news, peeking out the window of a house surrounded by SWAT guys."

"Come on. That shit won't happen. Pike's still Pike. Don't worry about him. He'll turn up. He just needs some time. Focus on the mission."

"I know, I know. I'm on the mission. One hundred percent."

"Good to hear. Look, I've got to go. The Oversight Council won't wait. I probably won't see you before you deploy." He stuck out his hand. "Good luck."

KURT HALE AND GEORGE WOLFFE crossed the Potomac River, entering into the District of Columbia. George was driving, giving Kurt time to reflect on what Knuckles had said. He had put on a brave face and told Knuckles not to worry, but the truth was that Kurt was very concerned. He wished there were something he could do to bring Pike back into the fold, but he had tried everything at his disposal, from simple downtime to in-depth therapy. Nothing had worked. Kurt knew Pike's days as an operator were over but didn't think there was any way he would end up like Knuckles had said. Pike just wasn't made that way, no matter how bad it got.

The shame of the whole thing was that he knew the Taskforce wouldn't have been where it was without Pike. It had been a long, hard fight to get the unit established, and Pike's initial successes had guaranteed its survival.

George broke him out of his thoughts, asking, "What are you brooding over? You look like someone just shit on your birthday cake."

"Nothing. I was just thinking about how far we've come. If Knuckles gets to Omega, it will be like closing a circle. Missing that terrorist four times is what caused me to quit the first attempt at the Taskforce and build what we have now. Dumb bastard doesn't even know he's the reason so many of his friends are now dead or captured."

"Yeah, I know. I'd like to be there to see him go down. That ain't it, though. I know you better. What's up?"

Kurt paused, then said, "Pike. Once we turned him loose we started taking out terrorists like they were delivered to our door. I don't know. . . . I guess I feel like I used him, then threw him away."

"Cut that talk out. Pike was good, but even you said he was a handful. He was always going off on his own. He never asked for permission to do anything. Just did what *he* thought was right. In my mind, we're lucky he didn't cause an incident while he was here. Shit, we *did* have an incident. We're just lucky it was during training."

Kurt knew that was bullshit. The Taskforce had existed for only three short years but in that time had executed more than twelve Omega operations, all perfectly. A third of those successful operations were done by Pike's team, a number twice as big as the next most successful team's. Other team leaders said it was simply luck—being at the right place at the right time—but Kurt had worked with Pike long enough to know it was something else. Most of the success was due to hard skills, but a crucial part was simply an ill-defined talent that couldn't be explained. Pike just made things happen. Yeah, he was a handful, but you couldn't argue with success.

George saw him bristle and backed off. "I'm not saying he wasn't good. I'm just saying that this effort is greater than one man. You can't let an individual—any individual—supersede what we're doing."

"Yeah, I know. I get it. I don't need my own speeches thrown at me."

Kurt had used the "greater good" argument to convince President Warren to begin with. He wasn't sure anymore it was right. The greater good had been used to defend a lot of actions in the past, including Pol Pot and Hitler. In contrast, the constitution of the United States itself was based on the individual—every individual. *When does the greater good become evil? When was it okay to kill one innocent to protect many? When the many said so? Or when the one has a vote?* It wasn't a trivial question, because Kurt and President Warren had managed to create an organization that, in the wrong hands, could be very evil indeed. He was walking a slippery slope, trying to keep his perspective on what was truly in the greater good against men, like that asshole Standish from the council, who didn't understand the meaning of the term.

His thoughts were broken by their sedan pulling up to the security gate for the Old Executive Office Building next door to the White House. The imposing granite structure housed some of the most important offices in the U.S. government, including the office of the vice president and the National Security Council. It was also where the Taskforce Oversight Council convened.

George parked the car. "Hey, I know how you feel about Pike. I didn't mean that the way it came out."

Kurt smiled, letting him off the hook. "Don't worry about it. I know what you meant. Let's go get this brief over with."

16

Within his palatial estate a few miles outside of Guatemala City, Miguel Portilla addressed the two Arabs in English. "To·ensure I understand, you're offering me a retainer to move items across the border into the United States for a period of three years. These items can range from human beings to boxes no larger than three feet by three feet and weighing no more than two hundred pounds. Is this correct?"

"Yes. We're willing to pay you a handsome fee regardless of whether we bring you something to ship or not," stated the taller of the Arabs in heavily accented English. He appeared to be the spokesman, with the other Arab simply looking on and listening.

Miguel was a smuggler, although applying that term to him was like saying Bill Gates was a computer salesman. He was the undisputed leader of high-end smuggling into the United States. First earning his reputation with the Cali cartel in Colombia, he now worked exclusively with Los Zetas, a ferocious drug cartel made up of former Mexican Special Forces currently at war with the Mexican government.

"If I agree to do this, it'll cost much more than you've offered, as I believe the implications will have a traumatic impact on my business. In addition, I'll get your items into the United States, but I won't travel more than forty miles across the border. I have no interest in being associated with your enterprise."

Miguel was no fool. He knew that he was being asked to smuggle people and equipment that would be used solely to inflict death and destruction on the United States. In so doing, he also knew that the United States would react in a frenzy of fear, turning its porous borders into an airtight Tupperware container that an ant would have trouble infiltrating. He cared not a whit about the damage and destruction, but was concerned a great deal about the future of his industry. He also knew that in this day and age, the one thing that could destroy him was being named as an associate of a terrorist group. He could bribe his way out of any smuggling charge or connection to Los Zetas, but he couldn't stand up to the pressure the United States would bring to bear if he was seen as helping terrorists who murdered innocent American civilians. Drugs and death in Juarez were one thing. Death on American soil was something else entirely.

Before the Arab could answer, one of Miguel's ever-present personal security detail came in and whispered in his ear.

"Show him in," said Miguel.

The door opened, and Eduardo was led into the room. He appeared healthy enough but still bore the scars of his jungle panic. He looked timidly at Miguel, then at the two Arabian men. Miguel made a big show of friendship toward the young Mayan, seeking to put him at ease. "Eduardo! How're you doing? I thought you'd still be on the professor's expedition. Don't worry. You can speak freely. These ignorant foreigners don't speak Spanish."

Eduardo was afraid to say the wrong thing to this powerful man. He had worked for Miguel in the past as a high-end coyote, smuggling migrant workers into the United States. Miguel was one of the few coyotes who could get you into the U.S. in style, not packed like cattle in the back of a non-air-conditioned U-Haul, destined to die of heatstroke in the middle of the desert. Of course, this service cost much more than the migrants could afford, so the first few years of their wages, instead of being sent back to the family, were mailed to Miguel. Failure to mail the wages guaranteed that there wouldn't be a family in need of funds in the future. Miguel had earned the moniker of "the Machete" by his methods of ensuring compliance.

"Sir, you told me to tell you if the professor found anything. Well, he found something."

Eduardo explained the entire expedition in detail, telling of his and Olmec's actions, the discovery of the temple, Olmec's death, and his subsequent journey here.

Miguel was intrigued. "Tell me again how Olmec died. What was it he found?"

Eduardo went through the description of the bag and Olmec's symptoms, reliving the terror again as he told the story. Miguel failed to notice the increased interest of his two guests in the description of the death.

"And you know where this temple is? You can take some of my men there?"

"No, sir. Olmec read the map, and he's dead. The only one who would know where the temple is would be the professor. I wish I could take you there, but I can't."

Miguel's demeanor turned cold. "But you said you had a GPS. Surely that would make this simple. Where is it? Are you hiding something from me?"

Eduardo felt sweat pop on his forehead. "Sir, the professor took the GPS back. I promise I don't know where the temple is, but I do know where the professor is. He's staying at a hotel in Flores waiting on a flight home. He's got the GPS. I promise I'm not hiding anything."

Miguel began smiling again. "I believe you, Eduardo. You've always been true to your word. So I understand, only two people have been to the temple, you and Olmec, and only one person knows the location, the professor?"

Eduardo visibly relaxed. "Yes, sir. I'm the only living person who's seen the temple, and the professor is the only one who can find it."

"Good. Very good. Please head home and speak nothing of the temple or the professor." He handed Eduardo a wad of cash and showed him to the door.

Miguel saw an opportunity that he would have to seize immediately. If he could get to the temple before the government or UNESCO found out, he could ransack it, use his smuggling network to get the pieces inside the U.S., and sell them at a handsome profit. If he did it quickly enough, the government or UNESCO would never know it existed. First, he had to locate the temple. That meant finding the professor. Second, he had to eliminate anyone else who knew about it and was in a position to talk.

Miguel motioned to the security man who had shown Eduardo in. "Kill him once he reaches the bus station.

Take his body into the jungle. Oh, and don't forget to get my money back. Send in Jake."

The security man nodded and went about his tasks as if he had been told to bring a glass of water.

Miguel spoke to the Arabs in English. "I'm sorry, but something of urgency has come up. You're welcome to stay in the guesthouse. I'll send someone for you when we can continue our conversation."

The taller Arab nodded and said, "I hope it won't interfere with our transaction, but we understand the demands of your business."

The head of Miguel's security entered the room just as the Arabs were leaving. A large man, at six feet four inches, Jake walked with the grace of a cat. The only gringo on the detail, he was also the only one with any true security experience. He had been expelled from the British Special Air Service for activities that he wouldn't elaborate on. The rumor making the rounds was that he had enjoyed interrogating suspected terrorists a little too much, using force long after the subject had spilled his guts. Since then, he had hired out to numerous organizations, finally landing as Miguel's head of security.

"You wanted me?"

"Yes. I need you to go to Flores and find a man named Cahill. He's an American professor staying in a hotel in the town. Probably a flophouse. Don't hurt him. Bring him back here with all of his equipment. Pay particular attention to any electronic items such as computers or GPS. I need him in the next forty-eight hours. Take my plane to the airfield at Santa Elena."

Jake simply nodded and left the room. That was another reason Miguel liked him. He never asked questions. Given some guidance, he simply executed, unlike all of the other pipe-swingers he employed, who would ask a thousand questions to ensure they didn't screw up. Jake was fire and forget, and just like a guided missile, once he locked on there was little that could be done to stop him.

17

In the fourth-floor conference room of the Old Executive Office Building, Harold Standish glared at Kurt Hale, infuriated. The man was arrogant to a fault. The Oversight Council meeting was winding up, and Standish had been stiff-armed on every question he had asked. It didn't help his mood that nobody else on the council seemed to think Kurt was being insubordinate. In fact, most seemed to agree with him. Tall, at six feet six inches, Standish looked like a cross between Ichabod Crane and Christopher Plummer, with a head of close-cropped salt-and-pepper hair and the sour disposition to match. At the official conclusion of the meeting, he closed his portfolio, stood up, and stalked out of the room before anyone could stop him.

He went down to his NSC office on the third floor, flew through the anteroom without addressing his secretary, and fell into his chair. Staring at his computer, he began to calm down. He was still, after all, a very powerful man. A political strategist of rare skill, he had risen from the trench warfare of American politics by mastering the art of manipulating information. He was the go-to guy when it came to playing dirty. By the time he was thirty, he was richer than he'd ever thought he would be. By the time he was forty, he was the undisputed master of political destruction. By the time he was forty-five, he was becoming aggravated at how he was treated. How could he be so rich, and yet still feel like the boy with the dirt between his toes, begging for scraps?

He vividly remembered the victory party for the previous president's second term. He was celebrating with the rest of the campaign staff when the president-elect motioned for his top advisors to follow him into his suite. Standish, who had been standing in the group, went along as well. Once the doors closed he found everyone looking at him like he was a turd in a punch bowl. The silence was extremely uncomfortable. The president-elect finally broke it.

"Harold? Is there something I can do for you?"

"Sir? Uh . . . no. I thought you had asked me to come in here."

"No, Harry, the campaign's over. Your job's done. We have real work to do now." Standish vividly remembered the president's patronizing smile. "If it wasn't for you, we wouldn't even be having this meeting. I mean that."

We have real work to do now. The words had hit Standish as hard as a physical slap. He had seen some of the advisors fighting to suppress a smirk. He left feeling a burning shame. He realized at that moment that money wasn't the Holy Grail. Power was.

Standish began putting his talents to use getting a key to the doors of power. He had worked hand in hand with the same people who had smirked at him in that suite and he knew he was just as intelligent as they were. Someday he'd jam those smirks straight up their asses. He didn't have the experience or backing to join the political fray, but there were other ways to get on the inside. When Payton Warren began his first run for president, Standish had eagerly signed on. Simultaneously, he began his research, looking for a position to which the president could appoint him, should he win. He found it in the National Security Council.

Created by the National Security Act of 1947, the same act that had created the Air Force, Central Intelligence Agency, and the Joint Chiefs of Staff, the NSC was designed to help the executive branch synchronize political and military affairs. What Standish found attractive was that the statute dictated who would be on the council by law, but, unlike other organizations such as the CIA and the DOD, it didn't specify any congressional oversight. It was one of the most powerful entities in the U.S. government, but the legislative branch had no control over its activities. In effect, it served one man: the president. Outside of the members mandated by law, the president could appoint anyone to the council for anything. *Perfect.* Since its creation in 1947, Standish saw that the NSC had evolved into a byzantine organization that fluctuated every time administrations changed, making it hard to ascertain who was doing what—exactly what he needed.

He had read about the NSC under President Reagan, and had become fascinated at how a mere lieutenant colonel in the Marine Corps named Oliver North, working as a junior staffer at the NSC, had managed to create a complete clandestine infrastructure and manipulate foreign policy on a grand scale. The fact that it had eventually unraveled, splashing into the history books as the Iran-Contra affair, did little to temper him. Clearly, the people involved weren't his caliber.

He had worked hard on the president's campaign, proving to be more indispensable than ever before, with his information critical in the political fight. After the election, he asked for and received an appointment as a do-nothing member of an inconsequential subcouncil on the NSC's statutory Committee on Foreign Intelligence. He went to work, using his skills to build what he wanted. In three short years he had managed to create the Deputy Committee for Special Activities, and had slowly but surely been included in the mission planning for all covert operations. If it was a secret operation on foreign soil, he knew about it. And knowledge was something he knew how to use.

He had come a long way since that late-night meeting. The memory still made his face flush, but that would fade. Soon, it would be him asking people to leave the room.

Standish was startled out of his thoughts by a knock on his door, followed by the president's national security advisor, Alexander Palmer, entering the room.

"Hey, Harold, you got a minute?"

Standish stood up and put on his kiss-ass face, wondering why his boss was here unannounced.

"Sure, sir. All the time you need. How can I help you?"

Palmer took a seat without being asked. "It's about the Taskforce meeting we just left. Kurt has some concerns about your line of questioning, and frankly, so do I."

That fucking crybaby, Standish thought. *What did he say?*

"Okay," he said, waiting on Palmer to continue.

"I let you on the Oversight Council because it seemed to fit the office here, but your primary purpose is simply to absorb what's said so you can see how it affects other activities going on. I don't expect you to weigh in on any decisions."

He picked up a paperweight off Standish's desk and twirled it around in his hands. "The council is well versed on the ramifications of these types of things. It seemed as if you were questioning our judgment."

Shit. I'm being frozen out. What did Kurt say? Still wearing a smile, Standish said, "Got it, sir. I just thought that Kurt and the council were being a little timid on everything. We have quite a few opportunities here that we could seize right now if we wanted. I don't think the council understands how important—"

Palmer interrupted. "Look, I know you don't have a lot of experience in government, and I see that as a good thing, but these activities are very, very volatile. The combined experience of the council is probably over a hundred years dealing with national security issues. You have to trust that we know what we're doing."

Maybe that's why nothing ever gets done, you pompous ass. You've worked so long inside the government you don't even realize you're a chickenshit. The entire council thinks that talking about doing something is the same as action.

"Sir, I meant absolutely no disrespect. I know I have less time in the government than other folks, but I *have* worked inside the NSC for the last three years. I've seen how things run. We seem to make more charts and briefings *about* doing something than actually doing something. I just think the Taskforce could be better utilized."

Palmer replaced the paperweight and stood, indicating the meeting was over. "I hear you. Sometimes I think the same way, and admire your attitude, but you've only been on the Oversight Council for six months. Give it some time before you decide we're all hand-wringers. See a few operations go down, then begin to contribute. Okay?"

"Sure. Yes. I don't want to get a reputation as a know-it-all. I'll sit back and watch for a while."

"Good. That's what I hoped you'd say. You're a valuable contributor and I don't want to lose you."

Standish watched the door close, thinking, *Valuable contributor, huh? Not yet, but I will be, you patronizing asshole*. He had seen the sausage factory of decision-making by the inner circle of the U.S. government and determined it was a recipe for failure. What was needed was decisive action, without a bunch of quibbling from Congress, or, heaven forbid, from the great unwashed of the American electorate.

Since Al Qaeda had started this war in 2001, Standish had seen the U.S. take a daily beating on everything it did in its defense. The public just didn't seem to understand that there was a threat. *Christ, even global warming is seen as a bigger danger*. After watching all of the timid, halfhearted measures employed by the United States, he was convinced that something more aggressive needed to occur, outside of the public eye. The Taskforce was the perfect tool for the job. If he could get control of the Taskforce, the nation could get serious about terrorism. He couldn't order around the CIA or the military, but he could definitely find a use for an organization that had no official affiliation with the U.S. government. *Shit, even Ollie North could do that*.

18

The Arabs had retired to Miguel's guesthouse and were embroiled in a heated conversation. Far from being ignorant, both had spent countless hours with a Rosetta Stone Spanish software program in preparation for this trip. While they couldn't pass as natives, they were now fairly fluent—something they had kept hidden from their host.

The shorter of the two went by the *kunya* of Abu Sayyidd, after Sayyidd Qutb, the Egyptian member of the Muslim Brotherhood, whose rabid proselytizing and interpretation of the Quran were, before his execution in 1966, milestones in future Islamic fundamentalist thinking.

The taller one, and the one who had done all the talking earlier, went by the *kunya* of Abu Bakr, after the first caliph who ruled following Muhammad's death, and the first caliph leading to the split between Shia and Sunni.

Ordinarily a *kunya* is a nickname meaning "the father of," as in Abu Abdullah meaning "the father of Abdullah," and is commonly used in Arabic countries. In actual practice it's a method for fanatics wanted by authorities to take an alias with a hidden meaning. The naming conventions in Arabic countries made it very hard to keep track of individuals, as a person's recorded name could be any variation of full name or *kunya*.

Unlike their heroes of 9/11, neither Bakr nor Sayyidd had been radicalized in modern Europe, where Mohammed Atta and his ilk were treated as inferior beings and outsiders, leading them to turn inward toward Islam. Abu Sayyidd and Abu Bakr heard the calling from the mosques in their own hometowns in Saudi Arabia, a radical influence unstemmed by the ruling House of Al Saud because of the simple fact that the threat led outside the kingdom, and thus was something to be encouraged no matter how much the United States protested.

In the Saudi government's thinking, if the radicals were given something greater to hate than the ruling class, so much the better. Not to mention that many in the ruling class sympathized with the cause anyway. Let the radicals leave the kingdom and get killed. It was a win-win situation.

Like many of the men who had made the trek to Iraq, Abu Bakr and Abu Sayyidd didn't start out as rabid ideologues. They were simply looking for a little adventure in support of a worthy cause. Their plan was to go to Iraq, fulfill their romantic notion of the fight to support Islam for a few months, and then return to their life in Saudi Arabia, working a normal job and telling stories of their heroic actions to their grandkids years later.

The naïve illusion of jihad was broken quickly. Most actions were accomplished by snipers shooting their targets in the back, improvised explosive devices hidden in the dark of night, or suicide missions that left dozens dead and dozens more brutally mangled with little discrimination between the infidel and the believer. One walk through the bloody devastation of a suicide bomber was enough to take away any idealistic notions of jihad.

Abu Bakr and Abu Sayyidd were lucky in that they weren't chosen for a suicide "martyr" mission. At the time, the terrorist pipeline had enough *shahid*, and thus they were allowed to fight, with IEDs and rifles. Once they had killed, their mind-set began to change. They had to justify within themselves the murders they committed, and their psyches simply couldn't accept that they had done wrong. The answer was simple: The cause was just, no matter what reality they saw on the ground that refuted the propaganda.

Sayyidd and Bakr, like many other radicalized fighters, had become nothing more than weapons of the most dangerous kind. Literal smart-bombs. Living, breathing, thinking weapons willing to trade their lives for their nihilistic goals, without any moral restraint remaining against taking innocent life. Had they the means, they would slaughter their enemies on a massive scale. The leadership of Al Qaeda had striven mightily to obtain such a capability. Sayyidd believed he may have found it in the story told by the native boy. All he had to do was convince Bakr.

19

Inside his fleabag hotel, the professor twitched at every noise he heard in the hallway outside, wondering how long he had before he was arrested. He couldn't believe the debacle that had occurred. The Mayans had come out of the darkness one by one, chopped to ribbons. So far only eight of the twelve original members had made it home. Counting Olmec, he could be looking at charges of manslaughter or murder of four people. He regretted the deaths, he truly did, but the real shame was that no one would care that he was correct about his theory.

After spending the night by himself, it had taken him a full day to get out, and that was mainly due to his GPS. Without it, he'd probably be trying to suck water out of vines right now. He had hotfooted it to Flores, a small town on an island in the Petén province, with access to the airport at Santa Elena. At fifty-eight, he was weary down to the center of his bones, and wanted nothing more than to return to his calm life in Charleston. He hoped that the news of the travesty wouldn't make it to this town before he could catch a plane out. Meanwhile, to keep his mind off his impending doom, he collated his information on the temple. Maybe, just maybe, he could get out of this alive and return with a real expedition of scientists.

As he always did, he maintained his level of secrecy, only this time he wanted to get all traces of the location of the temple out of his immediate possession. He downloaded the waypoint data and tracks from the GPS to his computer. Then he wiped the memory of the GPS so that it showed no trace of where he had been. He opened his laptop and booted up a very powerful encryption program by means of a sequence of keystrokes. The program itself couldn't be found by a cursory examination. He pulled the drop-down menu and selected the steganography feature.

The professor had first heard of steganography, or the hiding of messages in otherwise innocent carriers such as pictures or letters, while still an undergraduate student. He had read about the ancient Greeks, where Herodotus tells of hiding a message of Xerxes' planned invasion underneath the wax of a writing tablet to avoid scrutiny, and the legends of the pirates, where the head of a man was shaved and tattooed with a treasure map that was concealed when the hair grew back.

Later on, while on a dig with a savvy undergraduate of his own, he had been shown the modern usage of the technique. Every computer file, such as JPEG, MP3, or WAV, has unused data streams within itself, basically empty pockets that serve no purpose. The steganography program simply fills up this empty space with the data that one wishes to hide. Thus, while the picture of Aunt Sally still looks like a picture of Aunt Sally, someone who knows there is hidden information within the picture can extract and reconstruct it.

After the program booted up, the professor was asked what he wanted as his carrier file, or the file that would hide the data. He selected three MP3 songs from his hard drive. When asked what he wanted to hide, he selected the GPS data. He continued by selecting AES 256 encryption and the password key. Now, even if the data were to be separated from the songs, it would be encrypted in an algorithm that had never been cracked, and thus would be secure.

In thirty seconds it was done. He was asked if he wanted to create a physical key, and selected "yes." When prompted, he put a blank thumb drive in the USB port and the computer churned for a few more seconds.

He now had his data securely encrypted and could extract the data both virtually with a password on his computer, which held the steganography program, and physically by inserting the thumb drive into whatever computer held the carrier file, regardless of whether that computer contained the stego program or not. Once the thumb drive registered, it would self-extract the data.

The professor plugged in the phone line and dialed the closest ISP given to him by the front desk. It never failed to amaze him how far and deep the Internet had penetrated. It seemed like it was in more places than indoor plumbing. Once he was connected, he logged on to Hotmail.com and pulled up his account. He typed a short note and e-mailed the songs to his niece in Charleston, South Carolina. Jennifer was an anthropology student, so it wasn't outside the realm of possibility that she would appreciate the local Mayan music. Still, even if she thought it a little odd, she'd have no idea the information she was helping her uncle to hide.

Three minutes later the e-mail completed sending. He

closed out of the Internet, then used a shredding program to erase all traces of his stego activities. Nothing
related to the expedition remained on his hard drive.

He gave a sigh of relief and leaned back in his chair.
Maybe he should get himself a giant margarita and relax a
little bit. As he cataloged the bars in the small town he heard
a knock on his door, and his name called out. He nearly
passed out in shock. Just as his mind spun into overdrive,
with fantasies about the tortures he would experience along
with the ludicrous choices he faced, such as jumping out of
the third-story window, it dawned on him that the man
outside the door was speaking with an English accent. He
must be an expat who worked for the hotel. When he had
signed in, the professor had tipped handsomely to generate
goodwill, so perhaps the man was here to warn him about
something he had heard on the street. In the span of seconds the professor went from doom to giddy excitement.
He rushed to the door, intent on seeing who was there.

There was no peephole, forcing him to crack the door.
He found himself looking up into the ice-blue eyes of a
man a full head taller than himself. His clothes didn't
indicate that he worked for the hotel. In fact, he was
dressed like he was going into the jungle. His face was
expressionless, giving no hint as to why he had knocked.
The only indication of why he was there was a section of
pipe held in his right hand. Maybe he was a plumber.

"Yes?"

"Professor Cahill?"

"Yes. Can I help you?"

In response, the man kicked in the door, knocking the
professor to the floor. The last thing the professor saw
was the section of pipe coming at his head.

20

Jennifer Cahill opened her eyes and watched the ceiling fan above her rotate for half a minute. *This isn't going to cut it. I need to find something to do or I'm going to go nuts.* At first, she had enjoyed sleeping in. Waking up whenever she felt like it or rolling over and going back to sleep had been a nice reprieve. Now, with spring break almost over, she was beginning to feel a little restless. As an anthropology major herself, she had asked her uncle to let her go with him to Guatemala, but he had refused. She hoped he was having some luck, although she knew it was a long shot. Everyone else had written him off as a crackpot, but she believed in him, if for no other reason than because he had been so kind to her.

She threw off the covers and padded into the kitchen. She had a one-bedroom apartment in a row house on Pitt Street about two blocks from the College of Charleston, in the heart of downtown. The house had been turned from a regal antebellum statement of the past history of Charleston into a rat maze of individual apartments for college students. She was the only one still at home. Everyone else had left the city for party time at some spring break location. She didn't miss that. At twenty-eight, she wasn't that much older than her peers, but she was a world apart in maturity. She'd had enough of the spring break bullshit and *Animal House* lifestyle on her first try at getting a degree.

She put on a pot of coffee and went to open the front door to get some fresh spring air. It was only March, and the weather was already starting to warm up. The swelter was something that she enjoyed. She couldn't see how anyone could live in cold weather. She got cold in a movie theater—forget about living permanently in the snowbelt. Having grown up as a tomboy on a ranch outside of Dallas, Texas, where she had spent most of her time outdoors, she had become used to the heat. It was muggier here, but still pretty close. If she couldn't live in Texas, at least she could sweat like she did.

She turned to check her coffee and found a flyer at her feet. It was for a live band at a bar called the Windjammer on the Isle of Palms, a barrier island about thirty minutes from her house. She picked it up and saw writing at the bottom: "You should be going stir-crazy by now. The offer still stands—you can stay with us. Meet us at the Windjammer tonight. If you don't like it, you can always go home." It was signed by her girlfriend Skeeter.

Jennifer thought about it for a second. She was looking for something to do, and maybe it was time to get out a little. Yeah, she'd have to fight off all the ogling boy-men who only wanted to get drunk, then get laid, but she could handle that. She just wasn't sure it would be fun anymore. Those situations always made her think of her past. *Shit, who am I kidding? I think about the past no matter what happens. The damn weather makes me think about it.*

She poured herself a cup of coffee and was reading the flyer again when her cell phone rang.

"Hey, you're up. Let me guess. You're in your pajamas studying for a test that might come after spring break. Did'ja get my flyer?"

Jennifer smiled. "Hello, Skeeter. No, I'm not studying. I had a man over here last night. He's an exchange student from Nigeria. He's still asleep because we were up pretty late watching C-Span. I'm not sure what you mean by 'flyer.'"

"Bullshit. I left a flyer on your doorstep. Go get it. I'll wait."

"I got the stupid thing. It's in my hand right now."

"Well, what do you say? Come on out. The condo's already paid for, so it won't cost you a thing."

"Skeeter, you know how I feel about that scene."

"Jesus, Jennifer! When are you going to let go? I get you had a rough time, but come on. This is your last year of college! Your final spring break. You'll be able to sit in a cubicle and slave away to your heart's content in a little bit. Think about it. I'll call back and bug you later."

Jennifer was going to reply when she realized that Skeeter had hung up. The truth of the matter was not a day went by when she didn't think about her ex-husband and what he had done. Not a day without feeling sweat break out over the memory, wondering what her life would have been like if she had stayed in school the first time.

She had dropped out of the University of Texas after her junior year to marry the iconic frat boy son of a Texas oil tycoon, who had just graduated. Things had been fine for all of ten minutes before she realized he was sleeping around on her. It was as if her husband was trying desperately to hold on to his frat boy lifestyle while walking up the corporate ladder. Nobody held him accountable, least of all his trophy wife. Thinking about it now, she had been very shallow. She had been raised poor, but proud. The Cahill name had been drilled into her from an early age as something that mattered beyond wealth. She had believed it, then had thrown it away.

They held on for four long years, mainly because divorce wasn't accepted by the in-laws. She made do with the finer things in life, all the while knowing that everyone was laughing at her behind her back. On the surface she had everything a girl could want, or at least anything that could be acquired with cash—cars, trips to St. Lucia, jewelry, you name it. She was only missing the things that money couldn't buy, like respect. For a Cahill, this was worth more than wealth. She tried hard to get her husband to stop, then tried to adjust her pride to accept her lot, but neither worked.

It finally came to a head when she arrived home to find him in bed with his secretary. Cheating at a sleazy motel was one thing, but doing it in her bed was another. The scene was branded into her soul, still as raw as the day it had happened. The secretary covering up her obviously fake breasts, a small smile on her face, no fucking shame whatsoever. Her husband taking control, not even acting as if he had done anything wrong.

She had begun to pack her bags, telling him that it was finally over. He told her to stop. She told him to screw himself. He slammed her against her dresser and punched her viciously in the stomach, causing her to fall onto the floor. He calmly told her to unpack her things and left the room. She remembered lying on the floor in her own spit and vomit, gasping for air, the fake-tit whore stepping over her with a sheet around her body.

She fled the marriage with the clothes on her back, returning to her mother's house in McKinney, Texas. The next few weeks were a nightmare. The punch seemed to have done something internally. She had cramps so bad she was left doubled over in pain. Her period came early, and very heavy. She went to the doctor and in the same breath he told her that she had been pregnant—and had had a miscarriage.

Jennifer shook herself. The memories always caused her to sweat, making her heart palpitate. *That fucker . . . I should have . . .* She took three deep breaths. *Quit thinking about it. Think of anything else. . . . Think of positive things. . . .*

After the miscarriage, her family had been her anchor. She had lost her way, but they didn't care. They had rallied around her as soon as she had come home. She didn't tell her family about the miscarriage, fearful of her brothers' possible retaliation. Sometimes, when the darkness came, she toyed with the idea of letting them in on the secret, knowing they would kill that sorry sack of shit with a cheese grater. Looking back, she was glad she never did, but a part of her waited for the day when she could get retribution. On days like today, when she was left clutching a counter, taking deep breaths to control her fear, she wanted nothing more than to cause him the same agony.

In the end, while it wasn't a pleasant thought, she knew that the attack was the best thing that could have happened. She had understood that she could never win any legal battles in a system owned lock, stock, and barrel by the family, and that it was the fight alone that they were afraid of. It never entered their minds that something bad would happen to their son. They just didn't want the embarrassment of the publicity. So, as they had been doing since robber baron times, they bought her off. They gave her an impressive little nest egg of two hundred thousand dollars, telling her never to talk about what had happened. She agreed. She remembered the moment well, thinking she should have crossed her fingers behind her back because if she ever got the opportunity, she would bury the family and sow their graves with salt.

Now, standing in her kitchen a thousand miles away, she had had enough of the hate and fear. Maybe a night out would help. Just because the Windjammer had a bunch of drunken college men didn't mean they were all like him.

She glanced at her computer screen and noticed she had an e-mail from her uncle. She forgot about the Windjammer. *He's not supposed to come out of the jungle for at least three days.* Obviously, once again he had failed to find the temple. She smiled to herself, thinking of him hacking his way through the jungle on yet another attempt. No matter how many times he failed, Uncle John remained optimistic. She admired that in him. Then again, she knew she'd find anything her uncle did something to admire. He had gone out on a limb to help her, getting her a fresh start at his own university based solely on the fact that she was his niece, telling white lies that could have cost him tenure. She would never forget that.

She opened the e-mail and saw that it was nonsense. It said nothing at all about his trip, or his return. It was just a few MP3s containing some local music. She found this strange, but not unduly so, as her uncle was always doing goofy stuff. *Last time he came home he gave you a real shrunken skull. Be thankful this is just music.* Whatever had happened, he would give her the full story on his expedition when he got back. She hooked up her MP3 player and began downloading the songs. Her uncle must have thought they were some pretty good tunes if he'd e-mailed them to her instead of just waiting until he returned. With the music downloading, she went to pack an overnight bag.

21

Abu Sayyidd was electrified by the story they had heard. "Did you listen to that? The boy found some sort of ancient weapon in the jungle. A weapon that can be used to kill the infidels. What we've been sent here to do, we can accomplish in half the time, a month instead of years."

Abu Bakr wasn't so sure Sayyidd was right. He was a pragmatic planner, a man who had escaped death precisely because he had predicted and counteracted contingencies before they occurred. This mission had taken close to a year to develop, and he was reluctant to simply throw it away on the story of a native boy.

"Sayyidd, please. We don't have the time or equipment to go foraging through the forest for some sort of mythical weapon. We don't even know if that boy was telling the truth. We've worked too hard to get where we are."

Their purpose was to set up a mechanism to infiltrate the United States using the illegal immigrant pipeline already established. Once the cells were in place, they would conduct synchronized acts of terror that would dwarf September 11, 2001. The hope was for a sustainable, repeatable mechanism that would cause the U.S. to crack down harshly on all things Arabic (and even Sikh,

Hindu, whatever was seen as "strange"), which would in turn plant a seed of jihad inside the U.S.

Sayyidd persisted. "You heard the description of the death. The weapon is something like the poison weapons we learned about in the camps. Something the Sheik has tried mightily to obtain. We might now have the ability to do what no other has done."

"What on earth makes you think there's a weapon in the jungle?" Bakr said. "I've heard children with more logical skepticism than you."

"Have you never heard of the medicines that are found in the rain forest? It's said to be a wonderland of ancient plants simply waiting to be discovered. What's the harm of looking? If we find it, we may truly bring the far enemy to his knees! We were chosen for this mission based on our skills and judgment. We need to use both."

Never having worked with Sayyidd before, only trusting that his superiors had selected the right man, Bakr was suspicious of Sayyidd's eagerness to abandon all they had worked for up until now. He took a different tack. "Why is your idea, even as fleeting as it is, better than what we're already doing? The only difference is time, and the fact that the original plan allows multiple blows against our enemy. How will your blow of one time outweigh the ability to strike repeatedly?"

Abu Sayyidd inwardly smiled. He was making headway. He had been thinking about their mission for a long time, and saw the fatal flaw within the jihad as currently waged.

"Tell me, what's the greatest problem facing the jihad today? Is it truly the far enemy? His transgressions on the land of Mecca and Medina spit in the face of all true

Muslims everywhere, yet he is allowed to continue. Why is that? It's because the true Muslim has been seduced by Satan, choosing Big Macs over the purity of the Quran.

"The average Muslim doesn't understand the threat of the far enemy. We need the man on the street to take up arms. The grocer, shoe salesman, and barber. If all Muslims would throw one rock, we would succeed. The only way to do this is to show the far enemy's true colors, to prove that they want to dominate and rule over a Christian empire."

Al Qaeda's doctrine, developed by Bin Laden and his leadership, stated that the only way to return to the ways of the Prophet was to destroy the "far enemy" that supported, and in some cases propped up, the godless regimes that had come to power in the nations of the Middle East, the so-called near enemy. The United States was first on the list of the far enemy for its support of the Kingdom of Saudi Arabia, Israel, Egypt, Jordan, and a host of other countries.

Bakr sighed. "Okay. So what. You sound like any imam in our mosques. What's that got to do with this mystical weapon? How can a single blow get what you want? It takes multiple blows against the far Satan to get him to do anything. The people of the U.S. have no memory. How will you cause this to change?"

Sayyidd held up his hands. "Please. Let me finish. We need to force the United States to attack all of a Muslim faith, without discrimination. To force the average Muslim to take up arms—either for faith or survival. I think we can cause this to happen if we *don't* attack the far enemy in his homeland. We'll attack him through his Zionist proxy. If we unleash this weapon against the murderous occupiers of Palestine, we can guarantee that they'll react in a frenzy. It would be a catalyst of war against their neighbors, which will cause the far enemy to choose between his Zionist son or the pure Muslims. It's no question who he will side with."

Abu Bakr was impressed with the logic of Sayyidd, and actually a little surprised, but still didn't think simply attacking Israel would be enough, even with a weapon of mass destruction. He was intrigued, though, and mulled the idea over in his mind. The more he thought about it, the more he thought it might succeed, with an additional twist.

"I don't think the weapon alone would be a sufficient catalyst. We need to ensure the Zionists will attack another. A bomb, no matter how great, may simply cause them to slaughter Palestinians, and that is an old story."

Bakr paced back and forth a minute, then said, "Why not kill two birds with one stone? If we were able to bring about the attack you envision and blame it on the Persians, we could use the United States to eliminate those infidels while accomplishing exactly what you want. The United States has already forgotten about Iraq and begun to rattle their sabers toward Iran. With the Persians constantly talking about driving Israel into the sea and their current nuclear ambitions, it wouldn't take much evidence to convince the Zionists of their culpability. The attack would cause a major conflict, forcing all to choose sides."

Abu Sayyidd thought the idea was a good one but impossible to execute.

"But how will we implicate the Persians? We have no contacts with the Shia dogs, and I don't think they'd volunteer."

Sayyidd had a point. While Iran did indeed provide support to various terrorist groups, most notably Hezbollah, the regime had little affinity for the Sunni-based Al Qaeda. Bakr knew there were ways around this. "One step at a time. We're assuming such a weapon exists. I'm not averse to seeing if we can find the weapon, provided it doesn't jeopardize our long-term efforts. For now, let's focus on simply getting the weapon. If that fails, we can still continue on our original task. That remains the priority."

Bakr gave Sayyidd a stern look. "You understand that, correct?"

Pleased at the new path, Sayyidd said, "Yes. Of course. I wouldn't do anything foolish."

Abu Bakr went to the back of the room and opened a box. They had brought with them a test case—a collection of items that were not illegal individually but, put together, were sure to be confiscated. If the package made it to the contact inside the U.S., then AQ would continue to the next step with Miguel's network. Inside the box was a Canon Rebel XTi digital camera, four Garmin 60CS mapping GPSs, four 3M P100 medical respirators, a box of glass test tubes, and two remote-control garage door openers. Fairly innocuous items by themselves, but if the box were searched, the items together would trigger a response, which would allow the terrorists to judge the integrity of the smuggling network.

Abu Bakr was disappointed in the packing list. "Where's the police scanner? The GPS and respirators will be useful for finding the weapon, but we need the police scanner right now."

"Ahh . . . I did some research on the American laws,

and the police scanner we obtained had the ability to scan in the American cell phone spectrum. It's illegal to import those to America, so I took them out. I didn't think we'd really be using any of this equipment. It was just to see if the network was good."

Bakr was flabbergasted. "You took something out of the box because it was illegal? Something that we were illegally trying to smuggle in? What in all that's holy—"

"Don't begin to attack me!" Sayyidd said. "We were specifically told not to include illegal items so that if the box was found there would not be a legal reason to pursue its owners. It would simply get confiscated. I didn't know we would use the equipment."

Bakr waved his hand. "What's done is done. I won't mention it again, but if you wish to proceed on this path we need to find a scanner."

He pointed to the suitcase holding their laptop computer and Thrane M4 satellite phone. "Get on the Internet and find a local store that sells scanners. One that can scan in the nine-hundred-megahertz range that the cell phones here use. We need to hear what's being said from inside this room. It's the only way we can stay ahead of Miguel."

22

The professor woke up bouncing on the backseat of an old Toyota Land Cruiser, having no idea how long he had been unconscious. He was covered in a musty blanket that stank of horse sweat and moldy hay. He heard the Englishman talking on a cell phone.

"He's not permanently injured, but he's going to have a headache. I took everything with him and checked him out of the hotel. Outside of some ratty clothes and a few maps of the biosphere, all he had was a laptop, an American cell phone, and a GPS. He had no return plane tickets."

The professor tried to move and realized that both his legs and hands were shackled like those of a death row inmate, which he was beginning to believe he had become. He was convinced that he was headed to some dank prison deep within Guatemala, to be held on the charges of murder and antiquities theft.

The man on the phone continued. "No, he didn't have anyone else with him. He looked like he was about to flee. I didn't want to try to smuggle him past airport security, so I'm driving back. I'll be there in about seven hours. I'll see you then."

Eight and a half hours later, the professor sat in absolute panic. He was tied naked to a chair with a cloth bag over his head. He could make out light, but nothing else. He felt he had been sitting for at least forty-five minutes but in truth had lost all track of time. He heard a door open and felt a breeze on his naked chest. He made one final attempt to raise whatever dignity he could muster.

"I am an American citizen and a famous archaeologist. The embassy knows I am here, and in fact sponsored my expedition. They will come looking for me, and when they find me, they will punish you."

The only response he received was two alligator clips clamping onto his nipples. His heart began to hammer in his chest. He thought he was going to piss himself or throw up. A voice with a heavy Spanish accent stated, "You are Professor Cahill, a known antiquities thief and potential murderer. Far from sponsoring your expedition, the American embassy will more than likely sponsor your extradition to Guatemala to stand trial. Spare me your theatrics and you may yet walk out of here. I want to know where the temple is located. I've been through your computer and GPS and could find no reference to it. I have very little patience. Tell me what I want to know and I'll let you go."

It finally dawned on the professor that he wasn't in the hands of anyone remotely associated with the Guatemalan government, and that his overwhelming fears twenty-four hours ago paled in comparison to his present predicament. For all of his eccentricities, at his core the professor was a very intelligent man. In an instant, he computed that the only thing that would keep him alive was the fact that he alone knew where the temple was located. The minute he gave this up, he would be discarded with as much fanfare as a used condom.

As he began to form a plan, a searing jolt of electricity rocked his body, causing him to lock up in a rictus of pain, screaming out his soul. As rapidly as it came, the pain left.

The disembodied voice spoke again. "I can see you're thinking of ways to lie to me. Trust me, the longer you sit and think, the more I believe what you say is a lie. You have exactly three seconds to start talking, or I'll flip this switch and leave it on for an hour."

The professor gasped for air, sweat running freely over his body, his mind racing. He didn't have a plan. He didn't know what to say. His heart was palpitating, skipping irregularly.

"Three, two, one . . ."

"*Wait*. I'm trying to talk. Please . . . Dear God, don't do it again. I'll tell you whatever you want. I have two GPSs. I FedExed the one I used in the jungle to my niece in Charleston, South Carolina, from Flores. I don't have the information here, but I can get it. Please . . . Please . . . Please . . . I want to help you."

The professor couldn't believe how ridiculous this sounded. Why on earth would he do that? It made no sense whatsoever, but if he told them the truth, he would simply be made to retrieve the data from his Hotmail account. It was still in the sent folder. Once he gave that up, and he was sure he wasn't strong enough not to, he would be dead. He had to buttress the argument, so he began babbling to stem the punishment that was sure to come.

"You know what happened. A man died at the temple. I was not on a sanctioned expedition. The government would arrest me. I had to get rid of the data without losing it. I was afraid of getting arrested. I wanted to keep the location but didn't want to have any evidence on me. You have to believe me!"

He was met by silence. The disembodied voice circled around behind him. "Professor, that story is so ridiculous it insults my intelligence. I'm a smuggler. I know every single way to get something into the United States. I know there is no FedEx office in Flores. Why on earth would you think I would believe that?"

The professor now believed he would die. The man had freely told him he was a criminal. Obviously, he had no intention of letting him go. In a panic, the professor began to expand on his story, making it more unlikely, grasping at straws.

"I gave it to an American who was leaving yesterday. We had become friends drinking at the bars, and I didn't want any evidence on me if I was stopped at the airport. He promised to FedEx it as soon as he landed in the United States. You must believe me! I'm telling the truth!"

"All right. I'll give you the benefit of the doubt. What was this man's name?"

"His name? It was . . . Uhh . . ."

With that, the pain returned like a lightning bolt. The professor jumped out of the chair, his entire body bowed out in an attempt to get away from the agony, his ankles and wrists holding him in place. He let loose a keening wail, then collapsed back into the chair, his bowels releasing onto the floor.

"Why'd you shut it off?" Miguel asked.

Jake said, "I didn't. He's still got megavoltage going through him."

"Wake him up," said Miguel.

Jake shut off the juice and felt the professor's pulse. "We can't. He's dead."

"What the fuck do you mean, dead? We barely got started."

"Maybe he had a bad heart. We usually do this to men and woman much younger than him. Whatever, it's irrelevant. He's stone-cold dead."

"Shit. What do you suppose the odds are that he was telling the truth?"

Jake grinned. "As a matter of fact, probably pretty good. He didn't say anything that we can contradict, and people who follow the law usually panic when they realize they might be caught doing something illegal. The story is so damn stupid it just might be true. If you want to continue with this, it wouldn't hurt to simply check it out."

"Perhaps. I suppose it's worth following through. I'll give our friends in the U.S. a call. They owe me a favor, and this won't take much effort. In the meantime, I saw that our friends from overseas brought some computer equipment with them. Please go get them. Maybe they can take a look at his computer and find something we missed."

Jake left the room to go to the guesthouse while Miguel dialed an unlisted number.

"Let me speak to Vincent." He waited while the phone was handed off. "Yes, it's your southern helper, and it's time to repay the favor owed. I'd like you to get a package for me that's been mailed. It's coming by FedEx to a woman named Cahill in Charleston, South Carolina. She's the niece of a professor at the College of Charleston under the same name and may very well be going to the school. You don't need to be polite to her."

23

Sayyidd stared at the laptop he had been asked to examine, wanting to shout in triumph. The thumb drive he had found among the belongings next to the computer had come to life, asking if he would like to use something called "cryptmaker" to extract data. He had been right. The computer was hiding a steganography program. He hit "yes" and waited for the work to be accomplished. Three of the twenty JPEG pictures he had cut and pasted from the laptop had dissolved, leaving behind a notepad file welcoming him to the cryptmaker family and giving him a troubleshooting guide. He realized that these were probably the example photos that came with the software package, allowing a new user to play with the software without fear of losing any valuable data.

Two hours earlier, when Jake had asked if either Bakr or Sayyidd could help with a computer problem, he had jumped at the chance. After meeting Miguel's computer expert, a man introduced only as José, he had been led into a room containing a table heaped with clothes, a laptop computer, cell phone, and GPS. While examining the computer, he began to suspect that it held a covert partition used for a steganography program due to the large amount of random digital photos and MP3s. José might have been an expert at typical computer problems, but he hadn't spent a life on the run with the world's greatest superpower chasing him. While serving as the media chief for his cell in Iraq, Sayyidd had used steganography quite a bit. He knew the signs. He also knew that he had no chance on earth of figuring out the keystrokes for a hidden program. His only hope was a physical key, something missed by Miguel's men. He had asked José for a glass of water to get him out of the room. As soon as he had left, Sayyidd had searched the clothes on the table. To his absolute surprise, he had found a thumb drive missed by the computer expert and had loaded it on the computer.

He was now sure he was only seconds away from finding the temple's location. One of the pictures on the hard drive would hold the data. He only needed to find the right one.

He was about to go back to the photo files when he heard José returning down the hallway. He deleted all of the files from the thumb drive, palmed it in his hand, and backed away from the computer.

José handed him the water and said, "You ready to continue?"

Sayyidd shook his head. "Not really. I've found nothing in two hours. I can't do anything more than what you've already done. I think this is a waste of time but will continue if you wish."

José said, "I knew this was folly to begin with. Miguel appreciates you trying anyway. You may go."

Sayyidd hurried back to the guesthouse with the thumb drive. He knew that Bakr would be livid at his theft. If Miguel realized what had taken place, they would both be dead. Sayyidd was counting on nobody knowing the thumb drive existed. He told Bakr of his experiences and what he had found. As expected, Bakr initially flew into a rage at Sayyidd's risks, but calmed down when told of the manner the thumb drive had been taken and the fact that Miguel's computer expert hadn't searched it. There was nothing to be done about it now anyway. The thumb drive was theirs. Risking returning it would be worse than keeping it.

The stego program itself made no sense to Bakr, given Miguel's previous phone call. They had obtained a Bearcat scanner earlier in the day, and both had heard the conversation between Miguel and his friends in the U.S. describing a FedEx package. Why would Miguel be searching for a package if the temple location was on the computer? Bakr told Sayyidd to check the Web for a FedEx office in Flores, the last place the professor had been. Within minutes, Sayyidd answered that the only FedEx was in Guatemala City.

Bakr digested this. The facts didn't make sense. Let Miguel waste his time and money searching for answers in America. Bakr was sure that the data was hidden somewhere on the professor's computer, and that maybe they were as close as Sayyidd thought to pleasing Allah as no man had before.

24

The old man had been watching the boat-pretender for close to two months, waiting on him to do something interesting.

He called the man the pretender because he didn't act like anyone who owned a sailboat. He had seen plenty of people rich enough to own such a luxury in his job at the marina, and this man didn't fit the profile in any way whatsoever.

For one, the old man had never seen the pretender's boat leave the dock. Ever. Truthfully, he was unsure if the pretender even knew how to sail.

For another, boaters were a partying, gregarious bunch. When they docked, it was all about margaritas, bragging, and laughter. The old man had never seen the pretender smile. Never seen him talk to a single captain of another boat.

He'd figured out early on that the pretender was living on the boat. Something that wasn't allowed long-term, but the old man said nothing. Working dawn until dusk pumping gas at the marina, the old man had studied the pretender just to break the monotony. Every other day the man would punish himself with a workout routine on the deck of the boat, working until total exhaustion in the South Carolina heat, seemingly trying to kill himself, the sweat rolling off his body in rivers. He would then leave for a run that lasted about an hour. When he returned, the old man would watch him stagger behind the Dumpsters and vomit, sometimes on his knees. He didn't understand why until the pretender had passed by him finishing a run. The man stank of liquor, the foul smell wafting out of his pores like a fog.

After that, the old man began to lose interest, not wanting to waste his time on a drunk. Then one day the pretender had surprised him. Buying fuel for his boat, he had recognized the U.S. Army Second Division patch on the old man's hat and had asked if he had been in the Army.

The old man had grown wary, not wanting to be patronized as he had been by all the other rich folks who treated him like a piece of furniture, fulfilling their duty of patriotism with a pat on the head before demanding gas.

He had said, "Yes."

"Korea?"

"Yes. During some bad times."

The pretender had nodded with understanding. "Nobody can take that away from you. Even when you wish they could."

The old man was shocked. *He knows.*

A long time ago, on another continent, nobody had cared about the color of his skin. Rednecks and racists alike had learned that combat was color-blind. All that mattered was skill, and the old man had found that he inherently possessed something that others did not. Once upon a time he had been regarded as a savior, a man who could keep you alive, if you were lucky enough to be near him. He had been held in awe by better men than those who now demanded his gas. He was reminded of this by the nightmares that still caused him to lose sleep. He both loved and hated that time in his life, and somehow the pretender *knew*.

He began watching the pretender with renewed interest. The next time they met, he had asked, "Were you in the service?"

"Yes. The Army."

"Been to Iraq? Afghanistan?"

"Both, at one time or another."

"Seen some bad shit?"

"Not really. The bad shit's here at home."

The answer had confused the old man. He continued to watch, waiting on the pretender to do something interesting. Eventually, the old man began to believe he had been wrong. The pretender held no secret truth. He was simply a drunken loser, dealing with the same demons as the old man. That was until the day the pretender disappeared and the old man had found two dead bodies behind the Dumpster, both killed by hand. That caused him to rethink the pretender's status for sure.

I WOKE UP IN MY KING-SIZED BED and rolled over to kiss my wife. My arm hit the pylon holding the foldout twin bed, and I returned to the reality of my existence like I had done every morning for the last nine fucking months. Each day, in the brief moment between being asleep and awake, I had one split second of happiness before remembering what had become of my family. If I could

bottle each split second, I'd give the remainder of the day
to God, or the Devil, or whoever else was having a party
out of my pain. Twenty-three hours, fifty-nine minutes,
fifty-nine seconds, and some change for each split second. It would be a good trade.

I relive the grief process every single day, like clockwork. I'm still waiting for it to be a dull ache at the back
of my soul, like all the doctors promised would happen.
Instead, each morning the pain is as strong as that night
in Tbilisi almost a year ago.

I sat up in bed and looked at the picture of Heather
and Angie on my counter. I felt the pain begin to turn to
rage. That also happened like clockwork. It's hard to explain the level of the anger. It's like trying to explain
color to a blind man. I'm afraid to really put into words
the dark thoughts that come to me. I want to rip someone apart while they're still alive, to destroy something
so completely that nothing identifiable remains. Sometimes the thoughts scare me.

I hate the rage, but there's nothing I can do about it.
It won't go away. I've tried. I've seen doctors and gone
to support groups, but nothing quenches it. I've talked
to guys who say they used to be in the same boat as me,
who lost their wife to cancer, or their family in a plane
crash, and they say the pain will dull, the rage will dissipate. They mean well, but they're wrong. It hasn't dulled
one bit. I think it's because they aren't in the same boat
as me. They had their pain thrown on them without being asked. I earned every sorry bit given to me. They lost
their family to fate or God. I killed mine.

If I had listened to Heather and hadn't done that final
tour, they'd be alive. Shit, I could have done the tour and

simply come home for Angie's birthday—*like I promised*—
and they'd be alive. Simple as that. Because of it, my punishment is a rage that's hard to quantify. A blackness that
wants to eat me. Wants to eat everything, spreading its
rotting hatred until the entire world is burning. I don't
think it will ever go away. It's hard enough just to control. It sits just below the surface, a beast looking to run
free. Sometimes I fantasize about letting it loose, about
completely giving in to it. I haven't yet, but it's hard.
Very, very hard.

My residence is my latest attempt to get rid of the
pain. I took our savings and bought a sailboat. An extreme fixer-upper. I had this idiotic fantasy that I'd spend
my days sanding wood, working on the engine, and live
like some dumb-ass hermit at a monastery. In my imagi-
nation, the blackness would slowly dissipate the further
along I got, until I was some sort of mystical sailor who
finally understood the meaning of life. Apparently, that
shit only works in the movies.

So far, I haven't done a single thing with the boat. Well,
at least nothing positive. I have managed to turn the galley
into a giant garbage can. There are enough pizza boxes
and beer cans to keep it afloat if it springs a leak. Last
night, I had decided that today would be the day I would
begin work on the top deck, sealing it and doing other
maintenance. Now, in the morning light, I really didn't
give a shit about my crumbling deck. I'd rather go get a
beer. It was my day off from physical training, so I didn't
have anything I really needed to do. I kissed my finger and
touched the picture of my family. *Who am I kidding? I
never have anything I really need to do.*

25

Jennifer and Skeeter, along with six other girls, entered the front door of the Windjammer a little after eight at night. The floor was already crowded, but nowhere near as crowded as it would be in a few more hours. At least at this hour they could move around without pushing and could hold a conversation without leaning in and yelling into each other's ears.

Jennifer had shown up at Skeeter's condo on the Isle of Palms a little more than two hours ago. Skeeter appeared surprised that Jennifer had shown up, and went out of her way to make sure she was settled in, kicking out the coed currently sleeping in one of the guest rooms and giving Jennifer the bed. Surrounded by the other girls having a good time, Jennifer began to feel glad she had come. Now, standing inside the Windjammer, she wasn't so sure.

Four frat boys stood in the middle of the large dance floor, loud and obnoxious. Jennifer recognized the ringleader. His name was Tad, and he reminded Jennifer of her ex-husband both in looks and attitude. *Great. Just what I need to ruin the evening.* Tad himself seemed to think it was his destiny to sleep with Jennifer and came on to her at every opportunity. *Just ignore him. He's not your ex-husband. He's just a loudmouth.* She felt a tap on her shoulder.

"Hello . . . are you listening?" said Skeeter.

"Yeah. Sorry. What did you say?"

"What do you want to drink? I'll go fight the bar."

Jennifer laughed at that, because she knew Skeeter's idea of "fighting" the bar entailed "accidentally" brushing up against a man with her breast, saying "excuse me," then scooting through the gap made when the man turned around.

"I'll come with you. Maybe we can get a stool."

Skeeter moved through the crowd like she owned the place, using her hand or breast to part the crowd, depending on gender. When she reached the bar only one man separated her from her goal. Seated on one of the few available stools, he was holding a beer and staring unfocused at the bar top, apparently deep in thought. He was clearly easy pickin's, as he was here on his own and probably looking for a date. Skeeter brushed his upper arm with an ample breast and said, "Excuse me; can I get in here?"

Jennifer waited to see his reaction when he saw Skeeter. It was always funny watching a man's face turn from a normal expression to a drooling mass of testosterone upon looking into her eyes.

In this case, the guy looked up at her with no more expression than if he were talking to a cabdriver. Saying, "Yeah, go ahead," he scooted over, giving her space at the bar. As Skeeter moved forward he locked eyes with Jennifer, nodded, then returned to his beer. His stare made Jennifer want to take a step back. It wasn't exactly mean, just annoyed, as if they had interrupted something important. Older than most in the bar, wearing a simple T-shirt and sporting a day-and-a-half beard, he had a white scar that ran through his cheek, charting a path through his stubble.

Skeeter ordered a couple of margaritas and moved back from the bar. "What's up with that guy? He looked at us like he was wondering if we owed him money. I've had more interest paid to me by a transvestite. He'd better watch himself, or he's going to find himself on the short end of the Skeeter Slam."

"Come on. Leave him alone. He doesn't look like someone with a very good sense of humor."

"Yeah, I know. It's easier to screw with Tad anyway. Let's go make those guys drool."

"Can't we just stay here? I don't feel like putting up with Tad's shit."

"What's the big deal? He's just a blowhard. If he gets obnoxious we can leave. How about—"

Before she could finish, they both heard Tad's raised voice. He and his little group had surrounded another college student and were in a face-off. She heard Tad telling the student to get the hell out of the bar on his own two feet or leave in an ambulance. *Friggin' great. Now there's going to be a bar fight. Why did I come out here?*

From the other side of the group, the man from the bar suddenly stood up and walked over to Tad, saying, "Leave him alone. He's been sitting there listening to your shit for a half hour. You're even."

Jennifer stared at him, surprised. The penetrating gaze was gone, replaced by an unfocused alcoholic haze. She must have been imagining things, because this guy was clearly drunk. No wonder he hadn't hit on them. He probably hadn't even been able to focus on them. She knew that he was in trouble, because Tad would kick his ass just to make his night, and no matter how good a fighter the man might be sober, now he was swaying back and forth and would be lucky to land a punch. Jennifer saw Tad look at the drunk, sizing him up. She could tell that Tad had come to the same conclusion she had.

Tad said, "You know what makes me sick? Shitbags like you who come into the Jammer stinking up the place instead of hanging out at the VFW next door with the rest of the winos."

With that, he threw a hard right punch, catching the drunk full in the face.

To his credit, the man didn't fall, but he had no coordination to protect himself. Tad waded in, throwing right after left, almost all of them connecting in one way or another. The drunk staggered back, protecting his face and feebly throwing a succession of worthless jabs that Tad batted away. He finally fell over, whereupon Tad set about kicking him relentlessly in the ribs.

Tad's sycophant friends wasted no time jumping on the other college student, all of them falling to the ground and rolling around. The bouncers came screaming in, focused on the three-to-one fight, flinging bodies left and right to separate them, not realizing there were two fights occurring, and leaving Jennifer to watch the punishment Tad was dishing out. She flashed back to her ex-husband and snapped. Without thinking, she dropped her drink and ran the ten feet to the fight. She grabbed Tad's arm and jerked him back, screaming, "Leave him alone! You're going to kill him!"

Tad shook her off, intent on continuing the assault.

Jennifer threw herself onto the man, shielding his body with hers. Tad stopped, looking at her in a murderous rage as if he was considering kicking her as well. Instead, he made a hasty exit out the back onto the deck. In seconds, the bouncers had control of the other fight and proceeded to escort the offenders to the door.

Jennifer helped the bloodied, pathetic fighter to his feet, talking to the bouncer headed their way. "I have him. I'll get him out of here."

"You'd better. Before I have him arrested."

She didn't know why, but she began leading him out of the bar, apologizing to the bartender as she walked. Maybe she saw herself on the floor four years ago. Maybe she just wanted an excuse to leave. *Maybe this just wasn't such a great idea. . . .*

Skeeter ran over to her. "Where are you going? You didn't do anything! You need to stay. All the assholes are gone now and the music hasn't even started."

"Skeeter, I appreciate it, but I'm no longer in the mood. I'm going to get this guy wherever he needs to go and head on back to the condo for some sleep. I'll pack up and go home tomorrow."

Skeeter watched her leave. Another sorority sister asked, "Where's she going with that loser? Is she desperate? She can do better than him."

Looking at her friend, Skeeter replied, "She's just saving another lost puppy. Like every other time this happens, that puppy is going to end up doing nothing but peeing on her floor. I've seen his type. He'll give her nothing but grief."

26

Jennifer led the man to her car, a beat-up Mazda RX-7, which she had left at the end of Ocean Boulevard. He shuffled along a half a step behind her, making no effort to talk. She asked him repeated questions, but he just mumbled in response. She couldn't even get him to tell her his name. *Great. He really is a drunk. Maybe I'll just give him some change and point him to the nearest park bench.* When they finally got to her car, he attempted to wave her off, saying he was fine and could get home on his own. She was surprised by the sudden apparent sobriety. He was no longer swaying, and his eyes were fairly clear, although it was hard to tell with the swelling. *What is with this guy? He was a drunk one minute, and sober the next? Why fake being drunk?*

She said, "Look, don't act like you're putting me out. You're really doing me a favor. If you go off on your own, I'll have no excuse for not going back in there. I'm headed home anyway, so you might as well let me give you a ride—that is unless you live somewhere other than the Isle of Palms. I'm not running a taxi service to Charleston."

"I live at the marina, but I don't need a ride. My bike is down the street. I'm sober enough to drive."

"Are you nuts? Even if you were stone-cold sober, you'd probably wreck from the beating. Come on. I'm offering a ride for free. No strings attached."

"I don't need a ride. Worst case, I'll just walk. It will do me some good."

The penetrating gaze was back, forcing her to glance away.

"Walk? It's, like, five miles away. Quit bitching and get in."

He closed the gap between her and the car. With the car preventing her from moving away, he leaned into her personal space.

"Why do you feel compelled to help me out? You don't know anything about me. The world is full of monsters; why do you think you're immune to them? Do you think that just because you made some pathetic attempt at 'helping' me out I won't rape you? How long do you think it would have taken the bouncers to get to me? About a half second after you did? Don't flatter yourself. I didn't need the help then, and don't need it now."

He was towering over her, his eyes radiating anger. For a split second she was afraid, wanting to bolt, wondering if she had made a terrible mistake. But her fear quickly gave way to irritation. What the hell was this all about? All she was trying to do was to help him out. He definitely wasn't a charmer, but he didn't seem like the type who would smack someone around just for the hell of it. After living with her husband for four years, her antenna for that sort of thing was fairly well tuned. Either way, she'd had enough. *Ungrateful son of a bitch.*

"Back off! What the hell is your problem? If I thought

you were going to attack me, I'd have let Tad crush your ass. If you planned on raping me, why on earth would you tell me beforehand? Oh, and yeah, I did save your ass. In case you didn't notice, Tad was giving you a beating that was about to be the difference between a ride in my car and a ride in an ambulance. Thanks for your appreciation; now get the hell out of my way and start hoofing it to the marina, superman."

She pushed him back from the door, yanking it open and banging her head as she tried to get inside the small cockpit of her car. She reached over to close the door when he leaned in and stopped her.

"My name's Pike. Pike Logan."

"Pike? What, are your parents Romanian vampires or something? Thanks for the information, but at this stage I really don't give a shit. Please let go of my door."

"That's just what I'm called. Look, I apologize. I haven't had a good day and took it out on you. I could use that ride."

When she looked back up at his face, she saw the intensity had been replaced by pain and confusion. Maybe shame. She was left with the impression that he hadn't apologized to anyone in a long time, and he was waiting to see if the gesture was worth it. *Shit. I know I'm going to regret this.*

"Get in. I'll take you home." Once he was settled in the passenger seat, she stuck out her hand and said, "I'm Jennifer Cahill. What's your real name?"

He took it, saying, "I told you, it's Pike. Pike Logan."

She started the car and pulled out of the parking lot, keeping the conversation going. "Really? If I were going to book you for assault, that's what I'd write down? What was the name written on your birth certificate?"

"I've been called Pike for a long time. It's my name now."

They rode in silence for a few minutes before she tried again.

"If you live at the marina, you're either passing through or working as a sailor. Which is it?"

"Neither. I moved here about two months ago. I don't like paying rent and couldn't afford a house. A guy was selling a beat-up thirty-seven-foot boat that needed a lot of work. The plumbing was okay, and the slip was paid for a year. I bought it, and now I live there."

"Wow, that's pretty romantic."

"It puts a roof over my head."

Jennifer waited for more, but he said nothing.

"That's it? Nobody buys a boat just to live on. They buy it for a reason. Come on, what's yours?"

She saw him grimace at the question.

"I told you why. There isn't any deep meaning. It's just a damn boat. A place to live. Do we have to keep talking about it?"

She let it go. Luckily, they had turned onto Forty-first Avenue and were only seconds from the marina. The rest of the ride was spent in silence.

"All right, we're here. Where do I go?"

"Just park it anywhere. I can walk in from here. What do I owe you for the ride?"

Jennifer hesitated, and then said, "Does your boat have a bathroom? I really have to go."

She regretted saying it as soon as it came out. She

really just wanted to use the bathroom but was sure he would take it a different way. She didn't want him to think she was attracted in any way. When she saw his face, she realized that he was embarrassed as well.

"Ahh . . . yes . . . I do have a bathroom, but it's a dinky thing that requires you to pump it to get it to work, sort of like a floating outhouse. You're welcome to use it, if you want. Just don't complain about the mess."

"Okay. If you don't mind, I'll use it and go on home."

Jennifer walked down into the galley of the boat and was repulsed by the mess. *Doesn't this guy know that underwear doesn't wash itself? Man, how could he live in this filth?* She was really wondering what the toilet would be like, and figured she'd be doing the squat-and-hover like she was at a sleazy truck stop in between Mississippi and Louisiana. She looked around in an attempt to find something to talk about to break the awkward silence. She was just about to ask him if dirty socks were commonly used as insulation when she saw a picture of a very pretty woman on the shelf above the foldout bed.

"Is that your girlfriend? She's gorgeous."

"That's my wife. She's dead, and I don't want to talk about that either."

The words hit Jennifer like a cold shot of water. Next to the woman in the picture was a small child. She wisely decided not to ask who that was. Pike showed her the toilet, which was surprisingly clean, and how to operate the pump that flushed it. After she finished, she came out, trying to look cool leaning against the doorjamb, saying, "Thanks. I guess I'll head out now."

There was another moment of awkward silence. It looked to her like Pike didn't know what to say. She was wondering if he was going to spit out some sort of Tourette's syndrome rant when he finally said, "Well, I appreciate your help tonight. Thanks again for the ride."

With a wry grin, Jennifer said, "You don't lie very well. Thanks for the use of your bathroom."

Pike gave her a smile that reached his eyes for the first time. The effect diminished his Halloween mask appearance. *He ought to do that more often.*

"You don't lie very well either," he said. "I meant it."

Jennifer left the boat, wondering if she would ever see Pike again. She also wondered why she cared. He was attractive enough in a weird, Grizzly Adams sort of way, but he had a personality that seemed to swing between outright asshole to limited tolerance. He had moments of humor and kindness that almost seemed to be fighting their way out.

She had reached the front of her car before she saw the two men standing behind it.

She stopped where she was, immediately feeling unease and toying with running back to Pike's boat. "Can I help you guys?"

The taller of the two moved to the driver's side. "You can help yourself, that's for sure."

The shorter man, surprisingly fast, circled around behind her.

27

I pulled out my bed and sat down, thinking about Jennifer. *What in the hell was that all about? Who throws their body on a complete stranger in a bar fight? And then offers to take them home afterward? Especially someone like me?* That took a lot of guts—or stupidity. I wasn't sure which, but I was leaning toward guts. She didn't act stupid. I was starting to feel a little bad about the way I had treated her. I thought about the vile things I had yelled at her by her car and felt a wash of shame. *Jesus, what an asshole.* I was surprised she'd let me in her car.

I looked in my small mirror and felt the anger come back at the sight of my beaten face. Lately, after I got a few beers in me, I began thinking about beating the hell out of someone just to release a little of the pain. I hadn't sunk so low as to simply punch the first person I saw, but I could usually count on some blowhard to be around as the night wore on. I had found out early on that I must look like a mean bastard, because blowhards usually backed down when I confronted them. I solved that dilemma by acting like I was too drunk to brawl. The problem with this cycle was that some sort of switch goes off after I pick the fight and I end up taking an ass-beating. I just can't bring myself to crush whoever I'm fighting.

That's probably a good thing. All it would take was one fight to get out of control, and I would then be viewed as a menace to society, the fall from grace complete.

Outside, I heard, "Pike!"

What now?

Scrambling up onto the deck, I saw Jennifer running flat out down the gangway to my boat, followed by two other men.

Before I could say anything, she ran right by me, shouting, "Help me!" as she went down into my boat. I turned back around and faced the men.

They had reached the deck of my boat and stopped. They looked completely out of place for a marina. One was squat, with a bullet head and no neck. He had a ridiculous hoop earring in one ear. The other was taller, and more distinguished, with glasses and a little gray at the temples. Both were wearing suits.

The taller one spoke. "This is none of your business. Just step aside. We're her cousins. We told her some bad news about her uncle, and she took it the wrong way."

They both advanced onto my deck as he spoke, with the Neanderthal guy circling to my left.

"Get the fuck off of my boat."

Neanderthal spoke for the first time. "No, you get off. I promise, I'm much worse than that pissant college boy that kicked your ass. I'm not going to stop with a couple of punches. Step aside."

From Neanderthal's position I was having a hard time keeping both men in sight. They clearly had done this before, and I could almost smell Neanderthal's eagerness to tear into me. The fight was coming, because there was no way I was getting off my own fucking boat. I gave one attempt to stop it, since it wasn't really fair for Neanderthal to think the frat boy had won on skill.

"Look," I said, "I don't want any trouble. Just leave and there won't be any need to call the police."

Neanderthal said, "You've already got trouble," then swung a hard right cross. *Idiot.*

I raised my left arm, forming a triangle against my head in order to protect it. I took the brunt of the blow and wrapped my left arm around the man's right, trapping his elbow. I brought my right arm underneath the elbow and wrenched against the joint with great force, causing it to splinter upward, against the direction it was intended to go. Before the damage had even registered in Neanderthal's brain, I put his head between my arms at waist level in a guillotine choke, preventing him from harming me while I tried to determine what the other man was doing, an unknown threat still on the loose.

While we danced around, the taller man pulled out a double-edged Gerber Mark I boot knife.

"Let him go, or I'm going to carve you up."

I stared at the knife to make sure it was real, feeling a perverse sense of joy. In fact, it was more like elation, as if I had just rubbed off a winning lottery ticket. He had pulled out a lethal weapon, which legally allowed me to escalate to lethal force. *I can let the beast loose.*

I locked eyes with the knife-wielding man and grinned. Instead of cutting off the blood flow in the Neanderthal's carotid arteries and simply causing him to pass out, I jerked upward with all of my strength, snapping his neck cleanly. I continued to pull until I felt his vertebrae separate and his neck begin to stretch like a weak rubber band.

I dropped that lifeless sack of shit and took off at a dead sprint toward the tall man. He looked at me in amazement and brought his knife hand up, preparing to rip me open. I faked in, causing him to slash early. I dodged the sweeping blade and trapped his knife hand in between my own two hands. Controlling the blade, I ducked under his arm, bringing the knife with me and turning his arm into a pretzel. I continued to rotate until his joints gave, first at the elbow, then at the wrist. It sounded like a kid twisting Bubble Wrap. I completed the circle and ended up facing him head-on, still holding his knife arm, which had turned into a useless piece of bone and gristle. I looked deep into his eyes and rammed the blade straight into his fucking skeevy heart.

He remained standing for a full second, his mouth a perfect O, looking down in disbelief at the knife sticking out of his chest, still held by his own destroyed arm, his hand facing the opposite of where it should be. He fell over backward onto the deck.

I looked around for other threats and found none, either on the boat or onshore. All I saw were the two people I had butchered. My rage disappeared. I knew that I had crossed the final threshold. *I've just killed two people in cold blood. I'm a fucking psychopath. I'll be put down like a rabid dog, and I deserve it.*

I wasn't sure what to do. I figured I'd better call 911 but decided to check on Jennifer first. I called her name and descended into the galley. She came flying out of the forward hold, hugging me and crying uncontrollably. She stopped sobbing and began babbling something about her uncle and the danger he was in.

I held on to her arms and pushed her back a little until I could see into her eyes, saying, "Whoa. Slow down. It's okay now. What did those guys want?'

"I don't know. They said that my uncle was in trouble, and that if I wanted to help him I had to give them a package he had sent. I don't know what they're talking about. I never got a package, but when I told them that, they said that it was going to be very painful for me if I continued to lie. The shorter one began talking about what he was going to do to me if I didn't give them the package."

I already knew something screwy was going on, because Neanderthal had mentioned my fight at the Windjammer. These guys must have had Jennifer under surveillance, and an effort like that meant that somebody wanted something very badly from her. I found it hard to believe she was completely in the dark. *Great. Just perfect.* I had broken up some sort of sleazy criminal exchange.

"Who are those guys, and don't give me 'I don't know.' Bad guys hunting you for no reason only happens in the movies. What are you into? Drugs or something?"

Jennifer shook her head violently. "I'm not into anything. I don't know what they're after. Something about my uncle, I guess."

"Who's your uncle?"

"He's on a research expedition in the Guatemalan rain forest. I have no idea what they could want with him, or with me. I'm telling the truth. They were definitely after me because they knew my uncle's name. I don't know what's going on."

She broke down again and began to sob, sinking into a chair. I didn't buy a single bit of what she'd said. I didn't think the crying was an act, because they probably had threatened her with all sorts of vile shit, but I was sure she was lying about not knowing what was going on. After interrogating hundreds of suspected terrorists, I had a cynical view about a person's innocence when the facts didn't jibe. You wouldn't believe the number of times I have heard a terrorist say something stupid like, "I swear, I didn't know that the car in my garage had four hundred pounds of TNT in it. I just took it in for an oil change. . . ."

I figured Jennifer and her uncle were involved in some sort of drug smuggling scheme, and would leave it at that. *Research expedition. Yeah, right. Researching how to get some product across the border.*

Whatever she was into, I now had a new concern. I had just whacked a couple of unsavory individuals. These types of thugs had bosses who remained in power by being the biggest badasses in the jungle. They wouldn't let this go, but would be coming for me to make sure everyone knew what happened to somebody who interfered. On top of that, there was no way the cops would believe that I had nothing to do with whatever was going on.

I thought about my options, which is to say I realized I had very few. I could simply get on my boat and start sailing somewhere, getting someplace safe and starting over, but in the two months I had owned the boat, I had done absolutely nothing with it. It was less seaworthy now than when I'd bought it. Not that that really mattered, since I barely knew how to sail and had about four hundred dollars to my name. That pretty much eliminated the water option. I could leave the boat and do the same thing on land, but my finances made this even more unattractive. At least with the boat I'd be taking my house with me. Without it, I'd either be sleeping outdoors or running out of money in a matter of days.

I cursed and punched a bulkhead, the anger coming back with a vengeance. Jennifer recoiled at the violence, but I didn't give a shit.

"You're going to tell me what's going on before the cops get here. I'm not going to get rolled up into whatever bullshit, amateur-hour scheme you and your uncle are into."

"I don't know! Jesus, I'm supposed to be on spring break! If you don't want to talk to the cops, fine. I won't mention you. I'll just say somebody yelled at the jerks and they panicked and ran away. You've done your good deed; you don't have to worry about any police activity, since I'm sure that you've got an arrest record a mile long. In fact, I'm pretty sure I don't want any police officer to think that you and I are somehow involved in something either."

Is she drunk? I looked at her in amazement, then remembered that she hadn't been around for the finale of the fighting. "It's a little bit late for that. The two apes up top are dead. I killed them. I'm involved whether you like it or not, and I don't like to be involved in something I have no control over. Tell me what's going on."

Jennifer looked at me, stunned. "You *killed* them? How? Why on earth would you do that—"

"Because the assholes that wanted to talk to *you* pulled a knife on *me*. It's done, and now I'm involved in a mess I want no part of. Who's your contact? Who sent those guys?"

Jennifer simply sat there.

I backed off. Scaring the shit out of her wasn't going to get me anywhere. I leaned back, thinking about what I knew. My gut was suddenly saying she wasn't lying. When I thought about it, I realized the woman who'd helped me tonight didn't seem like the type involved in anything like drug smuggling. It just didn't add up. Someone like that would have waited until I was unconscious, then picked my pocket. I stopped that line of thought. *Don't be fooled by the package. You don't know her at all.*

Either way, it wasn't my problem. I needed to figure a way out of this mess and quit worrying about whether she was guilty. I went back to the deck, feeling the clock ticking rapidly. It was a miracle that nobody around the marina had heard the ruckus, but it was only a matter of time before someone wandered by. Thinking it through, I realized that it would be much, much better if I called the police, or if Jennifer did. Every second of delay was going to look suspicious.

I searched both bodies. The only things of value were a couple of wallets with driver's licenses from New York and New Jersey and a couple of cell phones. I checked the contact lists of both phones. They were empty, which indicated in and of itself that these guys had something to hide, although that was blatantly obvious at this point. I switched to the call history of the phones, hoping that these guys weren't that diligent with their operational security. The shorter man—Anthony, from his driver's license—had no incoming calls, and about twenty calls to 1-900 numbers on the outgoing list, thus was little help. The taller man, or Edward, had two incoming calls, one from overseas by the look of the number. His outgoing-calls list only contained two numbers, one of them matching up to the overseas incoming number. I went back to Jennifer.

"Do you know the country code of Guatemala?"

"I think so. It's either 520 or 502."

"Well, one of the guys has an international phone number starting with 502, so he's calling Guatemala. Does your uncle have a GSM phone that works outside the U.S.?"

"No. He always communicates over the Internet. Most of the places he goes don't have cell phone service, so he doesn't bother."

I hit redial on the phone, wondering who was paying the bill for this call.

Jennifer stood up. "What are you doing? Who are you calling?"

"I don't know who's going to answer, but I'm getting my ass out of trouble with whoever is after you. You might want to do the same. I'll pass the phone to you when I'm done."

I stood waiting for the connection to be made. Finally, a man with a heavy Spanish accent answered in English. "So good of you to call. I assume that it's done? Do you have some good news?"

"Uh, no. We don't have the package. And the guy who owns this phone won't be getting the package. He's now out of the picture for the long term."

I had no idea who this was, but there was a better-than-even chance that whoever he was, he was being monitored. I didn't want to incriminate myself on some DEA tape.

"I'm sorry; my English isn't that good. Could you please explain yourself?"

"Yeah, I'll try to make it as plain as I can. Your messenger acted like an asshole and I took him off the project. I'm not involved in any way, and just want to make sure that you know that I don't have the package, don't want the package, and don't even know what it is."

28

On his Guatemalan estate, Miguel cursed under his breath. *Those damn amateurs.* He should have known they would screw this up, but he was on a tight time schedule, and they were the only ones who could have reacted in time. His calculator brain began assessing courses of action. The guy on the other end of the phone, whoever he was, was clearly no innocent bystander, as he'd had the presence of mind to call and had fairly good operational security on the phone. Tony and Ed must have said too much, and now this guy wanted a piece of the action. On the other hand, why would he start out by saying he wanted nothing to do with it? Of course, he could be the police, but if that were the case it really didn't matter. Miguel wasn't tied to whatever antics Ed and Tony had pulled. The only loss was the package itself, and if this was the police, the whole operation was over anyway. He needed to determine who this guy was, and maybe turn this to his advantage.

"I'm beginning to think you have a wrong number. I'm sure I don't know what you are talking about, but am curious. If you don't know anything about the package, then how do you know there is one? That seems a little illogical."

"Look, the person who was supposed to get the package is sitting right here. She told me about it. I'm not involved and just want to make sure you know that I'm not trying to get the package, whatever it is. Your business is with her, not me."

Miguel had the opening he wanted but was still not sure this wasn't a trick. "All right, because I'm curious and have nothing else to do right now, I'll talk to her. Put her on."

"I will, but before I do, are we good? I'll get her on the phone, and I'm out of it? I didn't mean to do anything, but your messengers were insistent."

"Sure, you're good. Put her on. Since I don't know about a package or any messengers, I certainly won't be upset at you for anything."

Miguel waited a few seconds, then heard a female's voice. "Hello? Who's this?"

He was surprised, but pleasantly so. This seemed to be the real deal, and it didn't look like the entire operation had been brought to a halt. He still needed the package, but maybe he could get it through her. He dropped his innocent pretenses. "Is this the niece of John Cahill?"

"Yes, this is Jennifer. What do you want? How do you know who I am?"

"I'm a business associate of your uncle's. He told me that he mailed you a package by FedEx yesterday. Unfortunately, he mailed you something that he had promised me, and I need to get it back. My two friends were sent there to get it from you, but apparently you would prefer to steal what is rightfully mine."

The phone went silent. After a pregnant pause, the woman spoke.

"I don't know what to say. I don't have a package

from my uncle. If you would let me talk to him, maybe I can sort this out."

Miguel knew he had to manage this carefully. His only lead was the phone call going on right now, and both would likely flee as soon as they hung up. He didn't even know the man's name. He needed to turn this to his advantage, bringing the mountain to Muhammad, as his foreign guests would say.

"I'm not sure what else your uncle could add to the conversation. He told me he sent you a package, the method it would arrive, and the date. What I need is that package, and since you have seen fit to prevent my men from collecting it, I'm going to need you to bring it to me."

"I'm telling the truth. I didn't kill your guys; Pike did."

WHAT THE FUCK DID SHE JUST SAY? I jumped up in a spasm, trying to get the phone out of Jennifer's hands. She turned around in a circle, batting my hands away and continuing the conversation.

"I'm the person they threatened. I don't want to be a part of this either. Whatever my uncle owes you, I'll help him to repay. Whatever is in the package, I'll make sure you get a replacement. If you would just get my uncle on the phone, we can sort this out."

I saw Jennifer's face go white at whatever the man was saying. I quit trying to get the phone.

"Please, please don't hurt my uncle. . . . I'll do what you want. . . . Whatever you want . . ."

She looked me in the eye, her expression pleading for help, and said, "Pike wants the phone. . . . I don't know. . . . Please . . . Here's Pike."

She held out the phone with her hand over the microphone and said, "Talk to him. Please . . . do something. I don't know what to tell him. I don't know anything about a package. Don't let him hurt my uncle."

I snatched the phone and put my own hand over the microphone. "Why in the hell did you give him my name and tell him his men were dead? I'm trying to help us out and you're sitting there digging a grave for both of us. Focus on your own damn grave and leave me out of this!"

"Please . . . Talk to him." The fear on her face cracked my anger.

Shit. She's telling the truth. I looked at her for a second, making up my mind.

I removed my hand and said, "This is Pike."

"I didn't know the extent of the damage to my operation. Is what she says true?"

I gave up any pretense of operational security. If someone was recording this, I was already screwed.

"Yes, it's true, but I only reacted to what they did. The assholes came on my boat and tried to knock me out. When I stopped that, they pulled out a knife and tried to gut me. I have no idea what this is about, but I'm not going to be held accountable for your team losing their cool. I really didn't want anything to do with this. They escalated, not me."

"I don't give a shit about your excuses. I only care about the fact that your interference will cost me profits. I don't have my package because of you. I'll give you a choice. Either get the package and deliver it to me or I'll take the profits out of your skin."

Shit. That was the last thing I wanted to hear. What in the world had this girl gotten involved in?

He continued. "Don't test my patience. If you wish, you can run. It'll just increase the pain of your death. Put on the girl."

"Hang on, hang on. I'll get your package. We don't have it here. I just met the girl, and she's been out here all week."

"I'll make this plain, as I'm not sure my English would be able to get across any subtle nuances. Bring me the package or I will kill your uncle in a very slow, painful manner."

"Yeah, yeah, I get it. I don't speak Spanish, so I'll talk slow as well. It's not my uncle and I don't give a shit about him."

I saw Jennifer snap her head around, looking at me like I was a piece of dog shit on her shoe. I held up a finger and continued. "The package is probably at her house in town. We'll go see if it's there."

I waited a beat, hearing only silence. "You still there?"

"Yes. I'm now trying to decide if I want the package more than the pleasure of killing you. Let's get something straight: I will slaughter you and anyone you have ever known if you speak to me in such a manner again. Do you understand?"

Oops. I guess that wasn't so smart. "Yes."

"You and Jennifer call me when you have the package. If you don't call in the next six hours, you can start the clock ticking on your life. Tell the girl her uncle will be skinned alive."

I hung up the phone and looked at Jennifer's ashen face. *Yeah, I'll be sure and relay that bit of sunshine.*

29

It took relatively little time for us to determine that there was no package waiting at Jennifer's apartment. She went to her computer to see if she had a FedEx tracking number, or anything to indicate something was on the way, but came up empty.

Jennifer said, "What the hell am I going to do now? I don't even know what's supposed to be in the package, so I can't even fake it."

I needed to get some background before I offered any advice. "What was your uncle doing in Guatemala? I mean for real, no bullshit?"

Jennifer sighed again, like she didn't think I would believe what she had to say, which was smart, because if it was some sort of Indiana Jones bullshit, I wouldn't.

"My uncle has a theory about the demise of the Mayans. He thinks the Mayan priests created a weapon a long time ago that got out of control. For the last twenty years he's gone down to Guatemala to find a temple that he thinks will prove his theory." She saw the skepticism on my face and raised her voice. "I know it sounds ridiculous, but it's true. That's what he's doing in Guatemala."

This was getting downright stupid. "So, your uncle

believed that the Mayans had invented or found the world's first WMD? Did he look for crop circles during Christmas break?"

Jennifer's eyes clouded with a scowl. "I never said anything about WMD. I said a weapon. Many, many respectable scholars believed his theory."

I chuckled and held up my hands in a gesture of surrender. "WMD stands for weapon of mass destruction. It's a military term meaning any weapon that can kill a lot of people, like a nuke, or biological weapon. They're pretty hard to make. I'm not trying to get you mad, but is there a chance that your uncle was doing something besides looking for this temple?"

Jennifer shook her head adamantly. "No. No way. He was obsessed with the temple. He spent all year using every spare minute to research possible new sites. Nobody was paying for the trips anymore, so he had no reason to pretend."

"Was there anything about this trip that was different from the other trips? Did you talk to him at all?"

"Not really. He didn't have the money for a satellite phone. The only contact I had with him after he went into the jungle was an e-mail he sent a couple of days ago."

Jennifer paused a moment as a look of realization crossed her face.

"Actually, I did think it was a little odd, because it came before he was supposed to be out of the jungle. I just figured it meant he hadn't found anything."

"What did it say?"

"It was nothing. He had found some local music and sent it to me. He didn't even say anything about his trip."

"Let me see it."

Jennifer pulled up the e-mail. "See, it's nothing. The music isn't even that good. It sucks."

"Did he send you music on every trip? What was special about this music?"

"Nothing, now that you mention it. It was just some local music."

"Yet he'd been going to the same place for years and just now noticed the local music? That doesn't make any sense."

"Well, it might not make any sense, but that's what it is. My uncle is eccentric, so I wouldn't put it past him. The bottom line is that it's just a bunch of MP3 music. Nothing more."

"Pull up the properties of the music. Right-click on it."

Jennifer did as I asked, showing that the song she clicked on was about ten megabytes.

"Click on the next one."

It was nine megabytes.

"These files have been altered."

I was pretty well versed in various terrorist communication methods. I had come across steganography on multiple occasions from the computer equipment my team had confiscated, usually because some analyst with a fifty-pound head deep in a basement found it.

"I think your uncle sent you something hidden in these songs. The average MP3 song is about three to five megabytes. These songs are all twice that size, but not twice the length. I think he hid something in here, and whatever it is, it's what the man on the phone wants."

"Are you serious? How do we get it out? What do we do?"

"Whoa. Calm down. It might be nothing more than a bad copy of an MP3. If he got it from some corrupted server in Guatemala it could just have a bunch of extraneous stuff attached, or even some malicious software like a virus or Trojan horse. I'm just saying that steganography is a possibility. He might have embedded some message inside the songs."

"How can we tell?"

"We can't, without the program that created it. Whatever is in there will be encrypted and hidden."

I watched Jennifer deflate again. She said, "So what do we do now? That doesn't help us out at all."

What do you mean, "we"? I wanted to ask.

Instead, I thought about it for a minute, then said, "This might be enough. What we know is that the guy on the phone thinks your uncle mailed something. We also know he doesn't understand how it was sent or exactly what it was. I'm going to assume that he knows it was some sort of computer data, and he just doesn't know the form it's coming in."

"Okay, so? How does that help my uncle?"

"Well, you could plausibly tell the guy on the phone that you got the package, and that it was an MP3 player. You can see where it goes from there. If he seems to think that's okay, you take it to him, then use the stego portion as leverage to get your uncle back. In other words, let him get the MP3 player and see if he honors his part of the deal. If he doesn't, tell him the stuff is encrypted and you'll decrypt it when you get your uncle back."

"What do I do if I can't decrypt the files? This sounds like a dangerous game you're playing with my uncle's life. We don't even know if this is stegocryptography or whatever you called it."

"Yeah, it's a game, but the alternative is to say, 'I don't have the package. Feel free to send me my uncle's skin when you're done. I'm making some boots.' I'm offering some alternatives. If it is stego, your uncle made it and should be able to decrypt it. If it's not stego, you don't have a hand to play anyway. The fact remains that he thinks you have a package from FedEx, and you don't."

Jennifer looked at me in disgust. "Jesus, do you work at being such a jerk, or does it come naturally? I'm just trying to figure out the best thing to do, not questioning your manhood."

I let that go and watched her pace back and forth for a couple of seconds.

She said, "Trust me, it's painful to say this, but I can't see a better way." She stopped pacing and looked me squarely in the eyes. "Will you help me with this? Will you fly to Guatemala with me and help me get my uncle back? I'll pay the way. I have money. Please . . . I don't have anyone else to turn to. My uncle's a good person."

Shit. I knew that was coming. She didn't stand a chance in hell of getting this done. If left on her own, she would be eaten alive. Even so, getting involved was sure to be a dead end. I figured that if I left right now I could get out of here clean. I had dumped the bodies in the woods behind the marina Dumpster, so they probably wouldn't be found until morning and wouldn't be tied to me, at least not right away. The problem was that I didn't have the means to just up and leave. On top of that, I had the asshole on the phone who just might try to track me down. If I left now I would be looking over my shoulder for the next few years.

I felt squeezed by my lack of choices. I wanted to punch a wall again. *Maybe I should just dial 911 and haul ass.* That wouldn't do the uncle any good, but it would keep Jennifer from getting killed, no matter how much she thought otherwise. The uncle probably deserved what he got. It would also probably dissuade the man on the phone from hunting me down.

I prepared to give her the bad news. She was staring at me like I was a firefighter that was going to pull her baby from a burning building. *Jesus. Did she practice that look?*

I steeled myself, thinking that this really was in her best interest, and said, "Uhh . . . Yeah. I'll help you."

Huh? Where did that come from? You idiot.

Jennifer's face broke into a radiant smile. "Should I call or you?" ·

I thought about retracting my statement but didn't have the courage. "I'll do it. Let him know you aren't coming alone. Maybe he'll rethink any shenanigans he's planning."

I pulled out the cell phone, said, "Here goes nothing," and hit the last-call button.

30

Inside the guesthouse, Bakr turned off the police scanner. He had heard the entire conversation between Pike and Miguel and was puzzled by it. He gave Sayyidd a questioning look. "Are you sure there wasn't a FedEx location in Flores?"

"I'm sure. There was nothing like that, DHL, UPS, anything. I searched for all of them."

"Then what was that all about? Why are they talking about an MP3 player? What do you think's going on?"

Sayyidd thought about it, then decided it didn't matter. "The answer is simple: Allah is leading the way, praise His name. The explanation is irrelevant. We may not know why, but we do know what. The MP3 player has the data. We have the key. We just need to get the player and extract the data. It is being delivered right to us."

Bakr didn't really care for Sayyidd's blind faith but let it go. "Maybe. Maybe not. Either way, we need to inform The Sheik that we might be altering the plan. He should know that we've come upon an opportunity that we wish to seize. Let him give us further guidance."

Bakr was concerned that this new direction was outside the intent of his masters, and thus wanted to make sure he wouldn't be blamed for acting irresponsibly. To do so would endanger his status as a martyr when he died. As much as he mistrusted Sayyidd's simple belief in God's will, he still dealt in the world of religious fervor and wanted the blessing before continuing. This meant a risky message, something that was specifically forbidden on this mission. They had a file of six different e-mail accounts that could be used only once. Al Qaeda didn't know what was being monitored or who was being watched, and thus were treating every communication as compromised as soon as it was sent.

Bakr scribbled a message onto a notepad.

"Boot up the M4 and send this to the first address. You remember it, correct?"

"Of course. I've memorized all six."

Once the connection was established, Sayyidd typed in the message:

Praise be to God, prayer and peace be upon the Prophet of God. Operation Badr has taken a turn for the better. We are no longer looking to strike the far enemy in his homeland. We have found a catastrophic weapon that will wipe the Zionists into the sea at the same time it causes the far enemy to destroy the Persians. In the name of God, the Merciful, the Compassionate, we will rejoice in the destruction of all infidels, leaving the Caliphate assured. Please respond with a blessing for this new mission, or tell us the path to take.

The message went out to a Yahoo! address, where it would sit for a day, then be forwarded to another address, then another, before being transferred to a thumb drive and driven across a border to another Internet café, sent again to another account, transferred via cell phone verbatim, then copied to a CD, and eventually find its way into the hands of Al Qaeda leadership. Just as Al Qaeda feared, along this path it would be intercepted by U.S. intelligence, and end up in a massive pile of "chatter" to be sorted through for relevance, where it would sit at the bottom, waiting to be viewed by some low-level analyst in the depths of a windowless building.

31

After hanging up the phone with Pike, Miguel said, "They're bringing the package down here. They've agreed to meet us to deliver it, but I don't trust that. Get in touch with our people at the department of immigration. Have them be on the lookout for Jennifer Cahill from the United States."

"There's no visa requirement to get here from America if they come as tourists," Jake said. "We won't get any warning before they land."

"I know. We'll only have a small window to control the situation, but luckily all flights from the U.S. fly straight here into Guatemala City. We should be able to blanket every flight coming from America for the next three days."

Jake agreed, then added, "Should we build a net inside the local hotels as well? There's a small chance that they could get through customs without us being alerted."

"Yeah. That makes sense. Have it done. Stick to the tourist hotels."

"What do you want me to do when I find them?"

"Whatever it takes to bring them in to me. I want to get them in our hands before they have a chance to make any sort of plans or change their minds and talk to the authorities. Let's not inadvertently kill anyone else before we have our information."

Jake grinned. "I'll do my best."

THE HUMIDITY HIT ME LIKE A WET RAG as soon as we exited the airplane, causing immediate sweat to pop out. It did little to add to any misery. I had tried to get as much sleep on the plane as I could, but thirteen hours of flying or waiting around airports for connecting flights did nothing but make you feel tired. My mouth felt like someone had polished my teeth with dryer lint, my hair had a greasy feel, and I was dehydrated from the in-flight dry air. Jennifer didn't look that much better.

The man on the phone had given us directions to his house, telling us which roads to use to get out of Guatemala City. Once in the hills to the east of the city, we were supposed to simply stop and ask the first person we saw for the house of El Machete.

There wasn't any way I was going to make it that easy.

We had landed at the Santa Elena airport in the north of Guatemala after connecting through Cancún. I didn't want to land in Guatemala City, since I was pretty sure that Machete would have that covered, so we had purchased two sets of tickets. It would be a seven-hour trip down south, but at least we would make it through whatever initial net he had established without getting caught right off the bat. We picked up our Jeep CJ-5 we had rented over the Internet and wasted no time heading to Guatemala City on Highway 5.

I had never been to Guatemala before, and after talking to Jennifer, I learned she hadn't either. The sum total of her knowledge was wild-ass stories told by her uncle. None were of any help. My knowledge was limited to the fact that Guatemala had the distinction of being one of two countries—Iran being the other one—that the CIA had managed to overthrow in the 1950s. I wouldn't even have known that, except the story was a damn clown-fest and pretty funny to read about, with CIA agents mistakenly attacking British ships and revolutionaries attempting to ride into battle in beat-up station wagons. Funny except the fallout was a thirty-six-year civil war that left thousands of innocent people dead. I suppose it kept Guatemala out of Commie hands, so it was worth it. As long as you weren't Guatemalan.

JAKE WAS IN THE PROCESS of building his net inside the tourist hotels when his phone rang with the special tone reserved for his boss.

"Have you heard anything from our friends downtown?"

Jake told him no, but that he hadn't been checking in with them. He'd been too busy with the hotels.

"I'm wondering if they slipped through customs."

Jake swore under his breath. Miguel was as ruthless as anyone he had ever seen, but sometimes he had the patience of a four-year-old. "It's only been about twenty hours. Give it some time. They'll be here."

"I don't trust the people we've paid. I want our own people on every flight coming in. Make that happen."

"Sir, doing that now risks missing them both ways. I

haven't finished with the hotels. We need to stick with the plan."

"Jake, hear what I'm saying. Do as I ask. Now."

Jake acknowledged the task, then hung up, cursing. Why come up with a plan if you're going to change it because you're impatient? Give the plan a chance to work. *Jesus, why did I come down here?*

Pulling out now meant a risk he didn't want to take, as it would split the detection efforts before either one was complete. Nothing he could do about it. When Miguel made up his mind, it was done. In other assignments Jake would try to convince his boss of the correct path to take, but Miguel was different. Jake had seen Miguel do things to other humans that would have shocked Stephen King. He wouldn't admit it to anyone, but Miguel had the ability to scare him. Jake would do as he was told. He would just have to make sure he covered both the hotels and the airport as well as he could.

He looked at his list of hotels and called both team leaders, telling one to continue with the mission of the hotels and giving the other the redirection to the airport. The second team leader acknowledged the task and began calling his men.

Two of the members of the second team were pulling into the parking lot of a midrange hotel just outside of Zona 10 called Casa Bonito Clara when the driver's cell phone rang. The pair was preparing to go inside and spread around some cash when they were stopped by the team leader's call. The driver told the team leader where he was and the other hotels they had already visited. The team leader made a note of the hotels, then gave the driver his next instructions. The driver motioned to his friend to get back in, started the car up, and pulled into traffic, headed for the airport. As they left, they failed to notice the old CJ-5 being driven by two gringos pulling into the parking lot.

32

Pike had told her to stay away from the chain hotels and to find a small discreet hotel somewhere in the tourist areas. It looked like she had succeeded and she hoped Pike would be happy with the choice. She was still unsure about him. He seemed constantly on edge, like he would lose his temper if the traffic light didn't turn green soon enough. And he wasn't much of a conversationalist. He refused to talk about anything involving his past. When she had asked him how he was able to kill two men with his bare hands, he had gone into asshole mode, telling her not to look a gift horse in the mouth. In fact, the only time he had opened up was when they were preparing to leave, showing a small window into his inner self.

While she bought the airline tickets online, he had gone back to his boat to pack. She had to wait until he came back because she couldn't reserve the flight without knowing his real name. The ticket needed to match his ID. When he returned, she asked him for his passport.

"So you've finally figured out a way to get my name." He had reached into his pocket and pulled out a pristine tourist passport, tossing it to her. "Here you go."

She was surprised at its new appearance.

"I thought by the way you talked you were some sort of world traveler. This thing hasn't ever been used."

"I've traveled quite a bit, but not on that passport. You'll be the first to use it."

She opened the passport and looked at his personal information.

He said, "Yeah, I know, it's a damn strange name. Just get the tickets."

She went through the procedures for buying the tickets, typing in "Nephilim Logan."

"You don't have a middle name?"

"No. Before you ask, my parents were good people, but children of the sixties. When I was born, they had a lot of New Age, weirdo crap going on in their heads. When they married, they were full of hopeful ideas about how they were going to change the world. They ended up owning their own house-painting business, but I was stuck with the name."

"What's Nephilim mean? Something out of Norse myth or a type of laundry detergent?" Seeing him scowl, she backed up, saying, "I'm just kidding. Surely it has some special meaning."

"Yeah, it's from the Old Testament. It's supposed to be the name of a race of half-god/half-man people who roamed the earth during Adam and Eve times. They were supposed to be some sort of badass heroes, but all the name ever got me was a fight as I grew up. I've always hated it."

Jennifer had had no answer to that.

Now that they were actually in Guatemala, she wondered if she was placing too much faith in a complete stranger. *Complete stranger? That's putting it mildly. He slaughtered two people with his bare hands. What do I do if he goes off his rocker with me?*

She watched him pace the room, finally peeking out the window, causing her to wonder if she'd made a bad choice.

"Is this place okay?"

"Yeah. Just like I asked for. I'm just concerned that this place is some sort of local gem and will be under the eye of whoever was on the phone. Nothing we can do about it now, since we had to hand over our passports to check in. If he has this place under his thumb, we're made. At any rate, we don't have a lot of time before he starts to wonder where we are. Every minute takes away from your uncle's chances, so I think we had better get moving."

"Are you sure that going to his house is smart?"

Is she really questioning my judgment? I couldn't believe it. In the past, I had hated dealing with people who had no idea what they were doing in situations such as this, but I would tolerate it because I was forced to. I had dealt with country teams in American embassies all over the world who always asked the dumbest questions imaginable. Usually diplomats concerned with worst case scenarios or intelligence personnel worried about the impact to their operations; both looking for any reason to cancel a mission, but neither having the expertise to even ask the right questions. Now I didn't need to get anyone's approval. I decided to nip this in the bud right away.

"Look, let's get something straight right now. I'm the one who knows what to do here. I'm the one who can get your uncle back. I'd appreciate it if you wouldn't start questioning me at every turn. I know you're putting yourself out on a limb and want to feel some semblance of control, but that ain't gonna happen. You don't have a clue about what you're doing, and you're a damn menace to this whole operation just by being here."

I saw Jennifer recoil at my outburst, which made me feel like an asshole. Like I did outside her car at the Windjammer. My anger wilted, and for the second time in nine months, I felt like apologizing instead of ripping off her head. Before she could say anything, I held up my hands.

"Okay, okay. Sorry. That was a little overboard. I want to conduct a recce"—seeing Jennifer scrunch her eyebrows at my terminology, I scratched the shorthand—"reconnaissance of his house just to get a feel for who we're dealing with. He told us how to find his house on the last phone call, and we would be stupid not to use that information to get some insight into the enemy. All I want to do is a drive-by."

She didn't look convinced.

"Look, we're wasting time. Can we talk about this as we go?"

Jennifer backed down. "All right. Let's go."

33

The contact from Santa Elena said, "She came through here. She and her companion rented a Jeep here about ten hours ago. No information on where they were headed."

Jake swore, aggravated that he had missed the Santa Elena embarkation point. While no flights from the U.S. landed there, plenty of flights from neighboring countries did. He had thought there was little chance his targets were smart enough to transfer at another country and didn't like being outwitted.

Intent on getting any information he could on his prey, he asked, "Did you get the name of her companion?"

"No. He didn't speak and didn't fill out any paperwork. They paid in cash and the girl used her license. I did get a description. The rental man remembered him pretty well because he said the guy scared him. He's a white guy, about six foot two, one hundred and ninety to two hundred pounds, brown hair cut short, and blue eyes. He said he looked hard. He has a scar on his face that cuts down his right cheek. The rental guy said he didn't look like someone who took a lot of shit."

Jake took this in. This man was shaping up to be a

greater threat than they had anticipated. He was smart enough to have figured out a route that would evade Jake's net and had been strong enough to kill Miguel's men in the U.S. He was someone to watch out for. Jake decided to quit underestimating the man. He called Miguel.

"I found them. They came in through Santa Elena. They rented a Jeep and are now probably inside Guatemala City. Current whereabouts are unknown." Jake then relayed the description of Pike, ending with his assessment of the threat.

Miguel said, "I knew that fucker wouldn't call when he arrived. He might be as dangerous as you say, but look on the bright side: He's no professor—he'll live a long, long time before his body quits. I assume that since you know they're inside the city, it'll only be a matter of a few hours until you bring them to me."

"Consider it done. If you would do me the favor I ask that you leave the man alive long enough for me to kill him."

"Of course. He is yours."

ABU BAKR NOTED THE INFORMATION they had just overheard and thought through the ramifications.

"This man Pike doesn't sound like someone to trifle with. I'm inclined to forget about the treasure hunt and execute the mission given to us by The Sheik."

"Please," Sayyidd said. "He's only one man. An infidel at that. We can defeat him just as we defeated the soldiers of the Great Satan. We now know what he looks like. God willing, the rest will be easy."

Bakr didn't believe it would be as simple as Sayyidd said. They still had to beat Miguel's enterprise to the punch.

"We'll need to be quicker than Jake. Once he finds the location of the package we'll have little time to intercept it. Does this scanner work on batteries?"

Sayyidd said, "No, it doesn't, but it has an adapter for a car cigarette lighter."

"That'll work. Let's wait inside the car Miguel gave us. Once we hear the location, we'll need to move immediately while Miguel and Jake are coming up with a plan. You'd better pray that Allah is really looking out for us, or we'll be the ones begging for the pain to end."

34

I looked closely at the chain-link Cyclone fence, trying to determine if it was electrified or wired with sensors. After convincing Jennifer that this recce wasn't stupid, it would suck to get caught like an amateur before even observing anything of value. I saw nothing to indicate that the fence had any electronic monitoring at all.

Following the directions from the man on the phone, we had driven out of the city and into the countryside, leaving all traffic behind. We had found the road leading to his estate, the pavement winding away into the hills behind a ten-foot gate. I realized that the only way I was going to get any intel was on foot, so I pulled up another quarter of a mile and hid the Jeep on the side of the road in a turnout. I left Jennifer in the woods and told her I would be gone no more than an hour. She just about lost her mind, but I didn't give her enough time to protest before moving off into the cover of the woods. Hopefully, she wouldn't get in the Jeep and leave me stranded.

I approached the fence and sat for another couple of minutes, watching the road on the inside that paralleled its path. Satisfied that I was alone, I vaulted over the top and raced across the road into the wood line on the other side. I continued moving uphill until I came to a large open field falling away from the high ground. In the center was the house of El Machete.

House wasn't the right word. This was a gigantic fortresslike compound protected by an eight-foot brick wall. All it needed was a moat with a drawbridge. The centerpiece was a three-story mansion fronted by a circular drive. Next to the main building was a one-story bungalow that looked like a residence or guesthouse. Adjacent to the guesthouse was some sort of warehouse or garage, with multiple vertical doors and several chimneys. All told, the compound inside the walled area was probably three hundred by five hundred meters, with several other outbuildings. Machete clearly had money.

I glanced at my watch, thinking I'd better start heading back before Jennifer got antsy. When I looked back up, I saw a man round the corner of the wall dressed like a modern-day ninja. I thought my eyes were playing tricks on me. He looked like he had gone to Commandos Are Us and bought out the store. He was outfitted from head to toe in every conceivable type of black Velcro tactical gear, complete with a black balaclava hiding everything but his eyes. All of his equipment was state of the art, including the Heckler and Koch 416 rifle he had slung over his shoulder. The 416 had been developed jointly with H&K and U.S. Special Operations as a replacement to the M4 carbine, the shortened version of the M16 A2. Both fired 5.56mm, looked the same, and in fact, the H&K was designed the same to cut down on any learning curve for soldiers who were used to the ergonomics of the M4. It also allowed any components used on the M4 to directly transfer to the 416. The primary difference was that the 416 operated with a push rod piston instead of a gas tube like the M4, making it much more reliable. The weapon was fairly new and very expensive.

The 416 was outfitted much like the man, with every conceivable gadget attached to the rail systems, including an EOTech holosight and an AN/PEQ-15 laser attached to the rail system behind the front sight post. The PEQ-15 housed both an infrared and visible laser aiming module, and was a controlled export item from the United States.

This information alone told me a great deal about my adversary. On the downside, the fact that this guard in Guatemala had such exorbitant kit meant that his boss had serious money, serious contacts inside the arms world, and the intelligence to buy the best. *So much for the phone threats being a bluff.* On the plus side, the fact that the target looked like the Michelin man with all of that kit on told me that he wasn't a professional.

Anyone who used such kit for a living found quickly that less was more. Attempting to climb buildings or enter narrow rooms with ten tons of accessories flopping around usually ended in catastrophic failure. I had learned early to pare down my kit to the absolute essentials, leaving the rest of the Velcro for the wannabes who did more showing off than fighting. *Like this loser.*

I watched him as he continued walking down the wall and turned the corner out of sight. About ten seconds later, another guard rounded the corner to the south of the compound, opposite where the first guard had disappeared. Obviously, they maintained a roving foot patrol outside the residence and probably had a mounted patrol along the fence line.

I felt a split-second burst of fear as I realized I had been too hasty on my sensor analysis at the fence. Whoever was here had enough money to wire the entire jungle and could buy the expertise to monitor it. I then realized that if it had been wired, I would've already been caught. I decided not to test my theory and began moving as swiftly as I dared back down to the Jeep and Jennifer.

JAKE PULLED INTO THE PARKING LOT of the Casa Bonita Clara with a head of steam, hammering the brakes hard enough to cause a slight skid in the gravel. He had just finished talking to one of his team leaders and had discovered that the Casa Bonita hotel had been missed during the shift to the airport. *Because of incompetent idiots who couldn't follow simple instructions.* The team had reported their location at the hotel, and the team leader had assumed they had gone inside and established contact. They hadn't, and now he had a gap in the plan that might prove fatal. He felt like he was leading a bunch of children, forcing him to check and recheck everything to get the smallest task accomplished.

Walking to the front desk, he tapped his hand on the counter, waiting on the woman behind it to finish with a balding German complaining about his bill. Once he was gone, Jake addressed the woman.

"Hi. I'm looking for some friends of mine. They were supposed to arrive today, but I haven't heard from them. I was wondering if you could look and see if they've checked in?"

The woman smiled warmly. "I'm sorry—I'm not allowed to reveal any information on our guests. If you'd like, you can leave me a message for them with your contact information, along with their name. I'll ensure that they get it."

Jake smiled back, attempting to be as friendly as the woman, but failing because his smile did nothing but bare his teeth, giving him all the warmth of a great white shark.

"Perhaps I wasn't clear. The bloke who wants to find them is El Machete. I would hate to be the person who refused his request."

The woman's smile faded, replaced with a look of fear. She glanced around to see if her manager was in sight, then said, "What are their names?"

"Jennifer Cahill and a man."

The woman tapped on the keyboard and said, "They're here. Second floor, second room on the right. Room eight." Visibly shaking, she said, "Please leave now."

Jake grinned, thanked her, then went back to his SUV. He dialed Miguel's number.

Miguel answered after the fourth ring. "What've you found? Please tell me you have some good news."

"I have their location. I'm pulling in the teams and heading back to the compound. I'll be there in twenty minutes."

Miguel wasn't satisfied with that answer. "Well, don't make me beg. Where are they?"

"They're staying in a hotel inside Zona Ten called the Casa Bonita Clara. It poses some additional challenges due to its small size, but nothing insurmountable."

Miguel smiled for the first time in more than twenty-four hours. "Good. Very, very good. I'm looking forward to meeting this Mr. Pike. Come on back. We'll figure out how we're going to skin this cat. Shouldn't take long. Once we have the package, I want you on the road tomorrow looking for the temple."

"Okay . . . Got it. We're coming home now. See you in a few minutes."

SITTING INSIDE THE LOANED CHEVY SUBURBAN, Bakr and Sayyidd heard the entire exchange. Bakr started the giant SUV and drove down the winding road toward the highway while Sayyidd booted up the M4 satellite phone to search for the hotel.

Sayyidd said, "You're going to have to stop and give me five minutes before I can get the connection. This thing doesn't work very well on the move."

Entering the close-packed concrete landscape of Guatemala City proper, Bakr began to look for a place to pull over. Finding one, he waited while Sayyidd achieved a satellite signal. Seconds later, Sayyidd found the hotel's Web site.

"I have it. We're only minutes away. What do you want to do?"

35

Jennifer and I crossed the lobby of the hotel and headed to the stairs. I had made it back to her and the Jeep without incident, although she was spitting mad. I had found her hiding in the bushes, apparently unsure if the racket I made while approaching wasn't a bad guy or a jaguar. I had pulled a bush aside and found her staring up at me in fear, which had immediately turned into anger.

"You think you could give me some warning that it was you coming? What the fuck are we doing out here? Jesus Christ! I can't believe I let you talk me into this."

"Hey, calm down. It was worth it. Nothing bad happened."

She had continued on, and I had let her. I took the tongue-lashing, because she was right. That *was* a pretty shitty thing to do. I should have simply left her in the hotel room, like I was going to do now.

"I've got about forty-five minutes before I need to head out. You can do whatever you like, but I'd ask that you don't leave the hotel until I get back. We're getting close to wrapping this up, and I don't want to have any hiccups."

"Where're you going tonight? Do you have an idea?"

"Not really, but there are always tourist markets around the big hotels. I'll wander around a little bit until I find one that meets our needs. I want one that's open enough to require a large amount of manpower to cover it and give us multiple options for escape, yet small enough for us to see the exchange people before they spot us."

"I'd like to come with you."

I paused, acting like I was considering it, then said, "It'd be better if you just waited here. I'm not going to be gone that long."

"Are you trying to hide something? I'm getting a little sick of being stuck in the corner like a five-year-old. I might even be able to help you. Wouldn't it be better for both of us to know what the site looks like in advance?"

"Look, I appreciate the offer, but I'm going alone. Just stay here."

I walked to the door, now just wanting to get out of the room before she convinced me to let her come. I had my hand on the doorknob when she came back at me.

"Wait—I thought you said you had forty-five minutes before you had to leave. It's only been about two, or was that a bunch of crap just to keep me thinking you had some sort of incredible plan?"

Man alive, she tries hard to piss me off. "Look, I'm trying to save your uncle's life. I'm not going to fight you on this. Just sit down. Please. I'll be back soon."

"Well, you won't need the MP3 player for this, will you? Leave it here with me."

"What, now you think I'm trying to fuck you over or something? Jesus, *you* asked *me* to come here. To help you. If I wanted to cut my own deal, I'd do it without sneaking around. How about a little trust?"

She threw her handbag onto the bed. "Okay, fine. I do trust you. So you won't mind leaving the MP3, will you? Unless you plan on doing something with it while I'm sitting here twiddling my thumbs."

She was right—there was no reason to keep the MP3, but there was no way I was going to admit that now. I left without another word. For whatever reason, my rage had yet to show itself, and I wanted to get out before that changed and I lost control.

Exiting the hotel, I wondered what brain disease had caused me to fly down here in the first place. All I had to look forward to was a murder rap when I got back home, no matter how this turned out. *What the hell am I doing? Who gives a shit about someone's uncle?* I considered simply getting on a plane and going back to the U.S. I'd have to get Jennifer to buy the ticket, but I figured she'd do it. She clearly didn't like me being in charge.

I flagged down one of the unregulated taxis that regularly cruised the city. I asked where I could take my girlfriend to see some sights downtown. The driver said he knew just the place, called the Plaza Mayor, and set out toward the historic district.

He let me out at an open air market and pointed toward a towering, ornate cathedral a few blocks away. After walking west, I came upon a large open parade field with a fountain in the center. It did look like a great tourist stop, but it sucked for an exchange. There weren't any crowds to hide within, and it had a clear field of view from all directions. I stopped a woman and asked about the parade ground. The woman didn't speak English, and shrugged apologetically.

Another person standing nearby taking pictures must

have overheard me because he said, "You from the United States?"

I told him I was.

"Me too. This is the central plaza or Plaza Mayor in Guat talk. It really gets hopping on the weekends. I was here last Sunday and there must have been a thousand people around here, all out to have a good time. It's the best time to be here. If today wasn't Sunday, you'd see nothing at all." The man was younger than me, with a four-day growth of beard, a stuffed backpack at his feet.

I moved on with a wave, acknowledging his help, silently giving thanks for Birkenstock-wearing, dope-smoking granola-eaters. *Quite possibly America's number one export.* Crossing to the other side of the parade ground, past the large fountain in the center, I came upon a small Plexiglas monument containing a single flame burning from a hidden gas source. The inscription read, *"A los héroes anónimos de la paz"*—the anonymous heroes of peace—a monument to the peace accords of 1996 that ended the civil war here. If the place got as crowded as the backpacking college student said, I had found my exchange location.

I began to walk away from the monument, back toward the taxi stands. Moving through the packed streets full of vendors, I got sick of being accosted by every single one and turned into an alley as a shortcut.

I walked for thirty seconds before realizing it was a dead end. Turning back, I faced two local nationals moving in my direction. I pushed through them with a half-hearted "excuse me," getting a quick feeling that something wasn't right by the way they stared at me. As soon as my back was to them, I was thumped hard on the head and hit in the kidney. Rolling with the blow, I turned to face the pair, only to be tackled. They were uncoordinated, simply hitting and kicking me all over like in a schoolyard fight. I lashed out with a back fist and connected with one of them. He rolled off and shouted at his friend. I turned my attention to the other man on top of me, preparing to wrap my legs around the man's waist in a guard mount that would prevent him from pinning me down and allow me to finish the fight. Before I could do it, his friend jerked him off of me, and both ran back down the alley.

I stayed still for a few seconds to catch my breath, then laughed at how easy it had been for a couple of local pickpockets to take me down. As I sat up, it dawned on me that the first man had shouted to his friend in Arabic. I couldn't speak the language but had listened to it almost more than English in the past few years, and had no doubt that was what I heard. *What the hell? Why would a couple of rag-head toughs be running around Guatemala?*

I had seen stranger things and let it go. I checked my watch and wallet and saw that I still had both, so they had failed in their attempts. I picked up my backpack and looked through it. All appeared to be there. I honed in on the small outside pocket, torn open by the assault. A shock went through me. The MP3 player was gone. I ripped through the rest of the knapsack looking for the device. It wasn't there. I searched the ground around me, seeing nothing. I ran back the way I had come, scanning left and right, but still came up empty. I stopped searching. *What the hell am I going to tell Jennifer? How are we going to make an exchange? How on God's green earth have I managed to lose the device?*

I flagged down a taxi, gave him directions, and sat

back for the ride. Before I knew it, I was back at the hotel. I exited the cab and dragged myself up to our room, not wanting to tell Jennifer what had happened, knowing she would hate me for the incompetence that would cost her uncle his life.

I unlocked the door. She wasn't in sight, so I checked the bathroom. It was also empty. I was surprised, and felt the anger rise. I remembered I had said not to leave, but I could see her going out just to spite me. I was working myself into a fine, justifiable rage, building up an argument to counter the sting of losing the MP3 player, when I noticed a piece of paper on the bed. I picked it up and got the second shock of the day.

You said you would call when you arrived. If you would like to see the girl in one piece, please call immediately.

36

I stared at the note for a heartbeat and then sat heavily on the bed, holding my head in my hands. I had failed all the way around. I had misjudged the opposition and misjudged my own capabilities. *I'm a fucking fraud. I should've never come down here.* Nothing good was going to come out of continuing now. I ran through my options and settled on the best course of action: *Get the fuck out of here, right now. Get back to the United States.* I could fly back and relocate to another part of the country, starting over again. I wasn't without skills, although they had proven worthless here. I could hire on with a security firm. I had the credentials. They were hiring twenty-five-year-olds with only basic training on their résumé. I could go overseas and make some money, let this entire fiasco blow over, and build a nest egg at the same time.

I stood up and began packing my things. I wouldn't even check out. Let Jennifer's credit card handle the bill. She wouldn't need it anymore anyway. After packing my rucksack, I looked around the room to see if I could use anything of Jennifer's before I left. I dug through her purse, searching for cash. I pulled out her passport, seeing her face inside. I paused. From out of nowhere I thought about my family. Heather and Angie.

I squeezed my eyes shut, rubbing them hard with my hands. *This isn't the same. I didn't ask to be here. I failed Heather by omission. There's nothing I can do here.* Staying was stupid. Trying to do anything about Jennifer was dumber still. All it would do was cause more death, most notably my own. *What the hell can I do? I have no money, no equipment, no men, no support, no nothing. The man on the phone has everything.*

I opened my eyes and found myself looking into the mirror across the wall, a hollow, empty soul staring back. *What the fuck have I become?*

I was sickened by my own reflection, ashamed of my previous thoughts. *Heather would have left the man in the mirror.* I sat still, thinking of my family, then thinking of Jennifer. I had no doubt that she would have tried to help if the roles had been reversed, no matter the risk to herself. The thought caused a wave of disgust at what I had planned. *I can't go back like this. I have to do something. If I die, I die. Better than dying in an IED attack guarding a shipment of Baskin-Robbins ice cream in a war zone somewhere.*

I felt better right away. Even though the odds almost guaranteed my failure, I felt at ease.

I LEFT THE LUGGAGE, taking only the small backpack. I left the room as I had found it, with the note lying on the bed. I was surprised that I hadn't been attacked yet, since Machete clearly knew where we were staying. I took it as a good sign. I ran to our Jeep.

I merged onto 2 Calle and headed in the direction of the man's house, wondering just what the hell I was going to do. Thinking through my courses of action, I decided to simply continue with the plan. While the end state had changed, not much in the plan had been altered.

My original idea had been to find a place that would facilitate multiple exits, forcing Machete to spread out in an attempt to cover all bases. Since I was now about to attempt an assault on his house, I needed to get as many men out as possible to even up the odds. Plaza Mayor worked either way. The only difference was that I had to keep Jennifer in the house while the hired guns came to find me. I hoped I would accomplish that through a phone call. *I'm hoping for a lot to happen. Not a great way to plan.*

My first order of business was to get a weapon, and I was pretty sure I knew where to get one that was top of the line. Stopping the Jeep at the same pullout I had used earlier for my recce, I exited and raced through the woods to the chain-link fence surrounding the compound. I sat still for a few minutes to make sure I was alone, then pulled out the cell phone I had taken off the dead man in Charleston. I dialed Machete's number, using the lighted keypad to see in the darkening gloom.

He answered the phone on the first ring. "Hello, Mr. Pike. I'm so glad you decided to call. I was beginning to wonder what to do with Jennifer."

I fought to control my anger, needing to play a role. "Look, let's skip the small talk. I'm sorry I ever came down here. I want to give you the package right away. I'm located at the Plaza Mayor. I'll meet you at the peace monument with the flame. I'll be in the crowd. One man, and one man alone, should stand at the monument every half hour starting at eight P.M. You got that so far?"

"Yes. I understand. We'll meet you then?"

"No. The man should light a cigarette with his right hand. When I see that, I'll throw the MP3 player to him sometime between eight and ten. I won't come close enough for anyone to identify where the MP3 player came from. If I suspect that you're more intent on getting me than the device, I'll disappear and you won't hear from me again."

"And the girl?"

I paused, knowing that I was about to put Jennifer into extreme danger, but also knowing that I had to ensure she remained behind.

"I don't care about the girl. I just want to get you off my back. I thought about leaving the package in the hotel and hauling ass, but I want to make damn sure you get it. Once you get the player, we're through."

"Smart man. I'm good with that. We'll be at the monument. If I don't get the player, I'm going to find you. Don't fuck with me."

I gritted my teeth at the threat, thinking I would enjoy killing this asshole. "Understood. You only have about forty-five minutes, so you'd better get moving."

JENNIFER, lying on the floor shackled and gagged, saw Miguel hang up and waited to hear what he said to Jake.

"He's pretty smart. He has a good plan to keep himself in one piece, although I'm sure you'll find a way to defeat it." Miguel then relayed Pike's demands.

Jake said, "That makes it harder, but not impossible. The Plaza Mayor will be jammed with a thousand locals. I'm going to need everyone for this, or he'll get away. Security here will be a little light while we're gone."

"Take whoever you need. I want him almost as much as the package."

Jennifer saw Jake glance her way. "What about the girl? Are we taking her?"

She perked up, waiting to hear the exchange plan.

"No. He's a man after my own heart. He doesn't give a shit about her. He only wants out. I'll give her to the remaining guard force as compensation for missing out on tonight's fun."

What? Jennifer's brain refused to compute what she had just heard. She watched in a daze as Jake left the room, barking out orders as he went. Her mind finally clicked. *Jesus Christ. I'm going to die.* It failed to register that death was the least of her concerns.

She heard Miguel talking to the remaining guard. "Take her to the interrogation room. Pick four men who deserve a reward and give her to them."

Her predicament began to sink in. She tried to talk through the gag in her mouth, to get Miguel to understand there was some mistake. She was ignored. The guard grabbed the manacles around her wrists without even giving her a chance to stand up. *No, no, no. This isn't happening.* She was dragged kicking from the room.

37

After hanging up, I vaulted the fence and raced to the vantage point I had found earlier. Crouching in the woods, I waited, trying to see one of the guards patrolling the exterior grounds. I focused my eyes on the brick wall surrounding the compound, vaguely lit up enough to allow me to make it out. I used my peripheral vision to pick out movement, knowing that it was better in the night than my primary eyesight. Soon, I spotted a guard moving down the wall.

I moved in a crouch on a path to intersect the guard, covering the terrain as rapidly as I could without making enough noise to alert him. I closed within fifteen meters of his back and began stalking my prey. When I was five feet away, I closed the distance at a sprint. I wrapped my right arm around the guard's neck and pressed my shoulder into the back of his head, forcing it down. Kicking the back of his knee, I flung myself backward, pulling him horizontally toward the ground. Our bodies separated like a pair of scissors. We both hit the earth at the same time, the guard on his back and me on my stomach. The force of the fall generated enormous leverage applied through my shoulder directly into the man's neck, snapping it cleanly. I sat up, grabbed the dead man by his equipment vest, and dragged him thirty feet into the darkness. I began stripping the body, ripping away all of the junk to get to the ammunition for the 416.

JENNIFER LAY ON HER STOMACH inside the warehouse. She was still clothed, but her shoes had been removed to hamper any escape attempt. She could see the implements of torture in the gloom, along with dark brown stains at irregular intervals along the walls. In the corner she saw a pile of clothes and recognized her uncle's shirt. She began shaking uncontrollably. *What the fuck am I going to do? Something . . . there's got to be something.* Up until now, she had managed to maintain a semblance of self-control because she felt certain that the police or Pike would be arriving to help. People like her didn't end up shackled in a drug lord's house. At least not for long. Pike's comments to Miguel had popped that bubble; she now knew she was on her own. *Think. . . . Think. . . . Think. Gotta be a way out. . . .* The door opened, and she saw five Guatemalan men enter the room, all staring at her and smiling. *Oh, my God.*

THE THUMB DRIVE WORKED PERFECTLY, surprising Bakr. In his heart, he hadn't thought they would actually get the data, and in their rush to get to the hotel, he hadn't planned a next step.

As soon as they had arrived, they had seen a red Jeep driven by a man matching the description given by Jake. They watched him and a woman enter the hotel and had barely begun to discuss their options when the man exited alone less than five minutes later, giving them an opportunity they couldn't ignore.

Now they had the GPS location to the temple, but they didn't have a GPS. Bakr didn't want to return with the data to Miguel's house, but somehow they needed to get one of the GPSs inside their test package, along with the 3M respirators. While mulling the options over dinner, Bakr decided he would be the only one who went back. Sayyidd would remain in the restaurant with the data, waiting for him to return.

I FINISHED KITTING UP and conducted a functions check on the weapon, relieved when it appeared to work fine. I had stripped the man of his assault vest, then stripped the vest of the clutter it held. To my surprise, the guard had a plate-hanger underneath his vest, complete with front and back Level III armor plates, rated to stop everything up to 7.62 x 51mm, the primary round used in NATO sniper rifles and light machine guns. *What the hell is he wearing this for?* I wasn't going to question it. I was fairly sure I would need the protection.

I ditched just about everything the man had, throwing away a ton of bullshit accessories that might be useful on Batman's utility belt but would do me no good. The one thing I wanted that the guy didn't have was a radio, but that in itself gave me some relief about Machete's security posture. *Body armor and no radio? He's wearing the kit as a costume.* I kept only the three magazine pouches, each holding two magazines loaded with thirty rounds of Hornady match grade 5.56mm boat-tail hollow points.

For weapons I took the H&K 416 and a Cold Steel

push knife, a nasty instrument with a three-and-three-quarter-inch double-sided cutting edge and a "T" handle perpendicular to the blade.

Satisfied that I had all I wanted from the dead guard, I began to move toward the front gate, using the wall as cover, all the while scanning for cameras or other early warning devices. So far, no alarm had been raised, but it was only a matter of time before the guard I had killed was missed.

I held no illusions of what I was about to attempt. The standard operating procedure of my last unit prohibited entering a room as an individual. Two people could enter for extreme situations; otherwise three was the minimum, with four or five preferred. I was now going to assault the *entire fortress* on my own, using a weapon I had never fired, that might not even be zeroed, and certainly wasn't zeroed for me. I would be lucky if the wannabe I had killed had bothered to sight-in the weapon at all. I had no idea if the weapon had been properly maintained. Should it fail at any time, I would be a dead man.

As bad as that was, it was the least of my problems. Depending on how many men had left to go chasing shadows at the Plaza Mayor, I was outnumbered upward of twenty to one. In order to succeed I would have to maintain what we called relative superiority, attacking each man individually, or at most two at a time. Should an alarm go up, forcing me to fight a concentrated mass, I would lose.

Continuing down the wall toward the front gate, I heard a commotion on the other side. A man with a UK accent was shouting instructions in English against the background of multiple vehicles being loaded. I grinned. *Fuck, yeah. Get 'em all out of here.*

I waited until all the vehicles had left and was about to scale the wall when I heard movement to my right. I pressed against the brick, trying to squeeze into the shadows. Another guard came sauntering down the wall, moving without a purpose, his weapon slung and his hands in his pockets. I started breathing in a shallow pant, hoping he couldn't hear it, even though it sounded like an industrial fan to me. He came within five feet, then stopped and turned around, as if he was going back to the gate. *What the hell's he doing?*

Before he could make up his mind about where he was going, I closed on him, trapped his head, and stuck the push blade into the left side of his neck, slicing to the right and ripping out his windpipe and both carotid arteries. I held him upright, aiming the jet of blood away from me, then lowered him to the ground.

I quickly scaled the wall and raced to the first door I could see, a side entrance away from the massive, ornate entryway in the front of the mansion. I tried the knob and saw that it was unlocked. I paused, mentally preparing for what was to come, my conscious mind screaming for me to flee. Taking a couple of deep breaths, I knew that my next step, like a parachutist jumping out of an airplane, would be irreversible. *I can walk away now and live.* Not long ago I was one of the most highly skilled practitioners of armed combat on earth. There were maybe eight or ten people in the world who could equal my talent. I used that to psych myself up but knew in my heart it was a lie. Those skills had long since faded, and I didn't stand a chance in hell of rescuing Jennifer. I was going to die before I got through the first floor.

Fuck it. I raised my weapon to the position of high ready and turned the knob.

38

Lying on the floor, Jennifer stared warily at the men who had entered. So far, none of them had done anything against her, apparently because they were waiting on the word to start the fun. She had no idea what she should do. *Should I fight, or simply give in? If I fight, will that only bring on an ass-kicking before the rape, or will they back off?* She knew she couldn't keep up a fight for long, and that they could simply hold her down while battering her into submission. She might sustain enough damage to kill her outright. *But if I put up enough of a fight, they might be forced to hold me down while they rape me. Maybe I won't have to take on two or three guys at once.* She closed her eyes at the thought; her new definition of success being not all five men raping her at the same time. *Dear Lord, help me. Don't let this happen. Please . . . Please . . .*

I ENTERED A SMALL ROOM that appeared to be a butler area, stuffed with shelves holding all sorts of kitchen utensils. Swinging my weapon in an arc, I attempted the impossible task of covering three hundred and sixty degrees simultaneously. A frightened man dressed as a servant stood up, throwing his hands high above his head. He clearly wasn't a threat, but I had no way of detaining him and didn't have the time even if I could. My success rested primarily on my ability to keep the enemy from knowing an assault was under way, but speed was a close second. If an alarm was raised, the only thing that would keep me alive was keeping the enemy from knowing where to orient their efforts. If I maintained enough momentum, going as fast as I possibly could, the enemy wouldn't be able to pinpoint my position and would hopefully attack areas after I was through them.

I squeezed off a double tap to his head and raced to the next door before he even hit the ground. I suppose I should have felt some pity, but there was only relief at the fact that the weapon I held had hit what I aimed at. He was collateral damage. Nothing more. He knew who he was working for. *Fucker should have picked a better employer.*

I entered the next room and dropped a man in military kit racing for a weapon propped against the wall. I scanned the room for other targets, settling my sights on another man sitting in a large wing-backed chair smoking a cigar. Apparently a study, the room was paneled with dark wood and lined on one side by a giant bookshelf. The other side housed a fireplace, with the husks of a long-dead fire sitting on an iron grate like a blackened skeleton. The man was dressed in a business suit, smiling, with his hands outstretched, the Cuban cigar wafting smoke toward the ceiling.

"You must be the infamous Mr. Pike. Jake was right— you are full of surprises. I'm assuming you've come to bring me my package."

I eased off of the trigger. "Where's the girl?"

"All in good time. She's fine. First, where's my package?"

I felt the time slipping away, like lifeblood flowing from an open wound. "Where—Is—The—Girl."

The man leapt up in a rage, shouting, "Who the fuck do you think you are? You think you can enter *my* house, attack *my* people, and walk away unscathed? You think—"

Before he could finish his sentence, I blew out the back of his head with a high-velocity hollow point, watching him fall backward into the chair. *Who do I think I am? I'm the man with the gun, dumbass.*

I moved on, clearing room after room. The majority of the mansion was unoccupied, which made the clearing fairly fast. My assault was only into minute number twelve by the time I had cleared the first and second floors, encountering only two more men, killing both. I went to the third floor, clearing it and finding no trace of Jennifer. I couldn't believe I was still alive and felt my luck evaporating by the second. *Where the fuck is she?* Exiting the last room, I moved at a light jog in the direction of the stairs. While I was still twenty feet away, a servant appeared at the top. Seeing me, he whirled around and began racing back down the stairs, screaming at the top of his lungs. I snapped off a couple of rounds but missed. *Shit. Now the race is on.*

39

The lead guard bent down to unlock the shackles on Jennifer's ankles. She lashed out with both feet, hitting him squarely in the chest and knocking him flat on his back. She hadn't made a conscious decision to fight, reacting only by instinct. She decided her instincts were correct. Given a choice, she'd rather be beaten to death. *Motherfucker's going to work for this.* She rotated on her back, feet out toward the group.

The other guards laughed at the man she had kicked even as they moved in on her. Two circled around her. She tried to stay with them by spinning on her back, but it was impossible. One slapped her hard in the face with an open hand, stunning her. Two other guards grabbed her manacled arms, holding her down. The lead guard got back up, dusted himself off, and walked back to her. Standing over her, he spit into her face, then stomped on her stomach with his full weight, taking the wind out of her and causing her to double up. He bent down and unlocked the manacles on her legs without a further fight. Grinning at her pain, he pulled out a tactical knife and sliced off her clothes. She curled up in a ball, wondering how long her body had left before it was shattered.

*   *   *

STAIRWELLS WERE THE WORST AREA to fight through. There was no cover at all and only one way to move. It was a funnel that required several men working as a team to successfully clear. I had a choice—either sprint down the stairs in an attempt to beat anyone setting up at the bottom, or wait for them to attempt to come up. I split the difference, deciding to wait for them on the second floor. It was a calculated risk, as it would allow the alert to reach everyone in the compound, but I didn't like the odds of beating the enemy down three flights of stairs. If anyone was at the bottom by the time I got there, I would be easy to pick off. Better to let them do the hard work.

The stairs had one advantage in that it would limit the men coming up to two abreast, thus preventing them from bringing their total firepower to bear, and allowing me to fight no more than two at a time.

As I reached the second-floor landing I heard the rush of men on the hardwood floor below. I switched magazines, replacing the one in the weapon with a full thirty rounds. I waited in the darkness, my back to the wall, the stairwell opening up five feet to my right. I heard the shouting of the men below as they attempted to organize a collective response, then the pounding of feet on the stairs. I waited for a couple of heartbeats, getting control of my adrenaline. *Here we go. . . . Don't miss. . . . Don't miss.* I checked that my holosight was still functioning, then turned into the stairwell, flipping my weapon from safe to semiautomatic.

I saw seven men rushing up the stairs, the first three with a look of shock when they saw me coming. They were all outfitted like the guard outside. Without conscious thought, I shifted my aim to their heads to avoid any body armor. I began firing controlled pairs, pulling the trigger so fast the weapon sounded like it was on automatic. The first three men died instantly, two perfect holes appearing like magic between their eyes. One fell backward, blocking my shot at the remaining men. The four were firing wildly back at me.

Like inexperienced soldiers everywhere, their initial shots went high, but with this much lead coming my way, the odds were against all of them continuing to miss. I clipped one in the shoulder and was turning to move back to the cover of the second-floor hallway when one of the wild rounds struck me directly over my heart. The armor plate saved my life, but the force from the kinetic energy of the bullet still knocked the shit out of me, causing me to fall backward. Lying back, momentarily stunned, I poured fire down the stairwell in an effort to suppress the guards, desperate to finish the fight before one of them could calm down enough to shoot straight.

Realizing I was dead meat if I remained on the floor, I forgot about the cover and launched myself straight into them. The one I had wounded was holding his shoulder and crawling back to the first floor in an effort to escape. Of the other three, one was changing magazines and two continued to shoot ineffectually. One of the guards, shooting wildly at my charge, apparently thinking the noise alone would stop me, hit the man standing in front of him in the back of the head, killing him. Deadeye quit shooting, shocked at what he had done. *Nothing like a little luck.* I killed him while moving at a dead run down the stairs, close enough to see the look of shock on his face as his soul fled his body.

Continuing to move, I reached the third man before he could work the bolt release of his weapon. I jammed the barrel of the 416 into the man's forehead, causing an imprint of the flash suppressor on his skull and knocking him out. I double-tapped the unconscious man's head as I vaulted over him, feeling the weapon lock open on an empty magazine. Intent on stopping the man with the shoulder wound from getting away, I wasted no time trying to reload.

The man was on the ground floor and on his feet, moving toward a door off the huge, cathedral-like den at the base of the stairs. He was shuffling along like Quasimodo, looking back over his shoulder as if he was being chased by the devil, his shattered arm dangling uselessly beside him. I caught him just as he reached the door. Dropping the 416 on its assault sling, I reached across the man's face, pulling his head back by digging my fingers into his eyes and yanking upward. I hammered his windpipe above the thyroid cartilage with my other hand, crushing it. I let the man fall, his mouth working like a fish out of water, his lungs pumping to get air in through his destroyed windpipe.

I had now cleared the entire house and seen no sign of Jennifer. *Shit. Maybe they took her.* I knew I was running out of time. If I was still here when the men from the Plaza Mayor returned, I would be dead.

JENNIFER WAS YANKED UP FROM THE FLOOR by her hair. On her knees, her hands cuffed to her front, her face swelling from the earlier blows, she looked up at the lead guard before her. He leered down, holding on to her head by her hair.

He drew his finger across his throat and said, "You no bite."

He then unbuckled his pants, dropping them to his knees. The rest of the guards giggled like they were on a school outing to an amusement park, anticipating their turn on the ride.

Jennifer looked into the man's eyes, saying, *"Por favor . . . Por favor . . . Por favor."*

The man only laughed. She lost all hope. She was nearly catatonic, resigned to the atrocities about to occur. The man let go of her head and began to lower his dingy, stained underwear. She looked up at him again, praying to see some sign of humanity, some shred of decency that would make him rethink what he was doing. Instead, she saw his head explode like a burrito in a microwave. She stared uncomprehendingly as the man fell over backward.

Before his death could register, a cyclone of violence erupted around her, the head of man after man exploding as if touched by the hand of God. The local standing behind her grabbed her around the neck and jerked her to her feet, shielding his body with hers. He placed a knife against her throat and whirled her around toward the door. Her eyes focused on a man advancing toward them holding a rifle pointed directly at her.

40

I placed the crosshairs on the head of the man holding Jennifer. He was about thirty-five feet away, far enough that I didn't trust the zero of my weapon to make the surgical shot required to kill him without risking Jennifer.

When I had initially entered I had seen Jennifer on her knees with nothing on but bra and panties, five men surrounding her, one facing her with his pants down. I had come very close to leaving the zone I had been in since starting the assault, my rage exploding from the depths of my soul. *No, no. Not helping.* I suppressed it and set about killing the men as rapidly as possible, with all of the emotion of someone mowing the lawn. All were focused on Jennifer. None had a gun within arm's reach. They stood no chance. I killed the first four as easily as shooting a Bianchi Cup at an IPSC match, squeezing the trigger in an easy rhythm as the men scattered like roaches caught by a light.

Before I could complete the string, the fifth man had managed to put Jennifer in front of himself, using a knife to control her. He was shouting something in Spanish. Unfortunately for him, I didn't have a clue what he was saying.

I moved forward at a fast walk, closing the distance to

her, my weapon raised and ready. The man became shrill, shouting the same thing over and over, his eyes getting wide, attempting to drag Jennifer backward. When I was five feet away, I aimed for the eye orbit and pulled the trigger, knowing that when the bullet tore a channel through his brain it would sever the medulla oblongata, reducing his body to a useless sack of flesh and removing the risk of the knife reflexively jerking and hurting Jennifer. Blood and brain matter sprayed out, coating the right side of Jennifer's face in a fine mist. She sank to the floor, staring vacantly at nothing. The violence she had just witnessed, in addition to the trauma of her kidnapping, had caused her to shut down. I just prayed that I had gotten to her in time to prevent any assault.

I left her sitting down and searched the bodies on the floor until I found the keys to the handcuffs on her wrists. After unlocking her, I shook her shoulders, constantly talking to her. Eventually, she looked at me with recognition.

"We have to get out of here. Can you walk?"

She nodded in a vacant way. I realized that I had to get her some clothes and shoes. We still had to get to the jeep, and Jennifer would be ripped to shreds moving through the jungle at night nearly naked.

I helped her up, continuing to talk in a calm, deliberate manner. "We're still in danger. I'm going to have to continue clearing rooms as we leave. We'll find you some clothes as soon as possible. Stay behind me, but I want you to stay in the last room we're in, only coming in when you hear me call. Can you do that?"

She nodded again, this time with more focus. I smiled at her, encouraging her to engage me.

"I'm going to lead the way. When we get to a door,

I'm going to be aiming at it to prevent any surprises. I can't turn around to find you. I want you to keep your hands on my assault harness. When you're ready for me to proceed, squeeze my shoulder. Can you do that?"

She spoke for the first time. "Yes. Just get me the fuck out of here. Please, please, get me out of here."

I smiled again, lying through my teeth. "Don't worry; the hard part's over. You have nothing to worry about now. Let's get going."

I moved back to the open door, scanning the courtyard between the mansion and the warehouse facility. To the left I saw the guesthouse. Maybe it would contain some clothing.

"When we leave here, I'm going to focus my attention to our right, on the main house. I need you to focus to the left. If you see anything at all, jerk my harness and I'll reorient. I can't see three hundred and sixty degrees simultaneously, so you'll be the only thing keeping us from getting smoked from the left. Can you do that?"

When she nodded, I said, "We're going to run to that house over there. Do you see the door in the front? I'm going to stop on the left side of that door. Are you ready?" She nodded again. "Okay. Let's go."

I exited the warehouse and sprinted forward, my weapon moving wherever my eyes went, training on every window and door I could see as I ran by them. I fully expected to spot a muzzle flash at any second. *What the hell am I doing? Continuing an assault with my 2IC dressed in a bra and panties. I've lost my mind.* We reached the building without getting shot at, which was a damn miracle. At the door, I waited until I felt Jennifer squeeze my shoulder, then turned the knob and entered.

41

Jennifer jumped when she heard gunfire erupt in the bungalow. She pressed herself up against the wall, her mind racing. The room had gone quiet, and she realized she didn't know what to do if Pike never called. *He could be dead. Maybe there's a bad guy about to come out. No way are they getting their hands on me again.* She was on the verge of racing across the courtyard when Pike called her in, telling her not to look at the floor. Relief flooded through her. She entered, seeing a man dressed in black sprawled on the floor in the foyer, his arms splayed out as if he was about to be crucified. She saw Pike crouching next to a door up ahead, his weapon at the ready. She wasted no time running up behind him and giving his shoulder a squeeze. She watched him splinter the door open with a kick, then disappear. She heard no gunfire. After a pause, she heard him say, "Someone's living in this room, and I don't think it was the guy I killed in the foyer. Check out the closet and luggage and see if you can find something to wear."

Jennifer entered and went straight to the closet. She began going through the luggage, finding men's clothing. She pulled out a long-sleeved shirt and a pair of sweatpants. Digging deeper, she found a Quran, heavily worn and thumbed through, but didn't find any shoes. She moved to a box in the corner of the room, finding some kind of gas mask and a Genie garage door opener, just like the one she'd grown up with. She held them up, saying, "Pike, what do you think these are for?"

Pike turned from the door and said, "I don't know. Did you find some clothes?"

"I found a top and bottom, but no shoes." She dropped the gear back into the box, moving to the other piece of luggage. Digging through it, she didn't see any shoes. Nearing the bottom, inside a pocket on the side, she found two passports. She flashed quickly to her uncle, but both had pictures of the same stranger.

"Pike, what's going on here? Two passports for the same guy. One's from Saudi Arabia and the other's from the U.S. for some guy named Carlos. The picture's the same in both. What do you suppose these are for?"

Pike blew out the air in his cheeks. "I really don't know, and our time's running out. Please keep looking."

Jennifer dropped the passports and moved into the bathroom. Here she discovered a pair of ratty leather sandals, four sizes too big for her. She tried them on and found they would just about stay on her feet.

"Okay, I found something, but I'd probably be better off wrapping my feet in newspaper."

"Good enough. It's time to go. After you dress, we're going out the same way I came in, through the woods down to the Jeep. We'll be moving fast. If you have any trouble keeping up, say something. Otherwise, I'll assume you're good to go. Any questions?"

Jennifer paused, then said, "Yeah, actually, I do. Why don't we steal one of their vehicles right here instead of running through the jungle? They've got a bunch of Suburbans in the warehouse where you found me."

"That sounds like a plan. Do you know exactly where they are?"

"Yeah. Head back to the place where you found me, but go into the door on the end of the warehouse. I saw the vehicles when they dragged me through there."

"Okay. Get dressed. When you're ready, we'll go."

I covered the outside of the room, waiting on her to put on the clothes. I was running contingencies through my mind when it dawned on me that I hadn't done a single thing to find her uncle, the only reason we'd come down here in the first place.

"Jennifer—I've been in just about every room on this compound looking for you. I didn't see any indication of your uncle."

I felt sure the uncle was dead and didn't want to spend a single second hunting for him. I looked her in the eyes, knowing if she wanted to search, I'd do it. *Please, don't ask. We need to leave.*

Her answer surprised me. "He's dead. That fat bastard who runs this place told me so. If we get out of here alive, I'm going to do everything in my power to cause him a slow death."

On her face I saw a little of the rage I keep hidden inside me. "I killed him, but it was quick. After seeing what they were doing to you, I wish I had taken my time."

She looked up from putting on the sweatpants, a weak smile on her face. "Don't beat yourself up. If I didn't know better, I would have thought you were waiting outside for the perfect moment. You came in the nick of time. They didn't do anything to me."

I couldn't believe the relief that washed over me. I felt a valve release. "I'm sorry about your uncle. I wish I could have done something to help him."

"It's done," she said, finishing dressing. "Let's get the fuck out of here."

Following her instructions, we had no trouble finding the vehicle bay. Two Suburbans, each with the keys in the ignition. Seconds later we were out of the compound, heading down to the highway. A quarter mile after leaving we saw a single set of headlights approaching. Since we were still on the compound road, it had to be someone related to Miguel. I tensed up, telling Jennifer to hold on tight. My entire assault on the compound had lasted a little more than an hour, which, with driving time, meant that Machete's men had attended only two of the meet times at the Plaza Mayor. With any luck, they had another hour before the men grew tired. Whoever this was probably had no intention of trying to stop us. We passed the vehicle at a high rate of speed, the headlights masking whoever was behind the wheel.

42

Abu Bakr watched the vehicle recede in his rearview mirror, wondering why it was going so fast. He passed through the inner gate, seeing it open, something that had never happened in the week that they had been there. He parked at the end of the drive and went to the front door. Entering, he advanced cautiously into Miguel's study. First he saw Miguel apparently asleep in his chair, then a body on the floor, hands outstretched toward a weapon against the wall.

Bakr paused, catching the familiar slaughterhouse smell of bodily fluids slowly crusting. Somebody had hit Miguel's enterprise, but how on earth had they gotten past Jake and all the rest of the security? He approached Miguel, stopping short five feet away. The back of his head was a raw crater, the wall splattered with bone and brain matter, reminding him of the martyrs he had seen die in Fallujah.

It looked like Sayyidd was going to get what he wanted after all. Now that Miguel was dead, their original mission was destroyed. The long-term infiltration into the U.S. had depended on his smuggling network. No doubt, someone would rise up and take charge of the massive organization, but it would be years before the infighting was done and someone was crowned king. No matter what Bakr had thought of the idea initially, getting to the temple and finding the weapon appeared to be the best course of action now.

Bakr raced from the room to his bungalow, seeing it had been ransacked, with their belongings thrown about haphazardly. He went straight to the box designed to test Miguel's network and grabbed the GPS systems, test tubes, and the respirators, leaving the rest of the equipment. He then packed their clothes as fast as he could. He found everything but his favorite sandals. He looked under the bed and in the bathroom but couldn't find them. Why would someone want those? They were old, worn-out, and nasty, but had great sentimental value, as he had worn them on the hajj. He had no answer but had wasted enough time looking for them.

He grabbed the luggage, returned to the car, and raced out of the compound, heading back to the restaurant. Right after making the turn onto the main highway, he passed a caravan of Suburbans led by Jake. There was one answer: Jake hadn't been on the compound. When he found out what had happened, Guatemala City was going to turn into a bloodbath.

Abu Bakr returned to the restaurant, relaying to Sayyidd everything he had seen. Sayyidd was fascinated by the story, seeing it as another example of Allah's will. "Now we're the only ones looking for the temple. Everyone else is dead. If that isn't a sign of God's plan, then nothing is. We're going to succeed."

Bakr wondered how Sayyidd had managed to live as long as he had when he deferred all decisions to blind faith. "That may be true, but we still need to be careful.

Allah guides the righteous but turns his back on fools. We need to get rid of Miguel's vehicle and get out of Guatemala City. We need to plan our next move, not simply run into the jungle half prepared."

With that, he stood up, throwing some money on the table to pay for dinner. Sayyidd followed him outside. They unloaded the Suburban and took a cab to the main bus station in Zona 1. Sayyidd moved to a corner and loaded the GPS data from the thumb drive into the Garmin.

Moving back outside to allow the GPS to see the sky, Bakr waited for it to lock on to the satellite signals. It eventually beeped and showed them their current location.

Bakr went to the waypoint manager and looked at the waypoints now stored in the GPS. They numbered fifteen, without any special labels. He frowned. This gave them the general location, but without knowing which waypoint was the location of the temple, they would be thrashing around the jungle for months.

"This isn't going to work. We don't have the time or experience to go treasure hunting."

Sayyidd took the GPS. "Let me look at something."

Sayyidd went to the main menu and pulled up "tracks," a setting on the Garmin that left a bread-crumb trail wherever the GPS went. The latest track stored went generally straight, weaving here and there, passing through all of the waypoints. When it hit waypoint fifteen, it began a looping journey, moving north, then back south, continuing back crazily through the jungle before ending at the start point of the expedition.

Sayyidd smiled. "The boy Eduardo didn't put a waypoint at the temple, but the professor ran the GPS with the track feature on. It shows everywhere they went. It looks like waypoint fifteen was the last camp where the boys took the GPS. All we need to do is mark another one at the farthest location, where the track loops back onto itself."

Within seconds he did exactly this, labeling it sixteen. "Now we simply need to move to this location."

Sayyidd smiled broadly at his partner.

"We can be there in a day or less."

43

We'd been driving for close to an hour before Jennifer asked where we were going.

"We're headed to Belize. I'm going to a place called Puerto Barrios on the eastern edge of Guatemala. From there, we'll take a ferry to a town called Punta Gorda."

"What're we going to do there? Maybe we should just fly out from here."

"Maybe, but I've been to Belize a few times, so I know it better than this place. I don't want to be in this country when the word gets out about what I did. I'm sure a lot of people lost their livelihood tonight."

Jennifer leaned over and placed her hand on my arm.

"Hey, I never thanked you for saving my life. I'm sorry that I caused this mess, but I'm glad you were here." She smiled.

I felt an enormous wash of shame at what I had planned earlier. What was I going to say to that? *Yeah, I'm a great guy. By the way, I was within a split second of leaving you to get gang-raped so I could save my own ass.* I shook her hand off and told her the truth.

"Look, I'd like to say I came to help you because I'm a nice guy, but I'm not. You were rescued by the memory of a dead woman. I'm not a hero. I thought I was one once, but that stupid fairy tale was killed nine months ago."

We sat in silence for a moment. An incredibly uncomfortable silence. I wished I hadn't opened my mouth. *Just take the thank-you and let it go.*

"You can't expect me to sit here with that answer. What do you mean? Why'd you come back for me?"

I sighed, debating whether to continue. I decided to get it all out. "Nine months ago I was in a special unit in the military. I had been deployed at war since 9/11. My wife had borne the brunt of the deployments. While I was off doing exactly what I wanted, she had to stay home and pay the bills and raise our daughter. She asked me to quit, to not go on my next deployment, but I pulled on her patriotic heartstrings, giving her a pack of lies about how I was needed to save America. She let me go. A month into it, my wife and child were beaten to death by some sorry son of a bitch looking to rob a house."

I stopped, lost in thought, unsure of why I was talking about this. Jennifer said nothing. Eventually, I continued, feeling a little catharsis.

"Because I wanted to keep doing a bunch of bullshit stuff in the name of the United States, my wife and child were killed. If I'd stayed home they'd be alive. And nobody was making me go. The unit was voluntary. Because of my selfishness, I killed my family. That's the only reason I came for you. I was reminded of my wife, nothing more. I'm not a good guy."

JENNIFER WAS SHOCKED BY THE STORY. She thought she might be hearing something that hadn't ever been said aloud. She looked at Pike, gripping the steering wheel like he was trying to choke it to death, and didn't know how to respond. She knew that what he'd said wasn't true. *Nobody with those character flaws would do what he just did. Nobody else on God's green earth would even attempt it, saint or otherwise.*

She asked a simple question. "Would you have come for me if your wife was still alive? Would you have attacked that place all by yourself?"

Pike considered the question, reflecting on it for a few moments. "Yes. It's what I used to do. It's what I used to be when I believed in a lie. But I'm not that man anymore."

Jennifer smiled to herself in the darkness. She gave a simple response, not realizing the implications of the words. "Well, I don't think it was a lie. Welcome back."

I'M SURE SHE MADE THE COMMENT simply to break away from the awkward conversation, but it struck a chord deep inside. Back when I was operational, I had a quote from George Orwell hanging inside my Taskforce locker that defined the essence of what I believed I was: *People sleep peacefully in their beds at night only because rough men stand ready to visit violence on those who would do them harm.*

The death of my family had shattered that illusion, leaving me believing my life was nothing more than an act in a play that others directed. I had turned my back on everything I once held as sacrosanct, convinced that I had been used like a puppet because all of the terrorists I had killed had done nothing to prevent the death of all that I held dear.

Even so, deep in my soul, I desperately wanted to believe again. I wanted to feel the faith of my past, to be what I once was. Jennifer's comment sliced through the pain, opening up a window, albeit small, to the hope beneath. I liked the feeling. *Is it really that simple?*

I glanced over at her and squeezed her hand, choking out two words that meant far more than she could possibly realize. "You're welcome."

44

Passing through a small town, really just a collection of huts spanning the highway, I began to look for a vehicle to trade for our Suburban. I needed one that appeared mechanically sound but was old enough to allow me to carjack it without too much trouble. Something built before all the newfangled computers, laser keys, and complicated steering-wheel locks. On the outskirts of the village I saw a Ford Fiesta parked in the yard of a house that looked like it had been made from flattened beer cans. The car itself was at least twenty years old, dented and patched many times, with a coloring consisting of mottled spray paint covering the original finish like a bad rash. I drove past it a hundred meters and pulled over.

"I'm going back to get that car. You get behind the wheel here. When I start it, I'll pull out and flash you with the headlights. Let me pass you, then pull in behind me. We'll go about a mile down the road, then pull over and swap cars."

"Are you sure you can steal it?"

"Yeah. I've done it before. Shouldn't be too hard."

I pulled out the little Suburban tool kit from the glove box, consisting of a pair of pliers, a small hammer, and both a Phillips and flathead screwdriver. Leaving the car,

I fell into a light jog down the darkened highway to the Fiesta.

USING THE GIANT SIDE MIRROR OF THE SUBURBAN, Jennifer watched Pike approach the vehicle and peer through the driver's side window. She watched him rear back with the hammer, shielding his face from potential flying glass. Saw him shatter the window, only to be met by an ear-splitting alarm. Saw him running back toward her like a scalded dog.

She jammed the SUV into drive and hit the gas as he jumped in. She threw a rooster tail of dirt, fishtailing back onto the highway, weaving left and right. She started laughing uncontrollably, tears in her eyes, fighting to stay on the road.

Pike first looked indignant, moving on to aggravated, and ending with plain angry. "What're you laughing at? Christ! Watch where the hell you're going!"

Between hitches of laughter, Jennifer gave a poor impression of Pike's baritone. "I can rip that car off. Shouldn't be any trouble."

Pike shook his head, looking out the window. Jennifer continued to laugh, unable to stop, letting off pent-up emotion. The laughter was genuine but had a little bit of a brittle edge. She finally calmed down enough to look at him. Seeing his annoyance, she tried to mollify him. "Come on. You have to admit that was funny. You looked like a teenager caught in the girlfriend's bed by her father."

*   *   *

I TRIED HARD TO MAINTAIN MY ANNOYANCE, but it was a losing battle. Running through what had happened, I broke down with an embarrassed grin.

"Who in the hell puts an alarm on a vehicle like that? Who would steal that piece of shit out here?"

"Maybe there's a huge market for twenty-year-old American-made cars in Guatemala. Or maybe a lot of commandos come through here after blowing the hell out of Guatemala City and he's sick of them taking his cars for a getaway."

"Okay, okay. Let's find another car."

"Are you sure? Maybe we should stick with the Suburban while we're ahead. I'm not saying you can't do it. If you say you can, then I'm sure you can. I just don't want you to be forced to kill half the village to prove it."

She looked at me mischievously. "I'll bet you never ask anyone for directions, either, huh?"

She saw me grimace and said, "I'm just teasing. We'll do whatever you think we need to."

"We need it, and I won't kill anyone to get it. I *have* done this before. Trust me."

She lightly touched my arm. "I do trust you."

I didn't know what to say to that. I was completely unused to being on the receiving end of someone's trust, and it did nothing but embarrass me. Before the silence could grow uncomfortable, I saw an Oldsmobile Cutlass ahead on the left side of the road, circa 1984.

"All right, mission number two. Same plan. This time, if an alarm goes off, wait for me to get inside the vehicle before you act like Dale Earnhardt, okay?"

"You got it. You want me to honk when we pass it? See if I can save us some time with the alarm?"

Man, she's got some balls.

"Please just pull up a hundred meters."

I exited the vehicle and cautiously moved up to the Cutlass. The doors were unlocked. This was more like what I expected from the backwoods of Guatemala. Opening the door, I sat down behind the wheel. I took out the hammer and began smashing at the base of the turn indicator on the left side of the steering wheel stalk, attempting to get at the mechanism underneath the sheath of alloy steel. I opened up the steering column, with the cheap alloy coming off in quarter-inch flakes. I jammed a screwdriver into the mechanism usually rotated by the key and yanked backward. The car sputtered, coughed, finally catching itself as it warmed up. Satisfied that the vehicle would run, I took the wheel and began forcefully yanking it left and right, breaking the lock holding the steering wheel in place.

I hit the lights to warn Jennifer I was on the way, pulled onto the deserted highway and picked her up, and transferred the weapons and assault kit to the Cutlass. Within seconds we were back on the road to Puerto Barrios, leaving the Suburban abandoned on the side of the road.

JENNIFER SPENT THE NEXT COUPLE OF HOURS staring out the window, savoring the fact that she was still among the living. She couldn't control the thoughts and images flying through her head—her kidnapping, how close she was to being violently gang-raped by a bunch of savages, the vivid punishment Pike had brought to those same savages, the murder of her uncle—all competing for attention in her conscious mind. She turned on the radio of the Cutlass, looking for an outside diversion. She got nothing but static or Spanish music. *That figures. What I wouldn't give for an iPod right now. Wait a minute. . . .*

"Hey, you still have my MP3 player? I'd like to use it if it's handy."

She saw Pike look out the window and waited for him to answer. After a few seconds, she thought maybe she'd said something wrong, but couldn't figure out why.

He finally said, "I don't have it. I'll buy you a new one."

"Huh? Where is it?

"Man, who gives a shit about the MP3 player? In the end, it didn't matter what was on that thing. I said I'll buy you a new one, for Christ's sake."

"You don't have it? Seriously? What happened to it? Did you sell it or something?"

Pike sighed. "I was mugged, okay? It was stolen. I don't want to talk about it."

What? That's absolute bullshit. . . . There's another story here. She waited to hear it. After a moment of silence, she said, "Really? Are you telling the truth? *You* got mugged?"

"More like an attempted mugging. A couple of Arabs attacked me at the central market. Probably trying to get enough money to pay for some flight lessons. I chased them off pretty quickly, and they didn't get my wallet or watch or anything else valuable. All they got was the MP3 player. Let it go. I'm pissed off enough."

Jennifer started to ask another question, then thought better of it. "Hey, I don't care. I wasn't trying to get you mad. Let's drop it."

A lost thought tickled the back of her brain. Something about the theft of the MP3 that she wanted to follow up on, but hadn't. Like a person who just set her keys down and now can't find them, it tugged at her subconscious, an itch begging to be scratched.

45

Exiting the bus in Flores, Sayyidd was anxious to start looking for the temple. After checking in, he set about cataloging the belongings that Bakr had packed. He began to search at a faster past, clearly upset about something.

Bakr said, "What's wrong? What're you looking for?"

"I'm missing a shirt and a pair of American workout pants. Didn't you pack them?"

"I didn't have time to search the entire room. I took what was in front of me. I didn't see any other clothes, but they might've been there. I myself couldn't find my sandals. Don't worry about your Western disguises. We can replace them."

Sayyidd debated telling Bakr why he was concerned. In the end, Allah would either protect them or not. Did it matter whether he said anything? *Insha'Allah* guided his life. If God wasn't willing, then He wasn't willing. Nothing Sayyidd could do would alter that. Even so, it wasn't in his nature to hide things.

"I understand that I can purchase more clothing, but there's something in the shirt that we'll need. I had a scrap of paper in the pocket with the emergency e-mail addresses on it."

Abu Bakr's face contorted in anger.

"You *wrote down* the e-mail addresses? What were you thinking?"

"I know—it was stupid, but we aren't in the Land of Two Rivers, and nobody is actively hunting us. I did memorize them, but this mission was too important to rely on memory. I knew we wouldn't have the opportunity to conduct a meeting if we forgot them. They were our lifeline! Either way, didn't you say everyone was dead at Miguel's? It shouldn't matter. Allah has guided us to this point, and He will still guide us."

"You're proving to be an idiot. One of the dumb little neophytes who believe everything told them, driving a truck full of TNT because they're told they're delivering groceries. They make good martyrs but are not of Allah's chosen. Allah guides those who show they are worthy, not those who spit on his favor. Please tell me you didn't have the passwords with them."

Sayyidd couldn't bring himself to tell the truth. He thought Bakr was acting like an old woman, afraid of his own shadow, but didn't want to cause him to question the mission. He didn't believe he had the strength or courage to succeed by himself. Years ago, before giving himself to the jihad, he might have been up to the task, but his experiences in Iraq had paradoxically given him an Achilles' heel—his complete trust in Allah had left him with no faith in himself. He longed to be like men such as Bakr, but in his heart knew he wasn't. He held a secret shame that tore at the fabric of his being, an individual weakness that corroded the essence of his capability: He didn't believe he had the courage to be a *shahid*.

A suicide bomber's detonator wasn't pressed by Allah.

It was pressed by the man wearing the bomb. A man who executed Allah's will by his own action. A man like Bakr. Deep inside, Sayyidd questioned whether he had that same strength, afraid of the answer he would find when put to the test. He told Bakr a small white lie to protect the larger one festering in his soul.

"Of course I didn't keep the addresses with the passwords. I'm not that stupid. They're just e-mail addresses. They won't mean anything to anyone at Miguel's estate. Even if someone goes to them, they'll get nothing."

Bakr appeared to be mollified and let it go.

"We need to figure out how we're going to get to the temple and package the weapon. From Eduardo's description, it sounded like anthrax or ricin, only it acts instantly. Judging by the way Eduardo described the victim's distress, I'm almost positive it must be drawn into the respiratory tract and doesn't act on contact with the skin. Since it's not made by modern man, it should have particles large enough to be filtered by the 3M masks we brought."

Sayyidd had some training on WMD, but very little. Bakr had specialized in them at training camps in the Bekaa Valley of Lebanon, and thus Sayyidd deferred to him.

"If you say so."

Bakr smiled at Sayyidd's trusting ways. "I said I *believe* it must get into the respiratory tract, but I'm not sure. It could just as easily be some sort of nerve toxin that kills on contact. Are you willing to risk that?"

"If it's Allah's will that we die, then we die. I don't believe He would get us this far only to kill us deep in the jungle. I'm willing to risk it. Are you having second thoughts?"

Bakr internally cringed. Sayyidd's blind faith left him wondering how Sayyidd had lived for three days in Iraq, much less three years.

"No. This path isn't any more dangerous than what I've done in the past. I believe I'm correct. We should be protected."

Sayyidd pulled out the GPS.

"It looks like the temple's only twenty kilometers from here. We should be able to rent a four-wheel drive and get within ten kilometers before traveling on foot. If all goes well, we should have the weapon within a day. The only thing we're missing is food for the trip."

"We need more than simply food," Bakr said. "We need to purchase some equipment that will allow me to decontaminate whatever we find. Start thinking about what we're trying to do. We aren't going out to pick flowers. You don't follow my instructions exactly, we'll both be killed."

46

I woke early the next morning, while it was still dark. I was disoriented for a minute before remembering where I was. I snapped completely awake. I hadn't thought I was in my own bed, at my old house. I hadn't thought my family was still alive. I had no split second of happiness. I also had no gut-wrenching letdown. *I've lost my happiness.* I wasn't sure what to make of the trade-off. I didn't want to lose Heather, and that split second was all I had left.

I lay in bed thinking about the shift that had just occurred. Before I could get too melancholy, the last twenty-four hours of my life came back with a vengeance. I thought about the absolute insanity of what I had done, and the fact that I was still walking. It made no sense to me. How I had been allowed to live when I had practically begged God to kill me in the maelstrom of Machete's compound? Why had my family been taken when they'd done nothing more than go about their daily lives? It wasn't fair. *I should be dead.* I looked over at the other bed, watching Jennifer snoring softly. *We should both be dead.* I watched her roll over and felt a weird twinge, an unfamiliar pang. *Maybe it's payback for Heather.*

Dawn was starting to break. I slipped silently out of bed and went to our small bathroom. I splashed water on my face and stared in the mirror for a half minute. *Well, I'm up now. What to do?*

I went to the door and looked at Jennifer's slumbering form again. The twinge came back, making me feel uncomfortable. Making me think about Heather. Like a magnet repulsed, I wanted out of the room, away from the feeling. I went through the sliding door to our little outside courtyard, watching the sun break the horizon.

I sat down, enjoying the view for no other reason than it allowed me to focus on something else. I lost track of time and was startled out of my reverie by the sliding glass door opening. Jennifer came out, still dressed in the long-sleeved cotton shirt and sweatpants. She'd cleaned up the blood but still looked pretty ragged.

"How're you feeling?" I said.

"Better than I would have been, I'm sure."

She stood there for a moment, then said, "I've got something I want to talk to you about."

"Okay . . ."

She said nothing, clearly wrestling with the issue in her mind.

"Well? You have to speak if you want to talk to me."

She hesitated a second more, then said, "I think something bigger is going on than just us running from El Machete. I meant to bring it up last night on the drive, but it slipped my mind."

I walked to the door of our room. "What do you mean?"

She said, "Uh, well, how do you know that Arabs took the MP3 player?"

Please. Not this again. She must have really loved that thing. "I thought we were dropping that. I'll buy you a new one."

"No, no. It's not that. I just think that something's going on. I don't want you to think I'm crazy, and maybe it's nothing."

I shrugged. "I heard them talking. They spoke Arabic. No doubt in my mind. Now, what's the big secret?"

Jennifer hesitated, like she was embarrassed to say what was on her mind.

"Come on. Spit it out. What's up?"

"Well, don't laugh, but I don't think it was a random mugging. I think those guys attacked you for the MP3 player so they could find the temple. So they could ransack it and steal what my uncle rightfully discovered."

I looked at her like she had a second head. I figured she was going to have some stupid theory on how her uncle had survived and was now being held by terrorists in Beirut.

"Huh? What're you talking about?"

"While I was held, Miguel—El Machete—told me the story of my uncle finding the temple. He said that a native entered first, but died from being exposed to the contents of some type of sack protecting the entrance. This fits my uncle's theory exactly. The story had to have come from my uncle, because Miguel wouldn't know to make that up."

I didn't hide my disdain, forcing her to race to get the rest out. "Wait—I know it sounds crazy, but the room where I got my clothes had a Quran and two different passports for the same guy. One passport was from Saudi Arabia with an Arabic name, and one was issued by the

United States to some guy named Carlos. Now, you tell
me that you were mugged by Arabs in Guatemala. What
are the odds of that?"

I considered that. I had thought it just about as
strange as getting mugged by a couple of Girl Scouts but
put it into the category of "strange things happen." I
knew there was no way that WMD had been created by
the Mayans, and even if it had, it wouldn't have lasted for
a thousand years.

"Look, I don't know why I was mugged by Arabs.
Maybe they got stranded and needed some cash. Maybe
they thought they were doing their part for the jihad. It
really doesn't matter. We have no proof whatsoever of a
giant plot, and even if it's true, there's nothing we can do
about it."

"Why would Machete lie to me? He was about to kill
me. There was no reason to lie. Why did the Arabs quit
as soon as they got the MP3 player?"

"They didn't quit because they wanted to; they quit
because I was about to rip their heads off. As for Machete, he may believe what your uncle told him, but we
have no idea what yarns your uncle was spinning. He lied
about the FedEx package, for starters; he may have lied
about some mythical protection simply to keep Machete
from going after the temple. Don't build this up into
some giant terrorist conspiracy. Our first priority is to get
back to the U.S."

"I'm *not* saying they're terrorists, but those guys are
up to no good. Staying as guests of Machete is proof
enough of that. Just think about it some, okay? All I want
to do is tell someone. My uncle spent his entire life looking for that temple, only to get murdered when he suc-

ceeded. I don't want a couple of thieves to steal what he found. It's not fair. If I'm wrong, we only look like kooks, but if I'm right, we might be preventing something bad from happening."

"Stop. I know you want your uncle's death to mean something—trust me, I've been there—but sometimes bad shit just happens. He got killed by a sick fuck, and we dealt with that. End of story. Let it go."

She jerked like I had slapped her. "That's not it. That's not what I think. Nobody but my uncle believed the temple even existed. Now he's found it, and it's probably full of archaeological treasures. People have been trying to determine what happened to the Mayans forever. *I've* had to study about it with two different professors who both had different theories. That temple may hold the truth. It would be priceless, but now that history's going to be lost to a couple of grave-robbers who'll destroy the find for some paltry money. I can't let that happen. All I'm asking is that we consider how we could get the information to the right people."

I really didn't give a shit about the Mayans, but a part of me did identify with her determination.

"All right, I'll mull it over. In the meantime, let's go get you some normal clothes, get our passports stamped, and get on a ferry. We can't do anything on the run anyway."

Two hours later we were on the first ferry headed to Belize and safety. Once under way, I felt a huge weight leave my shoulders. I didn't want to scare Jennifer, but I had felt we were in very real danger every minute we were in Guatemala. Now that there was nothing to stop us from entering Belize, I felt our chances of survival had gone from about 60 percent to almost 100 percent. I relaxed for the first time in more than thirty-six hours, enjoying the sun and balmy weather.

My mind began to drift, thinking about what Jennifer had said earlier in the morning. I still thought the entire WMD scenario was crazy, but I had to admit that the Arabs' attempt to rob me inside Guatemala City, and the fact that they only took the MP3 player, was a coincidence that didn't stand the light of day. Coupled with the passports and Quran, I began to think Jennifer was on to something. She simply thought someone was going to rob her uncle of what he had dedicated his life to find, but maybe there was something more.

I hadn't said anything to Jennifer about what she had seen inside Miguel's compound, not wanting to build up the conspiracy theory, but the items in the box at the back of the room had all of the hallmarks of terrorist equipment. The 3M respirators were used to protect first responders against inhaled threats, but could be used just as easily to protect terrorists from harming themselves while constructing nuclear, biological, or chemical weapons. The garage door opener was benign on the surface, but I had seen it used plenty of times as a triggering device for improvised explosive devices. Put together with everything else, I began to think that Jennifer's instincts might be right. There was no way that the two guys who ambushed me were on the way to finding a thousand-year-old WMD, but I was beginning to believe that Machete was helping a terrorist enterprise, and that this enterprise was still on the loose. *Maybe I've destroyed more than a simple criminal syndicate.* The only question was whether the two Arabs still had the capability and the will to do anything now that El Machete was dead.

PART
THREE

47

Abu Bakr opened the door to their hotel room in Flores, completely spent from their ordeal. It had taken two days to get in and out of the jungle, much more time than he had thought. He was dehydrated, hungry, sliced up, and sore, but still felt a sense of urgency. He didn't know how long they had before Miguel's men found them. Being inside Guatemala was downright dangerous, with the risk increasing every minute.

They packed up hurriedly, checking out and taking a cab to the airport. Inside one of their pieces of luggage was the fruits of their jungle trek: a Tupperware container secured with duct tape and plastic sheeting. It protected the material they'd found next to a dead native boy deep in the jungle; something bad had happened out there, Bakr was certain. Something that might be the result of the weapon they dreamed of, and Bakr was looking forward to finding out.

They were about to purchase tickets on one of the local small planes when Bakr pulled Sayyidd out of line.

"What's wrong?"

"Take a look at what they're doing to the bags. They're putting each one through an X-ray."

"So? That's a result of our glorious victory against the Great Satan. We have no weapons. The X-ray will show a container of dirt. What are you afraid of?"

"I saw a man's bag searched after the X-ray. They weren't looking for weapons. They're looking for artifacts. This isn't for security; it's to prevent looters from taking treasure from the country."

"I say again, who cares? We have a bag of dirt."

"We can't chance it. Our package will look like a blob on X-ray. They'll be forced to check it out. We can't risk having them open the container, releasing the weapon. We can't fly out of here."

"What do you want to do? What else can we do?"

"We need to get to another country, where there's less security. Either Mexico or Belize. Let's get out of here and find a bus station."

Catching a cab, they made the short trip to the Santa Elena bus station. After a brief investigation, they found a bus heading to the Yucatán in Mexico at four in the afternoon, and another one heading to Melchor de Mencos on the Belizean border within the hour. Finding out that they could take a further bus into Belize City, and from there an airplane out, they bought the ticket.

Bakr, not sure if Sayyidd would remember, asked, "You have your American passport, right? Without that, you'll need a visa to enter Belize. I don't want to be embarrassed."

Sayyidd scowled, saying, "Yes, chosen one, I have the passport. I traveled the long way to get here as well. I haven't forgotten what to do."

"I meant no disrespect. I'll continue to ask questions, the same way I did in battle. It's why I'm still alive. I would expect the same from you. Please, let's talk about the mission."

"What do you mean?"

"I've been thinking," Bakr said, "and I believe we need to test the weapon. Now. Before we fly out. We don't even know if it's deadly. I put a sample in a test tube, hoping maybe we'd get a chance to analyze it with our specialists before we employ it, but really there's no reason for that. We test it here, and we'll know."

"You told me you saw the dead boy in the temple. Isn't that proof enough? Why risk letting the weapon out now?"

"Yes, I did see the boy, but we don't know what killed him. He might have had a heart attack or something else. I know it's a small chance, but we should be sure that the effort we're going through will be rewarded. We need to know the weapon is real. On top of that, I need to see how the weapon works. That's the only way I'll be able to determine the optimum method of deployment. Otherwise, I'll just be guessing."

They heard their bus being called. Getting up, Bakr said, "When we get off at the Belizean border, we'll find a place to test it."

Two hours later, Bakr was bouncing along inside the ancient converted school bus, roasting in the heat. The fan in the roof did little to provide any relief, although the local nationals riding with him didn't seem to mind. Looking around, he began to get an idea. He asked the man sitting in front of him how far they were from the border, speaking Spanish for the first time. When he heard they were only about ten minutes away, he told Sayyidd in Arabic, "We're getting off right now. When we stop, let me go up top to get the luggage."

"Why? We'll have to walk the rest of the way."

Bakr pulled out the test tube he had filled in the temple. "We're going to test the weapon right here, while the bus is still out in the middle of nowhere."

He moved to the front, gave out a lame excuse to the driver, and convinced him to pull over. Climbing on the roof, he pretended to mess with their luggage, passing one bag down, then pretended to struggle with the other. The driver killed the bus, not wanting to waste the gas, something Bakr was waiting for. Working swiftly, he securely taped a piece of twine to the test tube, then measured out the length of one of the fan blades in the roof of the bus. He cut the twine, tied the loose end at the hub of the fan, then laid the test tube on the edge of the mount. Now, once the bus started back up, the fan would jerk the tube off the mount and smash it against the frame, shattering the vial. Once that happened, Bakr hoped the poison would be blown into the bus by the rotation of the fan.

He retrieved his bag, climbed down, and called the driver to him—wanting to make him walk back to the bus to give them more time to increase their distance before it was started. He gave the driver a tip and thanked him, then began walking back the way they had come. The driver shook his head and moved back to the bus, muttering about crazy foreigners as he went.

Bakr and Sayyidd were walking as fast as they could when they heard the bus start up. Turning around, they watched it begin driving away. It moved about forty yards down the road before it began weaving back and forth. Then it lazily crashed into the wood line on the edge of the road, never getting up to more than twenty miles an hour. Nothing happened for a long five seconds; then the back door exploded open and two people fell out, clawing at their necks and writhing on the ground as if they were trying to scrape off ants covering their bodies. From the inside of the bus Bakr could hear what sounded like a group of pigs grunting, and could vaguely see arms and legs thrashing about, like a nest of snakes.

"Allah the Merciful," Bakr said in a subdued whisper. "It works better than I would have ever dreamed. And faster too."

48

Jennifer and Pike checked into their rustic villa in the small village of Punta Gorda, Belize. With Pike gone to sniff around the town, Jennifer was finally able to take off the filthy clothes she'd stolen. She filled the sink with cool water, soaked a rag, and blotted her face. She felt a sharp sting on her right cheek. She jerked her hand away like she'd touched a hot stove. *Damn, that hurt.* She leaned forward and looked at her cheek in the cracked mirror above the sink, seeing two small gouges ripped out, each about the size of a popcorn kernel. She had no recollection of how she'd sustained them, and hadn't even noticed the cuts when she'd cleaned off at the hotel in Guatemala last night. She leaned in closer. *Shit . . . that's going to leave a scar. Matches my nose.*

She was the only one who could still see the small white line across the bridge of her nose, a trophy from her childhood of competing with her older brothers. She thought of the tree she had fallen out of. Like lightning jumping from pole to pole, her thoughts went from that summer day, to her brothers, to her mother, ending with her uncle. And what had happened to him.

Uncle John's dead. Up until now, she hadn't had the luxury of dwelling on his loss. The thought hammered home for the first time. She felt the grief roil her like a wave, fighting to take control. She closed her eyes and leaned forward, resting her head on her arms. *Not now. Later. Think about this later, when you're home.* She took off her sweat-soaked undergarments and washed them in the sink, a mindless chore to keep her busy. She then stepped into the shower, trying to keep moving to prevent her mind from returning to the sorrow. Ten minutes later she toweled off and put on the simple floral print dress and leather sandals she had purchased. Picking up the stolen pants and shirt, she turned to throw them in the trash when a small bit of paper fluttered to the ground. Curious, she picked it up.

I CAME BACK FROM EXPLORING THE TOWN and entered our room, calling out to Jennifer. She came out of the bathroom freshly scrubbed and wearing her new clothes. I was a little surprised by the transformation. She had a couple of cuts on her cheek and a little swelling around her left eye, but she certainly wasn't ragged anymore. *Huh. She's a damn hammer. How'd I miss that before?*

"What're you looking at?"

"Uh . . . nothing. I was just surprised to see you without those Arab rags on."

"Well, speaking of Arabs, have you thought about what we talked about earlier?"

And she's crazy. . . . What is it with her family and conspiracy theories?

"Man, you're like a dog with a bone. I told you I'd think about it, but we can't do anything until we get to the U.S. anyway. Let's focus on that right now."

"I found something in the shirt. A bunch of e-mail addresses and passwords. I think we need to tell someone sooner rather than later. They may have already robbed the temple and smuggled out the artifacts."

I paused, torn because I wanted to stomp this latest request, but intrigued by the find.

"How many addresses?"

I knew that terrorists used hundreds of e-mail addresses to communicate, a move and countermove continually fought between intelligence agencies and Al Qaeda. AQ switched addresses so frequently it made me wonder how they knew which ones to use, but somehow they did.

"Six different addresses, with six different passwords."

"Well, that will be something we want to turn over to whoever we talk to in the States. *When* we get there."

"Pike, please, I think this is important. We need to tell someone now. Can't we go to the U.S. embassy? Won't they do something with it?"

I shook my head. "Unfortunately, no. They would listen to us, but they wouldn't do anything with the information. It'd be put into some report and buried in a ton of other information. You wouldn't believe the amount of reports that embassies get on crime and terrorism. We'll get quicker action by flying to the States first."

I could tell she didn't believe what I'd said. "Nobody in the embassy deals with crime? Who gets called when an American citizen is a victim of something?"

"The legal attaché. He's the representative of the FBI at the embassy, and if we go to him, he's going to be more concerned with the death and destruction we've done than any story of a temple vandalism. They'd listen to us for about five seconds. Then they'd put us in hand-cuffs. Remember, we don't have any proof of what you think. The only thing we have in concrete is that I've killed folks both in the U.S. and in Guatemala. Going to them isn't going to get the action you want. It's just going to get us in trouble."

"Well, couldn't we talk to the CIA? Wouldn't they listen to us?"

"Jennifer, trust me on this. I have a lot of experience working with country teams. We wouldn't even get in to see the CIA. They won't have a sign out front saying, 'Spying Done Two Doors Down.' They aren't acknowledged publicly. If we went to the embassy and said, 'We'd like to talk to the head spy,' we'd be shown the door."

"Look, how about this? We go to an Internet café and check out these e-mail addresses. If we see something in them that leans toward some type of illegal activity, we take that to the embassy. How does that sound?"

I gave up. "Okay, fine. We're safe here. We can either take some time out walking the beaches and seeing the sights, or we can waste our time trying to figure out this giant conspiracy theory. First can we get some lunch?"

"Sure. I'm hungry."

We practically ran to the first taco stand Jennifer could find, where I watched her suck down fish tacos like she was in some kind of competition. We finished in fifteen minutes, with Jennifer tapping her foot while I paid the bill. A little later, we found a tourist store with two ancient computers in the back. For the small price of twelve U.S. dollars per five minutes, we were allowed access. Sitting down, Jennifer went to the first e-mail account listed, at Yahoo.com. Putting in the password, we saw that the account was empty. Looking in the sent file, Jennifer saw one entry. She clicked on it, pulling it up.

"Look! It's in Arabic! This account is used by the guys staying at Miguel's."

"Great. We already know they're Arabs. All this proves is that they're e-mailing their family to tell them what they bought as tourists."

"Hang on, let me check the other accounts."

She did so but found nothing else. Every other account was empty. *Okay. Maybe she'll let this go now.*

She began typing on the computer, pulling up the Google search engine.

"What're you doing now?"

"I'm going to try and translate the Arabic. I have to do this kind of research all the time at school. I've never translated anything before, but trust me, there's a Web site that'll tell us what this says."

Jesus Christ. Stick a fork in it and call it done. "Come on. This is getting ridiculous."

"Just a second. We paid for five minutes. Let's use it."

She found a dozen translation sites and clicked on the first one that came up. Copying the Arabic from the Yahoo! mail, she pasted it into the translation box, then clicked on the "GO" button. We sat and waited for the slow Internet connection to work. Eventually, it timed out. She went back to the Google search page and clicked on the next one, trying again. Before this one timed out, it presented the translation of the Arabic text.

Jennifer, clearly disappointed, said, "Looks like you're right. A drunk must've sent this message. Let's go."

The pasted Arabic had turned into a translation in English, reading:

Praise be to Allah, peace and prayers be upon the Prophet of God. Trip took our rotary [for good]. We have sight to the enemy hits far in country his. We established weapon that the Zionist inside the searching will wipe the poison he causes the enemy far to the Persians destroy. In Allah's name, the Merciful, the Compassionate, we will rejoice in the destruction from all [['iynfydls]], Hope responds with blessing to new task, or says us the path to takes.

I stared at the screen. *I'll be damned. She found something.*

49

Jennifer said, "What? What're you looking at?"

"We need to print this and the original Arabic. Don't say anything else in here. We'll talk back at the room."

Jennifer was about to respond when I cut her off, looking at the woman manning the trinket counter. "Please, I know it sounds paranoid, but I'd rather do this somewhere else."

She printed both pages and we left, returning to the hotel. Along the way, I told Jennifer what I thought.

"It looked like a drunk had written the passage because it's a free Internet translation. Basically, it's a cheap-ass computer giving you exactly what it sees. The point of those things is to get you to buy a better translation. It's like you said, 'Last one home is a rotten egg,' and that was translated into Arabic as 'The long dead dropping from the bird is owned by the man who has the last house.' We don't know what idioms they used that the computer doesn't understand, but the direct translation says some things that support the fact that those guys are up to no good."

"Really?" Jennifer looked at me in surprise. "What did you see?"

"Let's get back to the hotel and I'll show you."

Twenty minutes later we sat at the cheap desk in our room, the translated printout in front of us. I pointed at what I had seen. "Look, ignoring the bad grammar, you find the following words: *weapon, Zionist, Persians, destroy,* and *infidels.* On top of that, you've got all the "Praise Allah" stuff. I'm starting to believe your crazy theory. At the least, I'm starting to believe that there might be some terrorists, and *they* believe your theory."

"Terrorists? Seriously? What do you make of the translation? Can you figure anything out from it?"

"Well, taking it at face value, I can make some assumptions. Rearranging it a little bit we get something that appears a little clearer." Working with the translation, I ended up with:

Trip took our rotary [for good]. (No Idea.) *We have sight to the enemy hits far in country his.* (We have the sight to hit the far enemy in his country.) *We established weapon that the Zionist inside the searching will wipe the poison he causes the enemy far to the Persians destroy.* (We have a poison weapon that the Zionists were searching for which will cause the far enemy to destroy the Persians.) *In Allah's name, the Merciful, the Compassionate, we will rejoice in the destruction from all [['iynfydls]].* (Praise Allah, we will rejoice in the destruction of all infidels.) *Hope responds with blessing to new task, or says us the path to takes.* (We hope you respond blessing our new task, or tell us the path to take.)

Putting it together, I came up with:

Praise be to Allah, peace and prayers be upon the Prophet of God. We have the sight to hit the far enemy in his country. We have a poison weapon that the Zionists were searching for which will cause the far enemy to destroy the Persians. In

Allah's name, the Merciful, the Compassionate, we will re-joice in the destruction of all infidels. We hope you respond blessing our new task, or tell us the path to take.

Jennifer read it, asking, "I don't get it. Who's the far enemy? Jewish people?"

"We're the far enemy. It's what Al Qaeda calls the United States and anyone who supports us. Basically, the West."

"So this is saying that they're going to attack us? What's the Zionist-Persian thing?"

"*Zionists* in Arabic would translate into Israelis. Persians are Iranians. Looking at what I came up with, I'm sure it's not right. There's no way that the Israelis are looking for a Mayan poison weapon." I paused, thinking, "Unless your uncle was Jewish. They could mean that *he* was looking for it. Was he Jewish?"

Jennifer shook her head. "No. If anything, he was athe-ist. I don't have any Jewish relatives as far as I know. What's up with all the 'Praise Allah' stuff? It sounds fake, like some-one stereotyping an Arab. Do they really talk like that?"

"Not every Arab, but devout Muslims do—which, by definition, a jihadist is. All those guys use about ten sen-tences for every one that means anything. You can't ask them the time of day without them spouting off four sen-tences kissing Allah's ass before they look at their watch."

I pushed back from the table. "Okay. I think we ought to stick with what we know out of the message. The fact that they mention kicking Persian ass means they're probably not supported by Iran. That knocks out Hez-bollah and the Shiites, and since they talk about the far enemy, they probably believe in the doctrine of Al Qa-eda. So . . . I'd say they're Sunni Arabs affiliated with Al Qaeda. They're also asking for a blessing on the mission, so whatever they're doing is not what they were sent to do. They're basically asking permission."

I leaned back, putting my hands behind my head. "So, we have a couple of AQ terrorists sent to Guatemala to do some sort of evil activity, who then got sidetracked by the story of the weapon, and are now trying to get the weapon to do something horrible against the U.S., the Israelis, the Iranians, or all three."

Jennifer halfway nodded. "Okay. What do we do now? Go to the embassy or wait until we get to the U.S.?"

"Well, I think we should try the embassy. I think I can get us in to the CIA. If not, we can always fly home. The key will be talking to the Agency. They'll be the only shop that won't care about the path of destruction we've left in our wake. Sound good?"

"I thought you said we couldn't find the CIA."

"I'm not saying it'll work. But I know how embassies operate, and how to find the CIA in the maze. If we get to the right guy, and I can get him to send a cable to headquarters, I can guarantee that the cable will be read."

"Okay. If you say so. What do we do now?"

"We take the first bus out of here to Belmopan. That's where the embassy is. I've been there a few times."

The shadows created by the dropping sun told me we weren't going anywhere today. I looked at my watch. "It's past seven now, so we've probably missed the last bus, but we can check the schedule for tomorrow."

She didn't look convinced but followed me out the door. Before I could lock it, Jennifer backed into me, her face ashen.

"The asshole that kidnapped me is in the lobby. He's talking to the clerk."

50

The hotel had only six rooms. A simple establishment built around an old colonial house, it had a balcony that extended out past our room and overlooked the front desk, with stairwells coming up left and right to our floor. Looking down I saw a Caucasian and a native discussing something with the clerk. The clerk pointed in our direction, and before I could move, the men were looking right at Jennifer and me. Time froze for a fraction of a second. Jennifer broke it, racing down the hallway toward the access to the roof veranda. The men immediately sprang into action, taking the far stairwell to cut her off.

Shit.

It wasn't the course of action I would have chosen, but I didn't bother yelling. Too late for that. Jennifer had committed us, and I had no choice but to follow, although going to the roof was possibly the worst choice. We couldn't jump off a three-story building.

We raced up the small stairwell and broke out onto the roof. I slammed the door shut and jammed a deck chair up against it. Jennifer kept going to the railing, looking down. I surveyed the area, determining what I had to fight with, which was pretty much nothing. We were on a small ten-foot-by-ten-foot veranda. No weapons, no room to dodge and fight two men.

Jennifer shouted over her shoulder, "You can climb down this, can't you? You've had some type of badass commando training, right?"

I couldn't believe how stupid that question was.

"Yeah, I can, but I sure as shit can't do it with you on my back. Get over here in the corner and stay down."

Jennifer bent down and tore off her sandals, throwing them over the side, followed by the knapsack she was using as a purse. "Don't worry about me."

Before I could stop her, she vaulted the balcony and disappeared. I ran over to the railing. Jennifer was already at the second level and scampering down the building like a monkey.

I was about to vault the railing myself when I heard the men hammer the door from the inside. The deck chair gave a foot. There was no way I could make it to the bottom before they reached the rail, and I'd be an easy target. I raced back, stopping on the side of the foot-long crack held in place by the deck chair, waiting on the men to break through.

They hammered the door twice more, finally causing the deck chair to fly off. The first man ran out with his pistol extended in one hand, breaking into the darkness of the deck and silhouetted by the light of the stairwell.

As soon as he was clear of the door, I grabbed the hand holding his pistol and used his own momentum to slingshot him up and over the railing of the deck, letting him fall the forty feet below. Turning, I saw the second man, the Caucasian, coming through the door, pistol at the ready. The sudden darkness from the light of the stairwell gave me an edge, as the man searched the gloom for a target he couldn't yet see. I kicked out hard and launched his pistol over the railing.

The force of the kick caused me to rotate slightly, getting rid of the immediate threat but exposing me to a counterassault. He wasted no time, giving me a roundhouse kick to my upper thigh that damn near crippled me. I went to a knee, collapsing my arms around my head to protect it. He followed with a snap-kick. My arms absorbed the blow, but it knocked me over. Hitting my back, I saw him close in for the kill, my position vulnerable for an endgame. I rose up on my arms like a crab and lashed out for his nearest leg with my foot, forcing him to back up and allowing me to regain my base. Back on my feet, we circled each other.

"I'm glad you got rid of the weapon," he said. "I'd rather beat you to death for the trouble you've caused. You should have hidden the Suburban. Not too many ways to go on that highway."

English accent. I said nothing, simply watching his technique. He had his hands raised chin high, balled into fists with his palms facing the ground. He bounced lightly on his feet, alternating between right and left, with one always poised to snap out and strike. A Muay Thai stance, so he had some training. *But Muay Thai's a stand-up game. Get his ass on the ground, and he's mine.*

He continued. "Where'd the little honey go? I'm looking forward to spending a little time with her. Once I get rid of you, she and I are going to get very well acquainted."

I ignored his banter, wondering why he wasn't forcing

the fight. It dawned on me what he was doing. *He's stall-ing. He's got backup on the way. No time to fuck around.*

I waited for him to dance forward again, then shot inside his striking range, blocking a palm strike and fol-lowing up with a right cross to the side of his head. I clinched him, grabbing his left biceps and controlling that arm, but before I could get my head into his chest he clocked me with a wicked elbow from the right, ham-mering right above my eye and causing an explosion of my vision. The blow broke the weak dam holding my blackness back, letting the beast loose. I now no longer wanted to escape. I wanted to destroy. I collapsed into him, protecting my head by pressing into his chest and completing the clinch. He gave me a useless blow to my back, and I was where I wanted to be.

I stretched my lower body back and drilled my knee into his inner thigh, hitting the tangle of nerves there, causing him to jerk in an attempt to escape. He raised his knee to attempt the same on me, but I was twisted away from the strike and waiting. I grabbed underneath the raised knee and launched forward with all of my might. He instinctively rotated to absorb the fall with his upper body, and I obliged, driving him full-force into the deck.

I ended up on his back in a rear mount, his body fac-ing the deck, the most vulnerable position I could ever imagine. He continued to fight furiously, trying to achieve dominance, but he had little skill on the ground. I pinned his arms with my legs and wrapped my right arm around his head, putting his forehead in the crook of my elbow and locking my hands together. *Good night, ass-hole.*

I bent his head back, listening to his rasping breath. When I got as far as I could, I hopped up onto the small of his back with my knee, freeing up his arms. Before he could react, I yanked to the rear, keeping his back pinned with my knee. He gave a guttural scream; then I felt his spine snap. The sensation sickened me a little, breaking my rage.

I rolled off him, gasping for air, a little ashamed of what I had done. Maybe a little afraid. *You didn't have to kill him.* I heard movement and immediately rotated into a fighting crouch, only to see Jennifer in front of me.

"Jesus Christ!" she said. "Are you okay?"

I relaxed and wiped the sweat from my brow. When my hand came away, it was coated in blood. *The elbow strike.*

"Yeah. Just a small cut. Head wounds bleed a lot."

"What about him?"

I looked at the body, maybe lifeless, maybe not, and couldn't bring myself to tell the truth. "I knocked him out. He's not a threat."

I walked over to the body and ripped a section of shirt, pressing it into my forehead to stop the bleeding. "Did you see anyone in the lobby? Anyone else coming up?"

"Huh?"

"The hotel lobby. Did you see anyone? Can we go out that way?"

"I didn't go through the lobby. I climbed back up."

Is she fucking kidding? "You climbed back up here? On the side of the building?"

"Yeah. There was a guy who came over the rail. I guess you threw him. He hit the ground hard, but he was still moving. I knocked him out with a rock and then waited on you to come down. When you didn't, I figured maybe I could help."

She was looking at me like she had done something wrong. I was having a hard time getting my head around the story.

"Well, get ready to go back down. This guy was waiting for backup, and they're going to be here any second. Can you get down a second time?"

She smiled with relief—whether it was because I hadn't chastised her or whether she thought we were on the way to getting clear, I wasn't sure.

"See if you can keep up," she said.

She repeated her monkey maneuver and was halfway down the building before I even cleared the railing, scampering over balconies and using drainpipes like a kid on a playground.

By the time I jumped the last six feet to the ground, she had her sandals back on and was ready to run.

"What do we do now?"

"Get the fuck out of here."

The hotel was situated on the eastern edge of town, right on the beach. I decided to go north, along the beach for a few hundred meters, before cutting back into town. After passing several buildings, I cut west through an alley, heading to the bus station. When I reached the edge of the building, I crouched and peered around the corner. Jennifer closed up right next to me, so near I could feel her trembling.

We slipped across the street and began working our way westward. It dawned on me that the trembling wasn't just from the recent action. Her experiences in Machete's house had scarred her deep inside, and seeing the Englishman had brought it ripping back out. She was barely coping. I decided to to get her mind off Machete. "Where'd you learn how to be a monkey? I've never seen anyone climb that fast."

"I got in a lot of trouble as a kid. My mom got me started in gymnastics to focus me. I kept at it for quite a while."

"Hmm. This is probably the first time in history that all the money flushed for some kid's activities actually paid off in the real world. You should thank your mom."

I grinned to show I was kidding. She scowled back, which was okay because that was better than the fear.

"It was a little bit more than that. When I dropped out of college the first time I had a bit of a bad stretch. Broke up with a guy and had the usual 'trying to find yourself' thing. I auditioned for Cirque du Soleil and was accepted. I trained up in Montreal for three months, learning all sorts of crazy things. That building was nothing."

I had seen several Cirque du Soleil shows, and the feats that were performed were unreal. Literally mind-bending. I'd watch an acrobatic trick and wonder if my eyes were deceiving me, if it wasn't a trick done with mirrors. The focus and dedication required rivaled anything in professional sports, or my world for that matter.

I stopped walking and turned around. We were inside another dark alley, which caused Jennifer to bump into me. I looked at her with a new appreciation.

She said, "What? It's not some French circus. It's a pretty well respected—"

"I know what it is. You were in it? For real?"

"I sort of was. I was accepted and finished the apprenticeship, but right before I was slotted for a show I decided it wasn't for me. I was pretty screwed up back then."

"Still, that's pretty amazing."

"Yeah, well, I decided to go back to college. That decision's worked out well so far, don't you think?"

She grinned at her joke. *Success*.

51

In Belize City, waiting at their gate for the flight to Cancún, Bakr said, "We've got some time. Let's see if The Sheik has responded."

Sayyidd moved to a secluded space within the terminal that had a look angle to the satellite. He went through the laborious process of getting online with the M4 satellite phone, then checked the first Yahoo! address they had used.

Bakr said, "What're you doing? That's the first address. They won't respond to that. They'll respond to the second address."

He looked closer at the screen, becoming livid. "Is something in the sent file? Is that the message we sent earlier? You didn't erase it?"

Sayyidd gave an embarrassed shrug. "We did this together. I forgot to delete it. You forgot to tell me to delete it. It's a mistake."

Deleting the message from both the sent and trash files, he said, "It's gone."

Bakr rubbed his forehead. He now saw that he would have to look over his shoulder for everything.

"Please check the other address."

Going to the other Yahoo! account, Sayyidd glowed

with anticipation when he saw four messages in the in-box. Three were for penile implants and counterfeit Viagra; one was an e-mail for them. Opening it, he read a simple paragraph, written in Arabic:

> Praise be to Allah and all thanks to Allah, your message brings hope to the breasts of true believers. Travel with the weapon to Imam Walid abdul-Aziz. Meet and discuss together the path to success. Peace be upon you in your journey. Imam Walid will send you a message in his own good time for the meeting. May Allah make this a day of pride and success for the Muslim Ummah.

Sayyidd looked up in confusion. "Who's Imam Walid? Where's he located? Are we supposed to guess?"

"Don't worry, my friend. He's a man that'll help the plan you've come up with, just as he's helped hundreds of other true believers in Europe. I know he lives in Norway, but don't know his actual address. We'll go to Cancún and catch a flight to Oslo. Send a reply to The Sheik telling him of the successful test. Before we leave, delete both messages."

Sayyidd did as he was told, saying, "I don't need to be treated like a child. I can learn from my mistakes."

52

I looked at the list of agencies, trying to smoke out the cover name the CIA was using at this particular embassy. I was looking for the name of an agency that sounded legitimate but was so innocuous it had no specific mandate. A name that nobody would call for anything. I knew most of the legitimate organizations, such as USAID, and focused on the ones I didn't. Finally, my eyes settled on the pompous-sounding Office of Southern Hemispheric Relations. That sounded like what I was searching for. The title was so broad that nobody would call them unless they had been given the number.

Jennifer asked, "How will we get to the CIA? You're right; I don't see them listed."

She didn't just say that. I looked left and right, relieved to see that nobody was within earshot. Trying to remain calm, I said, "Please don't say that name again. In fact, please don't say anything."

Chagrined, Jennifer lapsed into a sullen silence.

We had made the last bus to Belmopan without any other trouble, and had crashed in the nearest hotel we could find. Waking up this morning, it had taken little time to find the embassy and get through the outer security. Now was the hard part—how to get past Marine

Post One. I would need to get someone from the CIA to meet me in the lobby, because I wasn't on any approved access roster that Post One maintained.

I waited for the young Marine behind the bulletproof glass to finish what he was doing and ask me my business. I asked for the number to the office, moved to the phone provided, and gave them a call, Jennifer standing expectantly beside me. A man answered on the third ring. It took a little bit of convincing, made harder since I didn't want to say anything specific on an open phone line, but I finally managed to get him to meet us in the lobby. I gave him my description and hung up the phone.

Jennifer looked at me with a question.

"Someone's coming down. We'll see if it's the right guy or not."

Eventually, a young man came out of the elevator, dressed in chinos and a button-down shirt, looking like he would start to shave in a few years. He glanced nervously around the lobby, passing over me and focusing on Jennifer. He smiled at her, then continued to look around. *Great. An idiot.* I stood up and walked over to him.

"Looking for someone?"

He showed a spark of surprise, quickly covered up by bluster.

"I'm Eric. You apparently had some information you wanted to pass?"

"Yeah, can we go to your office?"

"No. Let's go over to the couch and you can tell me what you have."

I'd figured he'd do that and agreed. I was in a little bit of a quandary, since I didn't know if this guy was really in the CIA, and knew there was no way he would admit to it, so I would either have to dive in headfirst, or walk away.

Eric pulled out a notebook and pen, turning to me to speak when he noticed Jennifer walk up. He went into a random diatribe about the weather. I relaxed. *He's a flunky, but he's a spook.* Nobody else would have flexed at the approach of a stranger.

I interrupted the soliloquy. "She's with me. Don't worry about her."

He stopped talking, looking from me to Jennifer and back. I took the initiative, telling him why we'd come. As I went through the story, conveniently leaving out a majority of the death and destruction, I noticed that Eric kept stealing glances at Jennifer's chest and had failed to write down a single thing. I stopped talking.

Eric, smiling yet again at Jennifer, finally felt the silence and turned back to me. I leaned into his personal space.

"Look. You had better start writing some of this stuff down. There's going to be a cable coming out of this that I expect you to send. Understand?"

That flustered him. "Hold on a minute. *You* asked *me* to come down here, not the other way around. I'll decide what we do with your information, not you. Let's get that clear right now."

My rage began to bubble up, catching me by surprise, an unwelcome enemy determined to show who still owned my soul. Jennifer put her hand on my arm, probably seeing the signs and trying to blunt the edge. It worked, at least a little. I no longer wanted to kill him, just hurt him.

"Give me your pen and paper."

"Why?"

"Because I'm going to write your cable. I'm close to ripping off your head and shitting down your neck. To save us both the embarrassment, I'm going to tell you what to send."

Eric handed me the pad and backed away. Jennifer glared at me, clearly upset at the way this was turning out.

I took the paper and wrote a one-paragraph note. At the end of the note, I wrote, "PrometheusPike." Handing the pad back to Eric, I said, "Send that in a cable. I don't care who you route it to, as long as you include the crypt at the bottom. Do you understand?"

Eric nodded, completely subdued. "Is there some way I can contact you here? If I need to?"

I thought for a second. "Yeah, get me a hotel with an embassy rate and you'll know where we're staying."

"Okay, okay, I can do that. Give me a few minutes. I'll be right back."

Five minutes later, he returned with the confirmation number, the address to the hotel, and a little bit of his confidence back.

"Here's where we send all of our TDY folks. It's on my credit card right now. You need to put it on your card, or your cable's going in the trash."

I stared at him in silence until he began to falter, glancing over his shoulder at the Marine in Post One for help. He finally held out the address and confirmation number with a slight tremor. Jennifer shook her head and took the Post-it note, thanking him for his time. Then she turned without a word and began walking at a brisk pace out of the embassy.

Catching up to her outside, I said, "Well, that went better than expected. We very well might get a cable out, and as a bonus, we got a cut-rate hotel room."

Jennifer turned so quickly I ran into her. "Do you have to be such an asshole to everyone? He was just trying to help. We'll be lucky if he uses your note to blow his nose."

She was as mad as I'd ever seen her, slightly trembling but looking me in the eye and daring me to bark back, waiting on the inevitable rage she knew I had.

Instead, my anger not only disappeared, as it had in the past, but it reversed. For some idiotic reason I wanted to calm *her* down. To make her smile. *Jesus. I want her to like me.* I was so conflicted I wasn't sure what to do. I hadn't given a shit about any person on earth since Heather, and that was the way I had liked it. *What the hell? Am I going crazy?* Crazy or not, she had something that seemed to stop my slide into the abyss. Kept me human. Or at least reminded me of what human was. An innocence I wanted back.

"You're right. I shouldn't have done that. He pushed my buttons. I don't want to be a prick, but it just happens sometimes. I'm working on it. Can we forget about it?"

She looked confused, then suspicious. "Well . . . okay."

She waited a second, as if she expected a trick. When none came, her anger deflated a little bit. "Let's just hope he does something with what we told him."

I smiled, relieved. "He'll send the cable. It's too volatile not to send in this day and age. Easier to pass the responsibility to someone else."

53

Eric returned to his office, still flustered by the encounter with Pike. On the one hand, he didn't want to send the cable precisely because Pike had demanded he do so. *Yeah, maybe I was a little distracted by Pike's companion, but that's no reason to act like such an asshole.* On the other hand, if he did nothing and Pike's wild story proved to be true, there would be hell to pay.

Today was one of the few times he could send a cable out on his own. Ordinarily, he just wrote the cables for release by the chief of station, but Belize had been without a chief for six months, and would probably be without one for the foreseeable future as the CIA pulled experienced hands to fill the gaps created by dealing with a substate threat that couldn't be seen by satellites. With the deputy chief on leave, and Steve, the only other case officer, out doing what he was paid to do, he was now left alone at the wheel.

A year out of college, six months out of training, Eric had the requisite skills for his position of collating reports and sending cables but had little to no experience in the rough-and-tumble world of covert operations. He decided it would be better to send the cable and get scolded for clogging up the pipe than not send it and get hammered for missing a terrorist attack.

He typed up Pike's paragraph, adding some of his own observations, and launched it out, including the Counterterrorism Center on the distro, along with the usual Latin American Affairs desks. He included the crypt that Pike had given him.

THE CABLE TRAVELED AT THE SPEED OF THE INTERNET, instantly residing in the in-boxes of the people he had put on the distro. Because of the crypt, it was rerouted to several select boxes as well.

Seconds later, alarms began to go off in some of the most powerful offices in Washington, D.C. Some had official titles; others were simply oak doors with no indication of what was behind them. The crypt that Pike had given was unique to his last unit, and was guaranteed to get attention. It was a verification, sometimes a distress code that allowed operators working in deep cover to send a message through "ordinary" CIA channels during extreme situations, when established communications had failed. It had never been used. It was designed to get attention, and within a second or two of Eric's finger depressing the button on his computer's mouse, it had done its job.

INSIDE TASKFORCE HEADQUARTERS, the duty officer sat staring at a computer screen, bored out of his mind. The man was dressed in casual business attire, but like everyone else in the office, except the little old ladies downstairs, he looked like an athlete. He always wondered if maybe they shouldn't change their cover to something with professional sports. *Maybe be Jerry Maguire's D.C. office or something. Maybe hire Kelly Preston to roam around here, solidifying the cover.* Before his mind could wander to something less savory, the computer at his desk signaled an incoming message. He stood up and printed it out, giving a low whistle when he saw the crypt.

He took the cable directly to Kurt Hale's office. He knew Kurt was in the process of packing up to go on a date night with his wife, something they hadn't done in more than six months. He saw Kurt's expression change when he walked in, Kurt recognizing that his night might be shot.

"What's up, Mike?"

"We got a Prometheus message five minutes ago."

Kurt stopped what he was doing, running through his mind the two active operations currently ongoing. Only Knuckles was anywhere near an endgame. The other operation was still in the formative stages, laying the groundwork for execution two or three months from now. A Prometheus alert meant something had gone very badly for someone.

"Which team?"

"Well, that's what's strange. I think it's from Pike. It's not from anyone active here."

"Pike? Pike Logan?" Before Mike could respond, Kurt realized he was asking questions that Mike couldn't possibly answer. He reversed himself and said, "Okay. Let me see the cable. And holler down the hall at George."

"You got it. Here's the message."

Kurt read the cable, a short, simple paragraph. Skipping through the usual disclaimers about walk-ins, no established reporting record, and the ominous "Contact may have been attempting to influence as well as inform" trailer, he read:

> Contact stated he had information regarding a potential WMD terrorist attack. Contact had no concrete information about the attack, but stated that he had intercepted Internet traffic implying an Al Qaeda involvement in procurement of WMD for the application against United States, Israeli, or Iranian interests. Contact stated that he believed the WMD was not radiological. Contact stated that two unknown subjects of Arabian descent were in the process of procuring the WMD. Contact became evasive when questioned on his knowledge of the aforementioned WMD, refusing to state how he knew this information. Contact firmly believes that the procurement is time sensitive, and that the AQ members are actively pursuing this aim.

It was impossible that anyone on earth would know the Prometheus alert crypt unless Pike had told them, and in Kurt's mind, it was equally impossible that Pike would have told anyone such a secret. On the other hand, the Pike he knew might no longer exist. *Maybe he's slipped down completely, and is selling plasma on the street for his next bottle of Mad Dog 20/20, babbling secrets to anyone who will listen.* Kurt rejected that, as it didn't explain how a stranger was able to contact the CIA in an overseas embassy, then send the message. Everything pointed to its being Pike, however bizarre it appeared. Even so, they would need to confirm the identity before proceeding. Kurt turned at the knock on the door, seeing his friend and deputy commander.

"How long's it been since you made a trip to Central America?"

George looked puzzled by the question. "Well, not since we were supporting the Contras back in the good ol' days. Are they now the next terrorist threat? We going down to take them out?"

Kurt chuckled, filling him in on what he knew, then saying, "Call the station down there and let them know we're coming. Tell them to contact whoever's calling himself Pike. If it's him, we'll figure out what's going on. If it's not, we'll figure out where the breach occurred. Either way, this is too big of a problem to ignore. We should be able to get down and back in one day, two at the most."

"Easy enough. I assume we're leaving tomorrow morning?"

"Yeah, I've got a date tonight that I can't miss."

54

A few miles away, Harold Standish sat at his desk in the Old Executive Office Building, silently reading the Prometheus cable. He saw an opportunity. A way to get America back on war footing, and get control of the Taskforce at the same time. A way to strengthen the defense of the United States. *If the whiners on the Oversight Council are too timid to preempt an attack, maybe they need to see one up close.*

The more he thought about it, the more he liked the idea. America had lost its focus on terrorism precisely because it hadn't been attacked in close to a decade. The stupid electorate had the memory of a bovine, conveniently forgetting the threat, instead lambasting the very government that provided their protection. *A WMD going off would wake them the fuck up, that's for sure.* There would be a feeding frenzy just like 9/11. All the politicians would be screaming for action. The Oversight Council would have to bend with the pressure. The Taskforce would be turned loose. *With any luck, the council will be too busy doing their day jobs to look closely at Taskforce activities. I'll be the man left at the wheel. It's not like my day job takes up a lot of time.*

Standish paused, realizing he was thinking about the

slaughter of untold innocent civilians, not simply numbers in a news report. He pondered the cost and benefits. He decided the deaths were necessary. *Great leaders throughout history have had to make hard choices such as this.* He knew that Truman himself had made the decision to drop the atomic bomb based on this very same principle. *Hundreds of thousands of Japanese civilians killed to save millions of Americans. This is no different. There's a greater good here.* He, of course, would need to go on vacation for about a month to ensure he was out of the blast radius, should Washington be in the crosshairs. *This town could stand to lose a little deadweight anyway.*

He called his in-staff intelligence officer and asked him to run down any "chatter" on terrorist threats within the last three days involving the words *Israel, WMD, Iran,* and *poison weapons.* Within thirty minutes, the man arrived with fourteen NSA reports that had some tangential relationship to the search criteria. Most were clearly not what Standish was looking for, only detailing vague information of little value. Using the Prometheus cable, he necked down the reports until he found a NSA cut describing a WMD attack against Israel. He didn't have the background in terrorism to understand the reference to the far enemy, and was unsure why the intercept mentioned the historical state of Persia instead of the modern nomenclature of Iran, but since this was the only bit of intelligence that talked of pushing the Zionists into the sea via a single weapon—something that anyone could understand—he honed in on it, noting the reference to something called Operation Badr. He was pleased to see the intel was raw, meaning nobody had analyzed it yet, and thus nobody knew it existed.

"Ken, run a search on Operation Badr. Bring me what you find immediately."

Five minutes later Ken returned with a single message. "This is the only thing that's come in with those search terms."

Standish read the report, which simply said that Operation Badr was progressing and that a device had been tested successfully. He connected the dots. "Okay, do an open-source search on anything strange happening in Belize. Focus on a group of unexplained deaths. See if anyone in the press has reported anything like that."

After another wait, Ken returned, saying, "There was nothing in Belize. The only thing I could find was a bus crash on the border, but it was on the Guatemalan side."

"What's so fucking strange about that? I told you unexplained deaths."

"Well, everyone on the bus died, but nobody died from the crash." He handed the press report to Standish. "Apparently, they all died of some strange illness."

Standish read the news report and smiled. *The weapon's real.* "Ken, I want you to destroy any mention of these two intercepts about Operation Badr. Figure out who else got them, and erase them. Do it without their knowledge. Those reports never existed. Understand?"

Ken, a sycophant cut from Standish's mold, didn't question the directive. "Easy enough. I'll do it as soon as I get back to my office."

"Good. In addition, I got a cable from Belize today. Rescind that cable as well. Ensure it also doesn't exist." He gave the intelligence officer the cable cite number.

Ken asked, "What about the station in Belize? Won't they ask why it was rescinded?"

"I'll handle the station when they come in to work tomorrow. Just get rid of the cable right now."

"Okay—I'm on it."

Standish reflected on what he knew. On the one hand, it was a golden opportunity to accomplish exactly what he believed was necessary. On the other, while not out of control yet, it was an opportunity that had quite a few leaks. He had managed to stop the raw intel from being spread but couldn't be sure about the Prometheus cable. *If that thing's not rescinded in time, I'll never be able to deny I knew about it.* Luckily, it had come from Belize. CTC would probably shunt that cable to the back of the pack, focusing on Pakistan, Iran, and whatever else was brewing right now. *They won't give a shit one way or another about a rescinded cable from Central America.*

His primary problem was the Taskforce. They would get the Prometheus alert and would act on it. He had to shut them down right away. There was no love lost between himself and the unit, but they would listen to him, since they were still on shaky ground and couldn't afford an enemy of his stature. He could bring them down with a well-placed leak, and they knew it.

He called the Taskforce duty officer, went secure on his STE telephone, identified himself, and asked if the unit was planning any new movement in the next twenty-four hours.

On the other end, the duty officer Mike, knowing who it was, stated no. He didn't literally lie, as his bosses were traveling true-name as part of their true affiliation— Kurt as a member of J3 SOD, and George as a TDY member of the Office of Southern Hemispheric Relations— thus they weren't traveling under any of the covers used by the Taskforce. His answer was technically correct—there was no Taskforce movement. Standish next asked to speak to the commander and was told that he was out.

Standish hung up after leaving a message for Kurt to call first thing in the morning. He was satisfied that he was good for the time being. The cap was in place.

55

I woke up to the phone ringing, answered and perked up, replying quickly and ending the call. I saw that Jennifer was awake and leaning on an elbow, wearing a cheap tourist T-shirt with her hair sticking out all over the place, making me grin. Rubbing her eyes, she asked who was on the phone.

"It was the embassy. They want to see us at ten o'clock. The cable must have worked, because we've been invited behind the green curtain. We get to talk to the wizard."

Waking up fast, Jennifer tried to brush her hair in place, asking, "What's that mean? Who'd you talk to?"

"That was the asshole Eric." *Shit . . . Be nice. . . .* "Sorry. That was the nice man from the embassy, Eric. He asked us to come back."

"That's good news, isn't it? Do we need to do anything before we go?"

"No. I'm not sure what the cable caused. We'll just see how it goes. Either way, we got some action, so that's good."

She looked at me like I was hiding something, and I was, but she let it go. "Okay, Jason Bourne, I'll follow your lead."

When we got to the embassy, even I was surprised at who was waiting.

STANDISH CALLED THE TASKFORCE first thing in the morning, early enough to get Mike before his twenty-four-hour shift as the duty officer was over. Going secure on his STE, Standish asked to speak to Colonel Hale.

"Sir, he's gone TDY this morning."

"*What?* I thought you told me last night that he was out with his wife. Where is he?"

"Sir, he was out with his wife last night. Today he left."

Who does he think he's talking to? "Tell me where he is right this minute."

"Sir, I can't give you that information on this phone."

Standish was on the verge of frothing at the mouth. "I'm on a fucking secure line. You will tell me where he is, right this minute. Do you understand me? Is that clear?"

"Sir, I'm not trying to be difficult, but I must follow security procedures. Colonel Hale's location is top secret. Your phone is only certified up to secret message traffic. I'm not allowed to tell you his location on this line. Not my rule."

Standish realized he was done. The STE secure phone was certified by the NSA to pass information only up to the secret level. He couldn't order the man to break classification rules, since he would be on record violating the safeguard of national secrets. He also knew that he was being stiff-armed on purpose by the duty officer, but couldn't fight it. *At least not right now. You mess with the bull, you get the horns.*

"Listen to me, Mr. *Duty Officer*. Pick up a fucking pen. Write this down. I want Kurt Hale and George Wolffe in my office within twenty-four hours or I will go to the president and have all unit operations canceled pending an investigation of improper actions. Is that understood?"

"Yes, sir. I have it."

"Don't test me on this. If you value your mission, you won't push me. I *will* see Hale and Wolffe or you'll cease operations."

Standish slammed the phone down. *When I get control of that unit, he'll be out greeting people at Walmart.*

Done with the Taskforce, he turned his attention to the next problem: dealing with the CIA station in Belize. He couldn't call the station directly because they weren't in his chain of command and wouldn't have a clue who he was. He would have to do it through the Latin America Division in the headquarters at Langley. Luckily, he knew the chief of LA and could use him to clamp down on Belize. All he had to do was control the conversation correctly. Satisfied with his strategy, he picked up the phone and dialed the chief of LA on his gray line, a direct secure connection into the CIA.

56

"Holy shit! What're you doing down here?" I said. After giving me a handshake and an embrace, Kurt verbally poked me, saying, "Well, I've got nothing better to do than chase phantom Prometheus cables. It's what I do on my off time."

I got out, "Sir—" before he cut me off with a hand.

"Just kidding. How're you doing?"

I figured the question held more than it seemed, and that he wasn't asking how I was doing *this* morning. I answered truthfully, "Well, honestly, sir, I'm doing better now than I was a week ago."

"Still blocking punches with your face, huh?"

I smiled and touched the cut above my eye. "Long story, sir." Turning to Jennifer, I continued. "This is Jennifer Cahill. She's the reason I'm down here, and also the one who figured out what's going on."

He greeted Jennifer politely, then said, "Okay, how about letting me in on the secret."

I laid out the whole story, with the exception of the discovery of the e-mail addresses. After the bullshit shenanigans, I didn't trust Eric as far as I could throw him. There was no telling what the station here would do with that information.

After about an hour of give-and-take, Kurt got to the bottom line. "Given your lack of ability to do anything, I get the Prometheus alert, but, really, is there any proof that such a weapon exists? What do you want me to do now?"

I had known that was coming and, in reality, agreed with his skepticism. "Sir, I'm with you. I've been struggling with the whole Mayan WMD thing since this started. Whether that weapon is real or not is an open question. In my mind, what's not a question is that two intelligent terrorists with multiple passports *believe* it's there, and are trying to get it to kill as many people as possible."

"Okay. I can see that. Sounds like something that's happening all over the world every five seconds. Why bring us in? You know this isn't what we do."

"I didn't intend for you guys to fly down here to see me. I just wanted to talk to the chief of station. Sorry, but I played the only card I had. I think someone needs to check this out, to see if something strange happened on an expedition in the Petén region. If not, no harm. If so, investigate further."

Kurt looked at Eric, who said, "That makes sense to me. It's very little work to run this to ground. I'll give the station in Guatemala a call and have them check it out."

Kurt thanked him for the support, then asked George if there was anything else they were missing.

George said, "No, Pike's right. Let the station get some assets on the ground. We'll figure this out pretty quickly."

Satisfied, Kurt wrapped up the meeting. He told us to

come on back at nine the next morning to see where we stood. I walked with him out the door, stopping to allow him to retrieve his cell phone from the cubicles outside the station spaces. Since the cell phones could be used as eavesdropping devices, they weren't allowed inside any secure government facility.

Turning on his phone, Kurt said, "Well, I'm not going to blow smoke up your ass. I don't think there's much chance of some secret Mayan weapon being out there, but since we're here, might as well play the hand. No harm done by poking around a little bit."

He stopped when his phone chirped. "Jesus. I got six calls while I was inside there."

He closed the phone. "Let's get some dinner tonight. I'm sure you've got some things you want to tell me that you didn't want to say in there."

Smart man. "You read my mind. I held some cards back. There's a great little fish stand near our hotel. Give me a call at the hotel when you're ready to go."

I watched him walk off, dialing his phone.

INSIDE THE STATION, Eric finished his coordination with his compatriots in Guatemala to check out Pike's story. Talking to the deputy, he was disappointed to hear that it would be a couple of days before they could get on the ground at Flores, but was satisfied when he said they could make some calls to contacts up there for an initial snapshot. Eric thanked him, asking him to call back tomorrow at eight A.M. with any results, and hung up.

The phone rang with his hand still on it, startling him. Picking it back up, he was startled again when he found out that the chief of the Latin America division was giving him a personal call from Langley. Listening intently, he began to take notes.

When Jennifer and I got back to our room, I noticed the red light blinking on our old-fashioned phone. Jennifer went to the bathroom, leaving me to get the message.

Coming back out, she asked, "Who was that? Kurt? Is he going to take us out to a nice dinner instead of the taco stand?"

"I wish. Kurt's been called back to D.C. Something important came up, and he's got to get back immediately. He said to send him a message through Eric, and he'd take it from there."

"Well, he seemed like a pretty busy guy. I'm surprised he even flew down."

She could see that I was disappointed, and tried to make a joke. "He clearly knew better than to mess with you. I'm sure if you send another cable, he'll do something with it. Maybe you should tell him to meet us in the Caribbean, and that he needs to give us some tickets to get there."

"He'll do something with it, but cables are never as good as face-to-face. Whatever called him back will take front seat. It'll be hard to pry him away from that now."

I was surprised at the level of my disappointment, and wondered if I was more upset at our theories taking a backseat to something else, or that this adventure was drawing to a close. I hadn't realized how much I had wanted to go to that meeting tomorrow, and to continue on with this excursion. I think in my heart I was hoping Kurt would take me with him to figure out what was going on. *What a fantasy.*

I said, "Let's go get a flight out of here for tomorrow. No sense hanging around here now. Whatever we find out at the meeting tomorrow morning, the rest of this will be in someone else's hands."

"That sounds good to me. I'm ready to get back to my simple college life."

Her words gave me another kick in the gut. *I hear you. Boy, am I ever ready to get back to being a worthless fucking bum.* Once we left the embassy tomorrow, she would go back to her life and I'd go back to mine. All I had to look forward to was waking up in a rage every morning. I could already feel my self-worth eroding. The thought was depressing and must have showed on my face.

"What's wrong? Are you really that worried about the cable doing nothing? I thought Kurt was the Wizard of Oz."

I lied, "Yeah, I'm worried about the cable. You're probably right, though. No sense in crying over it now. Let's see what happens tomorrow. Come on. I'd like to get a plane that doesn't allow goats in the aisle."

"PALMER," President Warren said, "can you hang on a second?"

Alexander Palmer stopped at the door to the Oval Office, letting the other members of the president's National Security team leave.

"Sure, sir. What's up?"

Warren stood up and leaned against his desk. "The Taskforce got a Prometheus alert, but I never saw it."

"Oh, yeah. Standish told me about it. He's run it to ground already. Some sort of misfire. It wasn't Prometheus material. Sorry if I didn't bring it to your attention, but it was nothing."

"What do you think about him?"

"Standish? Ahh . . . I think if he wasn't around, you wouldn't be president, but he's not really giving us much in the administration. He's just taking up space on the NSC. Is that what you mean?"

Warren had been thinking about what Kurt had said months ago. About some unknown terrorist with the skill and patience to really do some damage. The thought scared him. As president, he'd created Project Prometheus at significant risk and let them run at full throttle. He had thought they were winning, that the risk had been worth every penny. But the commander didn't. Kurt thought they had just been lucky—as if the Taskforce was no match for a smart terrorist, and that that man was out there right now, planning. The revelation had caused him to lose sleep.

President Warren was a political infighter. A winner. He took no quarter and wasn't above dirty tricks to win—just like every other politician at this level. He had a lot on his plate—the economy, global trade issues, the constant bickering between parties—but only one issue really scared him: the loss of American lives because of something he had failed to do. And not in a political way either. It scared him in a personal way. He couldn't imagine being president on 9/11, watching the bodies fall from the burning towers. It was the one issue where politics had no business. And probably the one thing that allowed him to relate to Kurt Hale. Everything else he did in the name of democracy would make Hale's stomach turn.

He had reviewed his National Security team and begun to wonder if he'd ceded too much control. Everyone had become complacent when it came to terrorism, himself included. He'd allowed Palmer to run the NSC as he saw fit, but after hearing about Standish's questions at the last Taskforce Oversight Council meeting, he was beginning to believe the man was dangerous.

He said, "No, I don't mean what he's contributing to the administration. You put him on the Taskforce Oversight Council, and I'm wondering if that was wise. You work with him. I'm asking if he can be trusted. NSC business is one thing, but the Taskforce is something else. There's no room for error."

"Well, he has managed to work his way on the inside a hell of a lot quicker than I would have thought possible, but he's doing a good job. He keeps me abreast of all the secret things going on. He's pretty good at collating information."

"That doesn't answer the question. Is he a threat? Standish's answer for anything is brute force. He doesn't understand the complexity. Doesn't have the experience or background."

Palmer reflected for a moment. "No, I think he's okay. We both know he loves the feeling of being on the inside. He's like a political groupie, but that's about it."

President Warren locked eyes with him. "Palmer, don't let him become a threat. This isn't about payback or politics. I won't tolerate American deaths. That's got nothing to do with politics."

Palmer smiled. "Sir, don't worry about that. He's a coward at heart. He likes playacting. He doesn't have the balls to do anything for real."

57

Lucas Kane fiddled with his PDA, waiting on Standish to finish with a phone call. He played the keys with manicured fingers, looking like any other successful power broker in Washington, D.C. Actually, he looked like an actor in a beer commercial portraying a successful power broker in Washington, D.C. He had sandy blond hair, an athletic build, and a face that belonged in a weekly Hollywood tabloid. From across the street, women were automatically drawn to him. Up close, when they could look into his eyes, the attraction would usually wilt. His eyes were dead. Not unintelligent, just lacking in any warmth. His last date, after saying she would rather not see him again, commented that they reminded her of a three-day-old bruise. Purple and rotting.

Lucas didn't give a shit, as long as the date paid him back for the dinner and a movie once they returned to his apartment, which this one had, even if a bit reluctantly. *If the eyes are a window into the soul, I guess a bruise is pretty damn close.*

Standish hung up the phone, saying, "They're on the way over. Should be here in about five minutes. You sure you can do this?"

"Yeah, I'm sure. It's not brain surgery. The key is the

information you gave me. If the phone's a different model, or the pager information is incorrect, it might not work."

"That intel's good. I've seen them myself."

"Shouldn't be an issue, then. We'll know shortly."

He left the office and positioned himself on a bench in the marble hallway within view of the entrance to Standish's office, but far enough away as to be inconspicuous. He opened a magazine.

He didn't have to wait long. Two men approached Standish's office. He focused on the one matching the description of his target. They stopped and placed their two-way pagers and cell phones in the ubiquitous cubicles provided outside every government office that whispered the nation's secrets. He noted which cubicle his target used. He waited until they passed through the cipher-locked door, then waited an additional few seconds. When nothing happened, he walked at a quick pace and pulled both the pager and cell phone from the cubicle. He raced down the stairs to the equipment he had left in his vehicle parked outside.

His task was to clone the cell phone with a sophisticated Trojan horse virus, which would allow a separate cell phone to act exactly like the original. Anytime the target phone rang, the other would ring too. Anytime it dialed out, his would dial out. It would be like a three-way call every time the target used his phone, except that he wouldn't suspect it.

In addition to manipulating the phone, he was going to reverse the pager the target wore. Using the information given to him by Standish, Lucas knew that the device was specially constructed, capable of worldwide coverage through a satellite network, and equipped with a "panic button" that would send out a signal based on Global Positioning System satellites. Once triggered, it would give a grid reference to its location worldwide. Lucas was going to ensure that the pager sent a signal without the button being pushed, in effect making the pager a beacon without the target even knowing it. The trick would be ensuring the signal didn't enter the normal channels and thus cause an alert. Instead, it would be visible only to someone who knew it was broadcasting. Lucas didn't yet know exactly why this target needed to be tracked, but something told him that Standish wasn't finished using him on this particular assignment.

STANDISH LEFT KURT AND GEORGE sitting in the anteroom for five more minutes, just because he felt like being a prick. Eventually, he closed out the solitaire game he was playing and told his secretary to show them in.

He heard them enter, pretending to work on his computer. He let them stand for a few seconds before turning around. He pointed to the chairs in front of his desk and started right in, skipping any pleasantries.

"You received a Prometheus alert two days ago, yet you didn't notify anyone at all. If I remember your initial information briefings to me, those were supposed to trigger a response, but when I called the Taskforce, I got an idiotic duty officer who acted as if nothing was wrong. Either you're running an organization that isn't the caliber you so eloquently brag about in your brief, or you're attempting to hide things from a member of the council that oversees your activities. For your sake, I hope it's incompetence."

Standish watched both of them squirm a little, clearly not expecting to be attacked. *Good. They need to know who's the boss here.*

Kurt said, "Sir, we did get an alert, but it wasn't what you think. Neither of your reasons is accurate—the alert came from an old unit member. It didn't involve an active mission and thus didn't require a response from the Taskforce.

"As for you not getting any word about it, I apologize, but if you remember the brief you were just talking about, we get oversight solely on which target to attack and our method of engagement, based on potential second- and third-order effects that might be generated from the action. Once we get the go-ahead to proceed against a target, there is no further oversight, unless one of those variables changes."

Is he giving me a lecture? Like I'm slow? "Colonel Hale, don't treat me like a child. I understand how the Oversight Council works. I'm one of the members. Perhaps it's you that needs a refresher on who you work for."

Kurt backpedaled. "Sir, we meant no disrespect, but the Prometheus alert is a tactical control measure used solely by us in the Taskforce, and we didn't realize a report to you was necessary."

Standish steepled his fingers. "Well, maybe I should speak to the president about relooking at this little experiment's rules of engagement. It sounds to me like you think you get to decide what does or does not occur within your little secret world."

George broke in. "Sir, he's not trying to tell you that you had no right to know; he's explaining why you didn't initially get any feedback. We're here specifically to provide that feedback. Kurt and I just came from meeting the man who sent the cable. He has an interesting story to tell, and while it may have some merit, the odds of it being true aren't that great."

George continued, giving Standish a broad sketch of Pike's story, knowing that Standish had read the original message. He finished by telling Standish the coordination made with Guatemala and the way ahead.

"So, what's the Taskforce going to do with this? Anything?"

Kurt said, "Well, it depends on what the CIA finds out. Right now, there isn't a whole lot we can do and, with the information we have, not much we should be doing. This is more of a CIA issue. Unless you want us to start focusing on it, we're going to let them take the lead. We have enough on our plate without this."

Perfect. Just what I wanted to hear. "No, that sounds right."

Looking at his watch, Standish said, "I've got another meeting coming up. I appreciate you two taking the time out of your day to come down. We don't have to be looking across the fence at each other all the time. I want to work with you. All I ask for is a little courtesy and respect."

He paused. "Trust me—if I don't get it, you will cease to exist."

58

After the door closed behind Kurt and George, Standish buzzed his secretary and told her to show Lucas in as soon as he arrived. After a minute and a half, Standish saw him coming through the door and was embarrassed to feel his pulse rate go up. He wouldn't admit it to anyone, but Lucas scared him. *Bastard looks like he belongs in Alaska killing baby seals.* He was a cousin of Standish's wife, and extremely useful for certain tasks, but Standish didn't like being alone with him for any length of time. He watched Lucas plop down in a chair as if he were in his own office.

"No issues," Lucas said.

"Will it work?"

"No. You pay me just to pretend." He tossed the phone to Standish, reached into his pocket and pulled out another phone, dialing a number. The phone rang once before the one in Standish's hand began ringing.

Standish heard Kurt Hale answer after the fourth ring. Lucas said, "Can I speak to Betty?"

Through the phone he held, Standish heard Kurt say, "Sorry, wrong number."

Lucas hung up.

Standish grinned. With any luck, not only would he

get all information relating to the Mayan weapon, but he might also get other useful information relating to the Taskforce, or even Kurt's personal life. *I should have done this a long time ago.*

"Can you tell anything was done?"

"Not at a casual look-over. If the phone's software is scrubbed, they'll see it was manipulated."

"We're good there. No way they'll suspect this office of doing anything. What about the pager?"

"The pager's a little different. That panic beacon attempts to transmit on any signal it can find, like cellular, FM, you name it. With that much stuff blasting out on a constant stream, there's a chance someone will pick up the signal. It'll also run the batteries down about four times as fast, which might spike the target. I figured it would be better to restrict it to satellite only, so that's what it will transmit on. The batteries will still burn more quickly, but not enough to spike."

"Okay. What's that mean to me?"

"You'll only get a location when the beacon can see the sky. If the beacon loses signal, it'll just show its last known location."

"That's fine by me. The pager was just a benny anyway. I'll cut a check to the same account for your time. Is that acceptable?"

"Yeah. Same account."

Standish paused, internally making a decision. "Before you go, I need to read you on to something that might require your attention."

"All right. I'm still on your retainer. What's up?"

Standish's only weak link now was Pike himself. He had already gleaned both his and Jennifer's passport information from the station in Belize and had fed that into the gigantic, bureaucratic Homeland Security database, ensuring they would be stopped at whatever port of entry they attempted to use. His only purpose was to tie them up until the terrorists could set off their weapon. Getting arrested as a terrorist associate should do the trick. By the time they got an apology and a pat on the back, the bomb should have gone off. Still, Standish hadn't gotten to where he was by not planning, and he wanted to ensure he had a contingency in place. He'd play nice first but had no compunction about turning nasty.

"I have a couple of individuals I might need you to deal with."

Standish gave him a brief rundown on Pike and Jennifer, leaving out the reasons he wanted them stopped. Lucas didn't ask why or what they represented. It wasn't part of the mission and thus wasn't something that concerned him.

When he was finished, Lucas said, "What do you want me to do with them?"

"Nothing right now. I'll call you if I need you."

Lucas let the silence extend out a bit to show what he thought of that answer, then said, "Yeah, I get that. That wasn't my question. What do you want me to do with them if you call? What's the mission?"

"Get rid of them."

Lucas sat forward in his chair, looking a little agitated at the verbal dance. "What the fuck does that mean? Tell me what you want done. I'm doing the work. The least you could do is actually say it. You want them locked up, sent to the hospital, what?"

Let him know you aren't afraid to get your hands dirty.
"Kill them. Or do you have an issue with that?"

Lucas stared into Standish's eyes. "I'm pretty sure you know the answer to that."

Standish recoiled in his chair, mentally trying to distance himself from Lucas without appearing to do so.

"Yes. I guess I do."

A year ago, Lucas had been a SEAL serving in Afghanistan, where he had been accused of intentionally killing civilians. That in itself wasn't remarkable, since not a day went by without Standish's reading some bullshit report of Americans killing civilians. Ninety-nine point nine percent of those reports were propaganda put out by the enemy to stir up a little Islamic fury. The difference with the accusations against Lucas was they hadn't been brought forward by some unknown local with an ax to grind, but by his own teammates. Just before the investigation began in earnest, the two teammates died violently in an IED attack. The investigation took a new tack, now looking into the deaths of two American servicemen as well as the deaths of the Afghanis. Before it could build up enough steam, as a favor to his wife, Standish pulled Lucas out of the fire with a few well-placed words, allowing him to leave the military at fifteen years, his only true punishment being the loss of retirement pay. Now he was wondering if using Lucas might be a mistake. *He's liable to kill two hundred people to get this done.*

Standish decided to deal with that possibility up front. "I don't care how you do it, and don't need it to look like an accident or anything stupid like that, but you have to do it in such a way that it won't lead back to me. Ever.

And don't kill a ton of civilians just to get them. Under-stand?"

"What's your definition of 'a ton'?"

Jesus. He's a cold-blooded son of a bitch. "I'll understand a collateral damage number of five or less. More than that and you've exceeded the rules of engagement."

"I can do that. You got anyone you want killed right now, or is this it?"

Standish punched his secretary's buzzer. *Get him the fuck out of here.*

59

The next morning at 0815 we were both in the lobby of the embassy, with the same Marine flipping through the clearance sheets. Ten minutes later, after checking the massive amount of rosters at his disposal, the lance corporal turned to me and said, "I'm sorry, sir, but you're not listed."

I asked for the number to the office and called up. Getting Eric, I was told to hold fast, and he'd come down to me. I hung up the phone, a sick feeling in the pit of my stomach.

"Something's up. I think we're about to get the blow-off."

Eric exited the elevator and walked over to us with a big smile.

Shit. This is going to be bad.

"Hey, I guess you didn't get the word. The meeting's off."

Seeing me scowl, he said, "Hold on, now, it's not my call. My bosses in D.C. told me to cease and desist. Even the guys you brought down left last night."

"Fine. Got it. At least tell us what you found out from Guatemala."

"Well, the guys in Guatemala couldn't get to the Petén region for a couple of days. They were set to go when HQ stopped that as well. They did make some phone calls and found out that there was an expedition, which ended badly. Of course, they couldn't confirm anything. All they could find out was that one boy apparently was consumed by some sort of ancient curse and another disappeared after the expedition. Nobody knows what happened to them for real."

What the hell? Why would they have been called off? "So, preliminary investigation concurs with what we say, but it's not worth following up on? What's up with that?"

I knew Eric was just the messenger, and that he didn't like giving us this news. He continued in a calm voice. "Pike, please, all we have is that some sort of 'ancient curse' caused the disappearance of a boy. If we ran after every rumor like that, we'd be spending all of our time chasing Bigfoot."

"Okay. Fine. I'd like you to send a cable out to that effect. Can you at least do that?"

Eric shook his head. "Pike, I'd really like to help, but we've done more than we should have already. I'm not going to send out any more unsolicited cables. If HQ asks for clarification, I'll do so, but I'm not sending anything else out on your say-so."

I turned and walked away before I did something I'd regret, not even bothering to say good-bye to him. Jennifer caught up with me outside.

"What are we going to do now?"

"Nothing. We're getting on a bus to Belize City and going home. We're done."

I said the last two words with more force than necessary, causing her to look up sharply. I covered up the slip, speaking softer. "Look, this is over. Nobody cares and we can't do anything with it by ourselves. We gave it our best shot and got further than I thought we would. Let's just get home and see if we're going to be arrested for murder. We're in enough trouble already without pushing this any further."

"Well, I just don't think we should quit."

She saw me start to react and held up a hand. "Wait—before you go into asshole mode—hear me out. We believe that these guys are up to no good. Nobody else docs, and maybe they're right, but what if they're not? Can't we do something else? You're the expert. Have we exhausted all our options?"

I thought about what she said, feeling a little slimy that I wanted to continue more for the sense of mission than saving anyone's life.

"Well, if you want to foot the bill, we can go to D.C. and contact Kurt again. We don't have a lot, but we do have a few things he hasn't seen. We can give him the e-mail addresses for further tracking, get a real translation of the initial message, and tell him that the superficial investigation in Guatemala supports what we said. Is that what you want to do?"

This isn't right. I'm convincing her to chase shadows so I don't have to go back to my boat. So I don't have to face my life. If she's dumb enough to say yes, give her the truth.

We walked in silence for a minute. She said, "Yes."

Man, is she stubborn. "Are you nuts? You're going to flunk out of school. Our own government doesn't give a shit about this. Even if we do go to D.C., we don't have a clue where the terrorists are, or what they have. We won't get anywhere, and you'll just get a lighter bank account from paying the way."

Jennifer crossed her arms. "Yeah. I *know* that. But my family has a long history of doing stupid shit. Just ask my uncle." She looked hard at me. "What if someone like us existed before 9/11? Would you have wanted them to quit?"

Gee, thanks. I really feel slimy now. "No, I guess not."

AFTER EXITING OUR FLIGHT IN ATLANTA, we proceeded down the narrow gateway funneling us into the customs complex of the United States. We had a connecting flight into Washington but still had to pass through U.S. Immigration to continue. We moved up to the counter together, where I showed my passport. The man behind the counter ran the bar code and stiffened.

I watched his expression turn to stone. He asked Jennifer, "Are you traveling together?"

She said yes and handed him her passport. He ran it through the scanner, his face showing no emotion. Turning back from the computer, he became pleasant.

"I'm afraid that I'm going to have to ask both of you to follow me. We're going to need some additional information about your trip."

I felt the hair stand up on the back of my neck. *Shit. We've been flagged because of the dead guys in Charleston.*

Remaining pleasant, I asked, "Questions about what? We were only gone a few days. We can answer them right here."

The customs agent remained deadpan, giving me no

indication that he was a threat, but also no indication that he was friendly. "Sir, this won't take but a couple of seconds. We've had some trouble with U.S. citizens coming back from Central America. All we want you to do is take a little survey to help us facilitate future travel. I don't want to hold up the line here to do that. Once you're done, you'll be on your way."

As we moved down the hallway to the secondary interrogation rooms, I dismissed the Charleston angle, since suspected murderers would have been arrested and handcuffed immediately. We were walking free and clear behind the customs official. I relaxed, thinking that maybe Kurt had set up a method to contact us, since he had left Belize before I could give him a phone number.

Entering the secondary interrogation area, I stood behind the customs official, listening to him tell the man at the desk who we were and where we were going. I waited while the man typed in the information. I saw a reflection of the computer screen on the windowpane to the man's right. In it were the passport photos of both Jennifer and me, surrounded by words that were inverted due to the mirror image. I couldn't make out what the paragraph underneath our pictures said, but did decipher the words above them: "WANTED FOR QUESTIONING ON SUSPECTED TERRORISM ACTIVITIES." A spurt of adrenaline jolted my body.

Projecting an outward calm, I asked, "Can we use the bathroom before we do anything else? We haven't had a chance to go since we landed."

The agent said, "This won't take a minute. Once we give you the surveys, you can do whatever you would like."

I nodded, my mind racing. I knew what was about to happen. We would be separated and taken to different interrogation rooms. We would be locked in and questioned for hours. The interrogators would compare notes on the answers that we gave to see if they matched up. Using that information, they would continue the questioning. Since I hadn't bothered to develop a cover story with Jennifer, it would do me no good to lie. Whatever I said wouldn't match what Jennifer said. On top of that, Jennifer would more than likely tell the truth, believing that the truth would be the best course of action. Unfortunately, our story was so unbelievable that it would cause the customs agents to become *more* suspicious, not less.

I had no idea why we were flagged in the Homeland Security system, but had no doubt that the second Jennifer mentioned two Arab terrorists with a WMD, we would be locked up until we could prove we weren't associated with them. We could be detained for days, if not weeks.

We need to break out of here right now, before we meet the interrogators. The fewer people, the better.

To compound matters, I had to do it without harming the agents. This wasn't their fault. They got paid to intercept terrorists. *I'd do the same thing.*

The agent at the desk said, "Good to go. Rooms seven and thirteen. Rob and Kenny are tied up right now, but they'll be down in ten minutes. They'll meet you there."

The first agent nodded, telling us, "Follow me." He turned and punched in the code to the cipher lock of the door leading into the interior hallway, and presumably the secondary interrogation facilities. I checked out the man behind the computer, seeing that he had taken off his equipment belt and hung it on the wall behind him. *Mistake number one.*

I knew why they were acting so pleasant—it was to prevent a scuffle in front of any passengers or other civilians. What I didn't understand was why they had used only one agent to do this. They should have a man behind me and a man in front, preventing me from taking out both at the same time. *Mistake number two.*

Before the man could open the door, I threw my left arm around his neck and drew the Glock 19 from the holster on the agent's right hip. I raised my right leg and racked the slide of the Glock on the edge of my boot. I kicked the back of the agent's leg hard enough to cause him to lean backward, with me supporting his weight. I rotated the agent away from the door, placing the front sight of the Glock on the agent behind the desk. The action happened in a blink of an eye, quick enough to prevent the agent behind the desk from getting to his feet. He held up his hands, a look of terror on his face, convinced he was face-to-face with an insane suicidal maniac.

I barked out orders quickly, intent on dominating the confrontation. "Don't fucking move. I don't want to hurt anyone. Put your hands on top of your head."

60

Jennifer stood dumbfounded by Pike's actions. *Jesus Christ, he's gone nuts. He's flashed back to some sort of Rambo scene getting tortured by the Vietcong.*

"What in the hell are you doing! Have you lost your *mind*? My God! Pike! Put down the gun!"

Pike bared his teeth at her and said, "Take a look at the computer monitor."

The agent Pike was holding tried his hand at negotiation. "Look, we only have a few questions. Nobody's saying you're a terrorist. Put the gun down and we can sort this out peacefully."

Pike laughed. "I suppose this whole hostage-taking thing would be forgotten, huh? If I give you the gun, we can start over like this never happened? Promise?"

Jennifer cut in, turning back from the monitor. "What's this mean? Why are we on the screen as terrorists? What's going on here?"

Pike said, "I don't know. Something's screwed up, and we don't have the time to sort it out here."

He addressed the customs agents. "Both of you listen to me. We aren't terrorists, and I can't have you arrest us. I'm going to have each of you take off your clothes. I'm then going to tie you both up. I'm not going to hurt either one of you. Please don't do anything to escalate this situation. I really, really don't want to hurt you. Do you understand my instructions?"

They both nodded. "Okay. You at the desk, take off your clothes. Once you're done, lie down on your stomach with your ankles crossed."

The man at the desk complied, lying down with nothing on but a T-shirt and underwear.

Pike spoke to Jennifer. "Go outside and wait for me. Alert me if someone's coming this way."

Jennifer started to leave, then paused. *He wants me out of the way. . . . He's going to hurt them . . . maybe kill them. . . .* Before she could say anything, the agent on the floor became agitated, looking wildly at Pike and Jennifer, apparently making the same mental leap that Jennifer had.

"Stop what you're thinking. I'm not going to harm you, but I *am* going to embarrass you. I'm sending Jennifer outside because I'm about to make you take off your underwear. That's it. Do you want her to stay? Will that prove I'm not about to cut your throat?"

The agent thought about it, then shook his head.

"Okay. Jennifer, please go outside."

Jennifer left the room. She thought she'd made a mistake, turned back to reenter, and saw the cipher lock on the door. *Damn. He's going to do something bad. This isn't right. Stopping the terrorists isn't worth hurting innocent people.*

A short time later Pike came out, holding the agents' clothing and equipment belts, looking queasy and sweating. *Shit. He hurt them. I'm going to hell.*

"Come on. We've got to move. We're about to have every policeman in the city of Atlanta trying to find us."

Jennifer put a hand on his chest, stopping him.

"What did you do in there?"

Pike was brought up short by the ferocity on her face.

"Hey, easy. I just tied them up butt-naked. Nothing else. Made me sick to my stomach doing that to good guys." He looked up and down the hallway. "We need to go, *now*."

She felt an enormous weight leave her shoulders. *Thank God*. Then she felt a little shame at what she had thought previously.

She said, "What do you think's going on? We're terrorists now?"

He started moving at a fast walk back the way they had come, toward the passport area, shoving the agents' equipment and clothing into the first garbage can he came across.

"I don't know, but we need to get the hell out of this airport. The tricky part is going to be getting out of the customs and immigration area. With any luck, we can bluff our way through. Just remember to project an air of calm confidence. Customs agents smell fear like a bloodhound. Walk like you own the place, and we should be good to go."

She caught up to him, saying, " 'Smell fear like a bloodhound' . . . That's just great. It's exactly what I thought I'd be worried about at this stage in my life. When I said this trek was the right thing to do, I didn't mean I wanted to wear a prison jumpsuit. There is a limit."

He jerked his head around as he fast-walked up the hallway. "What's that supposed to mean? We're getting arrested one way or another. I just postponed it a little bit. Hopefully a great bit."

"I know . . . I know. It's okay. I told you we Cahills do stupid shit too. Of course, I'm pretty sure you've just set a record. . . ."

Pike cut her off by raising a finger to his lips. They had reached the double doors that led back into the customs area. Pike poked his head out, then said, "This is it. A new flight's in and the place is buzzing. You ready?"

Realizing what she was about to do, Jennifer's bravado left her. "Pike, I don't know if I can do this. We just broke the law in a big way. We held a gun on federal agents and threatened them with death. I don't think I'm going to be able to remain calm."

"I hate to break this to you, but we don't have a choice."

61

We slipped into the flow of people headed to the baggage claim.

"Remain calm. We're going to walk right to the man over there taking the customs forms. He'll let us through as long as we don't look like we're hiding something."

I gave her a reassuring smile. "You ready?"

She nodded weakly, looking like she'd rather go back to the interrogation room. *Don't worry about that. If this doesn't work, we'll be there soon enough.*

We got in line behind a family of four. Acting like I was a newbie tourist, I held up our blue-and-white cards and said, "Do we give these to you?"

The man nodded, saying, "No luggage?"

"Yeah, we have luggage. It's somewhere between here and South America. Don't get me started."

The man smiled and waved us through. We entered the security checkpoint and made it to the far side without any issues, now back into the airport proper inside Concourse E.

"All right, we need to get out of here and get lost in the city. Unfortunately, we're at the last terminal in this damn airport. We're going to have to cross all five concourses to get out of here. We need to start moving faster. Sooner or later they're going to lock this place down."

We jogged down the escalator to the underground trains, with one pulling up as we hit bottom. I ignored it, pulling Jennifer to the moving sidewalk in front of me.

"What are you doing? We get on that and we can be at the entrance in minutes."

"Yeah, I know, but it's too risky. They pull the trigger on an alarm and that train's going to stop, with us inside it and no way out. We need to run it to the end."

We started walking like we were missing a plane, fast, but not fast enough to cause someone to stare. I noticed that the camera systems here in the tunnel were clustered only around the train entrances and exits.

Right after passing the escalators to Concourse C the trains ceased running, with an alert flashing that they were having mechanical issues.

"Good call," Jennifer said. "Looks like you were right."

"Yeah, but if the trains have stopped, we're out of time. They know we're loose. They'll try to camouflage it for a couple of minutes to keep everyone calm, but eventually, this place is going to be covered in cops."

As we moved toward Concourse B I saw the trains start to move again. *Huh. What's that about?*

We reached the escalator entrance to the B Concourse just as another train stopped, exploding out with about twenty police officers. *Oh, shit.*

Instead of running past Concourse B, I pushed Jennifer to the escalator, going up into the concourse. Glancing back, I saw half of the force coming up with us, apparently not recognizing we were ahead of them. *No pictures out yet.* We reached the top and went left, away from the direction the police were headed. Unlike the tunnel, in the concourse the cameras looked like something out of a Vegas casino, one little dome sticking out of the ceiling every thirty feet. *Shit.*

I hugged the wall, attempting to cross the concourse to the down escalators on the far side, getting back to the tunnel while there was still a gap in the police presence. Before we reached it, a group of police crossed over, headed our way. I turned into an alcove, rotating in front of Jennifer and shielding her face with my body.

"Tell me when they've passed us. If they start walking toward us, the game is up."

I saw Jennifer's face blanch. "Shit," she said. "One's moving directly toward us. What do we do? Should we run?"

"Stay calm. If he's headed to us, we're done. Don't assume that's what he's doing, though. We wait until he asks us a question."

"He's still coming. He's walking right to us."

"Okay . . . okay. Bend down and mess inside your bag. Anything to hide your face. Act like you're looking for tickets or something."

Squatting down, I began to rummage through my carry-on next to her. I could hear Jennifer muttering under her breath.

"Shit. I'm going to prison. . . . Mom's going to love this. . . . Uncle's fucking dead. . . . I'm a terrorist. . . . The only man I know's a nutcase. . . . All I try to do is the right thing. . . . Why does this stuff happen to *me* . . . ? Who'd I piss off . . . ?"

I saw the cop out of the corner of my eye. I waited for

the tap on the shoulder. He moved right past me and kept going into the alcove. For the first time, I noticed it was a men's room. *Whew. Too close for comfort.* I reached over to get Jennifer's attention when I caught the tail end of her rambling.

". . . Why don't you just tie the fucker up butt-naked? Right here . . . get us out of this the same way you got us into it. . . ."

What a crybaby. "You going to bitch all day, or can we get the hell out of here?"

She snapped out of it, saw we weren't under arrest, and looked up at me with a sheepish grin. I saw her eyes focus on the sign above my head.

"Yeah. He went in to take a piss. We should go before he's done."

"Sorry. I didn't mean any of that. Just letting off a little steam."

I began walking down the concourse toward a restaurant, saying, "Well, you'll have plenty of time for that, because we're fucked. We can't get out without getting to the far end, and I'm pretty sure there's a platoon of cops at baggage claim by now. We need a way out that normal passengers don't use."

"I know a way."

I looked at her face and saw she was serious. "What do you mean?"

"There's a pilots' lounge down below Concourse A. Get down there, and we can get on the Delta employee bus. It takes us right out of the airport grounds."

"How do you know that? Are you sure?"

"My dad was a pilot for Delta. He was also a deadbeat sack-of-shit that I haven't seen since I was seven. After my parents divorced, his idea of quality time was dragging me through here while he worked. I've spent plenty of time in that lounge."

She had just earned her weight for the entire trip. "Can you find it? How do we get in? What's the procedure?"

"I can find it, but that was way, way before 9/11. I have no idea about the procedure now."

"You said A Concourse? That's the next one up. Let's go."

We saw that the escalator was now free of police, and hurried to get to the tunnel below before they returned. The escalator was a long one, about sixty feet down to the ground. Halfway down, a cop sauntered over and positioned himself at the bottom, his back to us. He acted a little bored until he turned around and glanced up. Then he looked like he was going to shit his pants. *Damn. Pictures are out.*

62

The cop pulled his weapon and aimed it up at us while we glided relentlessly toward him. Jennifer was in front of me, preventing any action. He was an older guy, about sixty, and I saw the pistol barrel shake with his adrenaline. *He's liable to shoot out of reflex.*

"Jennifer, raise your hands."

We both did, and continued our glide, with him shouting all sorts of commands at us and into a radio. Every time he moved his other hand to key the mike on his shoulder, the gun hand would quake violently. *Right-handed.* He backed up as we reached the end of the escalator, both hands back on his weapon, screaming at us to keep our hands in the air. I slipped in front of Jennifer at the end, attempting to calm him.

"We're done. We're done. Please don't shoot."

Once we were on the ground with him, and seeing our acquiescence, he seemed to grow more confident, saying, "Up against the wall. *Now.*"

He barked out orders like an overweight Dirty Harry. I turned to face the wall, making sure that Jennifer was to my left, away from the barrel I was about to move. I waited on him to key his mike, leaving one hand on his weapon. I heard him start talking. *Please be strong enough to take this.*

I rotated to my left, pushing his gun hand away from me while grabbing onto the wrist. I drove a light, stunning palm strike into his nose with my right hand, then closed it over my left, controlling the pistol. I rotated the wrist, locking up the joints in his arm like a twisted rubber band. I didn't move fast enough to destroy his arm but did move with enough speed to force his body to react, literally doing a flip to prevent his arm from being damaged. He hit the ground hard, the wind knocked out of him. I felt like shit.

"Sorry about that."

I picked up his weapon, ripped his radio from his belt, and took off in the direction of Concourse A, leaving him gasping for air on the ground. Jennifer stumbled after me.

"Holy fuck. We are definitely going to jail now."

"Yeah, probably so, because if we face another police officer, I'm not doing that again. We give up."

I shoved the weapon into the first trash can I could find but kept the radio. I saw Concourse A ahead, and the cops moving around it. *Need another way up*.

Luckily, the lack of trains had caused everyone to use the walkway, so the tunnel was starting to swell with people still attempting to go about their daily lives. We intermingled with a group headed toward the concourse, listening to them talk about terrorists on the loose. I saw a handicapped elevator ahead, without any police presence. When we came abreast of it, I stopped and pressed the button, the door opening while the group still flowed around us. As we rode up, the cop's radio crackled with the news that we were at Concourse B. *Perfect*. Within seconds we were standing outside of Gate A19, no police in sight, looking at the entrance to the pilots' lounge. The news wasn't good. *Fuckin' bin Laden.*

"That figures. Everyone has to swipe their badge before keying in a code."

The good news was that the door was down a small hallway, so we wouldn't be seen doing something unless someone was in the hallway with us. The bad news was that Delta Airlines was serious about security. Nobody entered the door without badging in. Not even when someone already had the door open. Everyone waited, one at a time, to key in their code. *Fucking pilots never listen to anybody. Why now?*

"We need a reason for someone to hold open the door. And we need to do it quick, before the police realize we aren't at Concourse B. They'll be back in force."

"What are we going to do?"

I watched a purser push an old man down the concourse in a wheelchair, and came up with an idea. *It worked on the exercise before Tbilisi. Nobody suspects the disabled.*

"Follow me."

I hugged the walls, staying out of the fish eye of the cameras every thirty feet. Getting to a smoking lounge, I found what I was looking for.

"Get in."

"What?"

"Get in and act like you need this chair."

Jennifer scrunched up her eyes, clearly wondering if maybe we weren't now on the desperate side of things, which we were. She sat down in the wheelchair.

"I'm going back to the ATM next to Gate Nineteen. I'll mess around there until someone goes into the hallway. If he's alone, I'm going to wait until he opens the door, then holler at him to hold it."

"This will never work. Delta doesn't have pilots in wheelchairs."

I began pushing. "Yeah, you might be right, but you'd be surprised at the number of times ridiculous shit I've pulled out of my ass has worked."

"Ahh . . . no. I don't think I would. Pulling stuff out of your ass seems to be your way of life."

We reached the ATM just as a single pilot began walking down the hallway. I pushed her forward.

"It's worked out pretty well so far."

63

"Hey! Hold that door, please. Let me get her through and I'll badge in."

The pilot looked at me, trying to decide, then held it open.

"Thanks. I appreciate it. Just let me get her inside."

I could tell he was wondering why a guy in civilian clothes wanted to take a female in a wheelchair into the pilots' lounge, but his chivalry took precedence.

He said, "You sure you're in the right place? You know there's no elevator in here, don't you?"

I pushed Jennifer through, saying, "Yeah, I know. She can walk short distances. She'll be okay. We're just catching the bus."

I saw the door close and said, "Give me a hand with her leg braces, will you?"

He came to the front of the wheelchair, where I was fiddling with the leg platforms. I stood up and grabbed the conveniently thick polyester collar of his uniform and cut off the blood flow to his brain. Once he was down, I ripped off his badge and stuffed him into an empty closet designed to hold the carry-on luggage of pilots coming and going.

"Okay. What now? Where do we go?"

Jennifer was stunned, looking at me like I was the Terminator.

"Come on! Where do we go?"

She snapped out of it, saying, "Down. There's a stewardesses' lounge on the right and a pilots' lounge on the left. Once we get in there, we need to move straight to the exit. There's a bus stop underneath the concourse."

Two minutes later we were waiting with a bunch of other Delta employees for the shuttle to the Delta parking lot, me wearing the pilot's badge around my neck with the picture side conveniently against my chest. After the longest three minutes of my life, we were on the next bus headed out of the airport. We sat in the back, away from anyone else, Jennifer still trembling from our narrow miss.

She said, "I don't think I'm cut out for this law-breaking stuff. It's going to give me a nervous breakdown."

I said, "Trust me; I didn't think it was fun either. You get used to it."

"What do we do now? Are we still going to D.C., or are we headed to Mexico to find a cheap house to spend the rest of our lives?"

"If you're game, I think we should continue on to D.C. Still want to do that?"

"Well, shit, we're outlaws now. It looks like the choices are turn ourselves in, run for the rest of our lives, or try to solve this thing. That's probably the only way to get any mercy. Maybe cut the jail term to half of our lives."

"Okay. I'm game. The folks looking for us know we're in Atlanta, so we need to do all preparations here, while it won't give anything away."

"What preparations do we need to do? How are we going to get to D.C. with the cops chasing us?"

"We have to disappear. We can't use any credit cards, cell phones, anything tied to either you or me. Right now, the police know we're in Atlanta, so it won't do any harm to use your ATM or credit cards here. It'll just reinforce what they already know. Once we leave here, we can't use anything that will trigger an alert with the authorities. First thing we need to do is go to an ATM and take out your max amount of money. Next, we need to get to a place that sells prepaid credit cards and cell phones. We also need to get a rental car for local use."

Something dawned on me. "You don't have your cell phone with you, do you?"

"Yes. I turned it back on when we hit the U.S. It works now."

"Turn it off and take out the battery."

"I haven't called anyone. Nobody knows it's on."

"Doesn't matter. Your phone talks without you using it. It constantly sends out a signal to make sure it has a tower it can talk to. This signal leaves a trail, essentially telling anyone who wants to check that your phone talked to such and such tower at such and such time. They can track the city you're currently in and neck it down to which tower you're near. Depending on the concentration of towers, it can put you within a couple of city blocks. That's *without* using any special gear. Trust me, turn it off and take out the battery."

I had intimate knowledge of the power within the U.S. government and knew that any slip-ups would cause us to be caught fairly quickly. Despite all that, the federal government wasn't omnipotent. Most fugitives were caught by doing something stupid, like returning to the scene of the crime, or going to a family member for help. Smarter fugitives managed to evade the law for extended periods of time, no matter how much effort was put against them.

A buddy of mine in the FBI had chased a man named Eric Rudolph, a homegrown terrorist who had murdered at least three people and wounded upwards of a hundred because of his twisted beliefs, including the 1996 bombing during the Atlanta summer Olympics. He'd managed to evade the FBI and local police for five years, despite a million-dollar bounty on his head and being on the FBI's top-ten most wanted list. *Great. You're hoping you're as good as that sick bastard. Perfect.*

64

Harold Standish slowly hung up his phone. Disappointed at the failure at the Atlanta airport, he wasn't overly surprised. Pike and Jennifer were proving to be more resourceful than he would have thought, but knowing Pike's background now, he should have anticipated it. He quickly punched in Lucas's private number.

"It's Standish. Remember what we talked about yesterday? I need you to execute. Come by the office and I'll give you the phone you worked on. They're headed here but I don't know when they'll arrive. I'm sure they'll make contact on the cloned phone."

After listening for a few seconds, Standish replied, "I'll be here. See you then."

Before the Atlanta incident, he'd had doubts that using Lucas was the best course of action. He'd contracted Lucas many times before for simple break-ins to gather information on opponents, but he had never asked him to do anything violent. After hearing what had happened in Atlanta, he saw Lucas as the only solution. *Let's see them get away from someone who doesn't play by the rules.*

* * *

SEVEN HOURS AFTER WE HAD EXITED THE METRO AT FIVE Points, we pulled into the Sheraton, in Greensboro, North Carolina—about halfway to Washington, D.C. We had robbed Jennifer's bank account of about five thousand dollars and converted that to pay-as-you-go credit cards and prepaid cell phones. Once that was accomplished, we found a "rent-a-wreck" car place and rented a nondescript sedan for in-town use, telling the man behind the counter our car was getting repaired. Finally, we'd stopped yet again to buy some clothes. Jennifer was probably getting sick of leaving our bags at every hotel we stayed at.

After checking in, as we rode up in the elevator, Jennifer asked a question that apparently had been bouncing around in her head.

"Are you sure you're not a drug dealer or something? How come you know all about hiding from the authorities? I know you didn't learn that stuff at basic training."

"I had to learn it for some other things we did. I've never had to do it as a real fugitive."

I could tell she didn't buy that answer.

"Sure. I bet. I can't wait to get back to Charleston. You're going to save me a bundle when you set up my free cable. I'm looking forward to it."

"I'm telling the truth. I'll be running out of tricks soon, trust me."

The door opened on our floor. Jennifer exited, muttering, "I doubt that."

BAKR AND SAYYIDD EXITED THEIR PLANE IN OSLO, Norway, exhausted from the trip. Given the seven-hour time difference from Belize, they landed at ten o'clock at night, almost twenty-four hours from the time they had left. Bakr had found them a small hotel on the outskirts of Oslo that catered to Muslim immigrants. Going through customs without issue, they flagged a cab and gave the driver an address.

For security reasons, Bakr had them exit the cab three blocks from the hotel. While they walked, Sayyidd asked about Walid abdul-Aziz, and why on earth they were in this country. It didn't make any sense to him. The place was frigid and full of blond-haired, blue-eyed infidels. It seemed the last place they should be.

"Norway is one of the few countries in Europe that allows us to blend in without undue scrutiny from the authorities," Bakr told him. "Believe it or not, it has a very large Muslim population. Larger than the people here realize, so there isn't a backlash yet. God willing, we'll own this country before they realize we're here."

"What do you mean? Own the country?"

"The faithful have been flooding into Europe for decades. We're the minority now, but we'll eventually outpace the native people. Sharia law has already been allowed in some countries. If we can't win by fire, we might win by simple numbers."

"So, we're safe here? The Ummah are all true believers?"

Bakr scoffed, "No. No way. Most of the Muslims came here to escape their life at home. They were told about the free welfare and decided to join in. Don't trust them just because they pray to Mecca. They'll turn you in simply to prove they aren't a threat."

Wearily unpacking their bags, Bakr checked to ensure the weapon was still intact in its duct-tape cocoon. Seeing no signs of a breach, he asked Sayyidd to set up the M4 satellite phone and check the e-mail account.

Sayyidd demurred. "Let's get some sleep first. The message will be waiting for us when we get up, and there's nothing we can do with it right now anyway."

Bakr started to argue but didn't have the energy. He was growing weary of his partnership with Sayyidd, wanting to be on his own again. He was unsure why his leadership had chosen Sayyidd for their original mission, but was becoming convinced it had been a mistake. A mistake that he would more than likely have to rectify. Crawling into bed, he turned out the lights.

65

Finished cleaning up, I gave Jennifer's door a light knock. I sensed her looking through the peephole, then saw the door swing open. Jennifer was smiling, standing barefoot while finishing buttoning the top of her shirt, her hair wet and smelling of shampoo.

"Hey, you're early. Let me get my shoes."

She moved away from the door without waiting on a response, which was lucky, because seeing her like that made me about as comfortable as a snail crossing salt flats. *Don't knock like this again. Call first.*

She came back to the door wearing a ball cap, her wet hair stuck through the hole in the back. The effect floored me. Heather had worn her hair the same way almost every weekend. *Jesus. I can't do this.* I knew it wasn't Jennifer's fault, but the combined effect cut me to the quick. She noticed me stiffen and looked at me with concern.

"Are you all right? What's wrong?"

I had no idea why my brain had made that connection. Heather looked nothing like Jennifer. It was just a ball cap—a stupid connection that passed quickly, like the jolt you feel when a car starts crossing into your lane on the freeway, then swerves back.

"Nothing. Let's go. I did a recce of the north lobby and found the business center."

Eight minutes later we were sitting in the the Link, a pseudo–business center, pseudocafé, with me on one computer and Jennifer on another. I logged on to the Embassy Suites Web site in Old Town Alexandria and proceeded to get us a couple of rooms.

I was finishing up the reservation, asking for adjoining rooms, when Jennifer whispered, "Pike. There's another message. It's in a different e-mail account. The first account's empty. The message we printed in Belize is gone."

I closed out my system. "Print it out."

After she hit "print" I said, "Scoot over. Let me try something."

I got behind the keyboard and typed www.whatismy ipaddress.com.

"What're you doing?"

"Well, we can't read the message itself, but with a little luck, we can determine where it came from. All I have to do is get the full header of the e-mail and paste it into this Web site. It should have the originating IP address, which, if we're lucky, is tied to an actual location. Sometimes it's good to go, other times it doesn't work, but it's worth a shot."

I clicked "get source" and waited for the computer to quit churning. The screen loaded with an analysis of the message.

Jennifer asked, "What's that telling us? Do you understand any of that?"

"No. The normal human language is at the bottom."

I scrolled down the screen until I saw "source." I felt Jennifer leaning over my shoulder, reading the screen:

Country: Norway
City: Oslo
Lat: 59.54.45
Long: 10.44.19

"You're a genius!" she exclaimed.

She got a stranglehold on my neck, giving it a hug. She pecked my cheek with a light kiss.

What the hell was that? I leaned away from her.

"I can't believe you just did that! It's like black magic or something. Why don't you raise your hands and say, 'Behave, and I'll bring back the sun'?"

"Hold on. All this really says is that the message went through Norway as a first gate. It doesn't mean it came from Norway. There's a good chance of that, but it isn't absolute proof. It's easy to fool this type of thing."

"All right, all right. It's still pretty cool. You're a walking library of cool stuff."

I didn't let it show, but I was secretly pleased with the attention. If I'd had a tail, I'd have been wagging it like a dog getting a pat from his owner. *I'm pathetic.*

"I'm going to delete this completely. If nothing else, it'll slow down the terrorists."

Making sure the message was gone from both the inbox and the trash file, I said, "I got a couple of rooms in D.C. Tomorrow, I'll give a friend from my old unit a call. He's an Arabic speaker and can decipher both this message and the one before. Sound like a plan?"

"Sounds like a good plan."

We headed back to our rooms to rack out. Jennifer opened her door, then turned around.

"Hey, Pike?"

I stopped working my key. "Yeah?"

"I'm sorry for that thing in the business center. I didn't mean anything by it."

She couldn't have made me more uncomfortable if she had asked to borrow a condom. Why bring it up?

"That's okay. You didn't do anything wrong. I'm just still a little touchy about that sort of thing, I guess. Not your fault."

"That's what I mean. I could tell I made you uncomfortable. I wasn't trying to . . . to . . . make you think of your wife. Anyway, I just wanted to make sure we're still on the same sheet of music. I shouldn't have done that." She broke into a smile. "But you do have some neat tricks."

ABU BAKR AWOKE BEFORE ABU SAYYIDD. He could feel the endgame in his bones and was itching to bring it about. Quietly setting up the M4, he logged on to the Internet and checked the next address on the e-mail list. Two messages were in the in-box, both supposedly from Nigeria telling him he had been named in a rich man's will. All he needed to do was wire some money to get his inheritance. Disappointed, Bakr checked the other addresses. None contained the message he was looking for. This was getting a little annoying. Working at a snail's pace was fine when one had that luxury, but they needed to get moving. It had been more than forty-eight hours since their last message.

He woke up Sayyidd.

"We have no new message."

Sayyidd rubbed the sleep out of his eyes, secretly

happy that his desire to go to bed earlier had proved to be the right call.

"How long should we wait? What do we do if he never contacts us?"

"I think we should send another message to The Sheik. If that doesn't work, we head out on our own. I think I can get some SEMTEX explosives from some helpers in the Balkans, but we won't be able to implicate the Persians. God willing, we'll still accomplish our mission."

Sayyidd was pleased that Bakr was now getting impatient, and was willing to strike out together with or without the message.

"Let's send the e-mail," he said.

Bakr turned back to the computer and typed a simple message:

We have successfully entered the country of Walid. He hasn't contacted us. We wanted to ensure that he knew we were ready to meet. God willing, please give us the path to take.

Bakr closed the laptop. "Now we wait."

66

Lucas leaned back from his computer with a new appreciation for his adversary. His research/administration assistant had sent him a data dump on his assigned targets. On the screen was the enlisted record brief for Nephilim Logan, the man he knew as Pike. The ERB was a one-page document used by the U.S. Army to encapsulate a soldier's career. In Pike's case, his assignments read like a who's who of the military elite. Initial assignment to the 3rd Ranger Battalion, on to Special Forces, with two years in Okinawa in 1st Bn, 1st Special Forces Group, followed by eleven years in 1st Special Forces Operational Detachment—Delta. His last assignment had been as some do-nothing communications technician on Fort Bragg. *Retirement job.*

His military schooling had produced more badges than he was allowed to wear at any one time on his uniform, to include a Combat Infantryman's Badge with a star, indicating combat in two different conflicts. He would clearly not be an easy target. *Another time, another place, and we'd be drinking beers together.*

Jennifer Cahill, on the other hand, had proven to be exactly as advertised: a college student. The only thing remarkable about her was her picture, since even the passport photo couldn't hide her good looks. Other than that, she had spent most of her adult life as either a student or a housewife.

Lucas was a careful, meticulous planner. He would become obsessed with the research on his targets prior to conducting a mission. It was what made him successful on assignments that were way outside the bounds of U.S. law. In truth, it was no different from what he'd done while in the military. Learn about the enemy in the hopes of exploiting a weakness and avoiding enemy strengths. To this end, he'd found it useful in his work to subscribe to various data-mining Web sites available on the Internet. It never failed to amaze him how much information was free for the taking to someone who wanted to look.

He was broken out of his thoughts by the phone ringing. Looking at the caller ID, he saw it was Standish. *Shit. Just what I need.*

"Hello?"

"Hey. Standish here. Have you heard anything yet?"

Why the hell is he bothering me? Standish had no expertise at all in man-hunting. His skills were in personal destruction from the shadows. Cowardly stabbing people in the back. The truth of the matter was that Lucas respected the target Standish had given him much more than he did Standish himself. But Standish *was* paying the bills. *I just need to cut out this micromanaging bullshit.*

"Standish. Listen to me. You gave me the phone less than twenty-four hours ago. I'm not sure what you think's going to happen, but your target is a hard, hard man. This isn't going to be easy. I'll get it done, but I won't be answering to you every five minutes. I'll call you when the mission's accomplished. If you don't hear from me, assume it hasn't been done. You got that?"

"Whoa. *I'm* the one paying for this. If I want information, you'll give it to me. I'm not going to throw money at you just to have you blow it without oversight. Do *you* have *that*?"

"Yeah. I got it. Fuck this. I quit."

"What? You can't quit. You owe me."

Lucas snarled, "I owe you *nothing*. You push that button one more time and you're going to see firsthand what I owe you. Understand? I don't want to hear that *ever* again."

Lucas waited a few seconds, hearing nothing but breathing.

"Call me when you have something."

"Fine."

Lucas was sick of hearing what he owed Standish. *Fucking politician.* A weasel like every other politician. *No honor. No belief in something greater than himself.* Just whatever favor could be gleaned based on which way the wind was blowing. Yeah, Standish had possibly helped him out, but the truth of the matter was there wasn't any proof that he had done anything wrong. The only people who could prove he had killed civilians were dead in an IED attack. He'd eventually have gotten off anyway.

He regretted having killed his teammates, but they had lost their way. *It was war, goddammit.* He had killed the civilians to get information on terrorist attacks. It had worked. The team broke up a terrorist cell that had murdered at least thirty Americans and would have murdered thirty more. He didn't understand why his teammates had chosen to turn him in, but he couldn't let it stand.

He had done the right thing. Two noncombatants for thirty Americans. *How could that not be seen as a good thing?*

He had been working the civilian side of the defense industry for more than a year now, and was beginning to hate it. Everything was about the almighty dollar. Nothing was about a cause, a goal greater than the individual. It disgusted him, and he wanted out. Even his actions in Afghanistan, while others might not understand them, were for something larger than money. At the least, it saved American lives, even counting the two who had died at his hand. The sacrifice was for a larger effort. Now his work did nothing but cause money to exchange hands.

It wasn't that he disliked the work. Truth be told, he'd never minded killing, any more than the average big-game hunter. He didn't draw any particular pleasure from the act itself but did enjoy the hunt. Now, though, the purpose was gone.

Since he had started contracting out, most of his employment had been nothing more than gleaning sleazy information for Standish, the greatest "success" coming when he found a political rival with a young boy. It disgusted him. He'd done only one violent act since leaving the Navy, on behalf of a foreign corporation looking to gain an inside advantage on a classified defense contract. Their only competition was a small outfit at Fort Bragg, something the foreign entity should have been able to outbid. The problem was that the competition was U.S. based, and thus the foreign company was convinced they were going to lose. Lucas had smoked the CEO of the U.S. contractor, securing a foreign win. The money had been extremely lucrative. Worth the woman and child he'd been forced to kill as well. The money Standish was throwing around was even better. *Enough to quit this shit forever.* He looked at this target as a blessing. The fact that two people would die caused him no angst at all. It was just work.

Lucas returned to the problem at hand. He had a pretty good background on both of his targets now and began to build a plan of attack. He would need his best folks for this one, as he was fairly sure a mistake against Pike had the potential to be catastrophic. He ran through his Rolodex of employees—all of whom worked for him on a contract basis—picking ten that fit the bill. He purposely left out the two who had worked with him at Fort Bragg. When push came to shove, they had balked at killing the woman and child. He had no idea where this would go and didn't need anyone who might hesitate.

He gave each of the men a call, telling them he had a job and the time to show up at the office if they were interested. He then began building a target package on both Jennifer and Pike. In the back of his mind, he thought about the money he'd make and the chance to get out. To get away from people like Standish. *Maybe I'll get my check and smoke him for free. Help out the country.*

67

I waited until I was outside of Fredericksburg, on Interstate 95 about forty-five minutes south of Washington, D.C., before I made the call. I had Jennifer dial the number on our new TracFone, then hand it to me. A man answered on the third ring.

I said, "Ethan, hey, it's Pike Logan. How're you doing?"

There was a pregnant pause. I'm sure he was getting over the initial shock of hearing my voice. I looked over at Jennifer, raised my eyebrow, and tilted the phone so she could hear.

"Pike? What's up? How're you doing?"

"Hey, nothing like a call from the past. I'm fine. I'm going to be in D.C. tonight, and I thought I'd drop by for a visit."

Ethan was an analyst inside the Taskforce. As such, he was support. Ordinarily, there was an unofficial separation between operators and direct support personnel, but I had always thought the distinction was bullshit, and had hit it off with Ethan. Being a geographic bachelor whenever I was in D.C., I had dinner with Ethan's family about twice a month. The last time I had seen him was in the mission brief for the operation in Tbilisi.

Since my implosion, Ethan hadn't said two words to me. It would do him no good to take sides on my demise, and so he had taken the route of discretion being the better part of valor. I didn't blame him, although I could hear the wariness in his voice as I finally convinced him to let us come by.

Jennifer, having heard my end of the conversation, said, "That's a friend? Don't get mad, but out of curiosity, how bad were you when you left? What happened?"

"About as bad as I was when we first met. You can expect everyone to look at me funny, like a cancer patient who might or might not be in remission. Everyone will be afraid to ask how I am."

I was surprised to find I was comfortable talking about it. That was a first.

"There wasn't any big blowout, like a drunk finally killing a carload of kids or something. I just sort of . . . fell apart. The Force did everything they could to help me, but it was all based on me wanting to get better. I didn't. Eventually, I just left."

Jennifer appeared lost in thought. She finally said, "You ever think about fate, or destiny? You ever think that God makes things happen for a reason?"

"I think about that all the time. In fact, it tears me up. Why'd you ask?"

She suddenly looked embarrassed and uncomfortable. "Nothing. Nothing at all. I just sometimes wonder."

I let the silence go for a second, then prodded her. "Wonder what? What were you going to say?"

"Well, what're the odds of me picking you up at the Windjammer? Me, someone who's about to get killed, picking up you, the one person with the skills to prevent it? Think about it—what are the odds that we'd collide at all? Given the entire United States? Shit, given just the city of Charleston? It's just weird, is all. It's a perfect storm. It makes me think."

"So what's the reason for this? Besides my company, I mean?"

"Maybe saving a lot of lives."

68

Later, after the settling in at the hotel, I decided it was time to get moving. "It looks like we have a few hours before we need to link up with Ethan. I'm going to the Taskforce Headquarters to leave a note for Kurt along with our cell phone numbers." I paused, not wanting a fight. "No offense, but I can't take you there. I have to go alone."

She smiled. "Come on. I'm not that big of a jerk, am I? I understand. I'll just hang around here. No big deal."

No way was I going to resist that opening. "No, no. That's not what I meant. Jerk isn't what I'd call you. Anyway, what you could do—"

"What's that mean?" She flicked her hand and back-handed my stomach. "Would you like to see me be a jerk? I don't think you'd enjoy it."

"Oww. Jesus. I don't like it right now." I snatched her hand out of the air to prevent her from hitting me again. "I was just kidding. What I was going to say was it would help if you went out and bought a laptop. One with wireless so we don't have to keep searching for Internet business centers. Can you do that?"

She squinted at me, the touch of a grin on her face.

Waiting a beat, she said, "Sure. Gives me something to do, anyway. We'll just meet back here?"

I realized I was still holding her hand and dropped it like a piece of hot iron. "Yeah. I should be gone no more than an hour. Get your stuff. We can walk to the Metro together. If you get off two stops after Reagan National you'll be at a pretty big mall. The stop's Pentagon City."

When she saw my embarrassment, Jennifer's little grin threatened to break into a smile, causing a clash of confusing feelings. I dealt with it the usual way—by getting pissed off.

"What? What're you grinning about? Can we go?"

She rolled her eyes, holding her hand in front of my face and making me feel like an ass. "Yeah. Let me get my purse before your head explodes."

We headed to the Metro station and hopped on the first train in, the Blue Line. We sat in the back, away from anyone else, and rode silently past the first two stops. One minute out from the Pentagon City stop I remembered what we were doing, and the fact that Jennifer wasn't a professional. I kicked myself for having taken her precautions for granted. She was going out by herself, into a world where someone wanted both of us very badly. A world full of invisible predators.

"Hey, the next stop is yours. Look, I don't want to scare you, but please be very, very careful. I've racked my brain about the Homeland Security alert, and can't come up with any reason whatsoever for that to have occurred. One name might be a coincidence, but both our names together is outside the realm of believable. I think that the alert has something to do with what we know."

"You said that was just a mistake. Why would anyone do that on purpose?"

I held up my hands. "I don't *know* it was done on purpose. On the one hand, it could simply be a mistake, some crossed wires from our visit to the embassy in Belize. There is also the very, very slim chance that it was sent by Kurt, and once we were in the interrogation rooms they would have simply put us in contact with him."

"And if it's not?"

"Well . . . the other reasons aren't that good. It could mean that someone knew we were traveling together, and so knew *why* we were traveling. Whoever that someone is wanted us to get arrested so that we're out of the picture."

Jennifer pondered a bit, asking a question softly: "You really think that alert was done intentionally to get us out of the way?"

"I honestly don't know. In my heart, I don't believe that, but I want you to act as if it's true. Treat the entire mall trip as if you're walking through a crack slum. Check out anyone coming near you. Avoid any contact with strangers. Someone stares at you the wrong way, get the fuck out. Go back to the hotel room. You tracking?"

She nodded.

I continued. "As soon as you're off the train, call my cell phone so you can simply hit redial in an emergency. Call me every thirty minutes. If you don't get through, if I don't answer, get out. Go straight to the hotel. Lock the doors and wait. I'll get in touch. If I don't hear from you, I'm coming straight here, to the mall. If anything happens, try to stay in the area, create a scene, whatever you can do to give me a clue on finding you."

"Whoa—are you serious? You think it's that bad? I can't believe this. All right . . . I'll try to leave a bloody napkin or maybe a finger for you to find."

"Come on. That's not funny. I don't think it's that bad, but it doesn't hurt to be prepared."

"Okay, okay. I can handle myself. I'll stay in crowded areas and scream my head off if someone tries anything. What about you? You're going straight to the one place that has people like you, the one place that can hurt you. What if they're the ones that did it? Maybe we should just call your unit."

I shook my head. "They change numbers every three months. I can't call. Even if I could, it's not the Task-force. No way. That's not what they do. If anything, they can figure out what's going on."

The train pulled into Pentagon City.

"This is you. Don't get hurt."

Jennifer smiled. "I'll be okay. Trust me; I can deal with a shopping mall."

She jumped out just as the doors were closing. I continued to stare out the window, seeing her pull out her phone to call me. My phone rang as the train pulled away. I gave her one more admonishment about being alert, then hung up. I was wondering if splitting up was such a hot idea. The cell phone contact plan was of more psychological help than anything else. It would allow me to know she was safe but wouldn't do anything to help me find her. If she didn't call, I knew there would be very little I could do.

I put myself at ease with the thought that nobody had

paid us a second's worth of attention on the drive up here, and both hotels had checked us in without question. While the police were probably ripping my boat apart in Charleston, we hadn't been on any news programs I had seen. I'd just have to hope our luck continued.

69

Lucas assessed his assembled team, satisfied that they could get the mission done. He had called ten men, needing at least five for the mission. Four of the ten were already contracted on another assignment. Out of the remaining six who answered his call, four were ex–U.S. Navy SEALs and two were ex–U.S. Army Special Forces. All were ruthless, intelligent, and very highly trained. After thanking them for coming, he started the PowerPoint slideshow, giving them the background on the targets.

He began with Jennifer, getting juvenile comments on her looks and heckling about why their skills were needed.

The demeanor changed when he got to Pike. The men became serious, taking notes and asking questions.

After the background, he gave them the mission statement.

"Both of these targets are to be terminated. There are no specific constraints on the termination. The only rules of engagement are that they are both out of the picture, and the act cannot be traced back to us. Collateral damage is acceptable as long as it is restricted to five or less.

"We know they're coming here, to D.C. In fact, they may already be here. Through information from other sources, we believe they'll make contact with an individual or individuals here in Washington. One of those individuals is tied to this phone."

He held up the cloned handset. "This is our only lead. We'll set up a duty roster, with this post manned twenty-four/seven. During the day, you'll stay here, just like that mission against the defense contractor six months ago. The bunks are still in the back, Xbox and cable still hooked up. At night, if you're not on duty, you're free to do what you want, as long as you can get back here in thirty minutes on a recall, sober and ready to work. Along with the man minding the phone, half the team will bunk here each night on a rotating basis.

"The actual mission will be fluid, no set plans or rehearsals. The Fort Bragg op was a pretty good template to use. Get this done, and we get a pretty good paycheck."

He turned to the SEAL directly to his right. "Mason, you're the team chief. Set up the duty roster however you see fit. Assign positions and issue out the necessary kit. Sean's out front with your beepers and cell phones, all new and clean."

Lucas paused. "All of you look at me."

He waited until he had their undivided attention, "This Nephilim character's picture is next to the definition of *badass* in the dictionary. Do not underestimate him. We need to take him out quick. If you get him in your sights, and can meet the rules of engagement, take him down. We can deal with the girl at our leisure, but make a mistake against this guy, or let him know he's being hunted, and he'll kill you. Any questions?"

Lucas spent the next thirty minutes answering a barrage of queries on everything from the title trace of the cars they would drive to the response time of EMS vehicles at an automobile accident. Holding true to the ethos of the special operations units they had come from, Lucas let the planning evolve from the bottom up. He gave out the guidance and let them sort through the gritty details.

Forty-five minutes later, they had the skeleton of an operational plan, with various straw man scenarios rehearsed on whiteboards and individual assignments dictated. They could now execute a multitude of plans on a moment's notice, with only the actual location of the operation unknown.

SAYYIDD WATCHED BAKR PACE BACK AND FORTH in their small hotel room, clearly impatient that a message hadn't arrived. Sayyidd had checked the account every hour on the hour, but they'd received nothing. Bakr stopped pacing and walked to the door.

"I'm going out. I need to get some air. This is driving me crazy."

"Allah has shown us the way throughout this journey. He'll continue to do so. There's no reason to worry or get angry. He'll speak again when He's ready."

When Bakr didn't respond, Sayyidd thought maybe he was getting through to him. He had convinced Bakr to choose this path, and now wondered if Bakr himself had the courage to believe in their destiny. Maybe he was looking for a reason to fail. Sayyidd had seen it before. Otherwise brave, righteous men cracking under the pressure placed upon them by the word of God. Not wanting to fail, but unable to simply leave, they ended up doing foolish things to ensure their place in heaven. He needed to prevent that with Bakr. He knew his limitations. Sayyidd had proven time and time again that he could accomplish missions against all odds, but always as a member of a team. Never as a leader. Or, in this case, on his own. Without Bakr, he knew he would fail.

He booted up the M4, praying that Walid had answered. He checked the next Yahoo! address and immediately deflated. It was empty. Behind him, he heard Bakr say, "Still nothing?"

Before Bakr could get angry again, Sayyidd said, "Let me check the other addresses. Maybe it went to the wrong one."

Sayyidd went to the next address on the list, watching anxiously as the new Web page loaded. There were two messages, one spam and the other from The Sheik. A shiver ran through him. Finally, an answer. He opened the message. It was short, and to the point.

Praise Allah, my pilgrims have made it to the land of Walid. I have passed your message, and Walid has replied that he gave you instructions, which you did not follow. He will contact you again, but requests that you send the e-mail address you wish to use to ensure there are no more mistakes. May Allah smile on your mission. All are aware of your journey, and all praise your quest. Wait for his contact, then smite the infidels with his help.

Sayyidd breathed a sigh of relief. It had all been a simple mistake. He felt a huge weight leave his shoulders. Everything was going to be okay. He turned away from the computer, smiling, only to see Bakr, his face drained of blood, staring at the screen as if he had seen his own death. Sayyidd had had enough.

"What is it now, you old woman? Can't you be happy about anything? Thirty minutes ago you were whining like a dog about not getting a message; now you're mad about getting one."

Bakr sat in silence. He finally said, "I'm taking the weapon in the morning. We've been discovered."

Sayyidd was stunned. "Taking the weapon? Have you lost your mind?"

"Walid sent us a message, but we didn't get it. Now we get the next message on the *next* e-mail address. Why? Why didn't The Sheik send the message in the order he dictated us to use? It's because there was a message, and he thought we had received it, thus that e-mail address was no longer usable. We didn't get it because someone else retrieved it. Someone has that e-mail address, and might have the others. I have no idea of the technology the Great Satan employs, but it's not impossible."

Left unsaid was the mistake that Sayyidd had made in Guatemala.

"Quit it," Sayyidd said. "You're constantly afraid of your own shadow. Why does everything have to be some evil plot against us? Why can't you trust in Allah to protect us? Just once?"

Bakr spoke in a dangerously quiet tone. "Dog, it's because of my caution that I live. I have killed more infidels in a month than you have in your life. I have no idea why Allah has shined a light on you and allowed you to survive with the mistakes you make, but I'm not going to repeat them."

Sayyidd felt a chill. Bakr was not a man to test, and Sayyidd could sense the mission falling apart, with Bakr about to make a decision that would leave him alone.

Without any support. Forcing him to face his fears. He held his tongue, awaiting Bakr's decision.

"I'm leaving tomorrow with the weapon," Bakr said. "Whatever happens here, we can't let the infidels steal the means of victory. It may simply be a mistake, but we should act as if it isn't. You will remain behind here to wait for Walid's message. Once you have that, meet him and finish the final planning."

"But where will you go? What'll I do once I meet Walid?"

"I'll head to Bosnia. There are plenty of old fighters there willing to help. You do exactly what we were going to do all along. Give him our request for evidence to blame the Persians, and figure out how we'll get into Palestine. Once you know that, contact me with the plan. God willing, we'll meet again and continue our journey together."

"But if you're right, I'll be arrested. I'll be the one who dies without striking a blow against the infidels. Maybe we should both go."

Sayyidd's voice cracked. He hoped Bakr took it as concern for the mission, and not a fear of being exposed as a fraud. It must have worked, because Bakr didn't sugarcoat anything, choosing instead to give him the hard facts.

"You may very well die here, or at the least be put in prison, but your part of the mission is worth that risk. Without you and Walid, I'll be forced to go on my own, with little chance of starting the catalyst that you envisioned. I need your help to make this work. Even so, we can take steps to protect ourselves."

"How? What should I do?"

"It's time for you to become what you were going to become in America: a simple college student, without any political aspirations. If they suspect us, the far enemy will focus on this section of the city. Check out of this Muslim hotel. Find one in the city that doesn't stand out and allows you to blend into the local tourist scenery. Set up your meeting with Walid away from known hotbeds and radical mosques. That should protect you more than any security procedures I could devise."

Sayyidd calmed down, feeling more secure. After all, Bakr had the weapon. Bakr would be the *shahid*. Sayyidd wouldn't have to push the button. He would be the facilitator, and with Allah's help, they would succeed.

"All right. I'll stay and meet Walid. How will you get to Bosnia?"

"Well, I can't fly, since they might be watching the airports. I'll take a ferry from here to Germany. From there, I'll take trains and buses until I join up with our Muslim brothers in Tuzla. It'll take a little longer but will be more secure."

"Give me five minutes and I'll get that set up."

Before he could boot up the M4 satellite phone, Bakr stopped him. "Wait. We need to ensure we can communicate first. I want you to establish a separate e-mail address, known only to you and me. Every twenty-four hours, I want you to send me a message. Include the town of Fallujah in the message somewhere. If I don't hear from you every twenty-four hours, or I get a message without the mention of Fallujah, I'll assume you've been captured or killed. I'll then immediately take the weapon and attempt to use it to the best of my abilities."

He stopped, waiting for Sayyidd to look up. When he

had Sayyidd's undivided attention, he began again. "Sayyidd, I don't want to make you mad, but the only way that splitting up will be a mistake is if you fail in this task and inadvertently send me to my death. Once I believe that you're discovered, I'll immediately flee to stay out of the hands of the authorities. There'll be no turning back. Do you understand?"

Sayyidd said, "I understand. Don't worry. I won't fail you."

Bakr relaxed, satisfied that he had made his point. "From here out, we must act as if we were still in the Land of Two Rivers. Watch around you. Look for the infidel with the knife. We've come very far in a short amount of time. God willing, we'll finish our journey in victory, but it will require diligence, and I'm sure we'll both be tested before this is through."

Sayyidd felt sick to his stomach at the thought of being left alone.

70

I called Jennifer as soon as I stepped off the Metro at King Street, asking her to meet me in the lobby. I had managed to leave my number at Taskforce Headquarters, but it hadn't been smooth. I was no longer a member of the elite little club. I didn't have the badges or passwords to get me into the inner sanctum, so I had to make a fuss. Even then, after getting through the first gate, and begging to simply leave a number for Kurt, I was ignored because Kurt officially didn't exist. I was politely asked to leave by Abigail, a gray-haired lady from whom I had bought Girl Scout cookies for years. I'd bought enough to put her grandkid through college, yet she acted like she'd never seen me. Eventually, the internal security force had shown up, giving me the not-so-subtle hint to get the fuck out. Before they pitched me headfirst out the door, Abigail finally broke through her stupid cover and said she'd take my number. I knew she'd get it to Kurt, so I guess I had succeeded.

By the time I reached the lobby Jennifer was already downstairs, carrying our new laptop.

Less than an hour later we were at Ethan's house. I took the lead to the front door, looking at my watch before I rang the doorbell. *Close enough for government work.* I rang the bell and waited.

Immediately, a dog began barking like his fur was on fire. I smiled. "Sounds like a rabid wolf, but he's really a teddy bear."

I heard Ethan tell the dog to shut up before opening the door. I waited, a little anxious at the response I would get.

Ethan gave me a big grin, holding his arms open. *Whew.* After embracing me, he noticed Jennifer for the first time.

"Who's this?"

"A friend of mine. Jennifer Cahill, this is Ethan Merriweather. Otherwise known as Haji."

Ethan shook her hand, then invited us both inside.

I bent down to ruffle the fur of a brown-and-tan mutt that looked like a cross between a bulldog and a miniature collie. The dog began to jump all over me, slobbering.

"Hey, Eddie, how ya been?" Looking up, I asked, "Kathy around? I'd like to say hello."

"No, unfortunately, she's not. She really wanted to see you as well, but Emily and Rachel had a big Girl Scout thing tonight. It's been planned for a month."

I nodded, relieved at the answer. It would be pretty hard for Kathy to decide at the last minute to attend something like that, and I knew that Ethan wouldn't outright lie to me.

Standing up from Eddie, freeing him up to run over to Jennifer and begin slobbering all over her, I said, "That's too bad. I'd really like to see her and the kids. I don't know how long I'll be in D.C., but maybe I'll get the chance later."

"How about coming by for dinner tomorrow night? I know we're out here in the boondocks, but she'll make your favorite—chicken pot pie."

I couldn't help but laugh because chicken pot pie was what Kathy always served when I came to dinner, whether I wanted it or not.

"You want some home-cooked food?" I asked Jennifer.

"I think that would be great, if one extra is okay."

I knew Jennifer's coming was implied. "Sounds like a date." I paused, then got to the point. "Can we go to your study? I've got some stuff to show you."

"You know the way. I'll grab some beers."

Once Ethan entered, I spread out both e-mail messages, one repeatedly folded and stained, the other a fresh computer printout.

"Haji, this is what we need translated. We got these from two different e-mail accounts. It's terrorist related, but we don't really know how."

He picked up the first sheet, spending a few minutes studying it. Placing it down, he picked up the second sheet. After about fifteen seconds, he placed it back down and returned to the first sheet, walking around the room and studying it.

I finally got fed up. "Well, what's it say?"

Ethan snapped out of his trance, looking at us like he didn't know where we'd come from. After a pause, he said, "Okay, one is clearly some sort of terrorist message. It talks about killing infidels and other things. The other is simply an invitation to coffee, with an address."

I already knew that one was terrorist related but was surprised at the other translation.

"What's the address? Is it in Norway?"

"It doesn't have a country listed, but it's a coffee shop somewhere in Europe. The verbiage is a direct phonetic translation, and isn't American. The meeting occurred today at thirteen hundred."

"What's the other message say? The first one?"

"Well, it's pretty ominous, but it's something I read every single day in chatter we get fed, so don't freak out."

"Yeah, yeah. The difference here is that I've met them; I know they're trying to kill people. I just don't know how. What's it say?"

"Here's what I *think* it says: 'Operation Badr will exceed our expectations. We no longer will strike the far enemy in his homeland. We came upon a weapon that will push the Zionists into the sea at the same time it causes the far enemy to destroy the Persians. Praise Allah, we will rejoice when all infidels are destroyed because of this, leaving us with the assurance of the Caliphate. Please reply, telling us this path is blessed, or tell us what to do next.' Is that what you expected?"

"Yeah, something like that. What do you make of it? What's an Arabic mind saying when it says that?"

"Well. . . . I'm not an Arab. I'm not really keen on telling you what I think because I'm probably wrong."

"Haji, cut the shit. I'm not a robot. I already know what *I* think. I'd like to hear what *you* think. I'm not going to run off shooting people because of it. You're an analyst, for Christ's sake. This is what you do."

Ethan held up his hands. "Okay, okay . . . Starting right off, they reference the Battle of Badr, the first significant defeat of Meccan forces by Muhammad, which led to Islam taking over the Arabian Peninsula way back when. Going further, this is clearly an AQ message. The references to the far enemy and the Caliphate point to that. Getting to the meat, in my mind, these guys have a weapon and they intend to use it on Israel. That, in itself, isn't unusual. Every Arab with a firecracker says that sort of thing. In this case, I don't think these guys believe they have a firecracker. I think they have a weapon that is dangerous enough to cause a phenomenal reaction, something designed to cause the Israelis to really, really go nuts."

"Okay. So far I'm tracking. That's about what I thought. What about the Persian comment? I couldn't make heads or tails of that. What do you think he's saying there?"

"Honestly, that part's a little disturbing. I'm not sure, but it could mean that the weapon will be blamed on Iran, causing Israel to attack them. The second order of effect for that, of course, would be that we would support Israel, drawing us in to a war with Iran. The end result, in the mind of the guy who wrote this . . ." He paused, looking at me. "Understand, I'm not saying this would happen, but I think they want to start the clash of civilizations everyone blabs about. They want to start a true holy war, using Israel as the bad guy. We'd be forced to defend Israel in any attack against Iran; and all other Arab states, because it's Israel doing the attacking, would be forced to choose sides. There's no question whose side they'll choose."

Ethan stopped, thinking about what he had just said. "Man, this could actually work. If they could blame the Iranians for a serious attack, especially with the nutcase in charge constantly talking about destroying Israel, it probably would start a chain reaction that would lead to a global fight between the Christian and Muslim worlds."

He paced back and forth for a second. "Do you really think that such a weapon is real? Do you think these guys really found something in Guatemala?"

"I don't know. I'm inclined to think they did, since a couple of indigs died on her uncle's expedition, and these guys have made arrangements to meet someone to continue on whatever journey they think they're on. If they failed in finding a weapon, or if the weapon wasn't real, why continue?"

"Shit, this is bad news. What're you going to do?"

"I'm not going to do anything. I'm going to pass everything you just said to the Taskforce. Kurt should contact me tomorrow. What you could do, if you don't mind, is simply reinforce what I'm going to say. I'll tell Kurt everything I have, but you know what my reputation is. He might blow me off, and I wouldn't blame him. Either way, this is a problem for the Taskforce, not for me."

Ethan mulled over his options. Finally, he said, "Yeah, I can do that. I don't know how soon I'll see the boss—you remember his schedule—but I'll certainly tell him when I see him."

ETHAN STOOD AT THE DOOR until they drove off. Once they were out of sight he went to the telephone to call Domino's for the second time that week. Before he dialed, he thought about Pike's visit. He picked up the handset, calling the Taskforce duty officer instead.

71

Mason hung up the cloned cell phone. Picking up the clean duty phone, he called Lucas.

"We got a hit. Pike was visiting a guy named Ethan Merriweather tonight."

"Is he still there?"

"No. He left. The man on the phone says that Pike talked about interesting stuff, and just wanted to relay that. Want to do anything with this?"

"Yeah. Alert the team. Tell them to get in as fast as possible. While we're inbound, figure out everything you can on this Ethan Merriweather. Find out where he lives and do a quick analysis of the area. I don't want to waste any time when we get to the office. Give us a target dump on both the man and his location."

"You got it. Anything specific you want me to hone in on?"

"Yeah, figure out if this guy's a badass as well. Check his military background. I guarantee he has one."

"Roger that. See you in thirty minutes."

It took Mason all of ten minutes to get a complete background on Ethan, to include his address, family members, and the last time he had paid his electric bill.

Thirty-two minutes later he was briefing the assembled team.

"The target is a thirty-four-year-old Caucasian male. His MOS is 96B, intel analyst. He is currently working in J3 Special Operations Division at the Pentagon. He's airborne qualified, but that's it as far as specialized schooling we care about. Basically, he's your standard intel weenie. No known firearms, no bills being paid to 'Johnny's house of jujitsu,' nothing dangerous at all.

"He has a wife and two children, both girls; ages eight and eleven. Of note, he does have a dog, but I couldn't determine a breed. All I could find were some vet bills for various things, which leads me to believe the dog is getting on in years."

Moving to the next slide in the presentation, Mason continued the briefing, covering the neighborhood and the house where Ethan lived in detail. When he finished, he turned the briefing over to Lucas.

Standing up, Lucas said, "This is pretty straightforward. We simply need this Ethan to tell us where to find Pike. Once we have that information, terminate whoever is in the house. Don't do it before we have the information, since you might need to use the wife or children for persuasion on the target."

Randy, one of the SF men, cut in. "What's our authorized level of persuasion? What if he refuses to talk?"

"There is no limit. Make him talk. Does anyone here have any qualms about that?"

The team looked around at one another, but nobody said a word.

"If you look at the team, you'll see the only two missing from the Fort Bragg op are Carl and Alan. When push came to shove, they didn't have the stomach for the work. Almost caused mission failure right when we were culminating."

Lucas made eye contact with each member of the team. "Does anyone have any qualms about terminating the wife and kids? No judgments here; not everyone can do this kind of work. If that's you, say so now, before we launch."

Once again, nobody said anything.

"Okay. Spend ten minutes figuring out how you want to tackle this problem. No more than that. It's pretty straightforward and the trail's getting colder every second we sit here. For all we know, Pike and the girl are already driving to another city. I expect you guys to be on the road in fifteen minutes."

72

I rolled over, groggy and unsure of what had awakened me, the noise blending in to my semiconscious dream. I realized my cell phone was ringing and snatched it up before whoever was calling could hang up, knowing it was either a wrong number or Kurt.

"Hello?"

"Pike, is that you?"

"Yeah, who's this?"

"It's Kurt. We need to meet. You went to Ethan Merriweather's house last night?"

"Yes, sir, I did, but it was simply to get all the facts before I talked to you today. I didn't do anything—"

"Ethan's dead," Kurt said. "I need to talk to you right now."

I was wide-awake now. "What? What the fuck are you talking about? I just saw him."

"I'm not going to talk on a cell phone. Let's do this face-to-face."

I stopped my questions. "When and where?"

"It's now about nine forty-five."

I fumbled for my watch, thinking that surely couldn't be right, but it was. Jennifer and I had decided just to sleep in until we woke up, but I never figured we'd both be out until this late in the morning. I must have been more tired than I thought.

Kurt continued talking. "I have to clean up a few things and make sure efforts are tracking over here. Meet me at eleven at Four Courts."

"I'll be there."

"Don't be late. I won't have a lot of time and I need to figure out what the hell's going on."

"I won't be late. I'm staying a hundred feet from a Metro stop."

I hung up the phone, my head spinning over what I had just heard. *Haji dead? He was healthy as a horse. Did he have a heart attack or something? Get hit by a car? Surely this had nothing to do with our visit. Did it?*

There wasn't any sense in trying to figure it out without any facts. I could sort it out with Kurt in an hour.

As I began putting on my clothes, the ramification of what Kurt had said finally hit home. *Haji was dead.* Having had multiple friends die in combat since 9/11, I understood the grieving process at the graduate level, but it didn't make it any easier. I had a hollow feeling inside, something I knew would bounce around for a long time, slowly diminishing until it only appeared when something triggered a memory of Ethan.

I remembered Kathy and the kids, wishing I had seen them last night. They would need support right now. I was sure the Taskforce was on that. They were very, very good about taking care of the families of fallen soldiers. Even so, I wanted to help, and wished the first time I was to see Kathy would not have been in the wake of Ethan's death.

*   *   *

IN CRYSTAL CITY, Lucas's team was gearing up for another run at Pike and Jennifer. Even though last night hadn't paid off immediately, it looked like it had worked in the end.

Lucas's research assistant was furiously working the computer to gather all data on "Four Courts" and hotels near Metro stops in the D.C. area.

Lucas was giving instructions while the men got their kit on and equipment organized.

"We know they're taking the Metro, which means they'll be walking to the linkup. We'll need a trigger position outside. We'll set up two shooters at Four Courts"—Lucas paused, staring at his research assistant—"wherever the hell that is—hurry the fuck up, Jerry."

"I got it, I got it. It's an Irish pub in Clarendon, right across from the Arlington Courthouse. I'm doing a quick scan of the surrounding area."

Lucas continued. "The two shooters there will be the primary killers. They'll be located at the nearest cover and concealment from the pub. Two others will be mounted in a vehicle. On the trigger's call, they'll approach and conduct a random drive-by shooting. The intent is twofold: One, camouflage the killing of the girl and Pike. To that end, you need to spray rounds loud and long. Two, to drive Pike and the girl into the real shooters. At the first shot of the drive-by, Pike will immediately take cover, moving to the nearest alley or other protected position. That's where the primary shooters will be located.

"Make sure you all take the same caliber of weapon. I don't expect a full-on ballistics check, but the cops will think something's funny if three innocent civilians are killed by a nine-mil in a random drive-by, while two others are dead from forty-cal fire."

Mason cut in. "Why not just smoke them with the drive-by? Make it simple?"

"If you can kill them from the car, so much the better, but I'm not counting on it. This guy's good and will probably be able to get out of the line of fire. I'm counting on his survival instincts to get his ass. Mason, you're the trigger. You need to pick them up at the Metro and follow them to Four Courts. More than likely that means the Orange Line stop by the Arlington Courthouse. Don't get compromised. Remember, this guy probably has spider sense. Do everything by the book. Use your judgment on when to make the call for the drive-by team. Jerry, you ready? We need to do some timing analysis."

Jerry turned on the overhead. "Yeah, I'm ready."

He pulled up a Google Earth image of Clarendon, Virginia, with several markers embedded. Using a laser pointer as if he were about to discuss stock prices, he began, giving a complete overview of the target area. From there, the team spent the next fifteen minutes coming up with a hasty plan, using the skeleton they had created the day before. Once all the questions and answers had been exhausted, and everyone was comfortable with his respective role, Lucas took back over.

"We're out of time. Any other questions? I know this is fast, but that's why you guys are making the big money." When no one spoke, he said, "Let's saddle up."

73

Hearing a soft knock on her door, Jennifer woke up. She saw Pike standing in the connecting doorway, the light from his room showing he was dressed.

She stretched, saying, "Where're you going? What's up?"

"Kurt called. He wants to meet right now."

"Well, that's good, isn't it?"

Pike hesitated, not sure how to break the news. He decided just to say it.

"Ethan's dead. He died last night."

Jennifer brought her hand to her mouth. "Oh, my God. What happened?"

"I don't know. I'm hoping to get some answers from Kurt. I'm headed to Clarendon to see him." He paused again. "I have to go alone. I'm going to be talking about a lot of old unit business. Kurt won't talk with you there."

"That's it? You tell me a man I met last night is dead, then switch gears to the meeting with Kurt? What about Ethan's family? Have you talked to them?"

"I haven't talked to anybody. I just found out ten minutes ago. Anyway, nobody will contact the family until the family lets the Taskforce know it's okay. I've been here before. Some wives want a lot of support; some just want to be left alone. Once that's sorted out, we can do whatever we think's best. I've got to go."

"Don't you think we should be doing something to help out his family? I don't even know them and I feel like I should help."

"Please don't fight me on this. There's nothing we can do right now. I'm not doing anything until I talk to Kurt. This might have something to do with our visit."

"*What?* What do you mean by that?"

Pike backtracked, sitting next to her on the bed. "It's just a big damn coincidence, is all. Look, you have to trust me on this. I can't stay. I'm running behind as it is. Please don't leave the hotel. I'll be back in probably two hours."

Pike exited to the hallway through her door, not returning to his room. Jennifer sat on the bed in a little bit of a daze, still absorbing what he had said. It didn't seem real. Outside of going to a funeral for her grandmother, and one high school friend who died in a car crash, Jennifer had had little experience dealing with mortality. Now it seemed like death was stalking her everywhere she went. Whatever she touched turned to ash. *Why would Ethan be dead?* It wasn't fair. He had a wife and a family. He didn't do anything to deserve this. *But neither had Uncle John. Or Pike when he lost his family.* She closed her eyes. *Please don't let it be because of me. Please, please.*

Her mind clicked on where Pike was headed, snapping her eyes back open. He might think Kurt was a peach of a guy, but she wasn't so sure. Yeah, Pike was a one-man wrecking crew, but what if he was moving into a trap laid by a bunch of guys just as good as him? He wouldn't even recognize it because of the trust he placed in the Taskforce. She grabbed her phone and dialed his number. She listened to it ring in her ear, then realized she could hear it ringing in his room as well. She jumped out of bed and went to his room through the connecting door. She saw his phone on the nightstand next to his bed.

"Damn it!"

She ran back to her room, ripping through her clothes in an attempt to get dressed before he got on the elevator. She left the room barefooted, running to the foyer, but Pike had already gone down.

HEADING TOWARD CLARENDON, I realized I had run out of the hotel so hastily I'd left without my cell phone. *Stupid, stupid mistake.*

Not only could Kurt not contact me for anything, such as changing the meeting time or location, but I couldn't make sure that Jennifer was safe. I thought about returning for it, but knew I didn't have the time. If I missed this meeting with Kurt, I might not get another chance.

By the time I got to the Orange Line I saw I was running late, causing me to worry about missing Kurt. He had stressed he had little time. *Should've never gone into Jennifer's room.* I paced back and forth, staring at my watch every few seconds like that would speed things up. Finally, the train arrived.

Luckily, the Court House stop was the first one past Rossyln. I exited the train at a trot. Glancing at my watch, I saw it was 11:03. *Shit. Kurt's probably already called.*

Probably leaving Four Courts right now. I broke into a run.

Exiting the Court House stop I could see the Four Courts pub about a hundred meters away on Wilson Boulevard. Two people were outside it, neither of them Kurt. If he had left in the last couple of minutes, I should be able to see him. *Maybe he's still there.* I waited for the light to change, allowing me to cross the street. After two seconds, I had had enough of waiting. A break in traffic presented itself, and I sprinted across. I continued to the entrance at a fast walk, straining to see if Kurt left the pub.

My attention was jerked to the street by a car swinging onto Wilson Boulevard at a high rate of speed, tires squealing fast enough to produce smoke. I saw the car immediately slow down, the right side window lowering.

I watched a man wearing a ski mask stick his head out, looking like an IRA terrorist in Belfast. *What the hell?* I stopped walking, processing the scene and preparing to react. The man stuck a Heckler and Koch MP5 out the window, aiming it at a couple to my front. He let the MP5 rip, spraying the front of Four Courts with rounds. Both the man and woman were hit instantly, spinning and falling to the ground.

Time stretched out, moving at half speed. I assessed my options and realized I was in serious trouble. I was standing in front of the plate-glass window of Four Courts with no protection in sight, nothing at all to stop the rounds that were about to tear into me. I knew my best bet was an alley to my rear about thirty feet away, but from the time of the first round until now, I computed that I wouldn't make it there before I was hit.

The man was still spraying rounds on full automatic, the bullets shattering the plate glass to my front, stitching toward me like a sewing machine. I saw the man's gun hand begin to lose control from the recoil, giving me a sliver of hope. The car continued forward at a slow rate of speed, only fifteen feet away. *Take him head-on.* If I was wrong, I was dead. I launched myself at the vehicle, watching the man's eyes widen as he saw me coming. He tried to swing the weapon directly at me instead of shooting rounds at the front of the building. I beat him by the blink of an eye. Just as the weapon was about to cross my body, I closed my hands on it.

Jerking upward, I tried to rip the MP5 out of the man's hands, the weapon cycling with the rounds blasting skyward, inches from my head. The man fought me to regain control, and almost succeeded, when his driver decided to accelerate, causing the weapon to be wrenched out of his hands. The car hurtled forward with its tires squealing again.

I watched the vehicle race away, then scanned for any other danger. I caught movement over my right shoulder and trained my weapon on the threat. A man was exiting the alley I had passed on my way to the pub. The same alley I had been going to use for cover. He had a pistol in his hand and was looking for a target. I let loose with the remaining rounds in the MP5's magazine, chipping the bricks around him and forcing him to retreat back down the alley.

The air was split by the sound of sirens approaching. I looked at the couple shot earlier, seeing the man sitting up holding his shoulder. The woman lay on her back, rolling left and right, her abdomen sprouting a red stain, dripping on the concrete. I knew I should help them, but had to make a hard choice. My conscience screamed for me to stay, but the man in the alley told me this wasn't random, and that I was the target. I decided to leave the scene. I dropped the weapon and took off at a dead sprint back to the Metro station across the street.

74

Two blocks away, Lucas was on an encrypted radio trying to get a handle on what had occurred. "What's the status? What happened?"

Mason came through first. "The target came alone. The girl wasn't with him. He didn't give me time to set up. He came out of the Metro at a dead run. I didn't have time to give the mounted team a warning order. By the time I called, he was almost at the pub. The mounted team was forced to rush, alerting the target that they were coming before they could engage."

The mounted team cut in. "The psycho didn't run for cover like you said. He ran right at us. He grabbed my weapon right out of my fucking hand. We were forced to exfil."

Lucas cursed. If they were lucky, Pike would think it was a random drive-by. That would be a break, but wasn't assured. The hope was crushed by the next call.

"This is shooter one. I saw what occurred with the mounted team. I tried to get a clean shot but was compromised. He suppressed my fire with the weapon from the mounted team." Shooter one's clinical description broke down. "He came close to fucking killing me. I didn't get off a shot."

Lucas dropped his mike in frustration. Pike definitely knew it was a setup now, and that he was being hunted. *Shit. This operation just went from easy to almost impossible.* Picking up his cell phone, he called Jerry. "Did you find the hotel they're at? Next to the Metro?"

"Lucas, there are about five hundred hotels next to Metro stations. There's no way I can neck it down without more information."

KURT TORE OUT OF THE FOUR COURTS PUB, trying to ascertain what had occurred. Seeing no sign of Pike, he moved immediately to the wounded civilians, honing in on the woman as the most seriously hit.

"You'll be okay. Help's on the way," he said, conscious of approaching sirens. He began initial first aid, checking her airway and putting direct pressure on her wounds as an ambulance screamed to a halt beside them. Paramedics leapt out to conduct triage.

Kurt told them what he knew, then walked away before he got tied up by the police. He pulled out his cell phone and called Pike's number. At the sound of a woman's voice, he was about to disconnect, thinking he had a wrong number. Then he remembered.

"Jennifer?"

"Yes. Who's this? Where's Pike?"

"This is Kurt. I don't know where Pike's at. Where are you? You're not with him?"

Jennifer voice grew alarmed. "No, I'm at the Embassy Suites. Pike left to meet you alone over forty-five minutes ago. What did you do to him?"

"Me?" He was shocked by the question. "For Christ's

sake, why would I do anything to him? Jennifer, listen to me. Get out of the hotel now. Don't even bother packing. Get out—go somewhere safe. Do it now. Write this number down"—he read out his cell number—"call me when you're safe. Let me know where you are."

It took several more attempts before she took him seriously, testing his patience. "Get out, Jennifer," he repeated. "Every second is dangerous."

"But Pike—"

"Leave him a note that only you and he would understand. But get out. *Now!*"

Jennifer's voice grew cold. "I hear you. I'm leaving. I'll do as you say, but if you've done anything to Pike . . . if he's hurt . . . I'm going to fucking *destroy* you. I don't know how, but I will."

LUCAS HAD REGAINED CONTROL OF HIS TEAM, reconsolidating in an empty parking lot eight miles away from the failed hit. He was running his options through his mind when his phone rang.

"Yeah, what do you have?"

Jerry was breathless. "They're staying at the Embassy Suites in Old Town Alexandria. The girl's there now but was just told to leave. Pike doesn't have his cell phone. The girl has it. He doesn't know she's been told to leave. I'm sure he's headed back there, but he only has the Metro. If you hurry, you can get both of them. Worst case, you'll only get him."

Lucas grinned, immediately barking out commands. "They're at the Embassy Suites in Old Town. Mounted team, go there immediately. Stake out the lobby and try to find the girl. She's probably already gone, but it's worth a shot. You other four head to the King Street Metro station. Pike's headed back. Pick him up when he gets off the Metro. Once you have him in sight, call the Embassy Suites team. He'll be headed that way. Close on him and finish the job. We can find the girl later, if necessary."

RIDING BACK ON THE METRO, my mind was running nonstop, trying to figure out what had just happened. I could come up with only one answer: Dr. Evil did exist and his name was Kurt Hale.

Earlier I had decided that didn't make sense, because Kurt wouldn't kill Ethan. I then realized that I didn't even know if Ethan was dead. All I knew was that Kurt had said so. Now it looked like he had said it to keep my mind occupied on Ethan's death instead of looking for threats. Every other fact pointed to Kurt.

Only one person knew where I was going, and that was Kurt. In fact, it was Kurt who had set the meeting up. Kurt had said he needed to straighten out some things because of Ethan's death, but if Kurt really had set this up, then Ethan was alive, and Kurt had used that time to set up his trap instead.

The thought sickened me to my core. The Taskforce was an anchor I had placed my entire trust within. If Kurt could do this, then there was no such thing as good. The world was just a mess of gray. I knew that Kurt wasn't inherently evil, but nothing else explained what had occurred. It wasn't a bunch of amateurs who had attacked me, but guys who knew what they were doing. I had to have been under surveillance to trigger the drive-by, surveillance that I had failed to notice because I was conveniently thinking about Ethan's death and the meeting with Kurt. The shooter in the alley was the final touch. It was clear that the drive-by shooter was simply the sweeper, designed to push me into the alley, and certain death. It was a miracle it hadn't worked. Had I been five feet closer to the alley, I would have immediately sought it out, looking backward at the drive-by shooter, not forward into the alley.

The more I thought about it, the more I began to build into a rage, feeling the anger grow white-hot. For the first time, wanting it white-hot. Savoring the feeling.

Kurt must have set us up in the Homeland Security database. When that didn't work, Kurt had used my loyalty to the Taskforce as a weapon to kill me. Kurt must have also turned off the CIA from investigating anything further in Belize. Few people in the U.S. government had the power to do all of that, and Kurt Hale was one of them. I was just lucky I had come alone. If Jennifer had been there, I would have reacted differently, and we'd probably both be dead.

I felt an electric jolt of adrenaline. *Jennifer's alone at the hotel.* I racked my brain, trying to remember if I had told Kurt where we were staying. I didn't think so, but I might have. I looked at my watch, wishing the train would move faster. I settled back into the seat, letting the rage flow through me, raw and thumping. If Kurt did anything to Jennifer, I was going to burn the Taskforce down.

THE FOUR MEN LUCAS HAD ASSIGNED to the Metro station entered and fanned out to positions that allowed them to dominate the platform without being seen. One, surveying the crowd simply out of curiosity, honed in on a woman across the tracks, waiting for the Metro going the other way. He keyed his covert radio.

"Brandon, look at the woman to your three o'clock. I think it's the target."

Brandon studied the woman. She was acting antsy and pacing back and forth. She carried a laptop case and a backpack that looked stuffed. "Yeah, that's her. Stand by. I'm calling for guidance."

Brandon dialed Lucas's cell. "Sir, this is the Metro team. I've got the female target here preparing to board a train. Do you want us to remain behind for the male, or follow her?"

Lucas paused a moment, considering. He went with the bird in the hand. "Follow her. As soon as you get the chance, terminate her. Make sure you can get out clean before you pull the trigger."

"Roger that. Train's coming. Gotta go."

Brandon called the team. "Board the northbound train. She's the new target. We stick with her until we can smoke her. Hurry—I can see the train approaching. Get to the other side."

They raced back downstairs, moving under the tracks, then back upstairs to the northbound side. All four members just managed to board before the doors closed. None noticed Pike exit the train on the southbound side.

IN THE LOBBY, Mason had just answered a call from Lucas when he saw Pike blow by him to the elevator.

Lucas was finishing up telling Mason the new plan.

". . . so they won't be able to give you early warning. They're on the girl now. When he gets there—"

Mason interrupted. "He's here. He just went by me to his room. We can't do anything in here. All the rooms look into a giant atrium. We can't even get to his room without anyone seeing us, much less break in. We're going to have to wait."

Lucas thought for a moment. "Okay. That's not bad. He'll either head to the other target, or she'll come back here. I'm betting he heads to her. Hold what you got and tail him. I'll coordinate with the other team. If you guys meet in the middle we can finish this thing. Don't wait for that, though. You get a chance, kill that bastard."

75

I went through my room into Jennifer's. It was empty. All of her clothes were gone and so was the laptop. I went back to my room. For the first time, I noticed that all of *my* clothes were gone as well. I saw my cell phone where I had left it, only now it was sitting on a piece of paper. Picking it up, I read,

Kurt called. I'm going to the place I went to yesterday. I'll be getting a bite to eat. Call me when you get this.

I smiled for the first time that morning. *Smart girl*. She was going to the most crowded place she could find, and she had managed to tell me exactly where without writing it down. She would be in the food court at the bottom of the mall. I didn't like the fact that Kurt had called, but hopefully she would be safe until I could get there. Kurt clearly just wanted to get her out of the hotel so he could kill her. He probably didn't count on me still being alive.

I picked up the phone and dialed Jennifer. She answered on the first ring. "Pike? Is that you?"

Thank God. More relief than I thought I had in me coursed through my body. I put on a calm voice.

"Yeah. How're you? Are you okay?"

"I think so. I just got off the Metro. Kurt called and told me to get out of the hotel. He left his number and told me to call him when I was out and safe somewhere."

That fucker. "You haven't called, have you?"

"No, not yet."

"Don't. Just go where you told me you were going. I'm on my way. Do not call Kurt."

"Pike, what's going on? I'm scared. I think someone's following me. I keep seeing the same guy. He jumped on the Metro at the last minute, and now he's been thirty feet behind me ever since. I don't want you to think I'm paranoid, but I think it's real."

I spoke slowly and clearly. "I think it's real too. Stay in crowded areas. Don't pay him any attention. If he thinks he's burned, he'll either do something drastic or be replaced by someone else. Better to know who's following you than to have to figure it out. Move to where you said you would meet me. Anybody tries anything, kick them as hard as you can in the balls, then run off screaming. Run in a zigzag pattern. I'm on the way. Can you do that?"

I heard her take a deep breath. "Yeah . . . Yeah, I can do that. I'm not going to ask why the zigzag pattern. I don't want to know what you're going to say."

"Don't worry. I'm coming. Hold tight. I'll be there in minutes."

IN THE COURTYARD OF THE ATRIUM, Mason saw Pike leave the room three floors up. He called his teammate. "Get ready. He's coming down."

The man was just outside the elevator exit, waiting. He watched Pike exit and head to a stairwell.

"He's not going to the Metro. I say again, he's not going to the Metro."

Mason cursed. "Stay on him."

"He's going to the parking garage. If I go into the stairwell with him, I'm burned."

"Hold on. Sit tight. Let him go. He spots you and we're going to have a gunfight right here. Don't take him on one-on-one. Remember, he took an MP5 from the mounted team this morning."

Mason thought about his options. He decided he needed to punt to his higher headquarters. He called Lucas and relayed the news.

In the Crystal City office, Lucas took the call, feeling punched in the gut with the latest report. *Jesus. Predicting this guy's actions is proving impossible.* He knew that he was now going to have to earn his salary. The hard way. It pissed him off. *Screw drinking a beer with him. Prima-donna SMU asshole. When I get him I'm going to castrate his sorry ass.*

"Let him go. Head back to the office. We need to regroup. This seat-of-the-pants shit isn't working."

I PARKED THE RENTAL and entered the mall. Standing at the railing of the first level, I looked down into the basement level of the food court, spotting Jennifer. I knew that if she'd seen one man, there were several more. Nobody with any training tried to conduct surveillance alone, and these guys had training. I gave her a call, watching as she answered.

"Hello?"

"It's me. I'm in the mall. Don't look around, but I'm looking at you right now." I saw her raise her head and couldn't resist teasing her. "I said don't look around! . . . Just kidding. . . . Listen, I need you to—"

"Jesus, Pike, this isn't a joke!" she said, speaking in a fierce whisper. "Come get me! The man I saw is directly behind me. He's been sucking on that small Coke for twenty minutes."

I spoke in soothing tones. "Okay, okay, slow down. Everything's just fine now. I need to identify who else is with that guy. I need you to get up and walk toward the stairwell to your left front. Just casually get up and walk that way, going up the stairs. Don't rush."

I watched the crowd. As soon as Jennifer began moving, a man to her right front stood up, moving with her, slightly behind. *One.* I watched Coke Man. Coke Man looked over at another man, who rose as well, moving toward the stairs ahead of Jennifer. *Two.* Jennifer was halfway up the stairs, one man in front, one man behind, when Coke Man rose. *Three.* He must be the last one. I faded into a store.

I called Jennifer. "You have three of them on you. We've got to slim it down. I need to get you with just one guy. Go into a store for a little bit to give me time to set up. I'll call back in a minute."

I heard a little panic in her voice. "Wait! Don't hang up. I don't know who they are. They might kill me here."

"Jennifer, trust me. They won't do anything here. If they were going to, they would've already done so. As long as they think you don't know they're on you, they'll be content to follow. If you push them, they might try something to keep you from running. You'll be all right. It's almost over. Go drool over some shoes or something."

She waited a second before answering. "Pike, you're an asshole. Don't wait too long to call, or I might run just to make you work."

"I'll only be a minute. I'm sure they're wondering who you're talking to, so act like this's nothing. One more call and we're done. Hang in there."

I hung up and sprinted to the nearest anchor store, a Macy's. Taking the escalator stairs two at a time, I exited on the second level. Looking around, I thought it would work. I could put my back to the elevator next to the escalator exit and not be seen by anyone coming up.

I gave Jennifer a final call.

"Hey, here we go. This is the endgame. I need you to go to Macy's. Take the escalator up to the second level. The escalator will act as a funnel. They'll hang back, so that by the time you exit you should have only one man on you, with the other two staggered behind. Exit the escalator and turn left. I'll be right there, so don't jump. Just walk on past into the store. I'll do the rest. Got it?"

"Yeah. I got it. I act like I'm shopping and you kick their ass. I think I can do that. You sure this'll work? What if two follow?"

"Then I'll improvise, but these guys are pretty switched on. I don't think they'll pull any amateur shit. Key here is to move naturally. These phone calls have got to be making them antsy. Don't act like you've got some sort of instructions to do something. Whatever you do, don't look down while on the escalator or look back while walking. You ready?"

"Yeah. See you in a couple of minutes. I'm moving now."

I pressed myself into the small opening for the elevator door and waited. Four minutes later, Jennifer exited, walking by me at a natural pace, looking like a shopper who didn't have a care in the world. She didn't so much as give me a glance, making me think she had missed me. Then I noticed she was giving me an "A-OK" sign with her hand, her arm still swinging easily. I blinked. *Huh. Cool as a cucumber.*

I moved into a slight crouch, resting on the balls of my feet. Nine seconds later, I could hear the man following talking to someone on a radio. ". . . No, don't wait on me. If you have a clear opportunity to kill her and get away, take it."

Damn. I missed someone. They must've had a floater in the mall.

76

The man exited the escalator still giving instructions on his concealed radio, looking a little strange babbling into thin air. ". . . We'll link back up at the garage. Just remember, no gunfire. . . ." It was Coke Man. He saw me, the recognition causing his eyes to widen. ". . . Holy shit . . ."

Great last words. I grabbed him by his shirt and whirled him around, pinning him against the elevator door. He immediately began to struggle, trying to tie up my arms. Before he could, I reached up with both hands and grabbed his head by the hair. I slammed it as hard as I could against the steel elevator support, hearing his skull crunch. I dropped him and took off in the direction Jennifer had gone, hitting redial as I went.

"Hey, I screwed up," I said. "They had a floater running around the mall and he's on you now. Get to a crowded area as fast as you can."

"I'll try. I took the first left and I'm in some baby section. Nobody's here." She paused, then said, "Oh, shit. Pike, I looked back. . . . I saw him. . . . He knows I saw him. . . . He's walking right at me. I can't get out of here without going by him."

I turned the corner and spied her about seventy-five

meters away. The man following her was closing in at a fast walk, giving up any pretense of being a shopper. She was right. The only way out was through him. She was pinned in by a corner wall that opened up to a balcony on the third floor. Unfortunately, no shoppers were up there looking down. The killer would feel safe.

"I see you. I see you." *Too far away. I'm not going to make it.* At least the man hadn't started running at her yet, giving me precious seconds.

She said, "Get ready. I'm going to set this guy up for you."

Huh? What the hell is she talking about? "Jennifer, listen to me—"

Before I could say anything, she dropped our backpacks and the laptop and took off running toward the wall below the third-level balcony. The killer began sprinting, rapidly closing the distance to her. I dropped the phone and followed suit, running flat out, as fast as I could. *What the hell is she doing?* There was nowhere for her to hide or defend herself. The killer closed the distance to five feet just as Jennifer veered directly at the corner. *Now she zigzags.*

I was thirty feet back, unable to do anything to prevent the man from catching her. I was just about to scream to distract the man when Jennifer launched herself in the air. She planted one foot on the left wall of the corner and pressed off, rising another four feet. She repeated the sequence with her right foot and got high enough to grab the railing of the third-floor balcony. She pulled herself over the rail, leaving the killer looking up, stunned. *And alone.*

I sprinted right at him. He was two feet off the wall,

his head cocked back, completely unaware that I was coming. *Wow. This is going to leave a mark.* I hit him just below the shoulder blades like an NFL linebacker, snapping his head straight back and driving him completely unprotected into the wall. I heard his ribs crack like dry kindling and felt a spray of blood from something damaged. When I dropped him, I saw his face was a gory mess. *Ouch.* I looked up and saw Jennifer, white as a bedsheet but smiling.

I smiled back, showing her that I thought this was just business as usual, although my face was probably white too. *Jesus, that was close.*

"Get your ass down here, spider monkey."

"I can't get down from here. Only up. Keep heading around the corner. There's a stairwell in back. Meet me there."

I ran back and gathered up my phone and our luggage, then ran in the direction she had indicated. I met her coming out the door. Knowing we were about five seconds from being seen by the other guys tracking her, I grabbed her hand and began dragging her toward the nearest exit.

"Come on, we aren't out of the woods yet."

We made it to the garage and the rental without getting spotted. I jumped into the driver's seat while Jennifer ran to the passenger side.

After closing her door, Jennifer leaned over and wrapped her arms around me in a fierce squeeze. She was trembling, adrenaline still coursing through her.

She said, "I thought you were dead or in the hospital. What happened? Why did Kurt call?"

I said, "Let's get the hell out of here while we still can. I'll tell you while we drive."

I started the car and exited the parking garage. "Before that, though, what on God's green earth was that Flying Wallendas bullshit back there? What were you going to do if you missed? Fall on top of his head?"

"No way was I going to miss. I told you, I used to do that stuff for a living. And somebody had to do something after your brilliant plan went to shit."

"Touché. So we had to flex a little bit. All part of the strategy." I grinned at her. "I will say that was some pretty switched-on thinking back there. Scared me to death, but worked out very well."

I told her what had happened and my fears about the Taskforce.

Jennifer didn't seem to buy the theory. "You were the one that said it couldn't be the Taskforce. Now you think it is?"

"I can't come up with any other explanation."

"Why on earth would the Taskforce do that? What possible good would it do?"

"I have no idea, which is why I'm going to call Kurt right now. Where's his number?"

Jennifer got out the number and dialed the phone, handing it to me.

I heard Kurt answer and said, "Guess you missed, huh, asshole?"

"Pike, is that you? What happened at Four Courts? Where are you?"

"You'll find me soon enough, you son of a bitch. I still want to meet, but on my terms."

"What's your problem? What's going on?"

"My problem is that you tried to fucking kill Jennifer and me. I'm willing to meet so you can tell me why. I'm sure there's an incredibly good reason."

"Have you lost your mind? Why the fuck would I do that?"

"Cut the shit. You were the only one who knew where we were meeting. You fed me that bullshit story about Ethan, then laid out the trap. I want to know why."

"Pike, Ethan is dead."

Kurt waited for me to say something, but his tone threw me off. He didn't sound like he was playing a role. When I didn't say anything, he continued.

"His whole family is dead. His older girl . . ."

"Emily."

"Yeah, Emily, was tortured to death. Both her eyes were punctured and four fingers were cut off from her right hand. Ethan himself was missing an ear and had all of the skin flayed from both of his thighs. The wife and other daughter were tied up and shot in the back of the head. This wasn't random. It had something to do with what you talked to him about."

What he said left me speechless. I tried to process it but couldn't.

"Pike? You still there?"

I refocused. "That's still just a story from you. I don't know it's true. All I know is that only one person on earth knew where I was going, and I walked into an ambush."

"There's another explanation. Either your phone or my phone is being monitored."

I considered this. "You still want to meet?"

"Yeah. Name the place."

"Meet me in ten minutes at the last place we saw Billy Donatelli. You aren't there in ten minutes, I'm gone. You come to that place, alone. If you're still a warrior, you'll feel a set of crosshairs on your skull. If I see anything strange at all, anybody attempting to set up a long-range shot or ambush, I'm *not* going to just leave. I'm going to let you get in position and then blow your head off. After you're dead, I'll leave. Is that understood?"

"Yes. It's understood. I'll be there. Don't turn the maintenance guy into the bogeyman."

I pulled into our destination, parking the car and hanging up the phone.

Jennifer looked around, confused. "What are we doing at Arlington National Cemetery? Where's the last place you and Kurt saw Billy?"

"Here. I was his troop sergeant major; Kurt was the commander of the Unit. He died in Iraq in 2004."

77

Kurt hung up the phone, realizing that Pike had picked the perfect meeting location. One, the reference to Billy was something that only he and Pike would know. Two, it was close enough to the Taskforce—only a mile as the crow flies—that Pike could force a very short timeline, thereby preventing Kurt from setting up any type of trap if he was so inclined. Three, Billy's grave would be in the middle of a vast expanse of white stones, no cover or concealment anywhere to hide a hit team. Four, the reservation was blanketed by patrols of either National Park rangers or military police, all investigating anything out of the ordinary in an attempt to prevent vandalism to the hallowed ground. Fifth, and perhaps most important, the location was sacred to both Pike and Kurt, and Billy's headstone would send a message that some things were worth more than whatever politics Pike believed Kurt was involved in.

Kurt grinned in spite of himself, wondering how long it had taken Pike to think of it. *He's still the best under pressure.*

He hit the timer of his watch and set out at a trot to his car, yelling at the duty officer that he would be back in an hour.

LUCAS AND HIS TEAM HEARD THE ENTIRE EXCHANGE at the Crystal City office. Lucas knew there was no way to figure out where both of these guys last saw the man named Billy Donatelli. He would have to rely on the beacon embedded in Kurt's pager. One thing was for certain: With two men in the hospital for a cracked skull and broken ribs, and two failed attempts, he wasn't going to launch out of here at the first opportunity. Pike had proven that he could thwart even well-laid plans. Now that he knew he was being hunted, he would be treated like the threat he posed. *Should've pushed Standish on the collateral damage. Should've used a car bomb.*

I STOOD STILL, looking but not seeing the cross bearing Billy's name, my mind a thousand miles away on a combat action years ago.

When I looked up, Jennifer asked, "How did he die?"

"On an assault. Nothing big, nothing fancy. It was an assault like hundreds of others. This one happened to be a hornet's nest."

I changed the subject, not wanting to talk about it. "We need to find a hiding place so we can watch Kurt and whoever else might come in."

I saw a knoll with a copse of trees about eighty meters away. It looked down on the site of Billy's grave, with unobstructed views three hundred and sixty degrees. It would work.

"Come on. Kurt should be here soon. If anyone else is coming, they'll be first, and we need to be hidden."

Eight minutes later we watched a single individual advance to Billy's grave. I recognized Kurt's walk. Rolling over, I winked at Jennifer and said, "You see me drop, get out of here."

She rolled her eyes, muttering, "Asshole. If I had any sense . . ."

I lost the rest, running out to meet Kurt. Within two minutes, he convinced me that he was telling the truth, which gave me no small amount of relief. Finding out he had turned would reset what I knew about the United States government and what we stood for, and that would have been as bad as the trauma I felt when my family died. I was just now beginning to believe again that what I had done with my life was worthwhile. A betrayal by Kurt would have crushed that forever.

After calling Jennifer, we got in the rental and exited Arlington. I asked Jennifer to drive, letting Kurt and me sit in the back and sort out what the hell was going on.

Once outside of the Arlington complex, I told Kurt everything I knew. I ended with Ethan's analysis and the attempts on our lives.

"So, we definitely have two terrorists, probably still in Norway, who think they have a catastrophic weapon and are intent on using it. On top of that, some sorry sons of bitches here in the U.S. want to ensure they succeed." I waited a beat, then said, "Well, I'm finished. I think that's enough information to work on. I'm ready to get out of this business. How soon before you can launch the Taskforce?"

Kurt's expression gave me a sinking feeling. He appeared to be considering what to say, which meant it probably wasn't going to be good. When he finally spoke, it was like cracking open a rotten egg.

"Pike, look, I don't think there's anything the Taskforce can do about this. I can't just launch willy-nilly, whenever I feel like it. There's the Oversight Council to think about. This is more of a problem for one of the Special Mission Units."

I was speechless. I'd thought he was going to say he couldn't do anything for two or three weeks, not that he *wouldn't* do anything *at all*. I finally spit out, "What the hell are you saying? Terrorists are about to kill hundreds, if not thousands, of people. We may be on the verge of World War Three. Ethan was skinned alive for this information, and you're worried about some pissant council oversight?"

Out of the corner of my eye I saw Jennifer flinch at my statement, then stare into the rearview mirror trying to catch my eye. I ignored her.

Kurt caught the look, apparently realizing we were now treading on classified information in front of a civilian. He held up his hands. "Pike, calm down. You know how it works. That's the way it is, and I'm not going to talk about it here."

"Fuck that. Read her on later. She's lost her fucking uncle and about lost her own life for this. She's not going to run around spouting at the mouth, and I want an answer. I've earned an answer."

He said nothing for a minute, making up his mind. "All right. You *know* the answer. Our unit was not designed for and is not capable of a rapid-alert scenario. That's why the damn Delta Force exists. It takes us months to develop the infrastructure and cover to penetrate a sovereign country and take down a target without it being exposed as an American operation. We can't simply pick up and haul ass to Norway like an invasion force. It would compromise the unit."

"Who gives a shit? Jesus, what's more important? Four people have died already. Two more were shot attempting to stop me from seeing you. I can't believe you wouldn't gladly throw the unit away to do this. I can't understand where you're coming from."

"Pike, it's more than the Taskforce. If we get compromised it will bring down the president. Not only that, but his entire administration, and would literally shock the nation to its core. Do-gooders would seize the opportunity to muzzle every other action against the terrorist threat. You think Internet wiretaps are hard to do now? After this, they won't exist at all. In fact, it's not hyperbole to say the best thing that could happen for Al Qaeda is for the Taskforce to be discovered in a foreign country killing terrorists. It would make Lillehammer look like a mild error in judgment."

I knew all about Lillehammer, and the irony wasn't lost on me that these terrorists had gone to the same country that caused Israel's Wrath of God operation to blow up in their face. In June of 1973, Israel had sent a hit team to the small town in Norway to kill Ali Hassan Salemeh, otherwise known as the Red Prince, the man responsible for the 1972 Munich Olympic massacre of Israeli athletes. Instead of getting him, they killed an innocent Moroccan waiter by mistake. Rapid police work uncovered the Israeli connection, with several of the agents being arrested before they could get out of the country. The repercussions were immediate and profound, starting with the permanent dismantling of the Wrath of God teams and ending with Israel being vilified on the world stage, compared to the very terrorists they sought to kill.

I didn't buy the argument. "Sir, I get where you're coming from, but there's a higher purpose here. Israel was simply conducting an attack based on revenge. We're trying to preempt a WMD attack, to save countless lives, for Christ's sake. It's not the same thing, even if we get compromised. The repercussions are worth it. Would you rather have World War Three or some egg on the president's face?"

"Pike, we don't even know if the WMD is real. All you have is what Ethan gleaned from a single paragraph. It doesn't make it fact." He paused for a moment; then his tone softened. "Look, I get that there's a threat out there, but the Taskforce isn't the correct tool to use against it. Let me get this information into the system. Let the CIA and the Special Mission Units handle it. That's what they do."

"Jesus Christ! You sound like all the jackasses that said the Taskforce doesn't need to exist. You *know* what happened with the first effort to create our unit. You put this information into the system and we're going to get our wheels spinning for weeks, until someone believes it's a true, distinct threat. You said it yourself. It's just a paragraph on a piece of paper and the word of a discredited operator. Nobody is going to take that seriously, and we don't have time to prove it. We can't waste a week developing corroborating evidence to convince the National Command Authority to launch. That bomb's going off before then."

I looked at Kurt to see if anything I said was registering. When I didn't get a response, I threw out my final trump card.

"In fact, because the Taskforce operates without constitutional constraints, we're the *only* element that can execute. Everyone else will be waiting on DEPORDS and presidential findings. Please. I'm begging here. Think about what you're saying."

"Pike, I have a greater obligation to the nation. If you had something besides simple extrapolation of what you *think* is going on, I might do something. I simply can't jeopardize the entire presidential administration and the future defense of the nation based on what you *think*."

I grunted, sick of the conversation.

"Get back to Arlington. Drop Kurt off," I said to Jennifer.

Turning back to Kurt, I said, "I'm not the only one who believes there's a bad fucking event coming. Someone tried very hard to keep me from talking to you. I guess they could have spared all the death and destruction, since you don't give a damn in the first place."

I could tell the words stung, but Kurt held firm.

"What're you going to do now?"

"I'll go to Norway and save the fuckin' world by myself—without any help from your Taskforce."

"You can't get on a plane. You'll be arrested from the Homeland Security database."

That answer caused me to start swearing like a sailor and punching the seat in front of me.

Kurt put a hand on my shoulder. "Hold on. Look, I can't launch a force, but I can support you from here. I'll get you to Norway on one of our aircraft. Give me those e-mail addresses. I can have them monitored twenty-four/seven. You said you deleted the meeting message, right?"

That mollified me a little. "Yeah. It's gone. They couldn't

have made that meet, so I'm thinking they're still hanging around waiting."

"Good. I'll keep an eye on the e-mails. When they set up a new meet, I'll relay the information to you. Give me an e-mail address."

I didn't have one. Jennifer turned around. "I have one. Will any address do?"

"Yeah, I don't care what it is."

Jennifer gave him a Hotmail address.

Kurt said, "Good enough. We'll monitor this twenty-four/seven as well. If you need any analytical help, send us an e-mail."

Kurt reached into his pocket, pulling out his world-wide pager. "Here. If you find them, and confirm there is a weapon, use this. You remember how, right?"

"Yeah. I remember."

"You alert us back here, and I'll assume you've found something. I'll launch a team your way."

He held the pager in his hands, not yet passing it over. "Pike, I meant what I said. Don't press this button just because you believe something's going on. Don't use it for your own personal vendetta. Once I launch, and we get compromised, there's an even chance that the U.S. government is going to go through a seizure. Make sure it's worth it."

78

Kurt gave me the pager, saying, "One more thing. You really will be on the Impossible Mission Force for this one. You get caught, and you're going to be hung out to dry. You won't get any official sanction from here."

"I didn't expect it. I won't get caught. I haven't been yet."

We pulled into Arlington and switched to Kurt's car. We spent the majority of the time it took to drive to the Dulles FBO listening to Kurt set up an aircraft for me. Finally, it was done, and I got to ask about the men who had tried to kill us.

He said, "I've been thinking about that quite a bit, but really have no idea. Whoever it is has a lot of power, but all the people with power like that simply wouldn't do it. It doesn't make any sense to me. I can't even figure out why they would want a terrorist attack to occur in the first place. The whole thing is screwy. Anyway, it's no longer your concern."

"Huh? It's exactly my concern. They aren't trying to kill you. They're trying to kill Jennifer and me."

Kurt's face became hard. "That's not what I meant. You focus on the terrorists. I'll find out who killed Ethan and tried to kill you. Don't worry about them. They have ceased to exist. I can't bring back Ethan's family, but I promise you the men who did that will pay."

Out of the corner of my eye I saw Jennifer visibly blanch. I'd purposely not told her the grisly details of Ethan's family to spare her feelings, but she had now connected the dots between the body count and who was dead. Maybe realizing for the first time that doing the right thing had consequences outside of our control, and that the good guy doesn't always win.

Kurt continued, pulling into the general aviation section of Dulles. "Whatever you do, don't call my cell phone until I have it scanned. Those assholes are tracking either you or me, and I don't trust my own equipment at this stage. I've got the thing dismantled in my pocket right now."

We pulled into Signature Air at the Dulles FBO. He parked the car and turned around. "Well, I couldn't get you a junky airplane. All we have available at short notice is the rock-star bird."

I grinned. "Perfect. Nothing like riding in style."

Jennifer looked from me to Kurt, asking, "What's the rock-star bird? Are we flying on a Greyhound tour bus?"

"Better than that. It's a Gulfstream IV. Just like the rock stars use."

Then the second part of her question hit me.

"And 'we' aren't flying on it. I am. You need to head on back to Charleston and go back to school."

She was silent for a second, the words not sinking in. When they finally did, she exploded. "What? Bullshit! I'm going with you."

I glanced at Kurt for support.

He gave her a look I'd seen a hundred times. "We appreciate everything you've done, but let's face it, you're not capable of providing help here. Pike will work better alone, without having to worry about you. You don't have to go back to Charleston if you don't want to. I have some safe houses here in D.C. you can use for a while. You'll have the protection of the Taskforce until this thing is over."

That seemed to really piss her off. "You didn't even believe the story in the first place. You have all of this talent and resources at your disposal and you're sending Pike by himself. You don't have the right to even talk to me. I'm the one that figured this thing out. I'm the one that got Pike to start this hunt. Me. Not you. All you've done is spit on our efforts, cloaking yourself in some bullshit tale of higher patriotism."

She ignored Kurt, turning her back to him and facing me. She looked into my eyes the same way she had when she asked me to go to Guatemala. I could see the hurt on her face, like I had broken her trust. *Surely she can understand that she's completely unprepared for this. It's not like we're going on a roller coaster ride and she's a quarter inch too short.* Her expression caused the twinge again, much stronger than before, making me want to end her pain. *Stop that. . . . Stay focused.*

She said, "I haven't been a liability. I've earned it. You can use me on this and you know it. They won't suspect a woman of anything."

I said nothing, conflicting emotions churning away. I considered the question, trying to leave my confusing, sorry-ass feelings out of it. Looking at it dispassionately, the truth of the matter was she had a point. I was already at a disadvantage for the work ahead. I had seen what the terrorists looked like when they mugged me, which meant they also knew what I looked like. *But they haven't seen Jennifer.* And she was right—the Arabs' inbred prejudice against women might help us.

True, she wasn't a badass counterterrorist commando, but she had the raw talent. Beyond the physical ability, which she had in spades, she was very good at solving problems under pressure. She had proved that less than an hour ago with her circus stunt in the mall. This trait, above all others, was prized in the Taskforce, and was the cut line that kept otherwise outstanding soldiers at the level below. With a modicum of internal talent, you could teach anyone to surgically shoot, run all night, or do hand-to-hand combat, but the ability to think on your feet and solve problems in real time was the prize. She had the mettle necessary for operations, lacking only the experience. She was a quick learner, though, and had gotten quite a bit of experience over the last few days. I made up my mind.

"She's not a liability. She's going."

Jennifer gave me a radiant smile, then turned and glared at Kurt.

Kurt exploded. "Have you lost your mind? She can't go. She's a damn civilian. She'll compromise the whole operation!"

"Sir, I appreciate your support, and your opinion, but you've already told me I'm hanging my ass out on my own. I'm also a civilian. It's my call, and I say she goes. I need the help. Unless you want to launch a team with me, that is."

Kurt grimaced but backed down. "You're going to be the man on the ground. Your call."

"Thanks. We'll contact you when we get in-country. What's the name of the corporation we're supposed to be flying with?"

He gave us both a down-and-dirty dump of the cover of the aircraft we would be on, ending with a caveat.

"Remember, you don't work for the corporation. You have nothing to do with the corporation. The plane is only stopping to refuel. You get off, and the plane flies away. You simply hitched a ride because you know someone who knows someone who got you a free seat. Happens all the time. You only need the cover story when you land. Once you're in-country, never mention the corporation again. You're tourists, or whatever else you want to be, but you're not connected to me."

Moving through the FBO to the flight line, I grinned. "Like old times. Except for that little 'you're on your own' thing."

Kurt wished us luck, holding his hand out to Jennifer. She graciously returned the shake.

He shook my hand, saying, "Look, I want to stop this as much as you do. Do what you do best and we can both rest easy."

I returned the handshake, feeling a little embarrassed at my outbursts earlier. "Sorry about yelling at you. I understand your position. I won't let you down."

I held his hand a little longer than necessary and locked eyes with him.

"Don't let me down either."

PART
FOUR

PART
FOUR

79

Inside his Crystal City office, Lucas closed out the tracking Web site in disgust. It had grown dark outside, and he wondered if he had missed the opportunity to take out his prey. The pager beacon had gone to Arlington National Cemetery, then had driven aimlessly about for the next couple of hours. It had finally stopped at the Dulles Fixed Base Operations center, where it had remained ever since. That meant one thing: the beacon, and presumably whoever was carrying it, had flown somewhere. Due to the length of time it had remained stationary, that flight was taking some time, either going across the country or out of it.

He picked up the phone to relay the bad news. When Standish answered, Lucas went secure and got right to the point.

"We missed both targets. The beacon signal itself has become stationary at Dulles, which leaves me to believe the targets are airborne moving to another location. Do you wish to proceed?"

For a moment he heard nothing but breathing on the other end, disgusting him. *Weasel can't make a decision. He'd last about eight seconds in combat.*

"Well, yes, I guess so," Standish said. "We need to get it done."

"Even if it means going to a foreign country? You willing to risk that?"

"Is that what they're doing?"

"I won't know until the beacon lands, but the last report was over four hours ago, so they're flying a long ways. What do you want me to do?"

"What have you done so far?"

Lucas proceeded to tell him about the lead they had gleaned from Ethan's phone call the night before, clinically using terms such as *asset information* and *neutralizing further exposure*. Before he could continue with the morning's events, Standish put two and two together and interrupted the conversation.

"Whoa! Wait a minute! Don't tell me you're involved in that multiple murder in Herndon. Lucas—"

"Yeah, that was me."

"Jesus Christ! They're calling it a Charles Manson copycat killing, for God's sake! They think a psycho gang's on the loose. Are you insane? Four people were fucking slaughtered. Tortured to death."

Lucas wanted to reach through the phone and rip out Standish's heart. *You coward. Just like everyone else. Want to get the job done, but don't have the balls for the work.*

"Listen to me, you self-righteous blowhard, you gave me my mission parameters and I'm still within them. I'm accomplishing the fucking mission. You don't like how I'm doing it, then you should've specified some restrictions beforehand. Now shut the fuck up and let me finish my situation report."

*   *   *

ON THE OTHER END OF THE LINE, Standish felt sick to his stomach. Not because of the deaths in Herndon, but because of the possible exposure to himself. He was barely listening to the rest of Lucas's situation report, frantically going through all of the ties that connected them, when something Lucas said clicked, bringing him back into the conversation.

". . . So we were forced to exfil without terminating either target. From there we regrouped, waiting on contact from the asset's phone you gave me. . . ."

Holy shit. He did the drive-by shooting in Clarendon as well? That can't be right. No way is that right.

"Wait . . . wait. Are you telling me you're also responsible for the shoot-out across from the Arlington Courthouse? You actually opened fire on a bunch of civilians?"

This time Lucas didn't shout. He spoke in a calm, deliberate manner. Standish recoiled from the venom he felt coming from the phone.

"I'll say this one more time. You gave me my parameters and my mission. I'm executing. You told me to ensure the hit wasn't traced to you, and *that's* why we did the drive-by. I'm following your lead. Don't question my methods again."

He thinks he's in charge. I'm losing control.

"Bullshit. You've *exceeded* my parameters. I told you that collateral damage had to be five or less. You killed four at the house in Herndon, then shot at least two at the courthouse, maybe more. You're *outside* my guidance, and my guidance stands. Is that understood?"

"Standish . . . there are two targets. A collateral damage of five per. That means I still have four to work with. Anyway, two of my guys are in the hospital because of your target, so I really don't give a shit about your damn *guidance* anymore. It's getting personal."

Standish couldn't believe how quickly the violence had escalated. He thought about telling Lucas to stand down but was afraid of his response. *He might ignore me altogether.*

"Okay, okay. I can see the miscommunication, but I'm the one in charge. I'm still the one funding this. You want to get him, the only way you'll do it is with my money—and that comes with my oversight. Got it?" He waited on a response, the silence making him wonder if he'd already lost control.

"All right," Lucas answered, "as long as we understand each other."

"Continue with your report."

After Lucas had finished, Standish gave him the go-ahead to execute—even on foreign soil—but told him that no more collateral damage was to be tolerated. He hung up the phone, wondering if Lucas would bother to listen to him. *I'm going to have to do something about him when this is over. Too much exposure. Too much of a threat.*

80

After a solid day and night of heading inexorably eastward, Bakr exited the train station at Tuzla, Bosnia-Herzegovina. Weary down to his bones, he gathered his meager possessions and walked to the first taxi he could find. Speaking in halting English, Bakr asked for a cheap hotel somewhere downtown. The driver held up a finger, saying he knew just the place.

Driving east, toward the heart of downtown, the taxi traveled about two miles before stopping in front of a nondescript four-story concrete building with a Cyrillic sign in the front.

"Here. They treat you well here," he said.

Bakr thanked him and was surprised when the man butchered the phrase *Allahu Akhbar* in return.

Bakr stared at the man, smelling of liquor and smoking a cigarette, thinking surely he was not one of the faithful.

"Are you a man of the book?"

"Yes, yes."

Bakr said, *"Allahu Akhbar,"* and exited the cab. He knew that the horrific civil war that had occurred in Bosnia during the 1990s had been primarily between the Serbian Christian population and the Bosniak Muslim population, but had never stopped to think that a "Muslim" in Bosnia was as far removed from his version of Islam as the far enemy itself.

Bakr entered the lobby of the hotel, seeing an establishment dating back possibly to the 1940s, solidly built of quarry stone, decorated with heavy drapes and dreary colors. The long registration desk, complete with old-fashioned boxes mounted on the wall behind for the guest to place his or her key, was manned by a thin, acerbic-looking man wearing the ubiquitous black leather jacket found all over Bosnia. Bakr checked into his room, happy to see that, although old, it was clean and tidy. The primary concern he had was that the door had a shabby, cheap lock, without a secondary locking mechanism. That would force him to take the weapon everywhere he went.

His first order of business was to check the prearranged e-mail account with Sayyidd. He had made initial contact twenty-four hours ago after leaving the ferry in Kiel, Germany, but that e-mail had been disappointing, with Sayyidd saying he was still waiting on a message from Walid. On the plus side, at least he appeared to be following instructions. The message referenced Fallujah and said that he had checked out of the Muslim section and moved closer to the city center.

Getting directions from the front desk, he found an Internet café four blocks away. Logging on to the account known only to him and Sayyidd, he was relieved to see the reference to Fallujah, then excited when he saw that Walid had sent the instructions for the next meet. It would occur at one o'clock today at a coffee shop in Oslo. Sayyidd ended by saying he would relay what had occurred later on, as soon as he was done.

Bakr leaned back in his chair, satisfied that their planning was still on track. His shift to Bosnia might have been unwarranted, but it was still the prudent thing to have done. It might also have removed one burden from Walid's back, as he thought he could get explosives and detonating material from a contact inside this country. He wasn't convinced that Sayyidd had the expertise to ensure the correct materials were taken from Walid, and there was no way they would return to Norway to remedy any mistakes. Better for him to see if he could gather the materials here.

While still a fighter in Iraq, he had been given the name of a person who was very active helping out Chechen rebels in their fight against the Russian infidels. All he knew was his name, Juka Merdanovic, and that he lived somewhere around Tuzla. He had never met the man but had been told he wouldn't turn away a Muslim in need.

81

As I was pulling into my fourth parking spot, my phone rang.

"Yeah, what's up?"

"Pike, he's waiting at a bus stop. I think he's going to get on. What should I do?"

Shit. I couldn't believe I had failed to plan for a Metro or bus scenario. That was absolutely what would be expected, since the terrorists more than likely didn't have a car. *Chalk one up to fatigue. You'd better pull your head out of your ass, or you're going to fail.* I told her to hang on a second, rapidly running through courses of action in my mind.

"All right, board the bus with him. When you see him get up to leave, give me a call. You stay on the bus. Getting on with him can be a coincidence. Getting off is asking to get burned. You exit at the next stop and head back to the one where he got off. I'll call you when I either find out where he's going, or I lose him."

"Okay. I can do that. Sorry I didn't see this coming and call earlier."

I smiled at her taking the blame. "*I'm* the one who should have seen this coming. Don't worry about it. We're still good to go."

We had landed in Oslo a couple of hours ago and had immediately checked Jennifer's e-mail account for a message from the Taskforce. Sure enough, the terrorists had received another message directing a meeting at a coffee shop at one o'clock in the city center, which didn't give us a lot of time to set up. We located the shop with only thirty minutes to spare. I'd put Jennifer inside, with me outside as a spotter, since I was the only one who knew what they looked like. Of course, that meant I couldn't conduct the actual surveillance because they would spot me.

When Jennifer found out she'd be in the coffee shop alone, she seemed to realize for the first time this was for real. I had reassured her, reminding her of the surveillance classes I'd given on the flight over, stressing again that it wasn't some arcane skill reserved for spies, but just common sense. She didn't seem to buy it, but she'd exited the car. At precisely one o'clock I'd recognized the shorter of the two guys who'd mugged me in Guatemala. I'd almost missed him, because I was looking for a pair. His friend was nowhere in sight, which could mean he was conducting countersurveillance like I had in the mall. No way to tell and nothing I could do about it anyway. I called Jennifer and triggered the surveillance.

After the meeting broke up, Jennifer had managed to track him for five blocks to the bus station, but she was now out of play. That was going to leave me doing the dismounted work, which would be hard to do without getting burned. I pulled out, driving slowly until I saw the bus ahead of me. Picking up the pace, I trailed the bus to the next stop, seeing both Jennifer and the terrorist waiting to board. Four stops later, she called.

"He's standing up. He's getting off."

"Got it. You go to the next stop and head back here."

I immediately scanned for a parking spot, whipping the car around and cramming it into a space barely large enough to hold a moped. I waited for the terrorist to commit to a direction before falling in behind him. The sidewalks in this area were much less congested than in the city center, with only a few couples using them. I knew that if he turned around there was no way he would miss me, but there was nothing I could do about it. I stayed as far back as I dared, praying the terrorist had no reason to feel he was being followed and would walk straight to his destination.

Luckily, that was exactly what he did. Striding with a purpose and ignoring his immediate surroundings, he entered a five-story building. I gave him a few minutes, then approached.

It was a youth hostel, a cheap hotel catering to college students and wandering backpackers. It was clean and neat, although a little threadbare, with a throng of young men and women coming and going.

I went across the street to a small restaurant/bar, took a table in the corner that had a view of the entrance to the hostel, and gave Jennifer a call, telling her where to find me.

SAYYIDD FLEW UP THE STAIRS of the youth hostel at a rapid clip, anxious to e-mail Bakr the good news. Walid had not only told him he could get "proof" of Iranian complicity for the WMD attack, along with the necessary explosive material, but he could get them into Israel proper with little trouble at all. In fact, he wanted Sayyidd to come with him tomorrow to the hinterlands of Norway to meet the man who would facilitate their travel. Unfortunately, the location of the facilitator was outside the footprint of the satellites for the Thrane M4 phone. While they covered a broad swath of the world, it wasn't 100 percent coverage. It meant he would be out of e-mail contact with Bakr for forty-eight hours, but he felt that was of little consequence.

Booting up the M4, he typed a jubilant message, giving Bakr the details of the meeting, including the fact that he might not get any further message in the next twenty-four hours. He reassured Bakr that he would attempt to locate an Internet café, but that the M4 would probably not link up with the satellite.

As he leaned back with a sense of satisfaction, Sayyidd's reflections on his meeting with Walid were interrupted by a growling in his stomach. He didn't bother to shut down the computer, since he would be gone less than forty-five minutes and wanted to see Bakr's reply as soon as he returned.

ABSENTLY LOOKING AT THE MENU ON THE TABLE, I was running through our next potential steps when Jennifer found me and sat down with a big grin on her face.

"Told you—you're a natural," I said.

"It was really sort of fun. I could get into doing that stuff."

"Well, that's good to hear, because I'm pretty sure you're going to get another chance at it."

I gave her a rundown of what I knew, telling her that

we needed to figure out, before we did anything else, whether the other terrorist was with his partner. In the end, we had to have positive proof these idiots had a weapon of mass destruction, or, equally, that they did not, which might mean breaking into their room. I couldn't risk that unless I knew the room was empty, and knocking on the door wasn't a preferred technique.

"What do you think?" I asked. "Any idea how the two of us can maintain twenty-four/seven surveillance on this place?"

"You're asking me? Why? You're the expert."

"Hey, I told you this wasn't rocket science." I glanced out the window. "I have some ideas, but I don't have a monopoly on smarts. If you—"

I saw the terrorist leave the hostel across the street.

Jennifer said, "What? What is it?"

"The guy you followed is on the move."

"Already?" Jennifer leaned over trying to see out the window.

"Shit, he's headed this way," I said.

I looked around for another exit, but we were out of luck. Short of running through the kitchen, the front door was the only way in or out. I saw the man halfway across the street and moving with a purpose directly toward our restaurant.

"He's coming in. Hide your face."

Jennifer picked up a menu and pretended to read it. I did the same, but my angle was horrible. At least Jennifer had her back to the guy. I was facing the entrance with the small menu the only thing hiding my features. I heard the front door open and tried to become invisible. I waited for some indication that he had walked deeper into the restaurant but heard nothing. *Why's he standing at the entrance? Move, dammit. Go to the bar.* The bell on the front door chimed again. Without lowering the menu, I glanced back out the window, seeing someone running toward the hostel. With a start, I realized it was the terrorist.

"Shit! We're burned! We need to stop him before he gets to his buddy!"

I raced past a group of startled patrons and flew out the door. I ran as hard as I could, slowly closing the distance. I saw him look back, fear etched into his face. He put on a final burst of speed, taking the steps to the hostel three at a time. He blasted through the front door, bowling over a couple at the entrance.

I came through the entrance right behind him, in time to see him fling open a stairwell door. I followed, a flight and a half of stairs behind, then narrowed it to one flight. I heard him open the door above me. I reached the fourth floor and exited the stairwell, catching a glimpse of a man entering a room midway down the hall. I had no idea if it was the terrorist or not, but had no other options. I took off at a dead sprint.

I reached the door just as it was slammed shut, jamming my foot in the opening and letting it bounce harmlessly against the sole of my boot. Drawing back, I threw my full weight against the door, causing it to explode inward, flinging whoever was behind it against the wall.

I followed the open door into the room and recognized the terrorist on the floor. I reached out to grab him, but he scrambled away, putting the bed between us.

For a split second, we just stared at each other in a

standoff, both of us panting. I saw the look of fear on his face turn to determination. I moved into a fighting crouch, preparing for the assault that was coming.

It never came.

Instead he shouted, *"Allahu Akhbar!,"* then turned and launched himself headfirst out of the window, shattering the glass with his momentum. The scream continued for four long floors, growing fainter, like a passing train whistle, until it was abruptly cut off when his body impacted the street below.

Before I could assimilate what had happened, I heard someone else at the door and whirled around, seeing Jennifer, out of breath from her run. She looked around the empty room, then at me.

"Where'd he go?"

82

Bakr exited the back of a pickup at the end of a rutted dirt drive leading to a crumbling two-story farmhouse. He thanked the driver for the lift, staring at the house as the man drove away. The people here and in the surrounding hills existed at the poverty level, barely scraping a living out of the hardscrabble ground. The residence was built entirely of stone and had been frequently patched with homemade masonry, with the residue of a past fire visible. Moving listlessly about in a pen next to the farmhouse were a couple of skinny goats and a small flock of chickens, all digging in the dirt to find a bit of greenery that had long since been eaten.

It had taken Bakr the better part of the day to track down Juka's residence, and he still wasn't sure this was it. Before walking up to the house, Bakr reviewed in his mind the tale he would spin to obtain Juka's help. Bakr had learned of Juka's existence through a Chechen who had come to Iraq to glean IED techniques that he could take back to his fight against the Russian invaders of his homeland.

Bakr knew that Juka was a supporter of Muslim causes, but not because of the religion. That just happened to be the common denominator between himself and others like him. Before the summer of 1995, it was unlikely that Juka had even considered his religion as something that defined him. In July of that year, the Serbian army had surrounded Juka's town of Srebrenica and set about on an orgy of violence, wantonly killing men, raping women, and burning everything touched by a Muslim hand.

Bakr knew he would need to play on Juka's emotion of Muslim unity, steering clear of any mention of Al Qaeda and the Great Satan. Far from wanting to harm the United States, Juka actually liked America, since it was American airpower, under the guise of NATO, that had come screaming in to punish the Serbians when the truth of Srebrenica reached the world. It disgusted Bakr, but he was sure that Juka didn't hold America to blame. Because of this, Juka would have to be handled carefully.

Bakr rapped on the rough-hewn door, hearing movement on the other side.

"Yes? Can I help you?"

Bakr was unsure about the man before him. His face held deep wrinkles, made more pronounced by the dirt ground into the crevices, his eyes sunken with large black circles underneath. The age fit, but Bakr had expected more of a sense of purpose, a little more fire, in the person he was seeking. What he saw was a man stooped by a lifetime of eking out a living from the ground, not a man steeled by a lifetime of fighting.

"Yes, I'm looking for a Bosnian named Juka. I'm on my way to Chechnya, and I was told by a friend that he may be able to help me."

Bakr watched the man go through a small transformation. He straightened up, giving Bakr a penetrating stare with pale blue eyes, apparently measuring his mettle with the gaze alone. He leaned against the doorjamb, now projecting a sense of confidence where before there had only been defeat.

"Really? And what would this friend's name be?"

"Milan Petrovic. He knew I was coming this way, and asked for me to pick up some things for him en route to Chechnya. Things that a Bosnian named Juka Merdanovic could provide."

The man stepped away from the door, holding his arm open in a gesture of welcome. "I am Juka. I'm at the service of any man befriended by Milan. Come inside and tell me how I may help."

AN HOUR LATER, Bakr stepped out of Juka's decrepit Lada in front of his hotel in downtown Tuzla, carrying a small wooden box, a gift from Juka.

"Milan will be forever grateful for your attention to his wishes," Bakr said.

Juka waved his hands, washing away the compliment. "I'm the one who will forever be grateful to Milan. I owe him my life. Beyond that, he's taking up arms to protect his people. Helping you help him is a small measure, and I'm glad to do it."

Juka leaned over to the open window.

"If you have any trouble finding the house, or getting in, call this number."

He handed Bakr a scrap of paper with a Bosnian international number written on it.

"The phone is located in a clean house near the one with the supplies you need. Nobody will answer, but the messages are checked every day. Don't say who you are. Just tell them what you need. It'll be provided."

Bakr took the number and waved good-bye, watching the Lada jerk forward, belching smoke. Juka had served his purpose. He had given him the location of a safe house on the northern side of Sarajevo. Inside this house were all the necessary components to fabricate any type of explosive device he desired. Bakr hadn't needed to prove his Chechnya credentials or state his requirements at all. Juka had taken it on faith that he was there on behalf of Milan, and had stated that Bakr could take anything he wished from the house. At one point in the conversation, while describing the inventory of the house, he stood up.

"I have just the thing for you. Something special that I don't keep in the house in Sarajevo. In fact, it's the only one I have ever seen."

Leaving Bakr alone in the rustic den, he rummaged around in a hall closet, returning with a wooden box. Inside was a wireless remote detonation device. Covered in Cyrillic lettering on the outside, it was small, with the receiver about half the size of a pack of cigarettes, and the transmitter slightly larger than a baby dill pickle. It was a state-of-the-art device used to clandestinely fire explosives from a distance. How Juka had ended up with it was anybody's guess.

While Bakr was happy with the option to remotely fire the weapon from up to two hundred meters away, he knew the detonator's true benefits lay in its channel-hopping capability and the fact that it used a separate signal for both arming and detonating.

Having played the IED game extensively in Iraq, Bakr

understood that these features would defeat the average countermeasure employed against radio-controlled improvised explosive devices. Known as a "jammer," the countermeasure basically broadcast a louder signal than the IED transmitter, preventing the receiver from getting the command to detonate, thus "jamming" it. A simple concept, it was analogous to a person listening to a radio station in the middle of nowhere. One second, the channel's putting out country music, the next Gothic rock, as the radio itself relayed whichever signal was strongest. The IED jammer worked the same way. It blasted out huge amounts of white noise on the transmitter's frequency, preventing the receiver from hearing the command to detonate.

The channel-hopping feature on Juka's device meant that the transmitter and receiver, synchronized together, frenetically hopped frequencies from the moment it was turned on, never transmitting on the same frequency for more than a millisecond. This ensured that the average jammer wouldn't be able to defeat it, as it wouldn't be able to sufficiently track which frequency the detonator was using, and thus couldn't override the signal. The second feature, the separate signals used for arming and detonation, meant that the weapon wouldn't be inadvertently set off by someone opening his garage or playing with a remote-controlled airplane. In order for the device to explode, it would take one signal, linked to a security code, to arm the bomb, and another, also linked to a code, to detonate it.

Juka had placed the detonator reverently in Bakr's hands, beginning to fidget once he realized that he had given it away. He made Bakr promise that he would save it for use on a special target, using all of the other mundane detonators he would find in the Sarajevo safe house for everyday terrorist attacks.

Opening the door to his hotel room, Bakr grinned at the memory. Yes, he would save this detonator for a special occasion. The perfect occasion. Placing the detonator on the nightstand, he went to the Internet café to check on the meeting with Walid.

Opening the latest message, it appeared that Sayyidd had done everything he had asked, and more, giving him a little guilt over his previous thoughts about his partner. He was a little concerned by the lack of e-mail contact in the next twenty-four hours, but seeing that this e-mail had arrived within the last hour, he was sure Sayyidd would check his account one more time before leaving, and reply. He typed a quick response, describing his successful meeting with Juka. He hit send, finally beginning to accept that everything was working out.

83

Jennifer asked again, "Where is he?"

I ran to the window, the broken glass crackling under my feet like popcorn.

"He jumped out the fucking window."

"He jumped? Are you sure he—"

"No, I didn't throw him out. As much as I would have liked to, I'd have to be the Incredible Hulk to chuck his ass out the window from across the room."

I saw a crowd gathering around the broken body, most looking down, but some looking up at my location, the drapes swinging gently in the breeze providing an instant point of reference. I snapped my head back before they saw me.

"We have about one minute before we'll be asked a lot of questions. Start packing up his stuff. We'll look at it back in the hotel."

"What about the other guy? What are we going to do about him?"

"I think he's here alone. There's no evidence of another person, no additional luggage, toothbrush, nothing."

Stuffing passports and any other paper I could find into my backpack, I said again, "Come on, pack that computer up. We need to move."

When I didn't notice any movement, I said, "What's up? We have *got* to go."

"An e-mail just came in, from a different Yahoo! account. He's still logged on and connected to the Internet."

"Close it all up," I said. "Don't turn anything off; just close it up for travel. Maybe we can duplicate it at our hotel, but we don't have time to mess with it now."

Finishing up, I held the door open for Jennifer. Just prior to letting it close forever, she grabbed my arm.

"Wait." She ran to the nightstand and grabbed a thumb drive. Holding it up, she said, "No telling what's on this thing."

"Good catch. That's probably got their whole diabolical plan."

She squinted like she was debating on whether to kick me in the nuts. Before she got the chance, I left the room. Once outside I turned left, choosing the opposite stairwell to the one by which we had arrived. We exited out the back, but were forced to walk through all the gawkers on the east side of the hotel to get to our vehicle. The smashed body hadn't been moved, appearing just as it had when I'd looked out the window minutes before. We pretended to be just as shocked as everyone else until we were clear of the crowds and could sprint to our car. Fifteen minutes later we were back in our hotel room.

I set the laptop on the coffee table and brought it out of sleep mode. The last e-mail was still on the screen.

"Toss me that thumb drive."

Putting it in the computer, I saw it was empty. *So much for finding the diabolical plan.* I copied the Arabic text from the e-mail onto the thumb drive, followed by the e-mail header information, then took the drive over to Jennifer, who had booted up our computer and was getting online.

"The thumb drive had nothing on it. Here's the last e-mail that was on the screen, along with the header. Can you send this to the Taskforce? Kurt said he'd have analysts standing by. Time for them to earn their pay."

"Sure. You think they'll be able to get anything out of this?"

"I don't know. I'm going to try to get back into the Yahoo! server and get all his e-mails before his password times out."

She sent the e-mail, then asked me, "What was that Web site that did the magic stuff?"

"What is my IP address dot com. You remember how to use it?"

"Yeah, I think so. I'll let you know if I get stuck."

I was pulling up the wireless toolbar on the terrorist's computer, attempting to get online, when Jennifer said, "The other guy, if that's who sent the e-mail, is in Tuzla, Bosnia-Herzegovina. Does that make any sense?"

"Yeah, actually it does. That's where all the muj went to during the Bosnian war. He's probably got some contacts there."

I tried to connect to the hotel wireless network but failed, being told it was "in use." "Will this hotel network handle two computers with the same password at the same time?"

She was staring at our computer and gave me an absentminded answer. "I don't know."

"His damn password is going to time out. We're going to lose the messages. Get off the Internet and let me go."

"Wait. I'm getting a message. Don't cut it yet. Why don't you try using the Ethernet cable? That's not tied to the wireless."

I felt the press of time and was about to rip her computer out of the wall when what she'd said rooted home. *Damn . . . little brainiac might be right again.* I plugged into the cable and began reconfiguring the terrorist computer, asking what the latest message said.

"It looks like that last message was from the other terrorist. He's found some explosive material and is ready to meet the first guy—I guess the guy that jumped out the window."

I continued messing with the other computer, only half listening to what she said.

"He's ready to build the bomb, and the window-jumper here in Oslo has some connection who can get them into Israel. The guy in Tuzla is thanking him for the work."

I saw the little wireless icon show a green connection. "Yeah! I'm online, and his account's still open."

"Didn't you hear what I just said?"

"Yes. I did. Give me the thumb drive. I want to copy all the messages in the sent-and-received files."

She passed it over, allowing me to load the new messages.

"Send that to them. See what they say."

She did as I asked, saying, "Pike, what are we going to do? I guess I had hoped that at some point we'd figure out we were wrong, especially since nobody else wanted to believe us. Every time we find something new, it tells us we're still right."

"Hang on. Let's see what the rest of the messages say.

We can figure it out from there. Let's face it—everything said so far could be for a single suicide attack into Israel. It may be nothing more than that. One bad guy is dead, and the other has no idea. We're still on the offensive here."

One hour later we got the answer from the Taskforce. It didn't get any better. The man who had jumped to his death had been very sloppy with his operational security. He had saved every e-mail sent and received, allowing the analysts at the Taskforce to build a pretty good picture. In a clinical report, the analytical transcript summarized what the e-mail exchanges contained. In general, it gave the strongest backing yet to Ethan's original take, buttressing the theory that the overarching goal was to deploy a weapon in Israel and blame the Iranians. The report read in a clinical, unemotional manner:

A. Terrorist A, having suspected that the pair was under surveillance, fled to parts unknown as a preventative measure.

B. Terrorist A, to ensure a self-healing operation, enacted a negative trip wire, whereby a penalty would be incurred if a code is not sent. Terrorist A will immediately cease all communication, assume the plan is compromised, and conduct the event at the earliest convenience, most likely at a target of opportunity. The penalty is reset every 24 hours. The code itself is undetermined, but most likely is some combination of words within each e-mail sent.

C. Terrorist A has coordinated for explosives at his present location but has not physically obtained them. The explosives themselves are held at a safe house, exact location undetermined. Along with the explosives he has obtained a complex detonation mechanism, type unknown.

D. Terrorist B has coordinated for transportation to Israel and coordinated for evidence to implicate Iran in the attack. Exact details and facilitation measures are unknown.

E. Terrorist B is going to finalize coordination for transportation methods and routes today, and will be out of e-mail contact for 48 hours. Terrorist B asked Terrorist A for an additional 24 hours before incurring a penalty.

F. Terrorist A has agreed to the additional time, with the caveat that Terrorist B make every attempt to make contact.

It is the consensus of the analysts that together, both terrorists have the means at their disposal to introduce an explosive device inside the borders of the State of Israel. It is further believed that they have the means to blame the attack on the State of Iran, at least initially. It is impossible to ascertain from the e-mails presented whether this blame will withstand rigorous forensic and investigative scrutiny, although it is the opinion of the analysts that such scrutiny may not occur, as the politics of the event will more than likely supersede any attempt at determining the actual facts, with initial reports becoming the perceived truth.

On the question of whether the event will be WMD related, the analysts could not reach a consensus. There is no evidence that the device is a

WMD, as neither terrorist refers to it as such, and a review of worldwide all-source intelligence for the last thirty days does not reveal any new indications of recent WMD activity. It may simply be a conventional terrorist operation with little second- and third-order repercussions. On the other hand, it is unusual for this much preparation, coordination, and infrastructure development be used to support a single suicide attack.

"Not good. Looks like we have forty-eight hours to play with. The muj motherfucker's going on a suicide run after that. No telling where."

Jennifer's face was pale. "We can't do this alone. Can't Kurt go get that guy now? Isn't this enough proof?"

"No. You heard his dilemma in D.C. That hasn't changed. It's sad to say, but a simple suicide attack won't cut it. He's not going to risk political upheaval on an event that occurs every day all over the Middle East. He's also not going to launch based on our hunch, especially when his own analysts can't agree that it's a WMD. We have to prove it."

"How on earth are we going to do that?"

"Same way we were here. He's obviously got the device, if there is one. We didn't find one here, so we need to go there, find him, then check out what he has."

"Where's 'there'?"

"Tuzla, Bosnia. Pack your stuff. We need to leave right now. We have a little over forty-eight hours before he goes nuts. Once he's convinced they're compromised, there's no telling where he's going to go."

Jennifer remained seated. "Are you serious? Where are

we going to go? How are we going to find this guy? At least here we had the message about the coffee shop. How are we going to find him in an entire city?"

"Pull up that e-mail trace again. It should have come with a map. It's not that accurate, but I've been to Tuzla. It's not that big of a place and probably doesn't have that many Internet cafés. It's a long shot, but we go to Tuzla, find the closest café to the map location given, and see if we can find him."

"What happens if we don't find him?"

"He blows up a bunch of people. Not much we can do about it. All we can do is try."

"Shit, Pike, we can't do this. We're going to fail. *Fail.* Can't you see that? Why isn't anyone else helping. . . ."

She put her head in her hands. I sat down next to her and rubbed her back.

"Look, this will all be over, whether we like it or not, within the next forty-eight hours. All we can do is try our best. Hang in there for a couple more days and it will end one way or another."

She sat up. I was relieved to see a spark back in her eyes. "Okay. Forty-eight hours. But when we get home I am kicking somebody's ass in the United States government."

84

Five thousand miles away, Kurt Hale sat at his desk with the latest intel reports from Pike. He rubbed his eyes, not liking the choices he faced, or the repercussions if he chose incorrectly. He wasn't surprised by the fact that there was no black-and-white description of the terrorists' intentions or capabilities. It was just the way of intelligence. From past experience, he knew there was never a smoking gun. You always had to make a judgment call, read the tea leaves, and hope you came close.

He knew that Pike would take the commander's intent he had given seriously, and wouldn't send an alert unless he proved there was WMD involved. Unfortunately, according to this last batch of e-mails, waiting until Pike's call might be too late. The team wouldn't have time to launch from the U.S. to wherever Pike ended up before the terrorist fled on his suicide mission, killing thousands and possibly starting World War III.

On the other hand, if Kurt did launch a team, he would quite possibly bring down the president of the United States of America and irreparably harm the future defense of the nation, whether the threat was real or not. Once he pulled that trigger, there would be no going back.

Kurt knew that hunting a human being was hard enough, especially one who knows he's the prey. Accomplishing the mission in another sovereign country, without leaving any fingerprints—the way the Taskforce operated—was exponentially harder.

Before starting up the Taskforce, Kurt had studied any and all operations that had a hint of being the same as what he would be called upon to conduct. He had learned—through others' mistakes—that just getting the guy wouldn't qualify as a success. The most glaring example post 9/11 that Kurt had seen was a rendition operation of a radical Egyptian cleric called Osama Moustafa Hassan—or Abu Omar—from Milan, Italy, by the CIA in 2003.

The operation itself was conducted successfully, with Abu Omar captured and flown to parts unknown, but the ensuing police investigation uncovered the entire plot, to include the specific names of CIA operatives involved. Using cell phone records, car rental receipts, hotel guest logs, and other old-fashioned police work, the Italians dissected the entire operation from start to finish. His abduction was ruled an illegal kidnapping, with most of the CIA operatives named in an arrest warrant. Since Italy is a member of the European Union, the warrants were valid in every other EU member nation. The end state was an enormous embarrassment for the CIA, with scores of operatives no longer able to set foot on the European continent.

The point was driven home to Kurt that the actual capture or killing was the easy part. He decided that the Taskforce would never attempt an operation without the requisite groundwork laid first, which took time. If a target presented itself before they could conduct the operation without compromise, it was passed up to wait for a better day.

Now the Taskforce had no time to prepare, no infrastructure in place. Kurt had no doubt that they could successfully snatch or kill the terrorist currently in Bosnia, but knew that it would take little police work to unravel that Americans had been involved. Once word reached back that a capture/kill operation had occurred involving American forces, the press and the U.S. government itself would unwittingly help the Bosnians in their investigation, with the Taskforce exposed as a paramilitary organization operating outside the bounds of U.S. law. The president would have no choice but to step forward and accept responsibility.

Kurt would have liked someone to talk to, someone to bounce ideas off of, but he had purposely kept his support of Pike a secret from his own men, including George Wolffe. If it blew up, at least they would be protected as unwitting. The only one he trusted above him was the one man who would bear the brunt of the decision—the president—and he was currently on a European goodwill tour. Contacting him meant going through the White House communications room. Using that, with everything recorded and God knows who else listening, would be the same as announcing Prometheus in the newspaper.

He thought about the Oversight Council and decided against discussing the problem with them. He had never called an emergency session, and after his last meeting with Standish, he didn't trust his ability to control the direction of the conversation without presidential support.

The irony wasn't lost on him that he was contemplating becoming what he feared the most—a single man making Prometheus decisions. *My fear of Standish has made me Standish.* He was at the top of the slippery slope, looking down. *What will the reason be next time?* It was his decision, and he was running out of time to make it.

85

Bakr awoke and rolled over to ensure the weapon was still in place underneath his bed. Seeing the Tupperware container, he smiled. He wouldn't need to worry about losing the weapon much longer. Today was the day that Sayyidd was to finalize both their method of entry into Israel and the means by which they would implicate the Persian infidels. He quickly dressed, anxious to see what Sayyidd had sent. He knew it would be another thirty minutes before the café opened, but he didn't have the patience to sit around in his hotel room. He decided to get a bite to eat at a coffee shop across the street from the café. He felt like breaking into a run after leaving the hotel, but forced himself to walk at a natural pace.

The service at the coffee shop was rapid, since there were only two other customers: a woman who was clearly closer to paradise than the usual Bosniak unbeliever, as she had her head covered in a scarf, and, on the other side of the room, a small man who looked like he spent most of his nights on the street, with a frayed black leather jacket and dirt-encrusted shirt, his gnarled hands holding the steaming cup of coffee as if he had purchased it more for the heat it provided than the coffee itself.

Bakr fidgeted until he saw the owner flip the Cyrillic

sign in the window of the café, signaling the start of business for the day. He threw some money on the table and rapidly crossed the street.

Two minutes later, Bakr leaned back in his chair, disappointed by the fact that Sayyidd hadn't e-mailed him back. There was nothing to be done about it. He would just have to wait until tomorrow for the news.

He left the Internet café, walking toward his hotel at half the speed he had used to get there. Caught in his own thoughts, he failed to notice the Muslim woman from the coffee shop match his pace on the opposite side of the street.

JENNIFER LET THE TERRORIST get a hundred yards away before picking up surveillance behind him. Learning all the time, she now stayed on the other side of the street, knowing it gave her a better ability to keep him in sight without his suspecting he was being followed.

Pike had been wrong on the number of Internet cafés. There were, in fact, seven within the radius of the e-mail trace. They had driven by each one and had discarded several, one because it was located next to a police station, a few that catered solely to tourists, and those that had their interiors monitored by cameras.

The process of elimination left two cafés, although Jennifer knew they were wishing away alternatives that might, in fact, be used. Luckily, both she and Pike knew what this terrorist looked like, allowing them to split up. The window-jumper wasn't the man that Jennifer had seen in the passport in Guatemala, which meant that she would recognize the remaining terrorist.

One location could be watched from a coffee shop situated across from the café. The other had no convenient location from which to view the entrance other than from a parked car on the same street. Not wanting to repeat what had happened in Oslo, with the terrorist recognizing him, Pike had given Jennifer the coffee shop location, buying her a quick disguise of a multicolored head scarf, a set of large, cheap sunglasses, and an ankle-length peasant's dress of the type that was ubiquitous in downtown Tuzla. She had dyed her hair black to complete the transformation, and now looked like one of a hundred Bosnian women roaming the city center.

Jennifer had been sitting in the coffee shop for only a few minutes, barely enough time to think through her surveillance plan, when a man resembling the passport photo came in. She wasn't sure, since the guy in the passport had a beard, and this man didn't. When he left the coffee shop and entered the Internet café, all doubt fled her mind. *That's him.* She called Pike and told him. Before Pike could find her, she saw the terrorist leave. *Showtime. You can do this. Not that hard.* Jennifer started window-shopping across the street, keeping pace within a football field of him, all the while running through her mind what she was going to do next.

Her mission was simple: Figure out where he was staying, right down to the hotel room. *And I need to be right behind him to do that.* She started to close the distance before she realized her dilemma. *What if he walks for the next four miles? I can't stay right behind him. He'll wonder what the hell I'm doing.* The longer she walked, the more she wanted to close the gap. *Fuck. This sounded easy on the airplane. He's going to turn into a hotel and I'm going to lose him.*

After three blocks, seeing the sidewalks beginning to swell with noontime shoppers that would give her some cover, she decided she'd pushed her luck for long enough. She crossed over, her fear of missing the opportunity now overpowering.

She picked up a position about thirty meters behind him, keeping him in sight through the crowds, but just barely. She called Pike and gave him an update, referring to the terrorist with the name she had seen in his American passport in Guatemala.

"Carlos has gone about four blocks from the café. I'm still on him. He appears to have a destination, but he's not moving with a purpose. Are you nearby?"

"Yeah, I'm right outside your Internet café. I'll be within a couple of blocks of you at all times. How're you holding up?"

"I'm okay. I'm about to fall asleep on my feet, but I'm okay. Nothing like exhaustion to tamp down stress."

"I hear you. I just about ran over a kid five minutes ago. Look—I'm having second thoughts about how far we should push this today. I think you should just pinpoint his hotel. We can find some other way to figure out his room. I think we're risking too much by you going in."

Why's he changing the plan now? "Would you think this was too risky if you were walking behind him, or is it because you're afraid of me getting hurt? We only have another twenty-four hours, and I don't think we'll get another chance. I'm going to finish this."

"Damn it, this isn't a *game*. There's no trophy at the end. If he figures out what's going on, he's liable to freak out and launch the device right in the hotel. Yeah, I'm worried about you, but I'd be just as worried about any teammate."

She watched Carlos pause outside of a hotel, looking left and right. She saw him glance at his watch like he was trying to decide what to do. She vaguely heard Pike continue.

"I'm just saying that I'm not sure a plan hashed out on an airplane after four days without sleep is the one we should go with. Let's figure out where he's staying and take a long, hard look at our options."

She didn't reply, focused on the terrorist. She saw him turn to the hotel entrance. *Holy shit. This is it.*

"Hello? Jennifer, you still there?"

"He just went into a hotel. I have to go."

"No! Jennifer, wait—"

Jennifer hung up the phone and rushed forward, reaching the door in time to see Carlos moving to a stairwell inside. Focusing on the backpack he was wearing, she gave a half thought to quitting, Pike's warning reminding her of the stakes. *Stop that. Get it done.*

To her right she saw a wizened old man at the front desk, reading a newspaper and paying her no mind. Crossing quickly to the stairwell, she heard footsteps above her, separated by a single landing. *How am I going to figure out his floor if I can't see him?* It dawned on her that she would only need to listen. When she heard his footsteps cease, she would simply exit on the next floor.

No sooner had she come up with the plan than she realized she was hearing nothing but the echo of her own footsteps. Carlos had exited the stairwell.

*   *   *

I FLUNG THE PHONE against the dash. *What the hell is she thinking? What was I thinking coming up with this dumbass plan?* I didn't even know where she was. From where I was parked outside the café I could see about forty different ways the terrorist could have gone. *Calm down. Think.* From what Jennifer said, they were somewhere within a four-block radius. How many hotels could there be inside that? Logically, they were probably west, toward downtown. I threw the car into drive and headed deeper into the city. *Please don't get hurt. Please, please.*

HURRYING TO THE NEXT FLOOR, Jennifer paused outside the stairwell doorway, listening for any sign that someone was just beyond. Hearing nothing, she gathered her courage and opened the door.

Carlos stood directly in front of her, fumbling with his key and softly cursing the old lock. At the sound of the stairwell door, he turned. Jennifer stumbled back, preparing to flee into the stairwell in a fight or flight response. *Get a grip. He doesn't know who you are.* Her eyes locked with the terrorist's. He smiled, nodding hello before returning to work his key. She smiled back and moved past him, seeing the hallway end about fifty feet away at a men's room. *What am I going to do when I reach that? Shit. I've got no reason to be here. Should've turned around.*

She kept walking, feeling his eyes on her back, wondering what the hell was taking him so long. *Get in your damn room.* As she approached the bathroom, her mind began to work in overdrive. *What if this is a men-only hotel? Or has floors separated by gender? He's going to know something's up. He's going to kill me.* She envisioned him stalking right behind her, knife raised to strike. With a superhuman effort, she kept walking forward, fighting the urge to turn around and look. She reached the end of the hall. *Now what? He's going to see you standing here doing nothing.* She turned to the last door and did the only thing she could think of, giving it a soft knock while stealing a glance back the way she had come.

The hallway was empty. She felt her knees begin to buckle and threw her hand up to the doorjamb for support. *Jesus, why don't I listen to Pike?* Leaning against the frame with her eyes closed, taking quick, shallow breaths, she didn't even notice that the door had opened until she heard someone speak.

Standing in front of her in his underwear, black socks held up by garters on his skinny legs, wearing a stained wife-beater T-shirt, was a man of about sixty. The man looked at her suspiciously and said something in Serbo-Croatian.

Feeling nauseous, Jennifer said, "Sorry, wrong room."

She speed-walked back down the hallway, taking care not to make any noise as she opened the door to the stairwell. Reaching the street outside, she walked as fast as she could without breaking into an overt run, not conscious of the direction she was going or the people she bumped into in her haste to put some distance between herself and the hotel. She made it about ninety feet before the enormity of the close call hit home. She stopped, reaching toward the nearest wall for support. She leaned over and threw up, splashing vomit on her legs and causing people on the sidewalk to immediately avoid her.

Racked with dry heaves, she sank to her knees. A

crowd began to gather around her, with several people asking her questions in Serbo-Croatian. *Get out of here. You're making a scene. You're going to blow this whole thing.* She stood up, brushing off the help and looking for an escape route. She heard a man on the street yelling something, then recognized it was Pike. *Thank God.*

She ran to the SUV as Pike opened the passenger door. She leaned back into the seat, shaking and gasping for air as if she had just run a marathon. Pike gunned the engine, pulling away from the hotel.

"You all right? What the fuck happened?"

"I'm okay." She closed her eyes, breathing deeply, repeating the phrase as if to prove it to herself.

"I'm okay."

86

In his Crystal City office, Lucas pinched the bridge of his nose, wanting more than anything to smash his computer into little pieces. No sooner had his team landed in Norway than the beacon had shown up in Tuzla, Bosnia-Herzegovina.

Through Standish he had confirmed that Kurt Hale was still in D.C., which led him to surmise that Hale had passed the device to Pike. This was a net positive, provided he could keep a bead on the pager and get his team in position quickly. The first update of its location had been Oslo, causing an immediate launch of the team. Now the damn thing was saying it was in Tuzla. *This is turning into a wild-goose chase.*

On top of that, someone here in the States was making inquiries about the death of the analyst and the shooting at the Four Courts pub. He hadn't been able to determine who it was but knew it wasn't official law enforcement. Someone had made a connection between the two and was closing in on his operation.

Regardless, he still had a mission to accomplish. He gave the order for the team in Oslo to redirect to Tuzla at their earliest opportunity. He then turned to his Rolodex and compiled a list of names for a backup team.

There was no telling where this was going to lead. He needed the flexibility to launch from inside the European continent while maintaining a reserve. He would fly with the backup team, directly coordinating the mission on the ground. It was becoming impossible to command and control the complex twists of the operation from five thousand miles away, and getting out of the country right now had a certain appeal. Not to mention the chance of getting out of the office and into the hunt.

I WAITED FOR JENNIFER to finish brushing her teeth before continuing the debriefing. When she returned to the bedroom, she looked a little bit like her normal self, the fear of her close call receding.

"Are you burned? Did Carlos suspect anything? Do anything when he saw you?"

"No, not really. I think I'm fine there. I'm pretty sure he thought I was a local. I didn't say anything, and neither did he, so I didn't give him any reason to think I was anything but a Bosnian."

"Good. I think we drive on with the plan. We wait for him to check his e-mail tomorrow. While he's in the café, I'll crack into his room and see if I can spot the device, or come up with anything else that screams WMD. Run me through what you saw for security. What were the door locks like, did you see any cameras, was there a lot of traffic, basically anything you can think of that might interfere with me getting in."

Jennifer sat for a moment, collecting her thoughts. When she was ready, she gave me a fairly detailed description of everything she had seen. I expected her to have tunnel vision, focusing on her survival after the contact with Carlos like most civilians would have, but she was able to clearly describe the exact number of doors in the hallway, the type of lock, the direction the doors opened, and even give a fairly good description of the old man she had inadvertently run into, to include what she could see of the layout of his room. I had gotten less information from trained operators in the past.

"So, you're positive you didn't see any cameras? Anything being fed to the front desk?"

"No. There's nothing like that. I'm sure of it. The hotel's fairly run-down. The only thing I saw was an old guy at the front desk, and he didn't even look up when I entered."

"You're positive that there was only one lock, and it was like ours here in the hotel room?"

"Well, I'm positive that's true about the guy's room at the end of the hall. I can't say for sure about Carlos's room, since he was standing in front of his door when I went by, but if all of the rooms are the same, then it has a lever, and a keyhole above the lever. That's it."

"And it looked just like our door lock?"

She pointed at our hotel room door. "Down to the engraving on the plate."

"Okay. I think I can get in with our key."

"How? Just because it looks like our lock doesn't mean our key will fit. I mean, really, I've seen enough *Magnum PI* episodes to know that won't work."

"If our key will fit into Carlos's keyhole, it will work. It won't open it, you're right, but I'm going to take our key and make a 'bump key.' If I do it right, we should walk right in." I grinned. "Trust me."

87

We attempted to have a normal evening at a local restaurant. Jennifer was subdued throughout the meal and I could tell that something was eating at her. When we got back to the hotel, she asked, "What are we going to do if you don't find any WMD in his room?"

"Honestly, I don't know. I've been thinking about it, and don't have an answer. Let's take it one step at a time. Right now, I just want to build the bump key and go to sleep. We're both exhausted, and it might be the only rest we get for a while."

Jennifer nodded absently. "Yeah, I could use the sleep."

"Look, quit worrying. We can't do anything right now and it'll just keep you awake all night."

"I know, I know, but . . . Pike, I'm scared. I really thought I was going to die today. I have never been so terrified. This guy plans to kill a lot of people. I don't think I realized what that meant until I thought he was going to kill me."

Here it comes. She's seen the elephant. Need to give her some confidence. "Quit it. Fear isn't bad. You just have to manage it, like you did today. This guy is going to *try* to kill a lot of people. We're going to stop it. Right?"

She stared at me, like she wanted to say something but wasn't sure how. I'd seen it before. Soldiers who had a near-death experience and wanted to talk, but didn't know what to say. Her next question threw me completely off.

"What was Heather like?"

I sat in silence for a second or two, wondering where this was going.

"I . . . I can't sum that up in a sentence. Why'd you ask?"

She didn't answer the question. Didn't appear to even hear it. "You know what I was thinking about at the end of that hall? I mean besides the scared-shitless feeling that I was going to die? I thought that if Carlos killed me it would destroy you."

"Come on. That's not going to happen. You're not going to die and I'm not going to self-destruct."

She ignored me. "I felt so selfish. I had run into the hotel because we needed to get the information and it was *my* life. But it's more than my life."

"Jennifer, it's never just your life. There's always someone else who'll be hurt. That's just the way it is."

She was staring at me now, making me uncomfortable. The twinge had come back with strength unlike anything I had felt since I had lost Heather. It was almost unbearable, a confusing mishmash of emotions that made me want to flee the room. *Stop it. Remember the mission. Focus.*

She continued. "I understand that my death would affect others. I mean, my death would also crush my mother, but I didn't think about her. This was different. The fear of dying wasn't as bad as the fear of causing you pain."

Where is this going? I had intended to give her a little support, a shot of confidence, like I had done many times to other soldiers in the past, but I was no longer on familiar ground. "Well, I'm glad I'm good for something. If pity gets the mission done, then I guess I'm a pathetic loser who'll fall apart at the drop of a hat. Can we talk about something else?"

"That's not what I meant. I . . . I don't know what's going to happen tomorrow and I just wanted you to know. . . ."

"What?"

She leaned in and kissed me.

"You're a good man. Much better than you give yourself credit for. Maybe better than anyone I've ever met. You didn't kill your family. You should let it go."

I sat still, frozen by her actions.

Jennifer laughed. "Wow. I finally made you speechless. I should have done that days ago."

"Jennifer . . . I . . . uh . . ."

She put a finger to my lips. "Shhh. I'm not looking for any deep thoughts. I just wanted to say that . . . in case . . . you know."

In case one of us dies.

I remained silent for a second, not wanting to dwell on tomorrow's potential consequences.

"You asked about Heather," I said. "She was . . . a lot like you."

The words seemed to bring a sense of calm to her. She put her hand over mine.

"Thank you. I think that's the best compliment you could ever give."

"You're welcome. Now, enough of the soul-searching."

I stood up, locking my churning emotions away and trying to concentrate on the mission. "We need to get some sleep. We have a big day tomorrow."

She remained seated, saying nothing, but with a different glint in her eyes.

"What?"

"I . . . I'd rather you didn't sleep on the floor tonight. Is that all right?"

The question took a moment to sink in. When it did, it separated my confusing emotions like oil and water. *Jesus, you want to.* The thought made me feel like a traitor, disgusting me to my core. *I can't sleep around on Heather.* The notion was ridiculous, but overwhelmingly there nonetheless. *Shit. What do I say now?*

Jennifer had just been through a harrowing event, and had now opened herself up in the most vulnerable way possible. The close call itself may have been to blame. I didn't want to hurt her. I sat down again, taking her hand.

"Jennifer . . . I . . . I . . . can't do that. . . ."

She blinked and looked at the floor. When she looked back at me, she was smiling, like I had confirmed something.

"I know. I just meant you could use a good night's sleep. Off of the floor. The bed's big enough."

We both knew what she really meant, but somehow my answer had avoided giving her pain. I smiled back, relieved. No matter what happened tomorrow, tonight I had done something right.

88

At seven A.M. Bakr got out of bed and completed sunrise prayers, wishing for the thousandth time that he were allowed the small dignity of a prayer rug as part of his cover.

At seven thirty, he walked to the end of the hall for his shower. He fidgeted in his room for another forty-five minutes, playing with the remote detonator and going through linkup options with Sayyidd in his mind. At eight forty-five, he packed up the weapon. Stepping onto the street, he looked left and right, then proceeded at a slow pace to the Internet café so as to arrive after it had opened.

JENNIFER SAT IN HER PEASANT'S DRESS with a different colored scarf in place on her head. The scent of vomit still occasionally wafted from her dress like the odor of a dead animal in the attic, the stench floating about with no clear source no matter how hard you walked around sniffing the room. She had done her best to clean the dress but had missed a spot somewhere.

She'd awakened before their alarm went off, the room artificially dark due to the heavy drapes, the corners showing the feeble light of dawn creeping in. Raised on an elbow, gazing at Pike's slumbering form, she could barely pick out his features. *This isn't fair. Why are we all alone out here? Why can't we just go home and forget about terrorists and WMD? Let someone else stop him.* She had lain in bed feeling a sense of impending doom, as if she had been convicted at trial and today was the day she reported to jail.

That feeling had remained throughout the morning, and persisted still. Sitting in the back of the coffee shop, she jumped when her cell phone rang, spilling her cup of coffee halfway to her mouth. She heard two simple sentences.

"He's on the move. He's going slow, so it'll probably be five minutes before you see him."

She acknowledged the call and hung up, the sense of dread building in her gut. Four minutes later she saw Carlos down the street, walking at a leisurely pace toward the café. It would take him a couple more minutes to get there, but that would only be more time for Pike inside the hotel. She picked up her phone and dialed, wishing it were still yesterday, not wanting to set things in motion.

OUTSIDE OF BAKR'S HOTEL, one of Lucas's team members from Norway sat looking at a map, trying to determine if he was in the location dictated by the computer plot of the beacon. He glanced up to get his bearings on the street, looked back at his map, then did a double take when he saw Pike exit a Pajero SUV fifteen feet to his front.

He had pulled into the parking spot five minutes before merely to pinpoint his location, one of several sites being reconnoitered by Mason's team based on the trail left by Pike's pager. This was supposed to be just a familiarization day, necking down possible locations and getting a feel for the area. Fumbling with his cell phone, he calmed down enough to dial, ducking to prevent Pike from seeing him.

"Mason? Yeah, I've got Pike. He's fucking right in front of me. The girl's not with him. He just went into a hotel."

He paused, listening. "I don't know if he's staying here or not, but if you want him, I need to get the team here ASAP. I'm not going to try to take him out on my own. I haven't seen the girl, but let's face it, he's the threat. Get rid of him, and she'll be easy."

He listened a few more seconds. "Yeah, I get that we can't track the girl, but this guy's been pretty damn dangerous from the beginning. You sure you want to attempt a capture?"

Hearing Mason's reasoning, he relented. "Okay, I can do that. If you get a team here, I should be able to close on him fast enough to prevent him from doing anything."

He listened a moment.

"If he gives me any trouble, I'll smoke him right here. If not, he can tell us where to find the girl. I don't recommend going in after him. We can ambush him when he comes out. Maybe we'll get lucky and they'll both come out."

I ENTERED THE HOTEL LIKE I BELONGED THERE, carrying the bump key and a small mallet I had purchased the day before. I moved straight to the stairwell, the distance and direction exactly as described by Jennifer. Exiting the third floor, I paused in front of Carlos's door. I strained my ears, listening for any movement behind it or from the rooms down the hall. Hearing none, I placed the key in the lock. It slid in easily. I moved it forward, feeling the clicks of the pin tumblers through the key. When I went past the last tumbler, I pulled the key back out until it clicked once. Looking left and right, ensuring I was alone, I raised the mallet and gave the key a sharp rap, applying torque as soon as the key seated past the pins. The lock broke free, the cylinder turning. I rotated the key and turned the lever, pushing the door. It didn't budge. I paused a half second and pushed again. The door was still locked. Puzzled, feeling the press of time, my instinct was to simply kick in the door. *Hold on. Solve the problem.* I went through possibilities in my mind. I remembered that European locks sometimes go two full rotations to open. I repeated the procedure with the bump key, feeling a sense of relief when the lock cylinder turned again, releasing the door. I entered the room.

Once again, Jennifer's description was spot-on. The room was small, consisting of a single floor lamp, an end table, a chair, and a twin-sized bed. No closet and no bathroom. I went to a duffel bag on the chair first, sifting through the clothes. Finding an American passport, I saw that Jennifer had been right. The name inside was Carlos Menendez. *Hispanic. Very smart.* I wrote down the name and passport number for future reference. I saw nothing else of interest. I moved to the nightstand, opened a drawer, and found a wooden box inside. I pulled it out, setting it on top of the end table.

89

Bakr sat at his usual table, staring at the in-box for the e-mail account between him and Sayyidd. The box was still empty. Bakr felt drained, cheated of the gift for which he had so patiently waited. What the hell was Sayyidd up to? Why hadn't he e-mailed? Bakr couldn't bring himself to think the unthinkable—that Sayyidd had been captured or killed. Surely he was just hung up on his trip with Walid. They were too close to paradise for something to happen now.

He calmed down, mentally chastising himself for his pathetic wheedling. The forty-eight hours were up, and he had told Sayyidd he would immediately leave, but he decided to give his partner more time. Too much was riding on Walid's coordination. If Sayyidd didn't send an e-mail by this afternoon, he would begin looking for routes into Israel on his own, planning his next steps. He would return tomorrow morning and check again, giving Sayyidd an extra twenty-four hours. If there was still no response, he would assume the worst and leave Bosnia, heading perhaps toward Turkey, then onward into Syria.

Leaving the café, Bakr chastised himself again for his

weak constitution, purposely picking up his gait to get away from the thoughts of self-pity.

INSIDE CARLOS'S HOTEL ROOM, I was carefully checking the box for any indications of booby traps when my phone rang.

"Yeah? How long? Okay. I'm headed out. No, I haven't found anything, but I really haven't had time to check it out completely."

I started the chronograph feature of my watch, figuring I had about two minutes to finish up. Sure the box was clean, I lifted the lid and found my first indication of terrorist activity. I pulled the remote detonation device out of the box and turned it over in my hands, considering what I should do with it. I looked for some way to disable it without Carlos being aware, but quickly dismissed the idea, since I couldn't read the Cyrillic writing and didn't know enough about its operational capability to ensure I did it correctly without his knowing. I placed it back in the box and returned it to the drawer exactly as I had found it.

Before I closed the drawer I noticed a scrap of paper with an international number written on it. I copied it down, assuming it had been placed there by Carlos, since the end table and room were completely barren, without a trace of rubbish.

I searched the rest of the room but found nothing at all. I had confirmed the detonation device the terrorist had referred to in his e-mail, but still could not prove or disprove any connection to WMD. I looked at my watch, seeing one minute and forty-three seconds had passed since Jennifer's call. *Out of time. I need to go.*

I left the room, getting as far as the stairwell before I remembered I hadn't relocked the door. I ran back and inserted the bump key, gave it a whack, and attempted to turn the cylinder. It refused to move. I repeated the procedure with the same results. A gunfighter's mantra floated through my head. *Slow is smooth and smooth is fast.* Ignoring the clock, I started over, carefully feeling the pin tumblers and setting the key perfectly. I gave it another whack, breaking the cylinder free. I turned it over once, feeling the cylinder lock up again. *No more time to mess with it.*

Trotting rapidly down the stairs, I considered my next move. I had no proof of WMD, but I was personally convinced that Carlos had it and was carrying it around on his back. I contemplated taking out Carlos by myself but quickly tossed that idea. It would be impossible for me to get close to him without being recognized and I had no idea if the device was armed and ready to explode, inside a glass container that could be thrown, or simply in a Ziploc bag that would break in a scuffle. The idea of wrestling Carlos for control of a device that could kill hundreds by just being released into the atmosphere was best left in the category of last resort.

I reached the second-floor landing and made a decision. *Alert the Taskforce.* I hated to do it, and knew I had promised I wouldn't without positive proof of WMD, but I decided that the circumstances warranted action. I pulled out the pager/beacon and hit the series of keys necessary to trigger the emergency signal. Nothing outward changed. It beeped once, returning to show the time. Reaching the first floor, I placed it back in my pocket and exited the stairwell.

Nodding to the old man behind the desk, I left the hotel and walked straight to my SUV, purposely not looking in the direction of the Internet café. I unlocked the driver's side door, looking down and hiding my face from anyone coming down the street. I was about to sit down when I felt the barrel of a pistol jammed into my kidney.

"You make a single fucking move, and I'll kill you right here. I know your capabilities, so trust me—I won't be guessing about your intentions. You understand? Nod if you do."

I did as he asked.

"Raise your hands where I can see them, but don't make it look like you're surrendering." The man jammed the barrel again. "Don't do anything stupid. I can kill you and get out of here clean."

I placed my hands on the door and roof of the car, feeling the press of time. I was facing the direction Carlos was coming from and would be impossible to miss. I didn't mind the gun in my back but needed to speed this up.

I turned my head slightly, about to say something when I was cut off angrily by the man with the gun, "Keep facing forward! Don't move a fucking muscle until my partner arrives."

I attempted to hide my face, saying, "Look, I'm willing to do whatever you want. I'll come quietly. Can we just get moving?"

"What the hell are you looking at? Raise your head."

I continued looking down.

"Raise your fucking head or you're dead. Do it now."

I sensed the fear in the man and could almost feel his finger tightening on the trigger. I reluctantly raised my head, seeing another man approaching out of the corner of my eye.

The man gave me a wide berth. "Car's on the way. Should be here in five seconds."

"Good. This guy scares the hell out of me."

I ducked my head again, counting out the seconds. I reached to five with no car when the man with the gun said, "I tell you to raise your head again, and we'll be throwing a body in a car. I'm not sure you can feel it, but that's a fat barrel in your back. There will be no noise."

I raised my head, hearing a car pull up.

I looked up the street, trying to see anyone resembling Carlos in the distance. Spotting no one, I scanned the people closer to me. I saw a man resembling Carlos approaching, no more than twenty meters away. I was about to push my luck and lower my head again when the man met my eyes. I recognized the terrorist at the same time he recognized me.

90

Jennifer picked up a loose follow as soon as Carlos left the Internet café, staying on the opposite side of the street. When he increased his pace to a fast walk, closing in on the entrance to his hotel, Jennifer felt the anxiety in her stomach begin to skyrocket. *Why hasn't Pike called? What's he doing?* Carlos was one block away and about thirty seconds from getting so close that Pike couldn't possibly leave without being seen. She kept his pace, almost forced to break into a trot, the speed of events ratcheting up her anxiety even further. She pulled out her cell phone, preparing to call Pike again, when she saw Carlos abruptly stop. She paused, watching closely. She saw Carlos spin around and take off running the way he had come.

Stunned, Jennifer looked down the street, trying to identify what had caused the reaction. She saw Pike standing next to his car talking to two other men, a second car idling next to him. She turned back to the terrorist, seeing him in a wild run, his pack flopping crazily on his back as he dodged through the foot traffic.

She watched him for a split second longer, then returned to Pike and the two strangers. She saw Pike drop his keys out of view of the men, then move toward the sedan in the middle of the street.

She felt light-headed, the crowds around her fading into the background, the pressure to make the right decision crushing her like a physical thing. Pike had said he hadn't found the WMD, which meant that Carlos must be carrying it. *And Carlos has seen Pike. He knows we're after him.* He was now running to parts unknown with a massive death trap on his back, under pressure to use it sooner rather than later.

She saw Pike get in the back of the sedan. She knew that the men who had him intended to kill him. Would kill him, possibly in the next few minutes. She watched the door close, frozen in place. *What can I do about that? Nothing.* In fact, they wanted her as well. Showing herself now, attempting some pathetic action to stop three trained killers from driving away with Pike, would only guarantee both their deaths. She felt a burning sense of helplessness.

She ran the choices through her mind, her brain working at the speed of light. *What would Pike do? He wouldn't dither back and forth. He'd make a decision and execute.*

She began a fast walk in the direction of Carlos, knowing what Pike would tell her to do. *Go after the terrorist. Save the many. Screw the few. Do what was best overall, not what you would like to do.* She broke into a run, going through in her mind what she should do next, evaluating options for the surveillance and tracking of Carlos. She looked back the way she had come, watching the car make a U-turn and begin driving away from her.

She continued running, straining for a glimpse of Carlos to her front. She glanced back one more time, seeing the taillights of the car flash, watching it make a right turn out of sight. Her conviction faltered. Unbidden, she had a vision of Pike lying in a roadside ditch. Her mind superimposed the graphic violence she had witnessed in Guatemala over Pike's visage, a nightmare flash in her mind of Pike's head exploded open, brain matter and bone splattered on the ground, his eyes looking skyward, unseeing.

The image hit her with a physical blow, causing her vision to blur, her breath to catch in her chest. She slowed to a walk, the image burning into her soul. She turned around and began sprinting toward the Pajero. *Fuck the terrorist. Someone else can stop him.* She knew the decision might mean hundreds of people died, but there was only one death she cared about, and she would do what she could to stop it, no matter how insurmountable the odds.

Pike had talked of saving the many as the best course of action, that numbers alone decided the value of the effort, but that didn't seem right anymore. It wasn't just about numbers. Jennifer knew beyond a shadow of a doubt that someone would die today. Probably a great many people, including her. If Pike was standing when the smoke cleared, the sacrifice would be worth it.

BAKR PAUSED TO CATCH HIS BREATH, leaning against the corner of a building. He had run flat out for ten or eleven blocks, randomly turning left and right to lose himself in the city. So far, he hadn't noticed anyone chasing after him—in fact he hadn't seen a single reaction to his flight whatsoever. He believed he was momentarily safe.

Clearly, it was no coincidence the man from Guatemala was now in Tuzla. He was here because of Bakr. But if that was so, why hadn't the man chased him? Why let him run away without a single response? Maybe the man didn't recognize him. Maybe they knew that the partner of Sayyidd and Walid was in Tuzla but didn't know exactly who he was. If that was the case, he was still invisible. He needed to get back into his hotel, retrieve the detonator, and head to Sarajevo. That would be a complete break from everything the enemy knew. He would once again be on the offensive, safe in his anonymity.

He considered the hotel room. It would be a great risk to return there, since the enemy could be waiting for him. On the other hand, he hadn't told Sayyidd where he was staying, and the very fact that he had seen them nonchalantly hanging around out front indicated a coincidence, since they would never have been so brazen had they thought he was staying there. The detonator was worth the risk. He would just have to be very careful in his approach, ensuring the hotel didn't contain a trap.

91

The men in the sedan had the presence of mind to handcuff me, but luckily they had done so after I was in the car, leaving my hands to my front. I would never have made that mistake, but I wasn't going to complain. *Hopefully, they'll learn this lesson the hard way.*

In front of us was another sedan holding three men, leading the way out of town. I was sandwiched between the two guys who had taken me off the street, both of them hard-looking with a military air. The man known as Mason, sitting on my left, was the only one who spoke.

"Pike, listen, this is nothing personal. I'm sure you understand. It's just a professional mission. You're going to die. That's a given. The choice you have is how. We need to know where the woman is. Tell us that, and we'll simply put a bullet in your head."

Well, there you go. Nothing personal about it. They just want to kill me.

"Go fuck yourself."

Mason nodded. "Yeah, okay. I figured my little speech wouldn't convince you. That's no problem. We have plenty of time."

We had left Tuzla and were headed south on a twisting two-lane road, the view alternating between rugged hillside and steep drop-off. The lead car was occasionally lost from sight around the sharp curves. After five minutes, we made a right turn onto a narrow blacktop that followed the ridgeline, heading deeper into the rugged terrain, away from the heavily trafficked main road.

Mason continued. "Look, I'll give you something to think about while we drive, just to ensure you know I've got the stomach for the work: I'm the one who talked to your friend Ethan. Trust me, it wasn't pleasant. I took no joy in it. The conversation lasted a long, long time."

You little coward. I stared deep into Mason's eyes, causing him to look away. "You should have kept that to yourself. I would've only killed you in self-defense. Now I'm going to kill every fucking one of you purely for the pleasure of it."

The driver gave a nervous laugh and said, "We'll see how tough you are in thirty minutes, asshole. Your buddy thought he was pretty hard, too, right up until we punctured his daughter's eyes."

Before I could respond, he jerked the wheel to the left, shouting, "Shit! Hang on!"

We were slammed back into our seats by a collision from the rear. The car swerved lightly right, then left, coasting to a stop on the side of the road.

Mason looked out the back window, saying, "What the hell happened?"

"We got rear-ended by some Bosnian bitch. Wait a sec and I'll get rid of her."

"Hurry up," Mason said. "We lost our escort. Assholes kept going around the curve without even looking back."

"Yeah, yeah. I'll throw some money at her. Give me a minute."

I turned around and felt a shock slap through my body. Jennifer was walking slowly to the back of our car, stooped over with a hand at her back, giving the impression of an injury.

Both Mason and the man to my right were focused on the activity to the rear. I didn't have a clue what Jennifer was doing but knew instinctively it was going to be borderline insane. *She has no idea what she's up against.* Before I could even come up with a half-baked plan, I heard Mason shout.

"What the fuck is that bitch doing! Jesus Christ!"

I looked back again and saw the driver doubled over holding his genitals. I watched Jennifer wind back up and kick him again, apparently attempting to drive the man's balls up into his neck. He fell over onto the ground. Jennifer proceeded to kick him in the head with all of her might. *Jesus, she's lost her mind.* His body was now on the ground and hidden from view, but Jennifer's leg pistoning back and forth like a jackhammer was not.

Mason threw open the door, screaming, "Watch Pike!"

The man to my right was still fixated on the beating the driver was receiving. The situation clicked—one man exiting the vehicle, the other focused on the fight. Neither one paying attention to me. *Big mistake.*

I drew my head back and slammed it full force into the face of the guy to my right, the hard, thick portion of skull right above my eyes caving in the brittle bones of the man's nose and eye sockets with a sickening crunch. Rotating toward Mason, I used every bit of strength I had to kick out with both feet, catching him halfway out of the door and launching him out of the car like I'd strapped his ass into an ejection seat. I ripped the Glock out of the lifeless hands of the first man and dove out the other passenger door just as Mason recovered and began firing into the back of the car, missing me but killing his unconscious partner.

I heard Jennifer scream, "Pike!" and then the sounds of gunfire. *Shit. Move faster. She's gonna get hit.* Rising up on a knee, I saw Jennifer running to the back of our rental SUV with Mason standing up trying to get a clear shot.

I raised the weapon in a two-handed grip, smoothly settled the front sight post on Mason's head, and squeezed the trigger.

"Good-bye, motherfucker."

The force of the round threw Mason into the ditch beside the road, his head cratered open with bits of bone and brain matter oozing slowly onto the ground, his eyes looking skyward, unseeing.

Seeing no other threats, I said, "Jennifer! Come out! It's okay."

I ran to the passenger side of the Pajero. "Hurry up. We need to get out of here before that second car comes back, and I can't drive with handcuffs on."

Jennifer jumped inside and turned the key. The starter ground over but failed to catch.

"Shit! I didn't hit you guys that hard."

"Forget this thing—get out and go to the sedan." I jumped out just as the other carload of men came flying back around the mountain curve at a high rate of speed.

"Too late," I said. "Come out this side. Get behind the Pajero."

Jennifer crawled across the seat, exiting the passenger

side and ending up on the ground next to me. Before I would lose the chance, I ran in a crouch to Mason, ripping the spare magazines for the Glock 19 from his belt.

The car came to a stop, both doors flying open, the men crouching behind them preparing to fire. The air grew silent, with the occasional whisper from the men carrying across the roadway.

I peeked around the Pajero, talking over my shoulder to Jennifer. "What in the hell was that all about?"

"Beats me," Jennifer said, breathing hard. "I was winging it, but it worked."

I pulled back around. "Man, I've seen some seat-of-the-pants shit before, but this is an absolute record."

I saw her laugh, apparently completely confident that everything would now turn out perfect. *She doesn't get it. She's used to miracles happening.* I knew the truth. I was facing three trained killers with two magazines of 9mm and shackled hands. I looked to our rear for an escape route and saw a hill rise about seventy-five feet. *We go that way and we'll be cut down for sure.* I knew what I would do if the roles were reversed—put suppressive fire on our position while maneuvering a force to flank us. Once they got on the high ground, with no cover between us and another gunman to our rear, we would be dead. There wasn't a lot I could do about it, since the odds of killing all three while they used the car for cover were just about nonexistent. *Shit. We're going to need another miracle.*

92

I poked my head up to get another read, immediately drawing a fusillade of fire. In that glimpse I had seen two men preparing to flank us. In order to do so, they would have to cross the road, traversing about forty feet of open ground. I leaned around the front of the SUV, keeping low, and saw them begin to move. I snapped off a few rounds, driving them back, but drew fire on my new position in return, forcing me to jerk back behind the Pajero.

Jennifer, still oblivious to our peril, asked, "What are we waiting for? What are we going to do?"

"Jennifer . . . we're in deep shit. I'm not sure what we're going to do. Once they get to the high ground in back of us, we're dead. The only thing that runs through my head is the ending of *Butch Cassidy and the Sundance Kid*."

Jennifer's smile faltered, the predicament finally getting through. "How are we getting away?"

I peeked around the front of the Pajero again, seeing the two men making another break, both armed with assault rifles. I was able to snap off three rounds before being driven back, thinking I had winged one of the men, but ultimately unsure. They made it across the open ground. I rolled back around, leaning against the frame of the Pajero. *Fuck. We're done.*

"This is it. I want you to crawl underneath the SUV. They're going to reach the high ground in about a minute. From there, they'll kill us both. Once I start shooting, I want you to roll out the other side and run across the road, into the underbrush. Run down the hill as fast as you can. With any luck the other guy will be focused on the firefight and won't be able to get a clean shot at you. Once you're in the woods, keep going. Don't stop for anything. Run until you hit another car or a town."

Jennifer sat still, the implications of the plan sinking in.

"What about you?" she said. "What are you going to do?"

I couldn't meet her eyes. "I'll find you in the town. Okay?"

"No, no, *no*. I'm not doing that. Let's both run."

Please don't make this hard. "Look, someone has to pin them down so the other can make the run. Since you can't shoot, that leaves me. Please, get underneath the damn truck. We're out of time."

Jennifer's face flushed. She started to say something else but thought better of it. She leaned close and gave me a peck on the cheek. I saw her eyes begin to water.

She said, "I'll see you in the town."

I leaned back, resigned to what was coming. Make no mistake, I wanted to live. But I had a greater responsibility to Jennifer. There was no way I was going to let her die. I was disappointed at how my life would end, but not tragically so. I had had a good run. My only shame was the mess I had become over the last year. *Just when I crawl out of the sewer, I get killed. What a waste.* God seemed to enjoy knocking me around. I just hoped my death would be enough entertainment. *Let Jennifer live. You're getting me. You'll have my entire fucking family. Isn't that enough? Please let her get out of here.*

I looked at the sky, seeing the contrails of a jet high overhead, wondering where it was going. I thought about Carlos, running loose with a device that would kill hundreds, if not thousands, hoping someone else would be able to stop him. I saw a helicopter in the distance, lazily circling as if looking for something. I felt a spring breeze against my face, light and warm, rustling the tree branches. *Why have I never taken the time to enjoy that before?* I wondered if my life had been good enough to earn the right to see Angie and Heather in heaven. I checked my weapon, saying another silent prayer for enough speed to give Jennifer a chance to escape. *Don't let them kill me quickly.*

I scanned the hillside and picked up a glint of metal in the sunlight at the top. *It's time.*

I dropped the half-empty magazine from the Glock, loading in a full one and laying out the other full one on the ground. I waited for the fight.

"They're at the top of the hill. Hold for about five rounds before running. Once you start, do not stop. Don't look back at me. Don't worry about the gunfire. Do you understand?"

I could hear Jennifer sobbing, ripping into my soul. *Jesus. Don't cry. It's okay.*

"Yes . . . I understand. Pike . . . don't die. I . . . I . . . Please don't die."

As I formed my answer, knowing that these words would be my last on earth, my pager began to vibrate.

What the hell? The screen said: *Mark your position. Mark your position. Coming in hot.* I stared at the pager for a split second before the truth sank in.

"Get out from underneath the truck! Take off your headscarf and start waving it. *Hurry.*"

She wiggled out, ripping off the scarf and waving it back and forth like she was in a lifeboat in the middle of the ocean.

"What's up? Why am I doing this?"

Someone else is God's entertainment. Someone who fucking deserves it. "It's the cavalry. Stand by. These assholes are dead."

The pager vibrated again with a single word: *Marked.*

The world had returned to level, all doubt and fear banished by that simple message. I had been given an incredible gift. *A miracle.*

The feeling of relief was short-lived as the air around us snapped with supersonic rounds puncturing the steel of the Pajero. *Shit. We're out of time.*

"Get back underneath the truck. *Move!*"

I shoved Jennifer bodily backward, then began raking the hillside with the Glock, hitting nothing but hoping to suppress the incoming fire. Bullets were chewing up the ground around us, causing a feral fear to surface. *So fucking close. Not fair.* I got Jennifer behind the wheel well, jammed underneath the axle, and turned to fight. The two men were coming fast, one firing while the other moved, flip-flopping down the slope. I snapped off the remaining rounds in the first magazine and reloaded, traversing the hillside to draw the fire away from Jennifer's position. I dove behind the cover of a large tree, the ground around me exploding in pops like someone was working a Weed Eater against the trunk. *Where's the fucking cavalry?*

I could tell who was moving and who was shooting because there was a pregnant pause in the fire each time they transitioned. I waited for it, then rolled to the right, attempting to keep them from flanking me or closing on Jennifer. I knew it was ridiculously stupid, but if I didn't even up the odds, we were both dead, and the small gap was all I had in my favor. If I did it right, I'd be facing the man on the move, and he'd block the shot of the guy providing the suppressive fire.

As soon as I aimed the Glock, I knew I was dead. I had picked the wrong side. The man to the left was moving, and I was facing the barrel of the man to the right, aimed directly at my head fifty meters away. Too far to hit with the pistol, but easy for the assault rifle. *Fuck.*

No rounds came my way. Instead, the man turned and aimed at the crest of the hill. For the first time I felt the deep thump of rotor blades. A Bell 427 helicopter sliced across the top of the hill, incongruously painted in bright yellow and white, with a logo emblazoned on the side reading Epeius Oil Exploration. The helicopter's blades bit into the air as it rotated violently, the open door facing the earth. I could see the team inside, held in place by the centrifugal force of the rotation, three holding SR-25 sniper systems at the ready. I couldn't hear the gunshots due to the rotor blades but saw the muzzles flash, two times each.

"Yeah, motherfuckers. Eat that."

The helicopter immediately circled around to the other side of the car hiding the single man. He jumped up and began to run, only to be cut down by the precision fire of the men inside, the 7.62 match-grade rounds flying unerringly toward his head as if it was a giant magnet.

Finished shooting what it could see from the air, the helo hovered over the road, its right door sliding open and a man hooking a thick fast-rope to the rescue hoist hanging off the side. Once attached, he threw out a kick bag holding the remaining coils. It fell to earth, the fast-rope snaking out of the bag on the way down. No sooner had the rope hit the ground than men began sliding down it, controlling their descent by hand and foot pressure alone, like a fireman sliding on a pole. One after another they exited the aircraft, until a total of five men were on the asphalt, fanning out and looking for targets.

When the last man hit the ground, the crew chief dropped the rope, allowing it to fall harmlessly to earth. The helicopter banked and flew out of sight.

I stood up, manacled hands in the air, saying, "You got them all."

The lead man turned, smoothly training his weapon on me. There was no overt threat in the gesture. The weapon simply moved as naturally as if the man were pointing.

I stared, mute at first, before words finally found me.

"Holy shit, *Knuckles*?"

93

Knuckles was trying very hard to remain serious, but he couldn't stop a giant grin from creeping over his face.

"Hello, Pike. Seems like I'm always bailing you out of trouble."

I was grinning like a schoolboy, too, but I didn't give a shit. "Hey, Knuckles. It's really good to see you."

Knuckles came over while the rest of the men fanned out, clearing the immediate area and searching the dead men and vehicles.

I stuck both of my cuffed hands out for a handshake, which Knuckles ignored. Instead he gave me a powerful embrace.

He held my shoulders. "It's really good to see you too. Alive, I mean."

"Man, you ain't lying. Ten more seconds and you'd be scraping us off the street."

"Who's the babe?"

Jennifer scowled, but I knew Knuckles was just kidding, trying to figure out what was going on.

"This is Jennifer Cahill, my partner in crime."

Knuckles smiled warmly, disarming her anger, and shook her hand.

I asked, "How in the hell did you get here so quick? I tripped my beacon less than an hour ago."

"Yeah, I know," he said. "It caused us to shit our pants. We were alerted by Kurt a day and a half ago. We're over in Tunis, doing 'Oil Exploration.'"

Knuckles raised his hands, making quotation marks.

"We were told simply to get our ass to Tuzla with the total package and link up with you. We got to Sarajevo this morning from Italy, refueled, and were heading in to Tuzla when your beacon went off. We homed in on it and saw the gunfight going on down here. The beacon wasn't precise enough to tell us who was who on the ground, so we paged you."

I couldn't believe how close we had come to dying. *I've used up my luck for the rest of my life. Or maybe it wasn't luck.*

One of the men came up with the keys to the handcuffs on my wrists. I gave him an embrace as well, like it was old home week. I waved in the direction the chopper had left.

"What's up with the helo? That's new."

Knuckles grinned. "Yeah, we got that since you left. It's a Bell 427. State of the art. You know the motto of the Taskforce—'Money's no object.' Anyway, we were tracking your favorite guy over in Tunis and about to pull the trigger when we got the redirect to here."

He paused, looking around at the battle site they had just entered.

"Enough about my story. What in the hell is going on here? Who are these guys?"

"I have no idea about the assholes here, but there's a terrorist in Tuzla that needs to be killed. We gotta get moving."

One of the men hollered at Knuckles, standing over the driver Jennifer had beaten into submission. He was awake and scared.

"Hey," I said, "I forgot about him. I guess there is someone who can tell us what's going on."

I pulled Jennifer out of earshot of the other men.

"Listen, I need you to get into the car across the street. Sit in the back and close the doors."

She looked at me warily. "Why? What are you going to do?"

"Well, I'm not asking you to leave because I'm going to make him take his clothes off."

"Pike . . . are you sure? I don't think this is right."

"Jennifer, he told me in the car that he blinded Ethan's daughter. You don't have to like it, but I'm going to make him tell me what's going on."

Jennifer's eyes widened, but she stood firm. "And then you're going to do what? Kill him? Just like that? In cold blood?"

"We don't have time for this. Carlos is still running loose."

"I get that, Pike, I really do, but I don't want you to kill him. You'll be just like him. You'll become him. Is that what you want?"

Can't she see he deserves to die? I thought about what had happened today. Who was alive and who was dead. And the gift. *Shit. Maybe she's right.* "Okay, look, I won't kill him. Just get in the car."

Jennifer hesitated, then jogged away to the car without looking back.

Knuckles and I walked to the man on the ground, now sitting up and staring at us, fear radiating off of him, his face swollen and bloody from where Jennifer had kicked the shit out of him.

I squatted down to his level, tapping his forehead with the barrel of my Glock. "Hey, tough guy. Didn't quite work out like you wanted, did it?"

He began babbling instantly. "Don't kill me. I'll tell you everything I know, but I swear, it isn't much. I'm just a contractor for a company called Trident Global Threat Analysis. Please . . ."

"Trident Threat Analysis, huh? How original. Let me guess—you're a SEAL."

The man nodded.

The Trident was the nickname given to the badge awarded after successfully completing Basic Underwater Demolition/SEAL, the arduous selection and training course that produced the Navy SEALs. Not too hard to figure out.

"How about that," I said to Knuckles. "He's a fuckin' retard. I can't believe a SEAL came that close to killing me."

Knuckles, an ex-member of SEAL Team Six, chuckled and said, "Maybe we should cut him a break for choosing the right branch of service."

"He's on the team that tortured and killed Ethan's family."

Knuckles's smile faded. "Maybe you should let me take a crack at him."

I returned to the driver, staring into his eyes, conveying no mercy. "Maybe I will. Depends on my man here. What's your mission? Who hired you? Who's the boss?"

Six minutes later I had all the information I could get from the guy. It wasn't much. He knew that the company was owned by a former SEAL named Lucas and that the mission had been to simply kill Jennifer and me. The good news was they were the only team on the ground, and the Taskforce had killed or captured everyone in it. As to how the team had found us, the man only knew that it was by electronic means. Somehow, Mason seemed to have an accurate picture of where Jennifer and I had been both in Oslo and in Tuzla.

Knuckles asked, "How could he get a beacon on you without you knowing?"

"I have no idea. It could be our cell phones, but I don't see how. We've had three different sets since this started, and bought each one with cash. The only other thing I've been carrying is Kurt's personal pager. It hasn't been out of my hands since he gave it to me, so it can't be that."

"You don't have anything else they could have altered?"

"No. We've been living like vagabonds. Doesn't matter now, anyway. The team's dead and we need to get moving. We can figure it out later."

Knuckles pressed a hidden switch on his thumb, giving his men commands through what looked like an ordinary Bluetooth cell phone earpiece. They coalesced around us, all reaching out and shaking my hand or giving me an embrace.

Knuckles gave a brief warning order of what was about to happen, then split the team between the two functioning sedans. After they began loading, he looked down at the driver, asking, "What about this guy?"

Fuck turning the other cheek. "Well, I promised Jennifer I wouldn't kill him, so I guess he stays. Doesn't mean I can't make it hard for him."

I aimed the Glock at the man's knee and pulled the trigger, shattering the patella. I ignored his scream. *You're lucky you didn't kill Jennifer. Nothing would've stopped me from carving you up.*

"Come on," I said, "let's go. We can talk as we drive."

I left the man writhing on the ground in pain, blood jetting out from the wound. Four steps to the car, I glanced at the sky. *No lightning. Must be Old Testament Day.*

We got in the car with Jennifer. Having heard the gunshot, she gave me a questioning look.

"Don't worry, I didn't kill him. If he's smart, he'll come out alive."

She said nothing.

I headed back to Tuzla, the other car following. "Before I begin, give me a rundown on what you've got here. What are the assets available?"

"Well, we were at Omega in Tunis, so we've got the total package on the ground. You saw the 427. We can use that in a pinch, but only to exfil whoever we get. We have no cover for status here, so I can't let that thing be seen doing anything operational. Dropping in here was pretty damn risky, but the gunfight sort of overcame that. It's supposed to only be passing through. Obviously, we have the team you just saw, but we have the same issues. We're all employees of Epeius, supposedly exploring for oil in Tunisia. We're really hanging it out here. There'll be no plausible deniability if this falls apart."

Knuckles was gently reminding me of the potential sacrifice should things go wrong.

"Sounds like you guys were about to pull the trigger.

Sorry for the change of mission, but, trust me, it's worth it."

Knuckles said, "You'll be sorrier about it when I tell you who the target is."

"Who?"

"Your old pal Crusty."

"Crusty? That bastard's still around? You guys haven't taken him off the board?"

"Yeah, he's still around, and he's moved up in the world. He's no longer just a low-hanging fruit to whack for the hell of it. His security ain't getting any better, though. We can fall right back into it, as long as we don't blow our cover over here."

Shit. He's not going to like what I have to say. "Well, it's going to be sticky. Our target knows he's being hunted. It's going to be very hard to take him off the board without a firefight. Whatever happens to your cover, it'll be worth it."

"Let me guess, you've found Bin Laden and he's here with a nuke on his back."

"Close. It's not Bin Laden."

He didn't need a map drawn out. "You're tracking someone with WMD? For real?"

"Yeah. He's going to deploy it soon. Maybe in the next few hours. And I don't know where the fuck he went."

94

We planned our next moves in a parking lot a block down from Carlos's hotel. It had been a little strange at first, since out of the five folks on the ground, four of them had been my guys—including Knuckles. I could tell he was unsure how to handle the situation, so I had deferred to him and simply fallen in as a team member. He didn't say anything, but I knew him well enough to see he was greatly relieved. I also knew he'd let me take over the team if I'd asked. But I wasn't ready. These men had worked and trained relentlessly for a very long time to hone their skills to a razor's edge. Part of that was individual, and part was teamwork. Either way, I was on the low end of the stick for both. *Taking charge would just be an ego trip. Knuckles is the man now.*

And he had grown quite a bit while I was gone. I watched him with the team and could see they were clicking. It was painful to admit, but my taking over would just make them less effective. I was satisfied with providing the intelligence, letting Knuckles handle the assault. I knew he'd defer to me if it came to that.

Knuckles finished giving instructions, wasting little time on fancy planning. "All right, remember we're dealing with WMD. Take that seriously. Pike's going to lead the way. We get to the room and scan it for heat. If we see a source, we go in hard. If the room's clean, we take it slow. No sense alerting the rest of hotel if we don't have to."

I'd be lying if I said I didn't get a kick out of the mission brief. It was like nothing had changed, and I was sitting on the patio at Tbilisi. *About to save the world.* Maybe that was a bit much, but it *was* a good feeling. Knuckles finally got to us. "Jennifer, I want you to engage the man at the front desk. Keep him focused on you until we're in the stairwell. We're going to enter in two groups, three seconds apart. Once the second group is in the stairwell, you can head on back to the cars here."

Jennifer nodded, apparently comfortable in her role.

"Pike, I want you to lead so we don't make a mistake on the door, but once you've pinpointed the objective, I want you to pull security while we're in the room. Okay?"

Security? That sucks. I didn't push it. "No issues. It's all yours. You got any kit for me?"

Knuckles grinned, obviously relieved that I hadn't demanded to be with the entry team.

"Of course," he said. "I knew you wouldn't have anything. You never did." He turned to a man carrying a civilian pack. "Give him the kit we brought."

Inside the bag was some communications equipment and an H&K UMP, just like everyone else was sporting. It was a small, lightweight submachine gun built primarily of space age polymer, which made it easier to break down and hide from X-ray inspection. While it lost the power of the cartridges chambered in carbines and rifles, the UMP had the appeal for the Taskforce of being easily concealable. There were other automatic weapons that were smaller, but the UMP chambered the more power-ful .45 caliber instead of the ubiquitous, but less power-ful, 9mm. The .45 had a much greater knockdown power and was a subsonic round, thus making the UMP easy to suppress without the need for special rounds. I pulled it out and did a functions check, knowing it was unneces-sary, but doing it anyway out of habit.

Once he saw I was ready, Knuckles started the ball rolling, telling Jennifer, "Showtime. We'll be thirty sec-onds behind you."

She glanced at me with a question. No fear, just un-sure of whether she should leave. Wanting my approval before she followed the orders of a stranger she'd just met.

I said, "Time to put your money where your mouth is."

She broke into a smile and started walking, saying, "Please. I'm just wondering if I should stay behind so I can pull your ass out of the fire."

Knuckles let her get out of earshot before saying, "Is she good to go? What was that all about?"

"Nothing," I said. "She's just good at winging shit. And proud of it too."

"Fucking great. Just what I need. You guys must be the perfect couple."

Two minutes later, the entire team was stretched out along the hallway of Carlos's room. I pulled security the way we had come, the team prepared to enter, with var-ious team members covering the other hotel room doors. One man turned on a sophisticated thermal viewer that allowed him to see heat sources through a variety of construction materials. It couldn't determine if the source was a man, but it would alert us if a large mass in the room was putting out more heat than the ambient temperature. Short of a space heater being operational, it would be a human, since the device wouldn't register such things as candles or lighters. The man swept the room quickly, then shook his head. Knuckles turned to the next man, twisting his hand as if he were using a key.

The man immediately dropped to a knee, pulling out a much more sophisticated version of my homemade bump key. It looked like a key on one end, with a baseball-sized lump on the other. He inserted it into the lock, pressed a button on the baseball, and swung the door open, leaning back as the entry team blew by him into the room. Five seconds later we were all in the room, discussing what to do next.

"He came back and took the detonator," I said. "Ballsy guy—I'll give him that."

Knuckles said, "You got any idea where he went, or are we now at the 'let's go fishing' stage?"

"I only know he has a safe house somewhere in Bosnia, presumably around here, but it could be anywhere."

"That's not much of a help."

Then I remembered. "Wait. I copied a phone number while I was in here. I'm positive it was something of his. It might only be his contact here, but it might also be the safe house. Either way, we hit that thing and we'll get something out of it."

"We've both hit jackpot with less in the past," Knuckles said. "Let's get the hell out of here before the locals start sniffing around."

Back on the street we linked up with Jennifer at the

parking lot. I told her what we had, then read off the phone number to Knuckles.

She asked, "What're you going to do, try to call that and trick him?"

"No," I said, "we're going to try to pinpoint it. The landline infrastructure here was pretty much demolished during the war, so this number is probably a cell phone. Just about every single cell phone built now comes with a GPS feature. What we're going to do is try to turn it on and have it send us its location. It might not work, because we need a digital network to slave on, and the phone needs a GPS. If we have both, we can dial the phone without it ringing and do some black magic."

While I was talking one of the team had pulled out a normal-looking cell phone, telling it to boot up a hidden program. He said, "We're good. We have a digital signal."

He dialed the number, watching the screen. "It's a cell."

He spent thirty seconds thumbing the keypad as if he were texting a friend.

"Got a GPS."

He continued to work it for another half minute.

He looked up with a smile. "We're in business. Got a grid."

He read the grid reference out to another man working a laptop computer with a world mapping program.

"It's a house in Sarajevo," he said, "north of the river about middle way through the city."

"That's outside the Republic of Srpska part of Sarajevo. It'll be a Muslim neighborhood," I said. "That fits.

We need to get moving. He's got a few hours' head start."

Knuckles said, "Well, unless he's flying, we can beat him. We sent the 427 to the old Eagle base. No Americans there now, since SFOR left, but it is an operational airport. We can probably beat him to Sarajevo. The key question is whether that's where he's going."

"Won't know that until we get there. Let's load up. You can follow me. I still remember the way to Eagle base."

An hour and a half later we were flying south, with me fuming over the bureaucratic nightmare of getting the helicopter fueled up and ready to go at the old air base. *Third-world bullshit. Maybe we should chase Carlos right into that damn terminal. Give 'em a sense of urgency.* Watching the ground race underneath, I relaxed. It would take less than forty-five minutes to get to the Sarajevo airport, even taking into account more bureaucracy. We should be very close behind him.

My mind wandered to the team we had killed, and how they had managed to find Jennifer and me. Eliminating everything I could think of, I was left with one possibility: They had somehow managed to track Kurt's pager. I couldn't see how on earth that would be true, since the pagers were treated as sensitive items in the Taskforce, but there simply wasn't any other explanation. Short of some miraculous new technology, it was the only weak point I could find, and if Kurt's pager was compromised, they were all probably vulnerable. With the team dead or bleeding on the side of the road, it was no longer a threat on this operation, but the compromise would need to be explored after we finished here.

95

Bakr waved his arms at a cloud of smoke spewed out by the departure of an inner-city bus. He surveyed the area, getting his bearings. Juka had given him directions to the house from the Sarajevo bus station, and Bakr had researched the city while waiting on Sayyidd to answer, but the image he had created in his mind didn't fit the reality on the ground. Finding a map on the wall, he quickly located the tram that would take him to the city center.

The trek back to his hotel room had been little trouble; the man from Guatemala and his henchmen were nowhere to be seen. He hadn't pushed his luck, spending less than three minutes in his room, packing up his things and taking the detonator. The bus ride itself had been inside a bouncing, belching machine that should have been retired years ago, but that was quickly forgotten in his eagerness to find the safe house.

Riding the tram parallel to the Miljacka River, he could still see the scars of war throughout the city, with mortar impacts slashing the street and bullet holes pocking the walls of older buildings. As the tram closed in on the old section of the city known as Bascarsija, he began to notice a healthy security presence. Pulling into his stop inside the old market area, he saw an overwhelming number of police. Too many for simple tourist protection.

His first thought was that he had already been tracked and was now on the verge of getting captured. Frozen in place for a second, the panic rising, he debated whether he should simply keep riding. He was broken out of his thoughts by someone else trying to exit.

Speaking in English, Bakr asked, "Why're all the policemen here?"

The Bosniak smiled and said, "Big ceremony today. It's the fifteenth anniversary of the Markale massacres during the war. They're just here to keep the peace."

Hoping the relief didn't show on his face, Bakr exited with the man, asking what the massacre was about.

"During the siege here the Serbians launched three separate mortar attacks on the Markale Market right up the road there. Killed a lot of people. They're putting up a memorial today. Something more formal than a Sarajevo Rose."

Bakr thanked the man and moved on. He hadn't known the name of the market but had read about the actions there, as well as the siege itself, in his research earlier. The Markale was the largest outdoor market in Sarajevo, and the attacks had killed hundreds of civilians who were simply trying to survive. He knew a "Sarajevo Rose" was the impact of the mortars themselves, now filled in with red paint and left as they were the day they were fired as a reminder of the callous act. Ultimately it had convinced the Western world to intervene in the bloody conflict.

It disgusted Bakr that the Muslims here would turn to

the West as their savior, going so far as to put up a monument commemorating their weakness. Maybe if they didn't act so much like the infidel, they wouldn't have needed the help of the infidel.

He walked through the old section of the city and entered into the close-packed neighborhoods to the north. Using Juka's directions, he approached what he thought was the safe house. It was hard to tell, since all the buildings looked the same, but this was the only house with a large concrete planter in the front yard, looking like a horse trough filled with dirt. Juka said it had been put up after a mortar round had landed in the street, but that it now served to keep people away from the front of the house. He could always call the number Juka had given him for the clean safe house somewhere nearby, but preferred to use that as a last resort.

Bakr glanced around, seeing nothing more than a couple of pedestrians walking away from him and a woman beating a rug on an upstairs balcony down the street. He went around the left side of the house and jumped the waist-high concrete wall of the courtyard. He moved to the northeast corner and squatted down. Looking closely at the ground, he searched for a length of twine coming out of the neglected patch of flower garden. Pulling gently, he followed it for a foot and a half, eventually pulling up a key. He smiled. He had the right house.

Bakr unlocked the back door and swung it open without going inside. He stood and listened for thirty seconds. Hearing nothing, he walked slowly into the house, smelling the musty, cloying odor of a space rarely used. He searched throughout the downstairs and upstairs, slowly walking and listening for anyone or anything. Eventually he was satisfied that the house was empty.

He moved to the front and peeked out the window, getting a clear view up and down the street. He saw nothing out of the ordinary. The woman continued beating her rug, dust swirling around her head, giving her a halo in the afternoon light, but nothing else was moving. He found the basement door and went downstairs, fumbling a second before finding a light. He took a moment to let his eyes get used to the dazzle.

Against the back wall, stacked from the dank floor to within a foot of the ceiling, were enough explosives to take out an entire city block. He saw blasting caps, AK-47s, blocks of Semtex, ball bearings, remote-control aircraft components, cotton vests, wiring, and anything else he might need to build his suicide weapon. It would take him some time to integrate his special detonator, but he had the expertise to make it work.

LUCAS WAITED ON HIS MEN outside of the Sarajevo customs area, where he was the first to make it through. The team didn't have to worry about anyone in customs searching their bags—they were using black diplomatic passports secured by Harold Standish through contacts inside the National Security Council.

He hung up his cell phone for the third time. For some reason he had no contact with Mason at all. The phone simply rang and went to voice mail. He chalked it up to a sorry cell network. He watched the first team member come through the customs hallway, carrying his duffel bag covered in military patches. *Way to go, 007.*

Real inconspicuous. He reflected again on the fact that he was dealing with the second tier. They were all special operations guys, but not the cream of the crop. They were good enough at executing simple missions, with specific instructions, but would not do well at contingencies or thinking on the fly. *They sure as shit aren't as good as Mason's team. Why won't that guy answer the phone?*

96

On final approach to the Sarajevo airport, I could see a flurry of activity on the tarmac. Instead of airport workers in yellow vests, I saw a bunch of guys in business suits casing the place. Getting on the headset, I asked the pilot what was going on.

"Some sort of ceremony in town today. They got dignitaries coming in from all over Europe."

Knuckles cut in. "That's great. Should make our illegal exfil with a captured terrorist that much easier."

I grinned at him. "Come on. What's the point of living on the edge if you don't lean over a little?"

He just shook his head.

The pilot said, "Might work out better for us. We're being directed to land at the old military side of the airport—away from all the security. Should be able to come and go freely from this end."

The Taskforce team exited the Bell 427 while the rotors were still turning, the whine of the engines slowly growing weaker. I was itching to get started. "We need some vehicles. Anyone know anything about this airport?"

One of the pilots responded, "Yeah, there're a couple of car rental places inside. The terminal's small, so it shouldn't be too hard to find."

I wanted to start barking out orders but held back, waiting on Knuckles.

"Okay," he said, "pilots stay here, ready to move. Keep the helo on strip alert, because we're probably coming back fast. Be prepared to flex to Tuzla. If I see the security's too tight, we'll exfil from there with the package. Retro, you and Jennifer go find a couple of rental cars. Something big enough to carry up to two more men than we have. You know what we're looking for."

Jennifer and the man called Retro had started to leave when one of the pilots shouted, "Wait. I'll go with you." Jerking a thumb over his shoulder at Knuckles, he said, "He always wants 'strip alert,' but we usually end up sitting around for days, begging for food from anyone who passes by. I'll get a car for us as well."

After they left, Knuckles asked me, "Well, what do you think? What's the play? Go in hard right now?"

He was doing all the right things, taking input from everyone, making me a little proud for no reason whatsoever.

"No. I think we should get the cars and conduct a recce to get a feel for what we're dealing with. From there we can make a plan."

Knuckles nodded. "Yeah, I agree." He started giving orders. "Break out the visor cams. We don't have a lot of time to go pure clandestine, so don't worry about a deep install."

Jennifer and Retro returned in two beat-up sedans within twenty minutes, with the pilot right behind them. No sooner had they exited the cars than four men began rigging one for clandestine surveillance. Using four cameras the size of lipstick tubes, they hid them in the upholstery and fed the lines into a digital recording device. The cameras would give a three-hundred-and-sixty-degree view around the chassis, allowing detailed planning against the target.

While the car was being rigged, Knuckles and I studied a map of the target area with Bull, the man he had selected to conduct the reconnaissance. Knuckles had picked him because he most closely resembled the indigenous population, and I'd given him the leather jacket I'd bought as additional camouflage.

Knuckles asked me, "You ever been here? What're the neighborhoods like? Is it like Fallujah where everyone knows you don't belong?"

"I haven't been in that neighborhood, but you know the city's a significant tourist attraction, at least as far as Bosnia goes. I'd say that most of the tourist stuff is centered on the sights downtown but they probably see strangers quite a bit all over the place. It's probably not suspicious to drive by, especially just once."

An idea hit me. "Hey, why don't you take Jennifer as some eye candy? She's pretty good under stress, and she's already dressed like a Bosnian woman. She'll lower the profile if she's in the car. If they have some sort of early warning going on, they won't suspect a couple."

Knuckles chewed the idea over for a few seconds. "Yeah, that'll work. Bull, you got an issue with that?"

"No. It's not like we're going into a gunfight. She'll be much more of an asset than a liability."

I saw Jennifer getting a little aggravated with the talk going back and forth, as if she weren't there or didn't have a vote.

"You game for that?" Knuckles asked her. "All you'd have to do is ride and keep your eyes open."

She said, "Yes. I can do that. Thanks for asking. I figured you were just going to tie me to the front seat no matter what I said."

Knuckles looked at me like he was going to scrub her participation.

"She's good to go," I said, smiling at her. "She just likes to be the one telling people what to do. She doesn't listen to me either."

Jennifer purposely ignored me. "You're Bull, right?"

"Yeah."

"What do you want me to do?"

BAKR PLACED THE FINISHING TOUCHES on his explosive package, attempting to make it as unobtrusive as possible. Ordinarily he would have embedded the entire device in ball bearings and nails in an effort to create as much death and destruction as possible. In this case, all he wanted to do was disperse his Tupperware container of death without destroying it. He opted not to build a suicide vest but to utilize the backpack he already had.

His biggest challenge was creating enough of an explosive effect to distribute the toxin over as large an area as possible without actually destroying it in the fire and pressure of the explosion itself. It was a delicate catch-22. Go too large, and all he would get was an explosion that consumed the toxin. Go too small and he would kill very few people. Luckily, he'd had in-depth instruction on how to tamp the material and protect it from the fire of the explosion as well as how to maximize the downwind hazard once the poison was airborne.

Taping down the blasting caps, he heard a vehicle approach down the road. He had been in the house for more than an hour and hadn't heard a single car yet. He paused his work and went upstairs to the window. He relaxed, seeing a beat-up sedan pass by with a Bosnian man and woman inside. They paid his house no attention whatsoever. He returned to the device, connecting his special detonator to the blasting caps.

97

Lucas wondered how far he could push his second-tier team. He decided to opt with their strengths: full-on frontal assault. Hopefully, it wouldn't come to that, as he had to assume that Mason's team was on Pike right this moment, tracking him for the kill. He asked his tech man what was taking so long for a beacon fix, only to be told for the third time that the pager track download was locked up. He took a deep breath and let it out, asking again, "How much longer is this going to take?"

"It's rebooting now. Shouldn't be but a few more minutes."

Lucas walked in a small circle, physically forcing himself to remain patient. The men returned from the rental agency, driving an SUV and a sedan. Together, they were large enough to hold the team plus equipment and perhaps one more person. The vehicles blended into the traffic around the airport, pleasing Lucas with the selection. *Figured they'd bring back a convertible Mustang or a two-seater Porsche. Maybe I'm selling them short.*

One of the drivers said, "Somebody just beat us to the counter. This is all they had available, but they should work."

Lucus mentally rolled his eyes. *So much for thinking they made a conscious decision.*

KNUCKLES PAUSED THE VIDEO at the target house, seeing the same two-story style with a courtyard in the back that appeared all over the area. The front of the house was clean, with a clear path to the door. No parked cars or fences to worry about. It was located on the east side of the street, with houses on both sides and behind it.

"What were the atmospherics of the neighborhood?"

"Quiet," Bull said. "In fact, we didn't see a single automobile. A couple of pedestrians and a few folks tending gardens, but definitely not a hopping place."

Knuckles stared at the still image. "All right. I don't want to do a mounted assault. We do an offset on the main thoroughfare to the east, then conduct a dismounted movement to the target from the south, the opposite direction of the recce drive-by. We move in two groups. One takes squirter control in the rear; the other enters the house from the front."

Knuckles paused for questions, then continued. "Remember, we don't know what's in this house, so we can't treat it as a hostile force. Discriminate on every target. We don't want to end up killing some old housewife."

Knuckles finished the briefing by splitting the team, putting me on squirter control. *Out of the fight again.* I didn't argue, knowing he was right.

I moved off to the rear of the lead car, checking my weapon and spare magazine placement, working to ensure I could reload in a minimum amount of time. Jennifer walked over, tentatively asking, "Hey, I'm not trying to bug you, but I didn't understand any of that."

I continued working on my kit. "Based on what you guys are saying about the traffic in the area, we don't want to drive right up to the target. We'll park on the main road to the east, then walk there. It should help us remain undetected. Me and another guy will move to the back to catch what we call squirters—really just a name for anyone trying to run. We'll lock down the back of the house while the team enters from the front."

Jennifer nodded absently, looking distinctly uncomfortable at how fast this was progressing.

"Relax," I said. "Your job's over. Don't worry about us. We do this for a living."

I heard the other men beginning to load the cars. "See you in a few minutes."

She locked eyes with me, saying, "Please be careful. Let them do the hard stuff. Don't do anything heroic. Don't let Carlos blow you up."

"Cut that shit out. You should be worrying about him."

I started to get in our car when she grabbed me by the arm. "Pike, I'm serious. You might have nine lives, but you've been going through them like a chain-smoker. A life can only have so much luck. We're both working on credit now. I can feel it. Promise you'll be careful."

I looked at her, realizing she was deeply worried.

"I'll be careful. This'll be all right. Trust me."

"I do trust you," she said, with a hint of a smile. "A little, anyway. It's just that you're acting different. I can't put a finger on it, but it's like you now think you're invincible. You used to be an asshole about everything, sure it was failure. Now you act like this is all just a ride at Disneyland."

"Hey, this is what I do. I've been killing terrorists a helluva lot longer than I've known you. Sorry if I get a kick out of it, but don't tell me to go back to what I was. You don't like it, I'm sorry. But *this* is who I am."

She recoiled, and I knew I had missed the point. The hurt and pain in her expression reminded me of Heather the last night I had seen her. I remembered what I had said after Jennifer had thought Carlos was going to kill her in the hotel—*It's never just about you.*

"Jennifer, listen to me. Carlos is about to kill a lot of people. We're the only ones who can stop him. And I mean *we* are the only ones who can stop him. You and me. You saved my life, and I don't mean just today. There's got to be a reason for that. I don't want to die any more than you do, but I'm the one that's here, and I'm the one that's got the skill to kill that asshole. You know I can't promise nothing bad's gonna happen, but if it does, you need to believe it was worth it. Okay?"

She sighed. "Yeah, okay. Just don't do anything stupid. Please. Before you jump off of a building, remember you can't fly. Can you do that? For me?"

"Sure. But you need a better analogy, because I *can* fly."

"Smartass," she said. "Good luck."

98

The tech man got Lucas's attention. "He's right here in Sarajevo. About three klicks from the airport and moving east."

About fucking time. He addressed the entire team. "Listen up. We aren't going to do any fancy work over here. If we execute, it'll be a simple frontal assault, but hopefully it won't come to that. Mason's team's in-country, and presumably tracking Pike right now. The last thing I want to do is screw up an operation he's already executing."

One of the men cut in. "So we're just backup for Mason?"

"Maybe, maybe not. I can't get in touch with Mason or his team, and I don't want to lose the targets again. If we can't link up with them, we'll get a fix on the beacon and hit Pike and the girl ourselves."

He saw the team start to grin, apparently anticipating an easy kill and the bonus that went along with it. "Don't get a hard-on yet. I've told you what happened in D.C. Remember that. This isn't a cakewalk. We close in on him and take him out with overwhelming force. I'm not risking another complicated operation. We smoke him and the girl, then immediately head back here and catch the first thing flying home."

Lucas gave the team a minute to break their weapons out and kit up, then said, "All right. Let's move. Remember what I said. You might think you're a killer, but this guy really is."

Twenty minutes later, Lucas's team idled in the parking lot of a restaurant on the northern end of Sarajevo. They had traveled the entire length of the city, the cars spreading out on the surface roads in an attempt to contact Mason and his team by both cell phone and radio. They had failed, and now Lucas had a choice to make. *I can spend my time trying to find Mason, or I can spend my time trying to kill Pike.*

He decided to execute the mission with the second-tier team, since he had no idea how long Pike's beacon would last. *Batteries might be going dead while I sit here with my thumb up my ass. Lose that, and the whole game's over.* He'd worry about Mason later. In fact, he wouldn't worry about Mason at all. He'd failed, and now, as in the past, Lucas would be forced to clean up the mess. He liked to think he was being logical, but the truth was he *wanted* Pike. Wanted to be the one who twisted the knife. And make no mistake, Pike wasn't going to die easy. Not anymore. As he saw it, all of his troubles centered on one man. The ongoing investigation that had forced him to flee the U.S. was precisely the result of this asshole's evading Lucas's net. The thought rankled him. Made him eager for the hunt.

He watched the beacon track on the computer in his lap and committed the team.

"Target's on the move. He's headed this way. By the speed of the beacon, he's mounted. We'll wait here until he dismounts. Once he's stationary, we'll roll. This car will lead, passing up his location. The trail car will follow, stopping short. On my command—I say again, on *my* command—we'll execute the mission. Nobody, and I mean nobody, will fire until I give the command. Once that command is given, everyone with a shot needs to fire. Is that understood?"

Lucas waited, hearing confirmation from every member of the team. "Okay. Good. I'll call once he stops. We'll take a look at the terrain, form a quick plan, then move."

Superimposed over the satellite image of the neighborhood, Lucas watched the beacon inch closer, seeing it stop short about a kilometer from their location. Within a minute, he saw the dot move again at a much slower speed.

"Stand by. He's now on foot."

Lucas felt the tension grow. The endgame was approaching. Pike was a dangerous man, someone to fear, but he couldn't possibly stand up to the concerted effort of the entire team. *Maybe he can kill one or two, but there's no way he can kill us all.*

He saw the blip stop inside the courtyard at the back of a house on the east side of a small street. This was it.

"All right. Team leaders get over here."

He pointed out the house, dictating where the vehicles would stop and where they would dismount and set up fields of fire.

"We wait until he comes out, all night if we have to. Once he's out, we open up, killing him. Pretty simple. Any questions?"

One team leader asked, "What about the girl? Isn't she part of the mission?"

"Yeah, she is, but I can't predict whether she's with him or not. If she's with him, smoke her. If not, we'll find her later. I'm through messing around with this guy."

RETRO AND I COVERED THE BACK DOOR and a corner window from the courtyard at the back of the house, waiting on the call from Knuckles. My earpiece gave a hollow echo, Knuckles speaking in a calm monotone, "Execute, Execute, Execute." The call brought back memories of assaults past. I tensed up, waiting to see if someone would attempt to run from the rear of the house. My mind's eye ran through what was occurring in the house, the team flowing like water through the rooms looking for a threat. I heard no gunfire, which could be either good or bad.

Five minutes later I heard the all-clear given, and the back door was opened by Knuckles.

"What did you find?" I said.

"Nothing. We found the cell phone, but it's the only thing here right now. No other targets. The house looks like it's lived in, but there's nobody home."

"Great. That figures."

"What do you think? A stay-behind?"

"I don't know. I suppose that's the best course of action. We don't have anything else. I could stay, you could give me another couple of guys, and we could sort it out when the owner returns. How's that sound?"

"I'm good with that, but maybe we're getting ahead of ourselves. Let's turn this place upside down first. Maybe we'll find something of interest. In the meantime, maybe whoever owns this phone will return while we're still here."

"Let's get busy. I'll start upstairs."

A HUNDRED METERS DOWN THE STREET, Bakr had finished with the device and was sitting before his dinner of moldy bread and nuts when he perked up at the sound of another car, only the second one he had heard all day.

LUCAS PULLED PAST THE TARGET HOUSE, parking on the east side of the narrow street. The position gave him a full view of the right side of the street and clear fields of fire to the front door of the target. His satellite imagery display showed the beacon superimposed directly over the house. Pike had moved inside. He waited until he saw the follow vehicle stop short on the other side of the target about a hundred meters away before telling the team to deploy into firing positions. He watched one man exit the follow vehicle and move nonchalantly to the corner of the house where his car was parked, taking cover behind a concrete planter. Another man sauntered across the street, attempting to cover the back of the target house.

BAKR PEEKED OUT the front window. His heart skipped a beat when he saw a car stop right in front of his house with three Caucasian men inside. That was not natural at all. He continued watching from the corner of the window, wanting to believe his paranoia was getting the better of him, but feeling the adrenaline start to flow. He saw one man with a rifle walk to the corner of his house and take a knee, peering over the planter out front. The man made an attempt at hiding the weapon under his jacket, but the barrel could still be observed poking out under the hem. Bakr had seen enough.

He raced to the basement, taking the stairs two at a time. Grabbing an AK-47 and four loaded magazines, he sprinted out of the basement and up to the second floor. Peering out a bedroom window, he saw the gunman directly below him.

The man was obviously preparing to assault the house with the other men from the car. Bakr knew he had to go on the offensive, and quickly. He could attempt to run out of the back of the house, but feared it was already covered with men he couldn't see. He could run out the front, but that would send him straight into at least three men. Either plan of escape would be better if he seized the initiative while they were still getting ready. He slowly opened the window, praying it didn't squeak.

99

The sound of an AK-47 rocking on full automatic caused me to hit the floor. *What the fuck?* It wasn't in our house, so it wasn't directed against the team. I peeked out a window, trying to identify the source of the fire, the upstairs vantage point giving me an unobstructed view down the road. I saw a man crumpled on the front lawn of a house across the street, two doors down. I leaned forward to identify the shooter, calling, "Contact—house to the northeast about seventy-five meters away. One man down. Unsure of shooter location."

Knuckles responded, "Not directed at us. Everyone stay cool. Probably some sort of gang fight or leftover animosity. We don't want to get dragged into that. Get eyes out three-sixty. Call in to let me know your position."

Bull called from downstairs, "Two vehicles to the front of the house on the east side. Three men. One man at the vehicle to the north, two men at the vehicle to the south. All are armed and focused on us. They're using the cars for cover. What's the call?"

Knuckles came back, cold and calm. "Stand by. Develop the situation. We don't know if they're police, criminals, or what. If they display hostile intent, take them out."

I was about to call my position when a hail of bullets shattered the window to my front. I dropped flat to the floor. "Contact, contact. North side of house. Fire directed at me."

I rolled to my left, coming up underneath the second window of the room.

I peered out the corner of the window, looking back toward the house with the fallen man. I caught a glimpse of a man jumping out of the back courtyard and sprinting away. Before I could process what I had seen, I caught movement directly below me and refocused. I saw a man crouched and running toward the back courtyard of the house next door. I called Knuckles, raising my H&K at the same time.

"One man, armed, moving toward cover. Not the original shooter from across the street. He's holding an MP5, not an AK. He's the guy that shot at me."

I tracked the guy until he paused at the courtyard wall, preparing to vault over it. I ignored Knuckles's radio calls, squeezing off three rounds during the split-second pause. The man tumbled down.

"North side's clear. One squirter from the original house moved north."

"Roger. Bull, continue to hold fire out front unless they fire first. I don't want to kill some psycho neighborhood watch. What do we have in the rear?"

The team members covering the back courtyard began to report. The immediate threat gone, I thought about the squirter I had seen. *A man with a backpack. Carlos.*

I cut in on Knuckles getting status reports. "Break—break. Squirter is the precious cargo. I say again, squirter is PC."

Knuckles came back immediately. "Still in sight?"

"No," I said, "he's running north. I don't know who these clowns are, but we need to clear out of here quick."

"Shit . . . Roger that. All elements, all elements—anyone with a weapon is now designated a hostile force. Engage at will."

LUCAS HEARD THE FIRST AK-47 rounds and snapped his head toward the sound. He saw the team member at the corner of the house two doors down doing a macabre dance, rounds stitching him throughout his torso. He saw two arms holding an AK out of a second-story window, the weapon rocking back and forth on full automatic. He was momentarily stunned. *What the hell is going on?* He shook off the confusion, rapidly analyzing his current options. He decided to withdraw. All element of surprise was lost. The police were more than likely on the way. They needed to get the hell out of here.

He keyed his radio to speak but was interrupted by more gunfire erupting out of his sight, on the north side of the target house. He recognized the sound as an MP5.

"Cease fire! Cease fucking fire! Who's shooting?"

"Sir, it's Sanford. I had a clear shot at Pike in the target house. I think I got him."

"I said don't shoot until I gave the command! Jesus! Everyone listen up. We're getting out of here. Move back to the—"

Before he could finish, another burst of fire came from the north side of the house. It wasn't an MP5.

He swore under his breath. *This is turning into a fucking debacle. What is it with this guy?* He was like a curse.

"All elements check in."

He saw the driver of the vehicle to his rear give him a thumbs-up, on a knee and covering the house the AK fire had come from. He saw the final man from his vehicle running back across the street from the south of the target house, hearing him in his headset. "This is Copfeld. I'm coming across right now."

With the dead man shot from the window, and including himself and his driver, he had everyone but Sanford.

"Sanford, this is Lucas. You copy?" He paused and tried again, "Sanford, Sanford, this is Lucas. You copy?"

When Copfeld reached his position he said, "We need to get the fuck out of here. I want you to run back to the other vehicle and get a view down the north side of the house. See if you can find Sanford. Don't penetrate across the street. If he's there, get him here. If you don't see him, he's on his own. Watch that house to the rear. You understand?"

"Yeah. Give me some cover while I move."

Lucas grabbed his sleeve before he left. "You do anything different from what I just said, and I'm going to kill you myself."

Copfeld stumbled back from the ferocity on Lucas's face. He began running toward the other car as fast as he could. He made it about twenty meters before Lucas saw his head explode and his body crumple to the ground, twitching from the impact of multiple rounds. Lucas had barely registered his death when bullets began slicing the air near him like a buzz saw. *What in the hell is inside that house? An army?* He immediately collapsed behind his car, trying to make himself as small as possible, the bullets shattering the glass and puncturing the sheet metal all around him. The drivers of both vehicles rolled out, rapidly bringing their weapons to bear on the men shooting from the house.

The fight lasted a total of fifteen seconds. The drivers returned fire to the best of their ability, but couldn't compete with shooters safely ensconced behind cover. First one, then another fell over as a hail of bullets pummeled their bodies like an invisible meat tenderizer. The other targets gone, the bullets began to focus on Lucas's specific position, chewing up the concrete of the street, the dirt around him, and the metal of the car. He knew he had seconds to live. He thought about returning fire and going out with his guns blazing, valiantly trying to accomplish the mission. A bullet clipped his arm, making the decision for him. He felt explosive rage at his failure, knowing that Standish had kept vital information from him. *Just another retired soldier, my ass.* He suppressed his anger, wanting to fight another day. Wanting the chance to bring some pain to the Honorable Harold Standish. He raised his weapon by the barrel and waved it back and forth over the roof of the car. The firing ceased. He stood up, laying the weapon on the roof of the car and raising his hands.

He saw the front door open and two men come out, both holding weapons and scanning the area before running to his location. They drove him facedown into the ground and flex-tied his hands behind his back.

BAKR RAN UNTIL HIS LUNGS FELT like they would burst. He didn't look back, didn't attempt to blend in, didn't try to hide his fear from other pedestrians. He just let his legs churn away, running deeper and deeper into the Bosnian neighborhood. Eventually, he stopped, bent over, his hands on his knees, gasping for air. He heard nobody following. Once again, he was confused by the reaction of the enemy. Why did they never chase him down? They obviously had some method to track him, but continually made blatantly amateur moves whenever they closed in. He could still hear the crackle of gunfire from the direction he had come. What on earth were they shooting at? Were they so pathetic that they would continue shooting an empty building long after he was gone? Was he misreading the whole thing? He couldn't believe that.

His next move boiled down to two choices: He could attempt to hide here, in Sarajevo, until the heat died down, or he could get out right now. Staying was appealing, since it would allow him to put some thought into his next move, and perhaps come up with a solid plan instead of simply running on a wing and a prayer. On the other hand, he had to assume that the enemy had some method of finding him, since they kept showing up all over the globe, from Guatemala, through Oslo, to here.

He decided he needed to run, to go to the station and get on the first thing leaving, whether that was a train or a bus. If they could find him, it would be better to be a moving target. The greatest risk was the station itself. If something wasn't leaving immediately, he would be vulnerable while waiting around. It was a choke point that he'd have to risk.

100

I crushed Kurt's beeper underneath my boot, having just confirmed that was how we'd been tracked. The man known as Lucas had pretty much spilled his guts in an effort to keep his ass from getting torn apart, and the beacon information had come as an unwelcome surprise. I didn't need any more. I squatted down, getting eye-to-eye with the man.

"You guys are like a bad rash. You keep coming back no matter how much I think you're done. Is there anyone else in this country looking for us? Anyone else we have to worry about?"

"No. Nobody else. Trident Global Threat Analysis is my company. I'd know if someone else was here. You killed everyone I had over here."

"All right, shithead. We're leaving here. If you're lying and we get in a gunfight, I'm going to pretend you're a principal I'm protecting so that I can kill you in my own sweet time later. Do you understand what I'm saying?"

Lucas nodded, but he didn't look particularly scared. *Hmm . . . need to keep an eye on him.* I stood up, talking to Knuckles.

"I don't know where Carlos ran off to, but he can't possibly have a ton of different safe houses here to choose from. My bet is he's either running to a hotel, or running to the bus station. Either way, the station's our first priority. If he's not there, we can stake it out to ensure he doesn't show up later, then begin working the hotels. What do you think?"

"What about the airport?"

"I don't think he'll go there. He won't risk being on some watch list after he's seen me."

"Sounds good to me. We need to get moving, though. We can't prove a negative. If he gets on a bus or train before we get there, we'll never know it and spend the next month trying to find him here in Sarajevo."

I bent down and jerked Lucas to his feet, showing little compassion for his discomfort. Knuckles called the team into the foyer and gave them the next potential mission at the station. I took over, giving the best description I could of Carlos, to include the pack he carried.

We left through the back of the house, the men falling into an easy perimeter around Lucas. We reached the vehicles just as four police cars, sirens screaming, flew by us to the location of the firefight.

Bull opened the trunk of one. I told Lucas to climb in. Lucas hesitated for a brief moment, starting to say he wasn't a threat and would behave. I gave him a straight punch right into his mouth, splitting his lips against his teeth. Before he could recover, I grabbed him by the throat and shoved him into the trunk. Bull slammed the lid.

RIDING THE TRAM BACK to the bus station, Bakr scanned outside, looking for a threat. Pulling into the station, he saw two cars drive into the parking lot out front. One continued to the far side of the parking lot; the other stopped short about seventy-five meters from the entrance. He saw the men from the cars fanning out, two headed toward the train station up the street and two headed into the bus station. He saw the man from Guatemala. He began to believe the man was the devil. He began to sweat.

He told the tram driver he had forgotten something at his hotel, then sat in the back, behind the crush of people boarding. Riding back to the city center, he considered his options. Beyond anything else, he didn't want to waste the device. Using it here would kill only several hundred, mostly Bosnians or other Eastern Europeans. He'd be lucky to kill a single Zionist. The impact would be minimal. Even so, the thought was growing in his mind. It was an eventuality that had to be considered. The man from Guatemala wasn't going to stop, and somehow he seemed to know wherever Bakr went.

He left the tram one stop early and proceeded north into the city, pulling out the number Juka had given him. Maybe someone would answer and get him out of here. He listened to the phone ring, then go to voice mail. He hung up without leaving a message.

He reached a walking promenade filled with people, all moving to the west, and remembered the ceremony. A germ of an idea began to form.

"ANY IDEAS?" Knuckles asked.

"Not really. Maybe it's time to pull in the Bosnian authorities."

"How the hell are we going to do that? And not give

up the Taskforce? What are we going to tell them? 'Be on the lookout for a swarthy man with a backpack'? We don't have a picture and we don't even know his real name."

We had finished our search of the bus and train station, and Carlos was nowhere to be found. I was certain he hadn't come here, and now we didn't have a thread to pull.

Knuckles said, "Maybe he went to the airport after all."

"Maybe, but once he got there he'd see all of the security for the dignitaries and go away."

We both stopped and looked at each other, a terrible truth dawning on us.

"Shit—he's got a perfect target right here. We need to find out about that ceremony."

Knuckles called the pilots and had them get on the SATCOM to the rear for some answers. Within minutes, his phone rang. When he hung up, I knew it was going to be bad.

"It's a formal ceremony for the fifteenth anniversary of the Markale mortar attacks. They're putting up a monument. France, England, and Germany will all have representatives here."

Great. A perfect target.

Knuckles continued. "Worse than that, the secretary of state is representing the United States. He's on the ground now."

"What? How could you guys deploy here and not know that? Jesus."

"He wasn't supposed to come here. He's supposed to be with the president on a goodwill tour. I've got that schedule and this isn't on it. Apparently, it just came up."

"Is it just him? Is the president here as well?"

"No, it's an entourage, but the SECSTATE's the biggest name."

"If this is someone's late-breaking good idea, the Diplomatic Security Service didn't have a lot of prep time for security. When's the ceremony?"

"It's going to happen within the next hour."

Before I could say anything else, the phone we had taken from the safe house began to ring inside Knuckles's backpack.

BAKR STOPPED A PASSERBY, asking, "Who's coming to the ceremony?"

"A lot of people. President Silajdzic is going to speak."

"So it's all Bosnians? Why all the security?"

The man looked at Bakr with contempt. "Of course not. France and Britain have representatives here. The American secretary of state is speaking. The world understands the importance of this day."

All Bakr heard was the guest list, his mind now working in overdrive. He began following the crowds to the west on the Ferhadija promenade, plotting his options. He knew that the odds of crossing into Israel were now slim. They were probably on high alert. Even if he could make it, he had no way to implicate the Iranians. He would make the news, but little else.

The deciding factor was the man from Guatemala. He was relentless, and Bakr felt in his heart the man would find him sooner rather than later.

He made up his mind. An attack here would have more symbolism. He could strike at least three leaders of the far enemy. His weapon would mainly kill Bosniak Muslims at the ceremony, but that in itself would be symbolic. They were cozying up to the far enemy and literally thanking the Great Satan for his so-called help. Because of this, they invited *takfir*, and would feel the repercussions. The attack would show what happens to Muslim *kafir* who stray from the path. It might even fracture the relationship between the West and this Muslim community, forcing them to embrace their true heritage. Forcing them back onto the path.

He reached within eyesight of the market and saw a crowd of about five hundred. Eighty meters away rested the raised platform the guests would use. A wall of security was checking everyone who entered into the inner ring. He recognized the security perimeter for what it was: standoff protection from a conventional man-packed explosive device. The distance was certainly good enough to thwart his blast, but the perimeter would provide no help at all against his poison.

KNUCKLES DUG OUT THE SAFE HOUSE PHONE from his backpack.

I said, "Don't answer it. That's got to be him."

Once it registered with a number, Bull began working to find its location with his special phone. Wthin seconds, he had a grid. Plotting it with a GPS, he said, "He's downtown."

I pulled out a tourist map, marking the location, then found the Markale Market. "He's in that area. He's going to hit the ceremony."

Knuckles said, "Maybe. Maybe not. If we go in right

now and get compromised, we may spook him into using the device. Maybe we should wait and see if he beds down tonight, then hit him with his guard down."

Knuckles had a point. We could make this a self-fulfilling prophecy if we screwed up. We now had a way to track him, as long as he kept that phone. It would be much, much easier to take him down in a hotel room than on a crowded street. On the other hand, any moment could bring a mushroom cloud. *Decision time*.

101

Bakr surveyed the wind patterns of the open air market. The entire area was covered by a high overhead roof of galvanized steel, but a slight breeze could still be felt coming out of the east. That was where he would set the weapon off. He moved around the crowd until he was situated as close as he could be to the security perimeter without gathering any undue curiosity. He stood for a few minutes, trying to appear as if he were just passing the time, when he noticed one of the security personnel glance his way a third time. He began to walk away, looking for somewhere he could wait that was close enough to allow him to get in position rapidly. Finding nothing, he kept moving. Eventually, he came upon a public restroom. It wasn't nearly close enough, but would have to do as a staging point. He was sure he would be able to hear the announcements when the ceremony began. Moving into a stall, he sat down and locked the door, waiting to hear the Great Satan's secretary of state taking the stage.

IN THE END, the potential for a massive amount of civilian deaths—at a ceremony commemorating the murder of civilians from a previous heinous act—made up my mind. The symbols of power from the United States and other European countries provided a target for Carlos to use, but as always, it would be the innocents who paid the price.

"We need to take him out. Now. It's a risk, but I don't think he's going to wait. The target's too juicy, and he's on the run."

Knuckles nodded. I knew he would see it my way. "Let's load up."

We drove along the river toward downtown Sarajevo, then cut in north to the grid of Carlos's last-known location. We were only allowed to go a short distance before hitting a roadblock, with all cars being turned away.

"Should've expected this," Knuckles said. "No way are they going to let a potential VBIED near the ceremony."

"At least they have some sort of security going on. Turn around and park it on the river. That'll only be about three blocks south."

After we had parked the vehicles, while Bull worked to get a new grid for Carlos, I said, "What about Lucas?"

"What about him?"

"We can't leave him alone. He's no pushover and a slippery bastard to boot. Someone needs to cover him, or he'll screw this whole thing up."

"I agree," he said, "but we can't afford to leave a teammate to babysit his ass. We need every man on this."

"Call the pilots. Get one of them to come here and swap cars."

Knuckles grimaced. "Pike, I can't do that. I can't risk the cover of the bird. Those guys are pilots, period. You know that."

"Shit, man, that guy's running around with a damn bomb on his back! Fuck the damn rules." I stopped, holding up my hands. "Okay, okay. I'll tell Jennifer to come get him. She can switch cars and take him back to the 427. The pilots can guard him until we get there. Can they at least do that?"

"Yeah, they can do that."

I called Jennifer and gave her instructions, a little piqued at Knuckles's rigid adherence to procedures. *This is one time he should be flexing like Gumby.* I let it go, knowing he had a point. Compromise the pilots and we wouldn't be able to fly out of here. *Jennifer's switched on enough to get the job done.* For the first time I realized that I trusted her as much as the Taskforce members themselves.

By the time I hung up the phone, Bull had pinpointed the new location. "He's just south of the market. Maybe one hundred and fifty meters away from it."

I looked at the map and said, "That's straight north from here. He's about two blocks up."

Knuckles gave final instructions, splitting the team into two-man elements. "Bull, you and Retro come in from east to west. Pike and I will come up from south to north. The rest of you box in from west to east. Hopefully we'll pin him in. Everyone, remember he's got a WMD. Whatever you do, don't hit the pack or his chest. If you have to shoot, go for the head."

The problem with the cell phone track was that it only gave us a snapshot in time. We couldn't do any real-time tracking, so whatever we had was only as good as the time we had it. Knuckles and I began walking up the sidewalk to the north, scanning the crowds. The other men were quickly lost from sight as they began their part of the mission.

Without any traffic, the streets were teeming with people going toward the ceremony. *Great. Rush hour.* The crowds were a definite problem. For one, it forced me to hide the UMP under my jacket, the folding stock jammed into my armpit. *I'm not going to be the fastest gun in the West running around like this.* For another, I could be walking right by the terrorist and not see him. Moving closer to the market, Knuckles and I both heard the loud-speakers signaling the start of the ceremony.

BAKR HEARD THE ANNOUNCER droning on and on about the significance of the day, first in Serbo-Croatian, then in English. Bakr waited, straining to hear any announcement that the dignitaries had arrived. He couldn't afford to leave and return. The man from Guatemala was some-where close. He could feel it. When he left this bath-room, it would be straight to the eastern corner of the security perimeter. Once there, he'd continue on, past any demands that he halt. Only when someone drew his weapon would he trigger the device.

He heard a different voice, then the words he was waiting for: the introduction of the guests of honor. He squeezed his eyes shut and said a silent prayer. Pulling the detonator from his pack, he conducted a self-test of the system. When it registered green, he opened the door and stepped into the light.

He was shocked by the number of people who had

shown up in the time he had spent in the bathroom. He would have to fight his way through the crowd to get close enough to ensure a successful strike. Setting off the device this far away would kill a lot of people but would most likely miss the targets, as they would vacate before they were hit with the downwind hazard. Pushing his way east, he continually scanned for anyone not focused on the stage. His confidence grew as the crowd cheered the speaker, with no threat in sight. He saw the perimeter fence with the security personnel ahead. Even the guards were staring at the stage. He pushed around a happy group, clearly having started the celebration early, and saw two men at the edge of the perimeter, both scanning the crowd as if they were looking for a friend.

He studied them before continuing, looking for anything out of place. They wore jackets, which wasn't unusual, but the bulges on their hips told a different story. Panic began to close in again. How had they tracked him so successfully? He backed up into the group and turned around, considering his options. Before he could decide, one of the drunks in the group pushed him, demanding he get out of the way. He bumped into another man, who pushed him back again. The scuffle was drawing attention he didn't need, making his choice for him.

He fought his way clear and went back the way he had come, attempting to get out of the crowd and circle to the west just to get close to the perimeter. He felt sweat popping out all over his body, thinking about what he was going to do if he was seen. Should he simply run? Attempt to make it inside the perimeter? No. They would kill him. He had heard the gunfire and seen the rifles from earlier. The only thing worse than killing a few measly hundred Eastern Europeans with his device would be dying with it strapped to his back, unfired.

He pulled the remote detonator out of his pocket, holding it tightly in his hands. Breathing deeply, he skirted the crowd. He saw the bathroom he had used to hide. He saw the door open about fifteen meters away. He instantly recognized the person exiting. The man was looking away, but he would soon turn and see him. Bakr frantically searched but there was nowhere to run, no way out through the crowds. Swiveling back, he met the eyes of the devil. Time slowed. The man reached underneath his jacket, bringing something out. Bakr raised the detonator, whispering, *"Allahu Akhbar."* He pressed the button.

I FELT A SHOCK OF ADRENALINE fire to my soul. I was staring straight into the face of the terrorist. I began to draw the H&K UMP, seeing the terrorist raise his hands with the detonator I had seen in the hotel room. *Why the fuck didn't I smash that thing?* My weapon snagged on the interior lining of the leather jacket. I knew I was dead. I might survive the blast, provided the man hadn't embedded the device with shrapnel, but couldn't get away from the poison, whatever it was. I yanked the weapon, tearing the lining, watching the terrorist with morbid fascination, like a man stuck on the tracks and seeing the train bearing down on his car. I saw him press the detonator, but nothing happened. *The idiot forgot to arm it first.* The terrorist realized it as well, frantically working the buttons on the device.

I brought the weapon up to shoulder height, slowed

my breathing, and drew a focused bead on the man's head, squeezing the trigger. I saw a blossom of red appear between his eyes just as his finger frantically probed for the button a second time, and he toppled over backward, landing on the pack.

102

Jennifer had made the rental car switch at the river three blocks away when she heard an explosion, loud enough to vibrate her car. She saw a cloud of smoke rise up the street. Then she saw that it wasn't smoke, but some sort of dust. It wasn't rising, but hovering, gently floating about, segments slowly falling to earth, reminding her of videos she had seen after the towers fell on 9/11. She floored the vehicle, driving as fast as she could to get out of the area.

She rolled into the airport exceeding the speed limit by thirty kilometers an hour. She had passed what must have been every police car and fire engine in Sarajevo, all headed to the explosion. She slammed on the brakes and ran to the Bell 427.

"The terrorist blew up the market. The WMD is out!"

For the first time, she noticed that the rotors were turning and the pilots were going through preflight. One said, "We know. The embassy's already been alerted and is requesting military support. We're getting out of here."

"What? You're leaving? What about the guys at the market?"

"We can't do anything about that. Our higher knows

the situation. It's in their hands now. Our orders are to get the hell out of here."

"Are you serious? What about Pike and Knuckles? You can't just leave."

The pilot stopped what he was doing and fixed her with an icy stare.

"Ma'am, Knuckles was a teammate. More than that, he was my friend. I understand the situation. There's nothing I can do about it. If anyone on the team is alive, they know what they need to do. We have a procedure for this type of contingency. My mission is to protect what I can at this point. I'm sorry, but that's it."

He turned back to his preflight. Jennifer stood in shock, unsure of what to do. She remembered the man in her trunk.

"Wait. I have the guy I was supposed to get. What about him?"

The pilot stopped. He turned to his partner and said something. Both exited the helicopter. One took the keys from Jennifer; the other drew a pistol and aimed it at the trunk. Swinging it open, they found it empty. The pilot gave the keys back to Jennifer without saying a word. He had finished preflight and was preparing to crank up the rotors for good, when he exited one more time.

"Look, I'm not sure what your whole story is or who you belong to, but let me give you some advice: I'd get on the first plane out of here. I'm sorry we can't take you. I would if I could."

Still trying to process what was occurring, Jennifer simply nodded her head. She stood still until she was driven back by the rotor wash of the helicopter. She saw it take off, and continued to watch it until it was a speck in the sky. She walked in a circle, unsure of what to do next. On the far side of the airport, she could see a beehive of activity around the dignitaries' planes.

She went into the terminal and bought a ticket on a Bosnian airline headed to Frankfurt, Germany. It was due to leave in four hours. She went back to the rental car and tried to drive back into the city. She saw the lights flashing a mile out. She got within a half of a mile of the downtown before being stopped at a police checkpoint. The man spoke little English. All he could say was, "Go, go. Poison." She turned around and headed back the way she had come.

She located the only hospital in the city and went to it. The place was a madhouse, with people in white running back and forth, and the wounded being brought in. She found someone who spoke English and asked about Americans. He told her he had not seen any Americans at all.

She drove back to the airport. She didn't feel grief. She didn't feel anything except exhaustion, both physically and emotionally. The flight to Frankfurt was a blur. While she waited for her connecting flight, the event began to sink in. *How had everything gone so bad so quickly?* She had cautioned Pike on the danger, but in her heart she had really thought he *was* invincible. He'd survived time and time again, pulling out miracles as ordinary events. If anyone was going to die, it should have been her. *How is this supposed to be justice? Where's the destiny now?* She put her head in her hands, trying to stop her thoughts. She heard someone talking to her and glanced up, seeing a Lufthansa Airlines ticket agent.

"Ma'am, are you all right? Can I help you?"

Because Pike had drilled it into her over the last four days, her first thought was she was making a scene. *Act like the other passengers. You're going to get burned.* She was then hammered with the futility of the thought. *What a joke. None of that helped in the end.*

"Yeah," she said, "I'm fine."

The agent looked as if he wasn't convinced but left her alone.

Thirty minutes later, he came back.

"Ma'am, are you on this flight?"

For the first time it registered that everyone had left the gateway.

"Yes. Sorry. I wasn't paying attention."

"No problem, but we're about to close the door. Are you sure you're okay? Is there anything I can do for you?"

Can you bring back the dead? "I'm all right. Sorry for the trouble."

She landed at Dulles International Airport completely spent. She had no idea what she was going to do next. She had a connecting flight to Charleston but didn't feel like getting on it. She felt like curling up in a ball and forgetting everyone and everything. She instinctively thought she should be crying or grieving over the loss of Pike, but all she felt was hollowness inside.

She joined the immigration line, moving forward like sheep to a trough. She saw CNN on a TV across the immigration area. She caught the flash of Bosnia-Herzegovina and focused on the story. She couldn't hear what was being said but saw a video of the market, men and women wandering in a daze, police waving the cameras back, firemen running, holding bleeding bodies, and an incongruous single individual in a space-age bio-suit. The screen cut to a photo, the name Harold Standish beneath it. She had no idea what that was about and didn't have the energy to care. She waited to see something about the president admitting the Taskforce's existence or some other catastrophic news conference, but the story ended.

She handed her passport to the man behind the counter. He scanned it and stiffened. She felt a stab of adrenaline, remembering what had happened in Atlanta, followed immediately by resignation. She had no strength to fight the bogus terrorist charge. *At least it solves my problem of what to do next.* Before the man could say anything, she said, "I'll come with you. Just take me wherever you need to."

He looked at her suspiciously, saying, "Follow me."

He led her down a hallway to a small room that contained two folding chairs and a table. He told her to wait, then left, locking the door behind him.

She sat for a half hour, mostly in a daze. She tried to remember her time with Pike, but her subconscious refused to engage. She was having a hard time seeing his face. She remembered the last thing he had said to her, and didn't believe it. *It wasn't worth it. We should have let him get away.* She laid her head on the table and began to cry. Sobs racked her body in convulsions. They slowly faded away, leaving her with the same drained, hollow feeling. She heard the door open and looked up, eyes red. She saw a man enter and smile.

"Jennifer Cahill?"

"Yes."

"I'm Mike. I'm from the Taskforce. You're not in any trouble. I was waiting on you to land. Kurt Hale wanted to see you as soon as you hit U.S. soil. I'm supposed to take you to him."

She showed no emotion. "Okay. How'd you know I'd be coming here?"

"We didn't. We have folks at every major embarkation point in the U.S. We left the terrorist alert in place. Sorry."

She waved it away and stood up. "I could really give a shit about that. Let's go get this over with."

As they left the immigration area he asked about her luggage. She shrugged. "It's in Bosnia. I don't have any."

They walked in silence for the rest of the way, exiting the airport. Getting to the car, he tried one more time to draw her into a conversation.

"I understand you ended up finding and stopping the terrorist."

She looked at him like he was an idiot. "I guess so, if you believe forcing him to blow everyone up early is stopping him."

He put the car in drive and didn't say another word. The rest of the trip was spent in silence. As they got onto the toll road, the weather turned sour, with rain beating the metal of the car. The only sound was the windshield wipers flipping back and forth.

Jennifer gazed out the window, ignoring the drive. Eventually, the car pulled into a checkpoint. She registered that the car had stopped, then realized where they were.

"Why are we here?"

"This is where Kurt is at the moment. I was told to bring you straight to him."

The guard waved them through to the West Wing parking area of the White House.

After a short walk, Jennifer stood outside the White House situation room, waiting to be asked to enter. The door opened and she saw a long table surrounded by wood-paneled walls with multiple plasma screens. She immediately recognized the president of the United States at the head of the table. He stood and approached her.

"Hello, young lady, we've been waiting for you. I'm Payton Warren," he said, extending his hand.

Jennifer didn't even begin to know what to say so she simply shook his hand, mute.

To his left was Kurt Hale. She looked around, recognizing the secretary of state and the secretary of defense. She saw other faces that she didn't know, but felt she should, vague recollections from Sunday news shows. *What's this all about? Why am I here?* She went from face to face, waiting on someone to tell her what to do. At the far end she saw a man with a horrendous visage. His face was scabbed, without any eyebrows. His arm was in a sling, a set of crutches to the side of his chair. He was smiling at her. The smile was real and familiar.

103

I saw Jennifer look from face to face, waiting for her to get to me, wanting to see the same glow I had experienced when she entered the room.

It dawned on me that I had been subconsciously holding back, protecting myself from the meat-cleaver of disappointment if it was a case of mistaken identity and someone else was at the Dulles Airport. Maybe secretly protecting myself against the trauma of having the newly formed scab covering the loss of my family ripped out raw had the unthinkable happened. In that moment, I realized that Jennifer had been right in Bosnia: Her death would have destroyed me completely. Left me broken beyond repair.

I watched Jennifer continue to search for some indication of why she was here or someone she recognized. She looked like shit. Like she'd spent the last twenty-four hours sleeping on park benches and knew the next twenty-four hours held nothing but the same. She finally got to me. I saw her face change from a lack of recognition to one of shock; then she fell backward into a chair. *Not exactly what I expected.*

From behind her, Knuckles jumped up, saying, "Whoa! Hang on there. You okay?"

I could tell she recognized him, but she simply stared like she was seeing a ghost.

He asked again, "Jennifer? You all right?"

Something clicked within her, and without a word, she jumped up and raced over to me.

Holy shit, she's going to hug me. It would hurt, but I didn't want to stop her.

She stopped short, smiling, tears running freely down her face. She leaned over and gingerly kissed my forehead on the crew cut of singed hair.

"You bastard. I guess you do have ten lives."

I grinned. "Yeah, I guess so. Took you long enough to get home. I was starting to worry."

She ignored everyone else in the room, simply taking my hands into hers and staring at me. After a second, she seemed to remember where she was, and what had led to this meeting. She asked, "What happened? What's going on? Why isn't everyone dead?"

Kurt said, "Well, we ended up being very, very lucky. Scientists are still studying the material, but it looks like the WMD was only deadly to those genetically predisposed."

"What's that mean?"

I took over. "The weapon they found was an ancient sack of spores from a plant that's probably extinct. It causes major anaphylactic shock in people predisposed to be allergic to it. Basically, it causes the same reaction as in someone allergic to bee stings, only a hundred times worse."

"Okay . . . that still sounds pretty bad. Isn't it?"

"Yeah, it is, but I managed to kill Carlos before he could set off the device. He fell on top of it, which somehow caused it to go off. His body tamped down the explosion, like a soldier jumping on a grenade. On top of that, it looks like folks from Europe aren't nearly as susceptible to the spores as guys from Guatemala, where they came from. Luckily, I fall into that camp."

Jennifer processed that, coming to the natural conclusion. "So, the whole thing was a waste of time? All that death and destruction for nothing? Ethan's death—"

The president spoke. "No, not at all. The bomb killed close to fifty people, but the team forced the terrorist to set it off far enough away from the ceremony that the representatives attending were able to escape before they were contaminated. Because of our unique security relationship with Bosnia, we were immediately asked for help. Most of the deaths *were* caused by the spores, but we were able to alleviate any concerns of a WMD rapidly, taking the emotion out of the attack. There'll be conspiracy theories for years about it, but the majority of the world thinks it was a conventional attack."

Kurt interjected, "Mainly because the terrorist put all his faith in the spores and didn't embed any shrapnel in the explosive. He also knew what he was doing. He kept the explosive power low to prevent burning up the WMD material, which worked in our favor, especially when his own body lessened the blast radius. If he had set off a conventional bomb with higher explosives and shrapnel, we probably would have had the same amount of casualties, so the story's plausible."

The president continued. "If he had made it to Israel, and had been able to implicate the Iranians, it would have caused immediate retaliation. He would've killed hundreds, and Israel would have feared a second strike.

Unlike Bosnia, they wouldn't have asked for our help or listened to any pleadings of restraint. Trust me, the WMD was real. Real enough to get us into World War Three."

"Okay . . . I guess that's good news. . . . Wait; that didn't come out right. I mean I'm glad the effort was worth it. I couldn't live with Ethan's death on my conscience if this was all for nothing."

She squeezed my hands, her face now alive, the broken look gone. "Ahh . . . this is a bit much to take in all at once. I'm not sure why I'm here. What do you need from me?"

The president spoke again. "Nothing. We were meeting here to discuss the repercussions of the whole affair when you landed. I asked for you to come here simply to thank you. You have immeasurably helped the country, and quite possibly the world. Your perseverance deserves my thanks as the representative of the American people." He gave his winning campaign smile. "That's all I wanted to say. If there's any way I can help you, don't hesitate to ask."

Jennifer winked at me, then smiled at the president with all the charm she could muster—which was substantial. *Uh-oh.*

"Well, sir, I appreciate it. I really do. Unfortunately, I promised Pike I was going to kick someone's ass in the U.S. government for leaving us hanging out there. I suppose I should start with you. Can you help with that?"

I closed my eyes. *I cannot believe she just said that.* When I opened them again I saw a roomful of the most powerful people on earth looking anywhere but at her. I could tell she was enjoying this immensely. She continued. "Then again, you guys did do the right thing in the end, so maybe I'll let it go. I guess all's well that ends well."

I squeezed her arm a little harder than was necessary, trying to shut her up before she did some real damage.

"Hey, guess what?" I said. "The folks you want to beat up took care of our little problem in Charleston. We don't have to worry about that anymore."

I thought she was going to rip into the rest of the group just for the enjoyment, and prayed she wouldn't. She grinned at me and said, "Okay, then, how about a nice hotel room?"

The room broke into relieved laughter. The president said, "I think I can manage that."

He grew serious again. "Ladies and gentlemen, I appreciate your time, but I have a press conference in an hour. I can't thank you enough for your service."

The meeting broke up with people shaking hands and saying good-bye. Shortly we found ourselves outside, me hobbling along on my broken ankle with Jennifer trying unsuccessfully to help. Eventually, everyone was gone and it was just us. She looked around, noticing we were alone.

"Where are we going? Better yet, how are we getting there?"

I said, "I guess we go hail a cab."

"Wow," she said, "that thank-you didn't last very long."

Jennifer began walking toward the gate with me hobbling along beside her, when someone shouted behind us.

"Jennifer . . . Pike?"

"Yes."

"The president asked me to give you guys a ride to the Hay-Adams Hotel here in D.C. You have the Presidential Suite, compliments of the White House."

"All *right*," she said. "That's more like it."

THIRTY MINUTES LATER Jennifer was admiring the view from the living room of our suite, the White House majestic in the last glimmers of twilight. Now that we were alone, she brought out the questions she knew nobody but me would answer.

"Hey, what happened to all the bullshit threats about the Taskforce bringing down the administration? Everyone kept saying we had to do all the work because using it was too risky. Why isn't there the big disaster everyone talked about?"

I knew what she was asking was highly classified, but it never crossed my mind to tell her a story. More than anyone else, she had earned the truth.

"It turns out that Dr. Evil is a guy in the National Security Council. He hired all of the trained killers. Their attempts in Bosnia gave the Taskforce a way out. We've blamed the whole thing on them, saying that a Lone Ranger hired a bunch of mercenaries to stop a terrorist. He's going to be indicted as a reluctant hero."

"That's the guy I saw on the news? Standish something-or-other?"

"Yeah. With all the press talk of the U.S. outsourcing combat power to independent contractors, it's plausible. The Taskforce is good to go."

She bristled. "Good to go? Are you kidding? What's going to happen to him? He tortured and killed a whole family. He tried to kill *us*. He should be strung up from the nearest tree. Now he's going down in history as 'helping America'? How's that justice?"

I didn't want to go there. I wanted to leave all of this behind for others to sort out. I tried to soothe her. "He'll get what's coming to him."

Jennifer squinted at me, her expression alone telling me she didn't think that was good enough. After what she had said to me on the hillside in Bosnia, I wasn't going to elaborate on what that meant. She wanted justice for the man's actions but probably couldn't stomach the Taskforce version. Luckily, she let it go.

"Okay. I guess in Washington getting indicted and suffering humiliation is what constitutes the worst that can happen."

I crawled onto the bed, trying to find a comfortable position that didn't rub my burns. "Why don't you get cleaned up? Maybe we can go get a bite to eat at a real restaurant for a change."

For the first time, Jennifer seemed to realize she was wearing the same peasant clothes she had worn for days. She ran a hand through her greasy, black-dyed hair.

"Yeah, that sounds good. Great, actually. What am I going to do about clothes?"

"We can go shopping first. Maybe put it on the president's tab."

"Even better. He owes me more than a hotel room. Give me thirty minutes."

She went inside the bathroom and I heard the sink start to run.

Jennifer hadn't asked the obvious question of why on earth Standish had wanted a bomb to go off in the first place. I had seen his initial FBI interrogation and it had made me sick to my stomach. Made me want to jump through the two-way mirror and slice him open with the broken shards. Of course, the Taskforce would have frowned on that. Not because I had killed him, but because I had done it in front of everyone. Bad form. I'd have to be satisfied with someone else delivering justice.

Standish had been completely unrepentant, shouting at the interrogators that his actions were necessary to protect American lives. He seemed to firmly believe that his efforts were not only legitimate, but good for the nation. The thought disgusted me. He sounded just like all of the terrorists I had ever chased. The only thing missing was him shouting, "It's God's will!" Like every other psychopath who justified his actions as nothing more than destiny.

I knew there was no such thing. "Destiny" was a tool used by the vicious or weak to explain a tragedy—nothing more. If God controlled our destiny, then wouldn't the good guy always win? Where was God when Hitler killed the Jews? Where was He when the planes hit WTC one and two? In the genocide in Bosnia or Rwanda? Was mass rape a destiny? Or just fucking evil? *Where was the destiny in my family being murdered?*

Jennifer had asked about the chances of us colliding, thinking that it was meant to be because the odds were astronomically against it, but I knew better. I had seen the truth. God, or fate, or destiny—whatever the hell you wanted to call it—had never crossed my path. *You make your own luck. Just like I did in Machete's compound.*

The thought sounded like a cracked bell as soon as it

came into my head. *No way should I have survived that.* The more I reflected on the last couple of weeks, the more it seemed there *was* some invisible hand looking out for Jennifer and me. Every time we were on the verge of failing, something happened that spurred us forward. It made me wonder. *Maybe there is a purpose. Maybe Jennifer's right.*

I didn't like the thread I was working, didn't want to stare too hard into the looking glass, because believing in one meant I had to believe in the other. That the loss of my family was for a reason, which was something I could never embrace.

I heard the shower stop, blessedly bringing me back to the present, or more precisely, my future. Kurt had offered me a job back at the Taskforce. A recall to active duty. The offer was compelling and conflicting at the same time. I could go back to being a rough man protecting our way of life, but the choice would mean losing Jennifer.

After all we had both been through together, I had become as close to her as any other teammate I had known. A part of me, I knew, wanted more than that. Another part, much more powerful, was repulsed by the notion. It would be a very, very long time before I could ever let go of Heather. Maybe never.

Even so, I wanted to continue working with her. She was as switched on as anyone I had operated with before, and we clicked as a team. I had toyed with an idea the whole flight home and now had the beginnings of a plan on how to make that happen. Jennifer held the key. She'd be graduating soon and looking for employment, but I knew she'd no longer be happy doing something boring.

She'd tasted what it was like to work for something greater than personal gratification, and while she'd probably get the same satisfaction doing her anthropological work, she'd miss the thrill. The question was whether she'd admit that to herself. I couldn't tell her what I had planned, because it was classified, not to mention she'd think it was nuts, but that was okay. I'd see if she was willing soon enough, and could get her the clearance if she was agreeable—later, after the groundwork was laid. All I needed was some start-up funds—and I had a good idea how to get those.

Minutes later Jennifer came out in a plush robe, smelling freshly scrubbed but looking puzzled.

She said, "Okay, I got it on Standish, but what about the other guy? The one in the trunk? He did the actual killing. What's the Taskforce doing about him? Just let him go free?"

Truthfully, in the aftermath of the explosion and the exfiltration, I had forgotten about Lucas. "He's in the same boat. He'll get what's coming to him."

"So they found him?"

"What?"

"They found him after the bomb went off?" She could see the puzzlement on my face. "You didn't know?"

"Know what? What the hell are you talking about?"

"Pike, Lucas wasn't in the trunk when I switched cars. He got away."

104

Thirty miles away, in the swank Chevy Chase section of Washington, D.C., a nondescript sedan pulled into the circular drive of the Honorable Harold Standish. Three men exited. They had already done their reconnaissance earlier and knew Standish was home alone. One manipulated the alarm system while the other two worked the lock on the door. All three entered. They moved directly to Standish's study, finding him facedown on his desk, a spreading pool of blood beginning to leak onto the floor.

The team leader called directly to the Taskforce Ops Center on his secure cell phone. "Someone beat us to him. He's already dead."

"How?"

"Gunshot wound. This guy must have made quite a few enemies."

"Can you still make it look like a suicide?"

The team leader studied the dead man for a few seconds. "Possibly. He's been shot in the temple at close range, and there's no exit wound, so it was a small-caliber weapon. That works." He pulled out the .22 rim-fire handgun they'd taken from Standish's bedroom earlier in the day. "The problem is that a ballistics check will show the bullet inside his head didn't come from the gun I'm going to leave in his hand."

"We can work that issue. Just make sure there aren't any other anomalies that give them a reason to look."

"Okay. I'll have to build a bullet trap, then squeeze off a round in his hand to get gunshot residue on him, but that's not an issue. He'll just be missing a phone book."

"Get it done."

Eight minutes later the sedan pulled away, the alarm reset, no evidence at all of a break-in. Only a dead man and a suicide note.

I WAS AWAKENED BY JENNIFER insistently poking me in the thigh.

"Pike, wake up! Look at the TV."

I cracked my eyes open, seeing a breaking news story about someone committing suicide.

"It's that National Security guy. He killed himself."

Big surprise. Couldn't see that coming. "Wow. I guess he couldn't live with the shame."

Jennifer looked at me suspiciously. I thought she was going to say something, but she must have thought better of it.

She turned off the TV. "Well, what now? Are we headed home?"

That depends on you.

"Kurt asked me to come back to the Taskforce," I said.

I saw her face fall and felt the tension leave my body. *This might actually work.*

"That's great," she said, without a lot of conviction. "I know it means a lot to you. Are you going to do it?"

"I think I have a better idea. Go to my jeans and check the front right pocket."

She did as I asked, pulling out a thumb drive.

"Is this the window-jumper's drive?"

"Yeah. The Taskforce guys looked at it. Turns out it's a physical key for a steganography program. You still have your uncle's e-mail?"

She nodded.

"You want to go find a lost temple?"

ACKNOWLEDGMENTS

First and foremost, this book is a work of fiction. There is no such thing as the Taskforce, the Oversight Council, or Omega operations, contrary to what Hollywood and some reporters want you to believe.

Pike Logan, however, is real. He represents a small fraternity that, more than anything else, is the catalyst of this book. I had the honor of serving with many, many Pike Logans, but make no mistake, I am not he. I owe them a debt of gratitude, not only for what you're holding in your hand, but for allowing me to serve alongside them. Greater still, the nation owes them a debt of gratitude for successful operations that will never see the light of day.

When I first put pen to paper, this was, of course, the finest novel ever written. Family swooned over it. Friends begged to read it. Fortunately, it didn't take long to realize it needed massive work to reach a level worthy of publication. Through a series of fortuitous events, I met Caroline Upcher, a freelance editor and published novelist in her own right. She has the distinction of being the singular reason you're reading these words. She not only helped me frame the story, but literally taught a knuckledragger like me how to write. If any new writers are reading these words for a clue of how I managed to get published, there's your big black X.

Even after all the work, someone still had to be willing to take a risk on an unknown. I'm indebted to John Talbot of the Talbot Fortune Agency for doing just that. When nobody else seemed willing to even want to open the Word document, he decided to see where it would go. Hopefully, it was worth the look.

As for the book itself, a huge thank-you to Major Beau Spafford, of the South Carolina Army National Guard and a James Island Redneck, who's currently getting shot at in Afghanistan. You won't find anyone with more common sense. Well, I should say more common sense who's willing to use the book as an excuse to go drink beer. He corrected innumerable inconsistencies.

To select people from my former life: thank you. The special mission world is close-knit and very unique. Writing for publication of any sort is frowned upon, but some friends agreed to read the manuscript to make sure I hadn't said anything that would compromise the safety of those still in harm's way—namely themselves. I say agreed, not supported, because my name on the cover is irritating enough.

A huge thank-you goes out to Dutton publishing and my editor, Ben Sevier. Honestly, I was worried when I signed the contract that I'd also sold my soul. I had visions of this big-name publisher ordering me to change everything in it that I held dear. Far from it, Ben took the manuscript to the next level, coaching, mentoring, and providing invaluable guidance. Again, I found myself learning.

Unlike what I originally naively believed, getting a

book published entails more than just hitting print. Although that's certainly an option, I'm grateful that the Dutton team chose not to take that route and have relentlessly supported the effort to see this succeed.

Finally, I'd like to publicly thank my wife, Elaine. One, for not losing her mind at the risk of leaving the military for a writing career, and two, for fixing all of my knuckle-dragging mistakes before anyone else had a chance to read them. When we were first married, she started a tally of what I owed her for various deployments and problems she was forced to solve in my absence, all based on the size of a diamond. I'm up to forty-three carats, which is roughly the size of the Hope diamond. So, if you see me in the Smithsonian "researching diamonds" for my "next book," you'll know why. Just don't turn me in when it comes up missing. I love you.

Read on for an excerpt from

ALL NECESSARY FORCE

A brand-new Pike Logan thriller
by Brad Taylor

Jennifer was halfway up the drainpipe to the third floor when she heard movement below her. She saw three men milling around the corner of the building, half in and half out of the shadows. Her foot slid against the pipe, making a soft clanking noise. She held her breath. *Please don't look up.*

When Pike had made the monkey comment, she knew they were talking about her. At first, she had violently disagreed, saying that Johnny was right. There was just too much risk. Pike had worn her down until she eventually agreed to at least see if she could climb the building before she made a decision. She knew it was a simple four-story square from her earlier visit, but she hadn't really looked for a way up on the outside.

It turned out to have a solid drainpipe on the back corner, which was hidden in the shadows from the street. Each floor had what looked like a six-inch ledge circling the building, with a six-foot alley separating the target from the buildings next door. The cameras in question were on the third floor.

She knew she could climb the building with ease. Pike knew it too and had worked on her until she agreed. In truth, she had secretly been a little thrilled by the challenge. Now, twenty-four hours later, her hands becoming slippery in the cloying humid air, she wondered what the hell she'd been thinking.

Her earpiece crackled, and Pike's voice came through like a megaphone. "Koko, you set yet?"

Jesus Christ, that was loud. She looked down and saw that there were only two men now. Neither glanced up. She clicked twice for no, then clicked rapidly four times. She heard the crackle again while still fumbling with her volume control.

"I understand you have a situation."

She clicked once for yes.

"Roger. I copy. Do you need assistance?"

She thought about it, knowing assistance would cause the mission to be scratched. She didn't want to be the reason for that. *If they didn't hear the first transmission, they won't hear me move. As long as I'm careful.* She clicked twice, and slowly began to climb.

Five minutes and two near-slips later, she was on the third-floor ledge, looking at the cameras seventy feet away.

"Pike, this is Koko. I'm on the third floor."

Stupid call sign. While at Solo, Jennifer had explained to Knuckles the importance of the Java man hominid and his possible link between apes and humans. She had made the mistake of talking about Koko, a lowland gorilla that could communicate in sign language. Knuckles had then given her the name as her call sign for the mission. It had done no good to explain that lowland gorillas weren't monkeys.

"Roger," Pike said. "Standing by."

Movement inside the building caught her attention. She could see the glass cases of the jewelry wholesaler in

the security lighting, full of samples for retailers to pe-
ruse. Just outside the door, behind the bars, stood a man.

"Pike, there's someone inside the building. At the
jewelry store."

There was a pause, then, "Roger. Security guard?"

"No. Stand by."

The man had bent down and opened a duffel bag. He
pulled out a hammer and a canvas sack, setting them
carefully on the ground next to the door. Then he pulled
out a cordless drill.

"He's a thief. He's got a drill. He's breaking in." Her
voice came out rushed and panicky, embarrassing her.

Pike's came back like he was ordering doughnuts.
"Roger all. Break-break, Johnny, we're aborting. I say
again, we're aborting."

"Roger. I copy."

Jennifer cut in. "Pike, I can't get down. There's two
men at the bottom of my drainpipe. I can't jump from
this height."

Pike's voice reflected urgency for the first time. "I
copy. What's the guy inside doing?"

The man had placed his duffel bag by the stairwell and
was kneeling in front of the door, working a drill bit into
the drill. The canvas sack and hammer were by his side.
Clearly, he intended to defeat the lock, set off the alarm,
then use the hammer to smash the glass cases in the jewelry store, stealing whatever he could before the police
arrived.

"He's preparing to drill the lock. When he gets
through that, the alarm's going to go off."

"Roger. Johnny, how'd he get in? Has he already set
off an alarm?"

"I won't know for sure without the SCADA, but I don't think so. My bet is that alarm is pretty damn loud. I doubt they'd have just a silent one."

The man had finished with the bit and began working the lock.

"Pike, he's drilling."

Pike came back immediately. "Go to the camera. Initiate the slave unit. Johnny, shut off the alarm. Don't let it go off."

Jennifer had begun moving before he was done, reaching the camera in seconds. She heard Johnny say, "Then what?" followed by Pike's "How the fuck should I know? One step at a time."

She found the wire with the red stripe leading out of the camera. *Should be the data line.* She pulled out the slave unit, a device the size of an average pager with a small antenna on the side. On the bottom were two claws designed to cut through the insulation to the metal beneath. She clamped the unit onto the wire, seeing a blinking red light. *This is great. The alarm's going to go off and I'm going to have a spotlight on my ass like a bad King Kong movie.*

She watched the man drill, her stomach knotting up. She saw the slave unit begin blinking alternately green and red, meaning it had the data line and was doing an encrypted handshake with Johnny's receiver. She knew that once it went pure green, it would take a few seconds for the hacking team in Washington, D.C., to gain control. *Come on, come on.* The man pulled back, shaking his hands and resting for a couple of seconds. Then he returned to the lock.

*   *   *

Knuckles, Bull, and I were just outside the front door, where I could see the leads to an alarm system. *How the fuck did that guy get in?*

Knuckles was grinning a little. "I told you this was a bad idea."

I nudged Bull. "Time to beat your record."

He pulled out a lockpick kit and selected a couple of tools. We could have used something like an electric rake gun, but those types of things left marks, and we were supposed to be in and out without any evidence. Luckily, Bull was the fastest I had ever seen at cracking an unknown lock mechanically. He could go through five doors in the time it took me to do one.

While he inserted the tools into the bolt lock, Knuckles and I slid a piece of Kevlar fabric that looked like a deflated tube balloon between the joint of the door and wall, just underneath the knob. Once Bull opened the bolt lock, we'd inflate the balloon using a compressed CO_2 cartridge, which would separate the joint far enough to spring the doorknob with a screwdriver.

We waited for the all-clear from Johnny, like a NASCAR pit crew. I heard Jennifer say, "I've got green. Shut it off. Shut it off. He's leaning into the drill. He's close."

Johnny said, "We're working it. Hold on."

Not enough time. I whispered to Knuckles and Bull, "Get ready to run to the drainpipe. Looks like a hot exfil."

Jennifer came back on. "Shit. He's in."

Jennifer watched the thief kick open the door. She tensed, waiting for the earsplitting sound of an alarm. She started when she heard Johnny through her earpiece instead.

"I have control. The alarm's off. I can see both the two outside and the asshole inside."

She sagged against the wall, watching the man run inside with his hammer and sack. After a few steps, he stopped, looking at the ceiling and wondering why the alarm hadn't triggered. Then he sauntered over to the first glass case and smashed it with a hammer. Reaching inside, he began stuffing his sack.

Pike came on. "All elements, we're going to take care of the burglar, then get Jennifer inside the building through a window. We'll exfil together out the front."

Seeing the bars on the windows of the jewelry wholesaler, Jennifer said, "Pike, the windows here are sealed for security. I can get down to the second floor without those guys seeing me. Then you wouldn't have to mess with the burglar."

"Sorry. I'm not helping these assholes clean out that jewelry store. We shut off the alarm for them. Find another window while we deal with him."

Huh. Didn't expect that. She looked up and saw a window above her cracked a few inches. "The fourth floor's good. I see an open window."

"Okay. We're inside. Wait until I call again, then meet us in the jewelry store."

Johnny cut in. "Koko, didn't you say the travel agency was on the fourth floor?"

Jennifer clicked once, not stopping her climb.

"You still have the thumb drive?"

Now on the fourth-floor ledge, she stopped and said, "Yeah. I'll see what I can do."

She snaked through the window and retraced her steps from a few days ago. Within short order, she was inside Noordin's office, waking up his computer. When it came to life, she saw a password screen. She shut down the computer, inserted the thumb drive, and rebooted. When the screen came back up, she was inside his system. She accessed the Internet and typed in the Web page Johnny had given her. The only thing on the screen was a button that said ENTER. She clicked on it. Nothing appeared to happen.

"Johnny, I'm inside and clicked on the Web page, but it didn't do anything."

"It's not supposed to. We got it. We're good."

She left the office exactly as she found it, rebooting the computer to bring up the password screen. She reached the stairwell and was about to head down when her radio crackled again.

"Pike, the other two assholes have entered the building. They're in the stairwell headed up."

WE HAD JUST FINISHED tying up the first thief when the call came in. *Shit, Jennifer's going to run into them.* A second later, I was thinking that wasn't a bad idea.

"Koko, this is Pike. Come down the stairs until you see them. Let them get a good look at you, then haul ass to the jewelry store. Come right through the door. You copy?"

After a pause, I heard, "Uh . . . okay. You'd better be right there."

"We'll be there. Hurry."

Bull and Knuckles looked at me as if I had started smoking crack.

"Bull, get over by the counter. Knuckles, grab that chain."

Knuckles got the idea and laid it in front of the door, me on one end and him on the other.

Jennifer came on, out of breath. "I'm on the way! And they're right behind me!"

Seconds later she came flying through the door. Once she passed, we raised the chain to ankle height. Both thieves hit it at a dead sprint, sending them sailing across the floor and crashing headfirst into the wall. Bull was on them immediately, but it was unnecessary. Like their partner, they were out cold.

Knuckles stood up, surveying the damage. "Man, what a clusterfuck. It's great being back with you, Pike."

Jennifer was sucking in oxygen as if she'd just run five miles, her hand on her knees, still pumped by the adrenaline, but the comment brought out a laugh. "Look at the bright side. At least we accomplished the mission."

Bull stared at her for a second, apparently sizing her up for the first time. "Yeah, I guess you did."

I winked at Jennifer. *Another believer*. She grinned.

"Well," I said, "if you guys think I can get us out of here without a lightning strike, I say we take these assholes out and drop them off somewhere. When they wake up, they won't come back here and certainly won't be going to the police about a bunch of gringos."

Bull said, "What about all the damage in here? This wasn't too clandestine."

"Let 'em think Batman showed up."